PRAISE FOR THE CARETAKER

*"In Sarah Gordon, Georg̅_____ a heroine
of such amazing courage_____ lf totally
immersed in her struggle_____ g a life-
changing accident. Sarah_____ ₙₐₛ ever gone
through pain and t___ ₜₒ come out stronger and better.
Don't miss this one!"*
—Cassandra King, author of **The Same Sweet Girls**

"George Weinstein's The Caretaker *is an intricate, grim-humored study
of precarious young love on the verge of collapse. Gracefully layered
with artistry, physicality and emotion, this book will compel readers
to question the very nature of love and loyalty as they limp with the
wounded protagonist through the minefield of her marriage and life
without one leg. Deeply hopeful and bitingly painful by turns,* The
Caretaker *will leave the reader cringing, laughing
and ultimately, grateful."*
—M.J. Pullen, best-selling author of **The Marriage Pact,
Regrets Only,** and **Baggage Check**

*"In this beautifully told story of a dancer whose career in ended by a
tragic accident, Weinstein looks way beyond the easy and obvious clichés
to the dilemmas of our closest relationships—spinning a moving, tender,
and ultimately hopeful tale of a woman seeking to relearn the greatest
art of all, the art of love."*
—Man Martin, author of **Paradise Dogs** and
Days of the Endless Corvette

*"George Weinstein's latest novel is a sympathetic exploration of a
carefully constructed life gone awry. The writing is visceral, the problems
are real, and there is no clear way forward. These characters break our
hearts and mend them all over again, reminding us that it takes courage
to establish an authentic place for ourselves in the world."*
—Kimberly Brock, author of **The River Witch** and
Georgia Author of the Year 2013

*"When will George Weinstein get the recognition he deserves? It should
be now. In* The Caretaker, *he explores a kind of claustrophobia created*

by disfigurement (is there losstrophobia?). He shows the damage this special kind of loss can cause to loves and marriages. We also see how hearts dancing together through the hardships can overcome."
—Charles McNair, author of **Pickett's Charge** and
Land O' Goshen

"*This is a novel of healing, redemption and discovery. The characters leap off the page! You can't help but bond with them as the story progresses. I thoroughly enjoyed the journey this book took me on. Highly recommended.*"
—Jackie Lee Miles, author of **All That's True,**
Cold Rock River, and **Roseflower Creek**

"*George Weinstein's novels are beautifully written and a pure delight to read, with characters so real you may forget they were born of the author's imagination. In this eloquent portrayal of loss and rebirth, The Caretaker gives readers an intimate look at the inner workings of a marriage turned to obsession. With his vivid descriptions and engaging prose, Weinstein will leave you eagerly awaiting his next book, and his evocative imagery will stay with you long after you've turned the final page.*"
—Valerie Joan Connors, author of **In Her Keeping** and
Shadow of a Smile

"*By creating a relationship of both intimacy and dependence, Weinstein reminds us of the central question of our emotional lives, that which often remains cloaked but is vital to our own stories—what to do when love pins us down rather than lifts us up. In the end, this is a hopeful story of a young woman with the courage to demand change, in herself, and others. A liberating, thoughtful and tender tale told by an observant writer tuned into the details of human frailty.*"
—Doug Crandell, author of **The Flawless Skin of Ugly People** and
Hairdos of the Mildly Depressed

"*George Weinstein possesses an uncanny ability to join the inner and outer worlds of his characters. George's impeccable attention to the nuances of human behavior is remarkable, as is his in-depth research on topics that lend credibility to his story.*"
—Terry Segal, author of **The Enchanted Journey: Finding the Key That Unlocks You** and **Hidden Corners of My Heart**

the Caretaker

the Caretaker

a novel by
GEORGE WEINSTEIN

DEEDS PUBLISHING | ATLANTA

Published by Deeds Publishing, Marietta, GA
www.deedspublishing.com

Cover art by Matt King and Mark Babcock

Library of Congress Cataloging-in-Publications Data is available upon request.

ISBN 978-1-941165-33-1

Books are available in quantity for promotional or premium use. For information, write Deeds Publishing, PO Box 682212, Marietta, GA 30068 or info@deedspublishing.com.

10 9 8 7 6 5 4 3 2 1

For Kate,
Who taught me the difference between loving and merely caring.

Chapter 1

SARAH GORDON'S INSOMNIA RESISTED EVERY remedy but sex. Four hours of deep sleep just coming to an end signified a new record. She had her husband Joe to thank for it. Since her car wreck, Sarah counted on him for everything.

She had awakened when Joe returned to his side of their large bed. The digital clock-radio he kept on his nightstand showed two o'clock. Joe fell asleep in less than a minute, like a computer shutting down. After a year of marriage, Sarah knew he had no trouble sleeping. No trouble doing anything, in fact.

Intending to appreciate the musk that still perfumed their bodies, she took a deep breath. Instead, she smelled food. Tomato sauce, sage, and succulent cheeses scented the air, mingling with molten chocolate, as if an Italian and a Belgian had staged a bake-off in the kitchen. She spooned behind Joe, hips against his bare buttocks, and nuzzled between his muscular shoulders. He exuded the warmth of ovens and steaming pots. With a lick, she tasted fresh salt: the perspiration of an industrious chef.

He murmured, "Love you," and absently slid his fingers over her plump left thigh. She was torn. One part of her desired to hold him and perhaps reach around front to explore the delights she would find, but she also wanted to know what he'd prepared in the kitchen so late at night.

An old dig sprang to mind about Jewish girls and how they treated the kitchen and bedroom the same: they didn't cook in either one. Maybe that fit her, but somehow she'd found a nice Jewish boy who did. At the moment, though, she didn't feel like making any jokes about it.

Sweat popped across her body in a sudden storm. Great, twenty-eight years old and already the hot flashes were coming. What was next, dementia? When she pulled away from Joe, the damp contact of their skin hissed in protest. His fingers clawed at her leg as she slid back to her side of the bed.

When Sarah pushed away the covers and sat up, the darkness hid her but she sucked in her once-taut stomach nonetheless. Gathering the flesh on the top of her thighs and pinching hard, she wondered how she had lost control of her dancer's body so quickly.

She scooted to the mattress edge. Only her right foot pressed into the plush carpet. Her left leg ended in a rounded stump, six inches below the knee.

Instead of a bedside table, she'd put an antique hall tree against the wall, keeping everything she needed close at hand. She retrieved a seersucker robe from its hook and pushed her arms through the terry-lined sleeves. In the umbrella stand was a large selection of crutches, many of them gifts from well-meaning family and friends to encourage her to get back on her feet. Well, foot. The artificial leg stood on its own beside them, dressed in a white sock and still-spotless tennis shoe.

Joe always referred to the ultra-expensive leg as "Fred." The aging prosthetist who had attended Sarah promised she would move with her new high-tech limb as gracefully as Ginger Rogers had danced with Fred Astaire. When she'd recounted the story to Joe, he dubbed the prosthesis "Fred" and the name stuck.

After contemplating the effort to dress her stump and then endure the agony of squeezing into Fred's socket, she elected, as usual, to use her favorite underarm crutches. The bedroom carpet under her bare foot gave way to cool red-oak flooring as she swing-stepped to the other end of the house to investigate the aromas of freshly cooked food. She transferred her weight carefully in the darkness; the rubber tips of the crutches thumped like heartbeats. Sarah had wandered their new home at night often enough to do so in silence, though she still feared cracking her toes against the furniture or slipping and falling.

It had taken months to get used to having so much space around her. The house was twice the size of her childhood home in Savannah and a mansion compared to the Atlanta apartments she'd lived in.

Near the dual ovens, which radiated heat through walnut cabinetry, she found the switch to turn on the overhead lights. Joe had cleaned up behind himself and left a note centered on an immaculate table in the breakfast nook. She passed long countertops and a large kitchen island. In the eating area, reflections in opposing banks of windows showed her fluid gait, with dyed-blond hair swaying against her shoulders. The mirrored images overlapped, becoming ever more distant until they disappeared into infinity.

Supported by her right crutch, she picked up the page of graph paper—Joe's stationery of choice—and read his meticulous copperplate printing:

√ 1. LUGGAGE: SUITS, SHIRTS, BELT, SUSPENDERS, TOILETRIES, ETC.

√ 2. CELL PHONE CHARGED

√ 3. SEMINAR PRESENTATION: LAPTOP, NOTES, HARDCOPY

√ 4. GPS AND PRINTED DRIVING DIRECTIONS TO SHERATON

√ 5. ATLANTA FORECAST—UMBRELLA?

√ 6. FRESH BATTERIES IN SMOKE & GAS DETECTORS, CLOCKS, & ANSWERING MACHINE

√ 7. COOK FOR SARE: LASAGNA, SAUSAGE BAKE, BROWNIES, & FUDGE PIE

As she considered the final item, her left hand trembled, rippling the page. She slapped Joe's checklist onto the table, for once not trying to realign something of his in the tidy way he liked. He'd waited until she slept to make all her favorite foods, to avoid her protests. When had he started caring *for* her, and stopped caring *about* her?

She snorted. As if she didn't know the answer to that one.

Multiple reflections taunted her in the windows. The body she had controlled so well as a ballerina had morphed into a voluptuous figure she hated. A mere glance confirmed she did not need another bite of Joe's cooking. She had packed on flesh the way she was supposed to be building up clay models in her art studio: with hefty slabs.

Only the night before, in bed with Joe, she had suggested, "Nothing but salads from now on; maybe a little broth for dinner. I'm like a water balloon ready to burst."

He'd kissed the top of her bosom and said, "Now there's more of everything I like." She told him she was serious, and he did Dracula, a common imitation of his, lips tickling her swollen breast. "But I vant a voman I can sink my teeth into."

As Mom would say: Oy, but didn't he have plenty to nibble on now.

Sarah scowled at her images captured in the glass. Twenty years in ballet, first as a student and then as a professional, had made mirror-gazing a horrible obsession. Few dancers could break the habit of sizing their bodies up and tearing themselves down.

Glancing lower, she winced and her stomach clenched. The windowpanes also showed the hem of her robe, where only her right leg emerged. Even nine months after the car wreck, the sight sucker-punched her. Intellectually, she knew her left leg had been amputated, and phantom pains would give her a reminder, but seeing it in a reflection somehow made it more real.

Beyond the glass, lightning flashed in the west, perhaps a summer storm approaching from Georgia. The oncoming downpour had long-since bathed Atlanta, her former home with Joe. She imagined it would soon race over the Savannah River and deluge their city of Aiken, before it moved across the South Carolina midlands. She loved rain, the way it appeared to alter reality, blending distinct objects and hues like the wet-in-wet washes of watercolor she promised herself she would paint.

After ten seconds, she stopped anticipating the deep roll of thunder. Heat lightning. No sound effects. No rain.

Another flash illuminated the entire front yard in a display even brighter than the security lights Joe had mounted on the roofline. Rapid blue-white strobes from the heavens bleached their lawn in an illusion of snow. Around the property edge, the ivory-colored, eight-foot-high privacy fence shimmered. Joe had hired contractors to erect it before he presented the house to her in April. The gift celebrated her completion of physical therapy. Sarah envisioned Tangletree Drive beyond the barrier and then the stone wall that ringed the gated community of Eagle's Lair. Past their neighborhood, she couldn't come up with any details. She hadn't ventured outside Joe's fence in three months of living there.

Well, I've been busy, she told herself. Preparing to do my art. It was only three months, hardly any time at all.

The smells of the kitchen helped her retreat from those thoughts. She crossed the hardwood floor to the double-oven, lowered the doors, and groaned as spicy and sweet perfumes teased her. Balancing like a tripod on two crutches and her right foot, she held open the seersucker robe to let the lingering heat breathe on her bare skin. An image of Joe came to mind: his mouth close to her breasts as he exhaled and moved lower.

Sarah glanced down at the stranger's body that had swallowed her own. Her neck and face pulsed hotter. Confined armpits dampened. In her nearly anorexic days as a ballerina, she could never get warm, but lately any little thing—sometimes mere thoughts—made her sweat like…Sarah wondered if a Jewish girl could be said to sweat like a pig. She didn't keep kosher, but the thought still seemed offensive. Sweat like I'd danced a tarantella, she decided.

Retreating to the refrigerator, robe still hanging open, she opened it and welcomed the cold air. Joe's four dishes sat on display atop glass shelves cleared of other food. He had even taped down reheating instructions on index cards centered over the shiny foil covering each container.

She lifted the foil from a circular pan: fudge pie. The surface glistened with a rich mocha sheen, a luscious color she wanted to add to her palette or recreate as a glaze for a stoneware pot. Irritation at Joe gave way to grudging admiration as she considered how hard he worked for her.

Unable to resist, she dug out a small portion of the brittle top and the still-warm filling. She sucked the sweetness from her fingertip, surrendering to the comfort it provided. God, give me strength, she thought, I could eat it all. She gouged out another hunk of chocolate bliss and experienced multiple mouth orgasms, the muscles there tensing and then releasing, over and over. A girl could swoon eating this stuff.

"I caught you," Joe said from the entryway.

Gasping, she wondered how long he'd stood there watching her. A sable-brown robe and matching slippers cloaked him. They were a shade darker than his eyes. He looked gorgeous as usual: wavy black hair and a square face atop a body still lean and strong as he approached forty, ten years her senior. Joe could've been a dancer if he had wanted that ecstatic, punishing life. He asked, "Are you biting your nails again, or sneaking into the food?"

She gripped the crutches, curling the fingers of her left hand tight to hide the incriminating one, and used one rubber tip to push the refrigerator door shut. It banged much louder than she intended. "Blame me for our high electric bills—I'm afraid I just can't help staring into the fridge." She gave a chuckle that sounded nervous.

"You weren't supposed to see them yet. I wanted to surprise you with all your favorites." He frowned as he approached her.

"You did surprise me. You've been doing that for a whole year."

He closed her robe, cinched the seersucker belt tight around her waist, and tied a textbook bow. "What about the six months we dated?" he said and leaned into her. His sudden kiss, though warm and wet, didn't last long enough.

"Of course. You swept me off my feet." They both looked at her lone foot.

In a quiet voice, he asked, "Have you stopped dancing with Fred altogether?"

"I was going right back to bed," she answered, sweat raking her ribs again. "So I grabbed the crutches, is all. Putting it on is such a production."

"As long as you're comfortable, I'm happy." He surveyed her features while he straightened her robe lapels and collar and fussed with her mane of bleached hair, which he willingly colored and trimmed with remarkable skill.

"Look, I'm grateful for the cooking, for all you do, but I really need to diet. We talked about this." With the left crutch propped against her side, she raked jittery fingers through her hair. When he began to reorganize her curls again, she cried, "Joe, knock it off."

He regarded her again, tucking his hands away in his robe. His pleasant tenor voice sank to basso profundo. "Why are you yelling?"

"I didn't mean to, but you weren't listening." She gripped her crutches and backed out of arm's reach so he would pay attention.

"I'm a multi-tasker," he said. "I can listen and fix you at the same time."

"Fixing is what I need, but you're not helping with that food. The reason I stopped using Fred is because it hurts. The socket's too tight now."

"I'll make an appointment with Dr. Ramos to have it enlarged." He smiled, looking relieved that she'd given him a problem he could solve.

"He can't enlarge a socket. Anyway, I don't need the next socket-size up—I need my body in the next size down. Four sizes down." She thumped one crutch. "Since we moved here, I've put on twenty-five pounds. On top of the ten I gained during rehab."

He held up his hands in surrender. "I'll make less from now on."

Her voice sounded a little hysterical in her ears. "Damn-near half my leg got cut off. I shoulda lost weight."

"I heard you! I'll throw it out tomorrow—all of it."

She took a few breaths. Blinking back tears, she said, "Sorry for shouting. I'm PMS-ing and I'm, I'm—"

One long stride brought him close again. He slipped an arm around her waist and said, "I know, you're not sleeping. You're just overtired." Without apparent effort, he lifted her against his side the way she'd once shown him: a premier danseur leading a pas-de-deux. Powerless now, her crutches dangling like the wings of a crippled bird, she allowed him to carry her to a captain's chair beside the kitchen table. Hand-carved wood surrounded her on three sides. He propped up the crutches and re-centered his checklist on the tabletop. "Let me do something for you," he said.

"You do too much already. I'm afraid I'll never catch up. Letting me stay home to paint and sculpt—"

Joe lowered to one knee and smiled up at her. "That's my plan, to make you indebted for life." He kneaded the sole of her right foot, not letting her pull away.

She frowned at her toes, calloused and mangled from thousands of ballet shoes and balancing en pointe for more than half her lifetime. Whenever she looked at them, she thought of Chinese foot-binding. Still, ay-yay-yay, that felt good. He massaged her Achilles tendon and worked forward to the instep. If his schlong could steam milk and dispense coffee, he'd be the perfect man. Yielding to his care, she quipped, "So what do you think, Prince Charming? Will the glass slipper fit?"

"On you, fair Cinderella," he said in a haughty British tone, "any footwear would look elegant."

"Concrete galoshes? One for me and one for Fred?"

Now he was the Godfather: "Only if you wanna sleep wid da fishes."

She said, "I won't need any extra weight to sink to the bottom."

Joe sighed and set her foot down. "I told you I'd throw the food out."

Sarah cursed herself. He'd been trying so hard to play nice. Looking him over, heat flooded her again, but it wasn't another anxiety attack. She murmured, "Sorry I broke the mood. Let me make it up to you." She reached behind her for a wall switch and flicked off the lights, arm curving in perfect ballerina form.

The kitchen remained bright for a moment, lit by another mute flash from the sky. In that instant, she fantasized about tasting Joe outdoors, seeing the glow of heat lightning across his body, pressing him against his tongue-and-groove fence.

Instead, as the room went dark, he opened her legs and parted the bottom of her robe. He kissed a spot on her left inner thigh that caused Sarah to jerk upright, tingling all over. Joe murmured, "Maybe I can put you in a deep sleep."

"Wrong fairytale." She shuddered again as his lips moved higher. He never acted horrified or disgusted by the stump, just as he never criticized her expanding figure. If anything, he showed more desire than ever. Joe's acceptance continued to be her salvation.

His hands slid beneath her buttocks, which used to be pure muscle. Sarah clenched them self-consciously as he drew her toward his mouth. When she draped her knees around his shoulders, spreading wide for him, her legs disappeared behind his back. That way, everything looked normal; her right heel rested near his spine, and she could pretend that her left leg extended in rigid anticipation. Closing her eyes, drifting into fantasy, Sarah actually could sense the toes of her phantom left foot curl with pleasure.

Joe whispered, "Ready to live happily ever after?"

Chapter 2

SARAH ONLY SLEPT TWO MORE HOURS IN BED, BUT not for lack of trying on Joe's part. Phantom pains had crushed her imaginary left foot, startling her awake. To distract herself, she pinched the excess flesh on her bottom with idle masochism and let her thoughts scatter. She finally eased out of bed, took up her robe and crutches, and swing-stepped over to a window.

The storm had gone without a yielding a drop of rain. Parting two slats of the wood blinds, she gazed at the dawn sky: an intense acrylic hue composed of two parts ultramarine, one part cerulean blue, and—she recalled from a video by a landscape painter—a dab of Payne's gray. To replicate it on canvas, she would need to use layers of glaze, applied wet-over-dry with a soft brush. The painter had promised the thin washes would set as clear as water and give the picture an inner light. She'd have to give it a try.

Wet snoring turned her from the sunrise. It wasn't Joe; he breathed without a sound, as if in consideration of her insomnia. The noisy sleeper lay in a fleece-lined, high-sided bed against one wall. Four tawny paws twitched in the air.

Sarah eased across the carpet, the foam pads of the crutches crimping the robe against her underarms, and peered down at Dorothy, a French bulldog. Eighteen pounds of muscle, fawn-colored fur, and Gallic disposition. Rumbling breath grated through small nostrils. The dimness of the room enhanced Dorothy's black facial markings: the mask that shaded a wrinkled, compact muzzle, Harlequin-style triangles above and below the closed eyes, and outlines that limned enormous bat ears like grand Moorish doorways edged in crepe.

Joe had brought the two-year-old French bulldog home from an animal shelter shortly after they'd moved into the house, so Sarah would have company. When she asked him why he gave Dorothy that name, he clicked the dog's wide-set front paws together and said in falsetto, "There's no place like home. There's no place like home."

From that first afternoon onward, the animal seemed to regard Sarah as the lowest rank in the pack, the omega dog. Dorothy was a daddy's girl. Sarah conceded that Joe's alpha-male qualities attracted her as well, though she'd dated too many assertive jerks to be sold on machismo alone. As she stared down at the snoring canine, she wondered what it would take for the bulldog to show her some respect. Obviously it was her missing leg that made her the weakest one in the pack.

"Let Dorothy get some beauty sleep," Joe said, startling her. Damn, he was always doing that.

Sarah returned to bed, passing her favorite Monet prints and the reproductions of Gauguin and Rubens that Joe had owned long before she knew him. Antique gold frames complemented the rose-colored walls that, in such dim light, looked sanguine. She imagined that she could be trapped in the belly of some great beast, like Jonah in the whale. Ahab in the whale, she amended, considering the stub of her left leg.

Back under the sheets, snuggled against Joe, she said, "Dorothy sleeps half the day and still looks like a troll. Since I only sleep for a few hours, I'm afraid I—"

"Stop it. You get more beautiful every second." He stifled a yawn.

She stared at his right eye, checking to see if the pupil and brown iris had turned outward. It happened whenever he was overly tired, stressed, or sick. On their second date, he'd warned her, "I get wall-eyed whenever I'm out of control," and showed her the black, triangular eye patch he kept in his pocket for those rare occasions. She'd researched his condition—*intermittent exotropic strabismus*—and learned that some people called it "lazy eye." Nobody, however, could ever pin the term "lazy" on Joe.

One time, he wore the patch for her in bed. Alternating

laughter with friskiness, they role-played the Pirate and the Distressed Maiden. Utter, consuming love had filled every day with similar adventures. The first time she saw Joe wear his eye patch for real, he had sat beside her bed at the hospital. His shadow fell across the section of covers that draped her legs and lay flat where her left calf and foot should've been.

He didn't exhibit the exotropia now, but she stared so long that he closed his right eye. "There's no double-vision," he said. "I'm fine."

"Still, you've gotta be exhausted." She stroked the roughness of his unshaven cheek. "Go back to sleep."

"I have things to do before leaving."

"Whatever it is, it can wait," she said. "Don't be so stubborn."

With his eye still squeezed shut, he gave her Popeye: "I yam what I yam."

Her laughter snorted out as she shook her head. "What you are is a gorgeous idiot who's as bull-headed as your dog."

He took the eye patch from his nightstand and slipped it on. The black triangle of cloth and its slim headband made him look vulnerable and dangerous at the same time. Maybe a freedom fighter or a mercenary. However, a glance at her leg warped the erotic role-playing possibilities from a bodice-ripper into something disturbing from Flannery O'Connor.

Joe centered the patch on his forehead, as if to cover an errant third eye. He said, "And would an idiot do this?"

"I know one who would." She giggled again, the dark images forgotten.

"The gorgeous, stubborn one?" Closing both eyes, he swung up his patch to give the third eye a peek.

"You'll make me pee in the bed." She pressed her knees together.

Whipping the patch from his head, he said, "Want to put this over it?"

"I'm gonna put it over your mouth!" Sarah yanked it away and slid the headband over her unruly dyed-blond hair. The elastic strap hugged her temples with a gentle embrace, but the patch tickled her eyebrow and the skin over her high cheekbone.

Joe regarded her, his boyish grin curling into a leer. His voice came out as a husky whisper. "Hey, Sare, that's kind of sexy." He pushed his hand between her legs, but she backed away.

"Sorry, Casanova, but I'm spent. What's got into you?"

"I'll be away for three days." His expression turned serious. "I'm going to miss you so much—I worry about you here on your own."

Removing the patch, she slid close again. She stroked him under the covers, thrilled as always at the immediate response. After her amputation, she hadn't felt feminine or sexual for months. No other lover would've tried so hard, let alone succeeded in pulling her out of the whirlpool of despair. She owed him so much. "Let me do you," she said. "You can get more sleep afterward. It's not safe to drive if your eye's tired."

"I'm fine." He ground his molars together, the muscles tight along his jaw line. "I can catch a nap at the hotel."

"How does that help you make the three-hour trip?" Pumping him, she said, "You never let me focus on you. Give in this one time."

While the rest of his body stiffened, he flagged in her grip. Sarah tried to scoot down to revive him, but he swung his feet to the floor and sat up.

She lay behind Joe, empty-handed.

Facing window blinds now lit by sunshine, he told her, "I'll get my projects done first. Maybe we can lie down before I have to go this afternoon."

"Sure. OK." She stared at the solid planes of his back, which tapered down to a nearly hipless waist and firm buttocks. The first time she saw Joe, he walked ahead of her in a bomber jacket and tight wool slacks, heading for a suite of engineering offices on Peachtree Street. His job was close to the ballet studio where she practiced. At the time, she'd fantasized about seducing him in a dance club. After the accident and his rescue of her sanity, she imagined creating a tribute to him, a heroic plaster bust. Now she considered even more rigid media, marble and bronze, materials she had no idea how to shape.

She had been used to sleeping with men who controlled every

aspect of lovemaking, but the others had taken—or insisted that she give—far more than they'd ever returned. "Sorry I annoy you," she said.

"You're fine. I'm just preoccupied."

"I'm afraid I don't show my gratitude enough." She reached out and traced the solid line of his backbone. "You're always so gentle. You never yell at me or make threats."

Joe turned and peered at her. "Who would do that to you?"

The man obviously had never spent time with a ballet mistress. Or any of her old boyfriends. She shrugged and said, "People I used to know."

He lay beside her again and held her. The cage of his arms provided comfort. She loved the press of his smooth skin around her, the velvet prison of his embrace. He asked, "Why would they?"

"I made them angry I guess." Her mother had raised her to be "a good Jewish girl"—studious and polite—which morphed into "a proper Southern lady" when she reached her teens. Countless ballets reinforced that image of gentle femininity, but sometimes she still forgot how to behave. She allowed Joe to lift her chin. He looked concerned, worried even, and then a frown darkened his expression. "See?" she said. "Just lying here I'm managing to piss you off."

"No, I'm upset at whomever caused you pain."

She had to smile. "Whomever?"

"That is grammatically correct, Madame." His playful tone told her that all was well.

"I never heard anyone actually say it before, is all."

He gave her a soft kiss. "I'd never hurt you. All I want to do is take care of you and keep you safe."

She relaxed against him but then her phantom left foot throbbed, trapped once more in its invisible vice. If she heard his words enough times, maybe she would feel safe again.

&

Sarah balanced on the digital scale before she took her shower.

As a five-foot, two-inch dancer, she had pirouetted around the hundred-pound mark. Once Joe started cooking for her, her figure began to fill out. At the time of the accident, she weighed 105 pounds. Now, she would settle in the short term for getting back down to 115, her weight at the end of physical therapy, and that was with almost half a leg missing.

On the scale, large red numbers reported 140.1 pounds, her heaviest ever. Mentally she subtracted a couple of ounces for her platinum wedding and engagement rings. She couldn't pry either of the damned things from her fat finger.

If she hung her head, she'd be forced to look at the stranger's body—the source of all her troubles—so she kept her gaze forward as she hopped to the shower. Joe had equipped it with a walk-in ramp and handicap bars. Though ballet had given her outstanding balance on one foot, the bars helped her confidence. And, she reminded herself, she wasn't balancing a mere 100 pounds any more.

A plastic stool allowed her to sit under the spray of water and wash her stump with care, using an antibacterial soap and an exfoliating washcloth. After the amputation, she figured the rounded end of her left calf, with its surgical scar like a broad smile, would need a thick callus to protect it in the prosthetic socket. Just the opposite was true: baby-soft skin held up the best. While she didn't plan to strap on Fred until her leg slimmed down, she wanted to be ready again for her dance partner if that day came. When that day came. When!

The worst part of each morning was washing the stranger's body. As a dancer she'd been all sinew and bone, nothing to lift and wash beneath, no folds of flesh. Toweling off, seated on the toilet lid, wasn't much better. So many places now where water could hide.

After cleaning up, fixing her hair, and applying a delicate blend of make-up, she hopped to the bathroom door and looked behind it. Joe usually hung clothes on the hooks for her while she bathed.

Previously, she had lived in T-shirts and torn jeans, often with tights and a leotard underneath. Adult fashions—even bras and panties—had felt alien. If she'd had a favorite color, she couldn't have said what it was. Who had time for such chazerei when there was always another ballet to learn? Thousands of steps to memorize, every part of her needing to be positioned just so and changing from one moment to the next. There really wasn't time to think of anything else.

The amputation only worsened her ambivalence, so Joe had offered to help out. A cream-colored rayon blouse, long denim skirt, and a matched set of underwear were there, along with her crutches and a low-heeled shoe in midnight blue. Joe always chose dressy clothes, even though she never went anywhere, and she wore everything he suggested. He knew her tastes better than she did.

Since they moved to Aiken, he shopped for all her clothing and shoes. In that steel trap of a mind, he carried a complete list of the sizes that defined her. Apparently he kept it up-to-date, because his purchases always fit her evermore-expansive figure. "He'll have to redo the list again soon," Sarah told her reflection in the vanity mirror. She brought her shoulders back and sucked in her stomach. "My diet begins today."

A breakfast tray awaited her on a stand beside the neatly made bed. In preparing the unrequested meal, Joe had given her a broad sampling of shapes in primary and secondary colors. A fluffy cheese omelet shared the plate with three rippled strips of bacon and two triangles of buttered toast. Joe had never been a lox-and-bagels kind of guy. On the side, he had placed a bowl of fresh blueberries, picked from his garden and dusted with powdered sugar. Cappuccino in a tall, white mug gave the still-life some vertical interest. The aromatic food and its promise of oral ecstasy brought tears she barely kept in check.

Beyond the bedroom windows, a Weed Whacker prowled along the foundation: Joe was completing the tasks he had assigned himself before his trip that afternoon. Sarah looked over the meal and the tidy bed. She noted the fresh sheets, the absence of laundry. Apprehension tickled like a loose hair caught in her eyelashes. At last she had achieved the pathetic goal her mother had wished for her.

A few years before, while recuperating at her parents' home

in Savannah after thirty-eight performances of *The Nutcracker*, she overheard her father exclaim, "If that girl spends all her time dancing, she won't ever find a place in the real world. It'll chew her up and spit her out."

Mom said in a Long Island accent that four decades in the South hadn't softened, "And if she should please the right man, she can play make-believe forever. Yes?"

Sarah surveyed the tableau Joe had created in the bedroom and spat, "So far, so good, Mom. At this rate, I'll soon be letting Joe bathe me and wipe my butt. In fact, he'll probably offer to shit for me to save me the effort."

She couldn't recall the last time she'd prepared a meal or lifted a finger to do any chore, at least not since Joe had installed her in their new home. No, really from the time of the car wreck. Nine months of contributing nothing to the household. Whose fault was that?

So do something, girl.

Do what?

You're a goddamn artist now—do your goddamn art. And do it on two goddamn feet.

The thought propelled her to crutch-walk to the hall tree beside the bed, where the neglected prosthesis stood. Its deep, cup-like socket appeared much too narrow for the stub of her chubby left leg. She imagined how much it would hurt her.

During her two decades in dance, her parents had never appreciated the effort that went into making each performance look so easy. Much more than tutus and moonlit scenes of love and tragedy, ballet was pain and blood and incredibly hard work. Maybe now she'd become too soft and couldn't abide suffering.

"Screw that," she snarled.

Even as she mustered her courage, though, she feared she was merely playing make-believe again: a role full of bravado, but ultimately a fraud.

Chapter 3

PERCHED ON THE MATTRESS EDGE, SARAH retrieved her prosthetic dressings from a stand on the hall tree. She went through the ritual of readying her leg with the single-minded focus she used to bring to preparing for a performance. The gel liner, with its clear, soft silicone interior and a taupe-colored fabric cover, rolled up over the smooth stub of muscle and rounded bone, then surrounded her knee, and ended at mid-thigh in a silken, cushioning grip. At the far end of the liner, past the curve of her stump, a ratchet pin lined with ridges thrust out, as long as an umbrella tip.

She kept her skirt folded back and pulled a thin nylon stocking over the liner. The sock toe had a centered, reinforced hole, which allowed the ratchet pin to poke through. With the dressings in place, she could now attach herself to the prosthesis. Attach Fred to me, she corrected.

Fred stood by in white sock and tennis shoe. Spongy foam to simulate musculature and an outer layer of cosmetic hosiery offered some camouflage, but it wouldn't fool anybody.

After rubbing a waterless hand-cleanser in the socket to kill any bacteria, she held the hem of her skirt and stepped into the artificial leg, extending her knee to push down into the smooth, contoured plastic that had once mirrored her stump exactly. The ratchet pin locked into the prosthesis with a series of clicks along the ridges. It would hold her there until she pressed the release button on the side of the socket. Five clicks would provide a deep, secure coupling. Sarah heard only two, so she gritted her teeth and bore down on her left side, managing a third click.

Painful squeezing—especially where the socket came up
the highest, against the sides of her knee—distracted her from
visions of the leg flying off in mid-stride. She hoped the eye-
watering pressure would remind her to stay on her diet. Glancing
at the breakfast tray, she sat again and picked at the food Joe had
prepared. She ignored the bacon and buttery toast, scraped off as
much cheese as she could from the omelet, and wiped the sugar
from the blueberries. The fruit stained her fingers purple and
burst in her mouth with explosions of sweetness, while the tall
cappuccino slid down bitter and smooth. The savory eggs were
gone in no time.

Still hungry, she allowed herself a slice of bacon and one piece
of toast. She imagined the melted cheese she'd scraped off would
be delicious when paired with more bacon atop the remaining
bread. Two, three bites, and the mini-sandwich was gone. A sole
piece of bacon remained. Despite her mother's reminders about
children starving in China, she decided she could throw it out.
Or at least save it as a snack for later.

So much for resolutions and self-control. She gave both
thighs a brutal pinch to punish herself for not staying mindful
about what she was doing. Could 150 pounds be looming in the
near future?

Near the garage, on the opposite side of the house, Joe
started his riding lawnmower. Hearing the sudden roar, Sarah
decided to get busy: she had art projects to do. Before she could
move around the house, though, she needed to match her shoes.
Without identical heel heights, she would wreck her hips and
spine.

Though the entire prosthesis only weighed three pounds, she
drew up her left leg with a grunt, mashing thigh against stomach
and chest. She untied the tennis shoe, and removed it and the
white sock from the end.

Below a seam at the ankle, where it met the costume leg,
Fred's foot had three layers. A hollow, flexible cover resembled a
generic beige mannequin foot. It surrounded a synthetic sock that
kept the foot mechanism clean and quiet, and the sock covered
the black carbon fiber skeleton. Shaped into a J, the forefoot

extended up into the leg where it attached to shock and torque absorbers below the socket. Bolted under the J were twin carbon flanges that arched backward to form a springy split heel. There was something beautiful about the design: elegant and efficient, nothing wasted.

I'm wearing art, she told herself. Maybe that could make the loss more bearable.

Planted beside her pale right foot, the fake one in beige appeared to be a bad joke rather than artistry. But when Sarah slipped a thigh-high stocking over it and then pulled a matching one up her right leg, the illusion improved somewhat. She stood and focused on balance. The prosthesis felt too long at first—her left hip had grown accustomed to having no weight-bearing support beneath it—so she limped for a few steps.

She also had to get reacquainted with the tightness that encompassed her left leg. It reminded her of going barefoot all summer and then wedging into Mary Janes for the first day of school. Every part of her leg felt the heel-strike, mid-stance, and toe-off of each step. Still, Dr. Ramos' coaching came back to her and trusting the prosthesis to do its job became easier by the time she had made a few circuits around the large bedroom.

Sarah plucked a matching midnight blue slip-on from a hanging rack inside the closet door. Using a shoehorn attached to a long shaft, she angled her right foot and then Fred into the leather confines without having to bend over and risk falling. The prosthetic foot would grant perfect balance only for low-heeled dress shoes and sneakers; wearing flats would make her feel as if she were toppling backward, while stilettos would pitch her forward.

Bedside again, she appraised her image in the full-length mirror that gave the hall tree its height. The imitation leg emerged from the calf-length denim skirt and, cloaked by the stocking, disappeared into the shoe. She cinched a narrow belt around her waist to check hip alignment, just as she used to do in ballet practice. Joe would say, "Perfect," but she knew otherwise. Somewhere inside was the thin, dedicated dancer, but she would never get free again. If that girl still had a voice, she probably was screaming the same thing that Sarah's leg seemed to cry out as the socket crushed it on all sides: "What have you done to me?"

Walking up to the mirror and back, she practiced until she didn't show the slightest limp. As a teenager, she'd once sat on her left leg while waiting for her turn in a ballet school audition, and then had to dance with that side awakening painfully. The throb in her leg reminded her of that challenge. At least she didn't have to do any jumps in real life—she couldn't imagine ever trusting Fred enough to support her in a grand jeté.

She carried the breakfast tray to the kitchen, which involved a measure of faith in her artificial leg since she didn't have her hands free for balance. Flatware rattled on the dishes, but she knew it came from her nervousness rather than a hitch in her stride. Again she imagined the ratchet slipping free and prosthesis flying off. And then the moment—falling, twisting, dancing in air—between safety and sudden impact.

Relieved to have reached the kitchen, she set the tray on a counter and paused with her plate half-tilted over the trashcan, ready for scraping. Joe drove past atop his mower, ball cap shading his eyes. A stab of guilt pierced her as she considered putting the piece of bacon down the garbage disposal. To spare his feelings, she wondered, or to hide the evidence? Feeling silly but anxious, she discarded the food in the trash, but pushed it down deep, making sure it was well covered. Maybe it would've been best to just eat the damn thing.

The dishwasher—which Joe had activated on top of everything else he'd done—was in its drying cycle, so she scrubbed her dishes by hand and toweled them, determined to do her share. Another phrase, "pull your weight," came to mind. Grimacing at that image, she put her flatware in the utensil drawer the way Joe did it, nestling fork against fork with tines aligned like ranks of soldiers. If he checked behind her, he would approve of her orderliness.

With everything put away, she left the kitchen, dress shoes clunking on the red-oak floors with a steady, even rhythm, despite the squeezing agony the socket was causing in her leg. An antique tiger-maple table and ten handcrafted chairs dominated the never-used dining room. A broad pass-through fireplace separated that area from the front of the house. She loved a romantic fire, but Aiken wouldn't have many cold nights; it was a place where rich Yankees brought down their racehorses to winter-over.

To her right, an expansive bay of windows opened onto a flagstone patio and the back yard of Bermuda grass, where Joe drove his lawnmower. Dorothy lay panting in the deep shade of the privacy fence, with a water bowl he'd set beside her. In the center of the yard, his large, raised bed of fruits and vegetables flourished in the glare of summer sunshine. He even did his own composting, regularly turning a big, steaming mound of leaves, grass, recycled plants, and kitchen waste in one corner of the garden.

A brown house sparrow hunted in the grass, seemingly oblivious to the approach of the riding mower. It was a plump, awkward little thing. Joe didn't slow his pace while the bird hopped, head twitching, scanning the pillowy Bermuda lawn. The sparrow paid no attention to the thunderous engine and slashing blades while the machine sped closer. If anything the bird grew more sluggish as Joe bore down.

A shout rose in Sarah's throat. She slapped the windowpanes. With inches to spare, the sparrow took wing and flapped in an undulating route, rising and falling and rising again, until it sailed over the eight-foot-high wall. Joe didn't pause in his systematic progress across the lawn, but his face jerked up, as if in response to the bird's sudden flight. He swung the machine into a rapid turn to cut another swath through the grass. Sarah swallowed hard. A heavy feeling crushed her chest, and her hands tingled.

Beside the bay window, a pair of cream-colored French doors stood. She tried to open them, rattling the knobs, though she had no plan of action. What would she do, lecture Joe about yielding to wildlife? Run ahead of him to make sure nothing else strayed into his path? The deadbolt was locked and required a key to open from either side. At that moment, with her pulse racing and head full of noise, she couldn't remember where her purse was or the location of any spare. The windows all had locks on them, too. Joe alone knew where those keys lay. Other than exiting through the three-car garage, with its electronic door opener, she couldn't get out of her own goddamn house.

Her reflection in the door glass showed the stranger's body divided within rectangular panes, each part in its own box. In her dancing days, she would've filled up only half that space.

Oy vey zmir, girl, get a grip.

Sweat had soaked her armpits, chest, and back. Shuddering, she took an unsteady breath. The next one didn't vibrate her insides as much. The third came easier. After a minute, she finally regained control.

Sarah recalled the corner of the bedroom closet where she'd stowed her purse and keys, beside a crude preparatory prosthesis Dr. Ramos had asked her to keep as a backup. Like a spare tire. As she calmed, she considered going out and sitting awhile in the sunshine, but decided not to be lazy. Joe treated his chores with the seriousness of a paying job; she should give her art the same regard. After another deep breath, she strode toward her studio with only a slight limp.

A hallway led her past spare bedrooms as well as a guest bath, the laundry room, and a den where Joe had set up a computer and displayed her ballet souvenirs along with his collection of antique banks and mechanical toys. He sometimes carried an old Cracker Jack game in his pocket for relaxation, negotiating a maze with a tiny marble or capturing nine BBs in divots arrayed across a baseball field.

She wanted those steady hands on her now, to reassure her and lift her spirits. Nothing else would do. The anti-anxiety medicines and antidepressants she had tried after the accident had caused too many side effects. She'd never responded well to prescription medication. Her doctor had even refused to give her sedatives or any more painkillers after she had become hooked on morphine in the hospital and then Demerol and codeine later on. "I'm afraid your brain chemistry is prone to addiction, Mrs. Gordon," he'd said. "I'm afraid therapy's the only option."

I'm afraid.

Obviously, dreading Joe's trip—three days of separation— had shaken her up. But, God forgive her, she knew she would welcome some time alone. Was that being disloyal or just needing some space? She didn't even know her own mind anymore.

Past the master bedroom, at the end of the long hall, she pushed open the solid doors of the solarium, her art studio. The only thing she'd ever enjoyed doing besides dancing was making art. Drawing, painting, and sculpture had kept her sane in high school and gave her something enjoyable to do while recuperating from the inevitable injuries from dancing. She was lucky: some ballerinas were so single-minded, they never developed any other interests.

She'd divided the five hundred square feet into quadrants for creation, storage, cleanup, and rumination. Over the concrete pad she had rolled out springy rubber mats to lessen the shock to her legs. The gentle bounce underfoot reminded her of ballet flooring. She wished she could revert to the delicate ballerina gait of toe-to-heel, toe-to-heel, but the prosthetic foot couldn't point. It forced her to walk like everyone else.

She'd put her painting station on the east side, where morning light streamed through the wall of glass. Lidded trays of watercolors and acrylics lay in rows atop oilcloth-covered tables. Alongside palettes and mixing bowls stood jars of sable-tipped brushes that thrust up like cattails. She kept jugs of distilled water nearby, ready to lift paint from the pans of solid color and dilute the concentrated mixes from tubes. Propped on a drawing table and several easels, which she had lowered to the height of her ergonomic chair, were three blank canvases.

On the north side, with its cooler sunlight throughout the day, she had established her sculpture center. A large table awaited studies she would do in gray-green polymer atop pine-board plinths, with plenty of space for larger stoneware models, which would hunker under cheesecloth. Wire-end tools and boxwood blades sat in nearby trays. She had hand-rolled slabs of earthen clay into sausage shapes, packed them in plastic bags, and stored them in airtight boxes under the workbenches. Beside them, bins held vermiculite, pumice, and other aggregates to give the medium just the right texture and plasticity. Sacks of baked, sifted gypsum lay there, too, intended one day to become plaster as smooth and creamy as custard.

In her own domain she could be as neat and organized as Joe. Actually she had accomplished a lot in just three months. She opened a box atop the table and pinched off a bit of gray-green modeling clay, eager to feel that cool dampness. The polymer cracked and crumbled between her fingers, dried out from neglect.

Aware again of the clammy sweat that stained her blouse, she carried the brittle fragments to the wash-up area on the west side of the glass-walled room with its stationary tub and trash barrels. She threw away the bits with some force, but they barely made a sound in the plastic can filled with balled-up paper from countless discarded paintings and sketches.

Sarah retreated to the solid wall of the south side, devoted to rumination, though at the moment she felt more like ruination. Joe had installed a velvety couch where she collapsed. She leaned back, sighing as she sank deeper in its embrace. Her eyelids drooped as she glanced at the matching wooden cases on either side of the couch, which housed dozens of glossy art books behind leaded glass doors. One day she would finish studying them.

Sleep almost overtook her, but the roar of Joe's mower caused her to gasp and jerk awake. It would've been so easy to lose another day just dozing, watching Internet videos of sculptors and painters creating wonders, and daydreaming of being one of them instead of actually making art. Thank God for Joe, he was always saving her from herself.

Glaring around her studio, she realized she had done all the organizing shortly after the move in April. In the months since they had settled into their new home, a place Joe had given to her where she could learn her craft, she had started nothing. Her canvases were barren and dusty, the clay was drying out, and she'd filled her trashcan with wasted paper. Her fear from earlier in the morning was spot on. She was a fraud. And a failure.

Well, at least it's nothing serious.

She gave her arm a pinch to jolt her out of her mood. Back in the day, she had danced until her feet were bloody and her tendons threatened to snap, and then she danced some more. And she was lucky to have something to fall back on, and even luckier to have a man who made that possible. She muttered, "So get busy, girl, and make something."

On top of one of the bookcases she kept sketchpads and a box of sharpened drawing pencils. She uncovered a blank page and hoped for inspiration. Maybe an oasis or a secluded glade, someplace she'd like to be transported.

Phones rang throughout the house. Joe had installed a unit in nearly every room because she never could remember to keep her cell phone charged or was always misplacing it. Now, whenever he called from work or while running errands, she could answer after only a few steps or less. A cordless model cheeped again from atop the other bookcase; the caller ID unit displayed her parents' number in Savannah.

She clicked the Talk button. "Mom?"

"How are you, Feygela?" Her mother always started the same way: the "cute little girl" Yiddish nickname Sarah had heard for nearly three decades, and The Question asked in a cautious way, as if Mom were braced for another tragedy. Still, there was the usual eagerness in her voice, too. She thrived on bad news and needed a double-shot of it.

Sarah knew The Question really meant: "How are you coping with the loss of your leg and your ballet career and everything you spent your entire twenty-eight years focused on?" Her older brother always asked The Question the same way, as did her ballet friends and instructors when they used to call. Notoriously superstitious creatures—dancers feared even amputations were contagious—they all had stopped calling, texting, or e-mailing long ago. Some had even un-friended her on Facebook, as if to ward off the evil eye.

Only Joe addressed things head on. And she'd just been entertaining disloyal thoughts about the one person who was straight-up with her. What a shit she was.

Pinching her thigh, she said, "Same old, same old, I'm afraid. You know, wallowing in self-pity, suicidal with depression, as big as a house."

"Normal men like a zaftig woman—never underestimate the power of cleavage. The reason you had all those meshugga boyfriends before you met Joe was because you were so skinny; a flat chest attracts the wrong type. How is he anyway?"

"Joe?"

"No, the mailman. Of course Joe."

The riding lawnmower thundered past the north wall of glass, with Joe sitting tall in the saddle. Sarah imagined herself the way she probably looked to him: a blowzy blonde slacker who sprawled on the couch instead of learning her craft. Plenty of cleavage-power, sure, but all she lacked was a box of bonbons in her lap and candy wrappers on the floor to appear totally worthless. She displayed the blank sketchpad to him, trying to justify herself, but he didn't look disapproving. With a tip of his cap, he gave her a toothy smile and roared toward the front yard.

When the engine noise diminished, she answered, "He's his usual perfect self." She didn't add that, when she met Joe, she was nearly two-dimensionally skinny and an A-cup.

Mom made approving sounds while Sarah thought back to her idea of an oasis or a glade. She glanced at Joe's perfect lawn for inspiration, but the eight-foot-high privacy fence spoiled that scene. Maybe someplace in Aiken? She couldn't recall anything about the town or countryside; her house could be enclosed in a big plastic bubble in the desert for all she knew. OK, then, pure imagination. Left hand and pencil darting over the page, she sketched a secret sanctuary deep in the woods, where a shaft of sunlight graced the center of a clearing.

Mom asked, "You're treating him right?"

Sarah cradled the handset between her right shoulder and ear and drew a huge mushroom in the sunlight, outrageously phallic but, hey, they were talking about Joe. "Mother," she said, adding polka dots to distract herself from the glans shape of the cap, "is that code for something?"

"It's important in a young marriage to keep your husband happy."

It was no use—either she had sex on the brain or her mother did. She snapped, "Are we talking about incidents of intercourse or number of orgasms? If it's the former, I think we might set a record. If it's the latter, I'm ahead by a ratio of about twenty-five to one, probably another record. You might want to call the Guinness people."

"Such a mouth you have on you. Who taught you to talk to your own mother that way?"

"You're the one who brought it up."

"Never would you say such things to your father, may he rest in peace."

"He's still alive, Mom."

"I know, but he's napping, which means he's not underfoot. May he stay that way awhile longer." Mom paused, as if waiting for a rim-shot.

Sarah crossed her right ankle over the hose-covered shank of the prosthesis. Fred had the same firmness as the arm of the couch. It was unbearable to think of her right leg under the artificial one, like being trapped beneath a piece of furniture. She rubbed her aching leg above the socket and asked, "Everything OK with you?"

"Mneh, I can't complain. Well, I could but who would listen? Not my children, that's for sure. Don't get me started."

"You're worried about me," Sarah said. "You know how I know? When you worry, you always sound like you're trying out for a gig in the Catskills, with the Yiddish and the 'oy vey' accent and everything."

"I'm not worried especially, just the normal level of concern a mother has for her daughter." Before Sarah could reply, Mom added, "But it's wonderful that you and Joe are having relations. Who knows, maybe next year I'll be there helping with a tatellah."

The pencil cracked in her grip. She shoved it behind her ear and eased her fingers open. They trembled. "Sorry, Mom, I'm afraid a baby is the last thing I need right now. Or want."

Mom sighed. "What do you want, Feygela?"

"I want..." Just what the hell did she want? The sound of the mower reminded her of the bird that had escaped over the fence, the rising and falling and rising again as it gained altitude. "I want to be the way I used to be."

"When you danced, yes?"

"I didn't just dance, Mom, I flew. I freaking flew." A sob escaped and tears filled her eyes. Pull it together, girl, and lock it down. Mom doesn't want to deal with this and neither do you. Sarah blinked hard to clear her vision and inhaled wetly. "Maybe I can create some art that makes me feel that way again."

"God willing."

See? It was one of those pat phrases that meant they were done talking about it. Not that they really had gotten started. Not ever.

Mom stuttered, paused, and then said, "So, um, it sounds like all is, uh, well there in Ache-in, a town that was named for its founder's bursitis no doubt."

"Aside from the self-pity and suicidal depression—"

"And the big as a house. I heard." Some steel returned to her voice. "What are you doing about it?"

"Which one?"

"Take your pick or go for the whole shmeer."

"I'm going on a diet, I'm launching a new art project, and I'm starting to say only positive, ego-reinforcing things to myself." She added a waif-like fairy pirouetting atop the spotted mushroom. Feminine but petite. Definitely an A-cup sprite.

"That's nice. Will this grocery list solve one of the things or all three?"

"I don't know. It's a work in progress." Tiny toe-shoes appeared on the graceful creature. After slipping the pencil over her ear again, Sarah pulled at the bra that constrained her own abundance. She then thrust her hand under her skirt to free the cotton wedged between her buttocks, just in time for Joe to roar past.

Catching her in the act, he fluttered his shirt as if she made his heart race. The mower reached the end of the window, and he spun it about, whipping the vehicle around so fast she imagined she could hear skidding tires. In a flash, instead of watching Joe and battling her panties, she was inside a memory of nightmarish whirling on a rain-slick road, her hands frozen on the steering wheel. Then came the sudden impact like a slap from God.

Mom said, "As long as it doesn't bother Joe, I guess it can't do any harm."

"Which part?" She shuddered. Her face and neck were slick with sweat, as wet as that street had been. To counter her thoughts, she wiped her forehead and cheeks with the back of her hand, withdrew the cracked pencil from behind her ear, and drew a placid spring beside the mushroom.

"All of it, the diet and the project and the positive. You always over-thought everything, even as a little girl."

"You used to say I never used my head."

"Same thing. Listen: the secret to life is to go with the flow."

Sarah gave the ballerina pixie some wings and went to work on the surrounding forest. She said, "Your hippie past is showing. Next you'll tell me to tune in, turn on, and drop out. I think I smell patchouli wafting through the phone."

"I was more of the sage-and-sandalwood type. Also, remember to keep Joe happy."

"And we've established what that means. Mom, I've gotta go. Joe is here and he's lowering his pants."

"Give him my best, dear."

"That's an image I don't even want to contemplate. Love to you and Dad." She slid the phone from between her right ear and shoulder, thumbed the Off button, and bent her neck to the left until it cracked like the pencil. It brought instant relief, but all too soon she was aware of her damp clothes, the cabbage-stench seeping from her skin, the painful clamping around her stump, and just how damn heavy she felt, as if the pull of gravity had doubled. All she wanted to do was lie down and sleep.

Glancing at her lap, she spied the fairy dancing by itself in a glade. It looked so happy there on its own.

Then she knew.

Like a flaw finally exposed after viewing a canvas in the mirror, she could at last name the guilty pleasure—her disloyal feeling—about Joe's imminent departure: "relief."

Deep down, she really was looking forward to the next few days.

Alone.
Unobserved.
Free.

Chapter 4

"EVERYTHING ALL RIGHT?" JOE HAD CALLED ONCE an hour from the road. Now, with his third call, he reported reaching the outskirts of Atlanta. He said, "I forgot how much I hated the traffic here. Even Sunday afternoon is rush hour."

Sarah lay on the couch in her studio again, no longer inspired by the fairy sketch, trying to lose herself in the strange visions of René Magritte. When she resettled the art book in her lap, the page flipped and revealed the image of a voluptuous woman's nude torso trapped in a box. Yeah, sister, tell me about it. She slapped the covers closed and put it on the floor. "You're still tired," she said to Joe. "Be careful."

"I am full of care."

He sounded wounded, so she replied, "You sure take care of me." She didn't add that she took and took but never gave back. "Will you rest some when you get there?"

"I'll have a couple of hours before dinner. Maybe I could visit your favorite shoe store in Buckhead."

She clicked her heels together a few times, startling Dorothy, who sat in a dog-bed along the west wall of glass. The bulldog sighed and returned to her surveillance of the front lawn while Sarah said, "You got me a new pair last week."

"I'll stop by an art store and buy you some new brushes."

"I've got more right now than I'll ever use." She knew the truth in that.

"If nothing else," he said, "I need to pick up more hair coloring. When I get home on Wednesday, I'll touch up my homicide blonde." Dyed by his own hands, his twist on the "suicide blonde" joke.

Instead of laughing, she wished she had as much confidence wielding color. Out loud, she said, "That's fine."

"You sound annoyed. I'm interrupting dinner, aren't I?"

"No, I haven't eaten yet."

"But you're going to, right?"

"I will. I'm waiting to get hungry, is all." She sucked in her stomach and remembered their nap. His arm had lain across the waistline of her skirt; she had practiced shallow breathing so her abdomen could remain concave beneath him. He slept two hours while she watched. So boyish in sleep, relaxed and angelic. One of her fingertips had followed the black waves of his hair, and she'd asked herself how she could have felt relief at the impending departure of such a sweet man.

She wondered now if that was an early-warning sign for marital troubles. Maybe she'd read something similar in a *Cosmo* quiz. Of course, magazines like that were designed to create insecurity and then dole out tantalizing tidbits of advice, ensuring enslavement to a lifetime subscription. Great, she thought, add paranoia to my Top Ten Problems. She'd have to drop "Sloth" to make room for it.

All she wanted was to be a better wife, a more complete woman, someone he could respect. Cradling the phone between shoulder and ear, she seized the skin on the top of her right forearm and twisted hard.

"Hold on, Sare, here's my exit. I'm almost there." After a pause, he said, "Don't worry, I won't just bring home Clairol. I'll surprise you with something."

"The only thing I want is for you to come home safe. You know how crazy some of those Atlanta drivers are."

I was one of them, she reminded herself as they wrapped up their conversation. Sarah knew he believed it, too. When they began their intense six-month courtship, she'd driven them to exotic Atlanta hot-spots in her black Miata. The sports car and her mounting credit card bills had added up to a nearly six-figure debt from which Joe had rescued her.

She recalled how he would hold his breath while she executed double-clutching power turns, daring reverses, and rapid lane changes. With the top down, she loved how the wind whipped her then-brown and very long hair behind her like an Isadora Duncan scarf, and rippled the hand-woven peasant blouses she often wore over dark slacks. No bra—she didn't need one then. He would keep a hand on his head, trying to control his carefully combed locks, while his other hand left the impressions of fingertips embedded in her leather upholstery.

At the end of their second date, as the roadster idled outside his condo, which would soon be their first home together, he said, "You work so hard, what with your ballet practice and performances. The least I can do is to be your chauffeur."

"Sounds like you plan to take care of me." She relaxed in the driver's seat next to Joe. Wanting to kiss him, she stroked the back of his hand and smiled so wide it hurt.

Joe obliged her with tender lips and gentle fingertips that traced her cheek. He whispered into her mouth, "Who knows? It could become my life's work." His next kiss, and the way he held her, left no doubt that he'd taken control.

Because he worked on the same block of Peachtree Street where she practiced, he'd pick her up from her apartment in funky Little Five Points every morning. They often dined in the nearby bohemian cafes, where he cajoled her into eating more than her usual few ounces of food. One conversation flowed into another as they spent the evenings together, cruising the offbeat shops or curled up at her place. Then he began to stay through the night or took her back to his place.

He knew nothing of the world of dance, a refreshing change from the obsessive balletomanes who tried to romance Sarah or the other performers. Though Joe drove her to rehearsals and performances, and sent flowers to the dressing room on nights he couldn't attend, he showed her a life beyond that insular world.

At a small party in her apartment one night, while Joe had gone into the kitchenette to refresh Sarah's diet cola, her best friend in the Atlanta Ballet shook the dreadlocks surrounding her wide-open face and snatched Sarah's wrists in two coffee-colored fists. She said, "You grab hold of this one and never let go."

"I'm glad you like him," Sarah said, proud of her achievement.

"Like him? You're lucky I don't conk you over the head and run off with that man."

While Joe packed her glass with ice the way she liked it, Sarah confided, "He makes dating easy. To have a great time, all I have to do is show up. And Joe even takes care of that. I can't remember when I last drove the Miata."

In their year of marriage, Sarah only had gotten behind the wheel once.

Now, she promised Joe for a final time she would eat, then said goodbye and hung up. Sarah limped as she crossed the studio. Painful squeezing had returned to her stump. She had removed the leg during his nap to relieve the tightness, but then forced herself to reattach it after he had gone.

Looking through the open studio doors, it was a straight shot to the kitchen. The long hallway telescoped like a perspective drawing, funneling her vision. In a Hitchcockian moment, she imagined that she literally looked "down" the hall, as if standing on a precipice, consumed with vertigo.

The corridor gave way to a huge expanse, like dropping through the roof of a cave. She would freefall into the dining room and tumble through the kitchen entry. At the opposite end, a closed door stood. If her plunging body smashed that barrier open, she would crash-land against the far wall of the three-car garage. Except for lawn equipment and garden tools, the enormous space was empty. .

She had destroyed her sweet black Miata the one time she'd driven as a married woman. Destroyed her leg and her career, too. Hell, her life.

Her imagination had such power that the first step into the hall did seem like a leap of faith. Surprised she didn't spin out of control, she laughed out loud and kept walking.

Dorothy left her post at the studio window and trotted past Sarah en route to the floor-to-ceiling windows in the living room, which afforded a better view of the gate through which Joe had gone. After Sarah once had told him about Dorothy patrolling from window to window whenever he left the house, he had placed a fleecy, high-sided dog bed at each stop on the bulldog's rounds. "Good soldier," Sarah called to the small backside with bowlegs and a flat tail no bigger than her thumb. Dorothy didn't acknowledge her.

Outpaced by a lapdog, Sarah continued to the kitchen, where she'd laid her copy of the deadbolt key on a countertop. She called to Dorothy, "How about dinner al fresco? And I don't mean watercolor on wet plaster." Retrieving a plate and fork, she continued, "Come out with me, Dottie, and I'll teach you the only Italian I know: art and dance and food."

Because Joe had served a light lunch of gazpacho, she'd avoided an argument about her new diet, which would've hurt his feelings all over again. She now checked the refrigerator to see how much remained for dinner. The huge dish of lasagna and the fudge pie sat there still, seeming to mock her determination. She yanked open the top-mounted freezer and found Joe's sausage bake and brownies. He had broken his promise to throw them out.

Hunger pains knotted her stomach. In her ballet days, that signaled a satisfying control over food; lately it meant that she wanted to binge. With a defeated sigh, she set both refrigerated items on the granite counter, uncovered them, and inhaled. Even cold, the food exuded delicious aromas. The last time she smelled the tomato sauce and chocolate, she lay in bed, still limp from sex.

Joe had cut the lasagna into huge portions, squares as big as her hand. He had sliced the pie into four massive wedges, one cut bisecting the divot she'd made with her finger the night before. Initially, she wondered if he really thought she ate so much in one sitting. Then came the grudging admission that they often shared seconds and sometimes thirds, so maybe she did. Well, not anymore.

Sarah searched a few drawers muttering, "I gotta learn this damn kitchen," before she found the long butcher knife. She cut the lasagna squares into much slimmer rectangles, rinsed off the blade, and began to bisect the pie wedges.

Her breasts quivered as she sawed the thick dessert into eighths. "Traitors," she hissed at her chest, and subdivided the slices once more. As a reward for her sacrifice, she edged her finger against the long, flat sides of the knife and licked off the truffle-sweet chocolate. The treat slid down into her stomach, she imagined, like falling through the roof of a subterranean cave. She tried not to think about the calories converting to even more cleavage-power.

As early as middle school, she'd skipped meals to maintain the expected ballerina form, while envying the voluptuous girls who turned the heads of every boy in Savannah. Her pretty face and waist-length hair as brown as burnt sienna still had attracted attention, but she always felt like a sidetrack on her boyfriends' journey to full-figured nirvana. After Sarah's second serious beau dumped her for a girl who was built for comfort, she overheard him tell another boy, "Now I know the difference between a three-dollar bill and a ballerina. The three-dollar bill is a phony buck; the ballerina is a…" Her mother caught her crying about it, and kvetched at her for being "all angles and attitude."

When Joe began to cook for Sarah in the months leading up to their marriage, she filled out a little. Mercifully, the Atlanta Ballet didn't require weigh-ins, but her peers noticed, and the company seamstress cussed her. During one intermission, as Sarah and the other dancers stripped in their shared dressing room and then tugged on skin-tight outfits for the next act, an emaciated ingénue called, "Look at Sarah, the B-cup Ballerina!" The nickname stayed with her.

In the large wedding photograph on the living room mantle, Joe looked like a tuxedo model, and Sarah, still with her long brown mane, wore a low-cut bridal gown. Clearly her ever-more Rubenesque build pleased him.

How zaftig could I become before he was turned off? Maybe he had a secret fat fetish—and an amputation thing, too. Maybe he'd keep plumping me up and hack off a limb every so often to maintain his interest.

Nonsense. Surely he hadn't fallen in love with just a body.

Especially since she barely resembled the woman in the wedding photo, and he seemed to love her more than ever. Didn't he? She silently asked this of the double kitchen sink, which had a kind of robotic face now that she studied it: a steel nose, as solid and straight as Joe's, separated two sunken eyes, with a shiny sieve-like opening in the left basin and, on the right side, a dark rubber hole as black as Joe's eye patch.

She said, "Am I just waiting to get rejected again?" Warm, soapy water sluiced over her hands as she washed the large butcher knife.

Another question escaped from her mouth even as she thought it. "Goddammit, Joe, why'd you break your promise?" The wet handle slipped from her grip. Falling point-first, the knife plunged into the black rubber hole, dead-center through the right eye.

The disgusting image and over-the-top anxiety made her retch. Doubling over, she struck her forehead on the steel rim of the sink, reinjuring one of the same spots from when she wrecked her car. The area blazed again like a branding iron, and Sarah slumped to the floor.

಄

She dreamed of the Saturday afternoon three months into her marriage when she had taken a rare break between ballet rehearsals. Nursing a headache, she slouched in the spare bedroom of Joe's Atlanta condo, which he'd converted into an office. She watched an Internet video of a sculptor demonstrating how he built up a figure using a wireframe skeleton affixed to a pine-board plinth. Sarah rolled gray-green sculpture clay between her palms as she memorized his words and actions. A smudge streaked her forehead where she absentmindedly rubbed at the pain behind her eyes.

The artist repositioned the figure's arms and turned one of its palms up, to capture an instant of epiphany. Then he began to nudge the sleeves with a boxwood blade to reshape the folds. Sarah took it all in, fingers playing with the clay, and thought that, after another decade or two on the stage, she might like to master this other art form.

Her cell phone rang, playing the "Swan's Theme" from *Swan Lake*. Normally she'd let the caller leave a message, but with her head pounding, she decided she needed a break. She set down the clay and paused the video. Walking into the master bedroom with her usual dancer's gait—toe-to-heel, toe-to-heel—long brown hair swaying behind her size-four body, she noted Joe had made the bed again. She'd told him not to bother. Ballet-free weekends meant "sixers": making love six times across two days, morning, noon, and night. She punned, "Coming, coming," to the phone as it continued to play Tchaikovsky.

When she answered it, she heard background noise from Joe's cell, a surf-like whoosh punctuated by rattling steel and car horns. He'd gone to his favorite haberdashery miles away to order a new suit. "The city of Atlanta," he warned her, "has armed everybody on the east side, including children, with jackhammers and shovels. Forget kudzu; the spreading menace is orange traffic barrels."

"And signs like 'Road under destruction next hundred miles,'" she said, playing along as the sound of his voice eased the ache behind her eyes.

"Looks like I won't get home until six at the earliest, Sare. Would you mind buying some things for dinner?"

"Give me the list. It's lonely here—I'd like to get away." She took up the pad of graph paper and a mechanical pencil he always kept bedside, and noted the groceries he dictated to her, including all of his contingencies: "If the kale isn't good, get a bundle of the Swiss chard—green, not red—and if that has too many wilted leaves, try…"

Finally, with her hand cramped and headache refreshed, she said, "And if the gourmet produce sucks, I'll pick up a microwave pizza."

"OK," he said, a smile lightening the weary tone in his voice, "but only if it has Portobello mushrooms and—"

Sarah snorted and ended the call. Before going out, she checked her face. The clay on her forehead brought to mind an Ash Wednesday penitent, not a nice Jewish girl. She applied make-up with rapid skill, an art learned backstage. Never warm enough, she pulled on a jacket.

The first day in October had turned sunny after morning showers. Beads of rain sparkled in myriad constellations on the windshield of her Miata and its ebony hood. Water still dampened the quiet street and trickled through the gutters, where it carried bits of trash. Watching a torn lottery ticket drift past her tires, she saw the rubber had begun to deflate on all of them, sagging like the waistlines of ex-dancers. She couldn't recall the last time she'd taken her car for a spin, let alone checked the tire pressure. It was only a short trip to the store; she could stop by a gas station to inflate the wheels. Joe never had asked for help before. She didn't want to disappoint him.

After tossing her purse on the passenger seat, she pulled the seatbelt across her svelte torso and sniffed. The interior smelled as musty as antique pointe shoes. "Time to air you out." She lowered the roof despite her shivers and executed a sharp one-eighty turn. Rusty in her reflexes, she held in the clutch too long. The engine roared as she accelerated, and the tires squealed until she completed the high-revving maneuver.

She would only have to drive twelve zigzagging blocks to reach a gas station and the supermarket. At the Piedmont Road intersection, the one busy street on her route, a power outage from the morning storm caused the traffic light to flash red. Instead of treating the intersection as a four-way stop, the drivers on Piedmont took advantage of one less obstacle on their struggle through midtown Atlanta. Vehicles stacked up behind Sarah, and heavy traffic crisscrossed the wet thoroughfare. Sunshine flashing on the pavement made her headache throb worse than ever. She slid on dusty sunglasses from her console as she signaled a left turn.

A small window of opportunity appeared, with empty lanes in both directions. However, traffic quickly was massing again from the north and south, water spraying from wheel wells as the cars charged. Behind Sarah, two drivers leaned on their horns. She gunned the accelerator but rode the clutch in her haste, costing precious time and speed as the oncoming drivers bore down. Cursing, she turned the wheel hard to the left and shifted into second. Her Miata skidded through the wet intersection. She headed south, out in front of the others by a dozen car-lengths.

Sarah shouted, "Winner!" A moment later, the back end of the convertible lost traction. With a neck-wrenching spin, her car faced the oncoming traffic that hadn't stopped for the flashing light. Time slowed. She noted each driver's face, hasty men and women who opened their mouths and eyes wide in panic as they stomped their brakes.

Now time sped up as the roadster whipped around, facing south and safety. The wheel spun in her hand, as useless as bumper-car steering since the deflated tires could not take hold. In a blink, she faced north again, with the traffic on top of her.

Sarah's scream mixed with the screeching of tires and blaring horns. The momentum of the spin flung her hair around as the curb came into view. Her Miata would slam up onto the sidewalk, and the others would shoot past. She would survive. The sense of elation returned, but it only lasted for an instant.

The convertible smashed into a concrete light pole, obliterating the driver's-side fender. Airbags exploded around her as she cried out again, and her roadster bounced back into the street. A minivan caved in the short black hood. The impact stole her voice and consciousness.

During her blackout, she dreamed of Isadora Duncan, the bohemian icon who restored dance to a high art in the 1920s. Cursed by a tragic legacy with cars, Duncan had lost her two children when their unattended vehicle rolled into the Seine River. Years later, a flamboyant silk scarf Duncan had wrapped around her neck and body snagged in the rear wheel of her chauffeured sedan. As the open-top car sped along a Parisian street, fast-winding silk strangled the dancer and yanked her over the side. She was hurtled to her death on the cobblestone pavement. In Sarah's vision, Duncan danced with a scarf hiding her left leg from view.

A symphony of sighs and beeps, the music of machines, greeted Sarah when she blinked awake after the car wreck.

Lying in a hospital bed, she couldn't take a deep breath—tape swaddled her ribs. Tubes carried clear fluid into the back of her hand and trailed under the thin covers to her left leg. Something immobilized her neck, but, peripherally, she saw Joe perched bedside. His expression and the patch shielding his right eye emphasized the direness of her condition. She wanted to apologize for upsetting him and failing in the one thing he'd ever asked her to do.

Bone-deep bruises darkened her skin, but she couldn't feel them any more than she could sense his shadow falling across her. Instead, she experienced a delicious euphoria—as if she were made of laughter and light—all the way down to her toes. Except something was wrong with her left leg. Below her knee, a big lump rounded the nappy gold coverlet and blocked the view of her foot. She might need to call about missing rehearsals the following week. Hopefully she wouldn't have to skip too many of her daily ballet classes. Joe would explain what happened and what it meant; he knew everything.

୧୬

On the kitchen floor in her Aiken home, Sarah woke to familiar sensations—the prosthetic socket squeezing her knee, her phantom left foot trapped under something heavy—but also odd ones: a waterfall surged onto a metallic plain, and insistent birds called. Long oak planks, cool against her face, narrowed in the distance, guiding her attention to a fawn-colored troll that stood on two stubby legs. It had no arms. The troll cocked its head at her; oversized ears pivoted forward and then slid back. It turned its face away, perhaps looking for something more compelling than a cripple with a bruise on her face.

The troll pivoted and revealed a well-muscled body and hind legs: Dorothy. The French bulldog ambled to the front of the house to resume her vigil for Joe. Sarah blinked as the birds stopped singing—the answering machine picked up the incoming call. Over the sound of falling water in the sink, she could make out Joe's voice announcing greetings from the

Gordon residence and apologizing for not being able to take the call. He answered his recorded self, leaving a new version of his lovely tenor in the machine memory. His words were indistinct, but his tone sounded concerned.

She felt her brow, where a small, sensitive lump had formed. Pressing the bruised place caused resurgent pain that nearly blacked her out again. Deep in her ears, a persistent ringing grew louder: the alarm bells of concussion. She crawled to the refrigerator and sat up, steadying herself against the wide door while forcing down nausea. With a cupped hand, she pushed her knuckles against the inset water dispenser. Clumps of crushed ice cascaded into her palm and onto the floor beside her. The ice she caught turned to slush as she held it against her aching head.

Several applications later, frigid water soaked her face, clothes, and the floor. When she felt well enough to stand, she searched kitchen drawers until she found re-sealable sandwich bags. She filled one with ice and pinched it closed. Holding it to the bruised patch, she slumped back against the counter, and her right hand sought purchase behind her. It plunged into 350 cubic inches of cold lasagna.

"Shit!"

She swiped the glass dish into the sink, which snapped off the base of the protruding knife and submerged the lasagna, with its crater-sized hole, under a waterfall. The clatter reinvigorated the pressure behind her eyes and the alarm bells that wouldn't cease. Swaying, she rinsed her hand and kept the ice bag against her forehead.

From the answering machine in the living room, a faint beep reminded her of Joe's call. Puddles seeped under the refrigerator. The paper-towel roll she yanked came free from its holder and uncoiled two-dozen sheets across the counter, the fudge pie, and the floor. In the sink, her dinner lay ruined under water, as irretrievable as Atlantis.

Sarah tried not to cry in pain and frustration but finally gave in. Not just a fraud, no—she was a train wreck, a fuckup. A complete and utter failure.

Chapter 5

JOE HAD CALLED TO MAKE SURE EVERYTHING WAS all right. His recorded voice asked, "How was dinner? I guess I caught you taking Dorothy outside. Remember how bad the mosquitoes get at sundown. Call me around ten, OK? If you have an emergency, I'm carrying my cell." He told Sarah he loved her before hanging up. Joe always said, "I love you," as though for the first time, clearly meaning it.

She slumped on the plush living room sofa, dressed in her seersucker robe. Her crutches lay nearby; she'd abandoned the artificial limb in the bedroom. The painful squeezing had ended, but a thousand tiny demons armed with needles jabbed at her leg to punish her for the long, tight confinement. A small gel strip protected a spot on her stump where a blister had formed.

Sarah removed the fresh bag of ice from her forehead. The swelling was receding, and the ringing had quieted a bit, but the skin between her hairline and brow burned from the cold. After setting the ice bag in a crystal bowl, a wedding present from Joe's father that was displayed on an end table, she reclined against the overstuffed cushions again. She'd thrown out the lasagna and put away the pie uneaten. Despite her fast, she felt bloated.

Another hour remained before the Project Management Institute welcome banquet wrapped up and she would have to call Joe. Tchaikovsky's *The Sleeping Beauty* played pianissimo from his first-rate stereo. She'd put it on as a joke, since she felt the exact opposite of the title, but the music soon reminded her of several versions of the ballet she had danced. The memories both soothed and depressed her.

Dorothy sat at her post and watched the spotlighted gate in constant anticipation of Joe's arrival. While ravenous for anything Joe ever set down, the French bulldog didn't eat the food Sarah had given her. Apparently they both were fasting, though probably for different reasons.

Sarah watched the dog for a moment then chided herself for staring out the window, too. He would be away for another two and a half days. "Hey, Dottie," she called, "we have lives of our own. We don't have to mark time until your daddy gets back." She twisted around to check the mantel clock again. Fifty-five minutes to go. "OK, we could mark time by watching someone else do art on the Internet." The bulldog sighed, and she replied, "Yeah, I don't feel like it either."

On one end of the fireplace, their large wedding portrait beamed down. The grinning faces didn't bother to hide their lascivious desires, which she and Joe had satisfied only two hours after the photograph was taken, and that at one time had been illegal in the state of Georgia.

At the other end of the mantel sat a large, painted bowling pin—anyway that had been Sarah's first impression of the award Joe had brought home one time from his job in Aiken. He worked as a project manager for Matryoshka Engineering, a firm run by Russian expatriates who did lucrative work for the federal government and local industry.

"The figurine's called a matryoshka," he'd informed her, "a Russian nesting doll. Everybody on the project team got one. It's an atta-boy, or whatever the Russian equivalent is."

"They give you toys instead of bonuses?"

"It's not a toy." He hugged it in his arms. "It's a major award."

"A leg lamp is a major award, Joe. This is a wooden teddy bear." She grinned at him and made baby-rocking motions. When he thumped down the figure on the mantel, she held up her hands to declare a truce. "Don't get upset. I'm afraid you can't tell when I'm only teasing."

Since then, the managing partners had presented Joe with

other handcrafted, bowling-pin-shaped figurines. They arrived so regularly, Sarah suspected the expatriates of having ties to a source in the Russian black market.

The nesting doll on the living room mantel, a laminated acrylic of a peasant woman in a blue dress, stood ten inches high and seemed to stare down at Sarah. When she got up, the doll's gaze followed her. Along its base, "Matryoshka Engineering" was written in gold cursive script. Sarah thought of all the figures trapped inside the doll and felt a sudden claustrophobia.

Balancing on her right foot, she removed the top from the outer figure and then from each of the progressively smaller characters contained within it. The last one, a waif-like girl, was hollow and tiny, so small that there wasn't room for "Matryoshka Engineering" like the others. It simply bore the company initials.

Sarah arranged the five un-nested dolls in a row on the mantle, imagining a sweatshop of women with palettes and narrow brushes hunkered over bisected wood forms. She saw their paint-stained fingers and the hard lines of their mouths as they concentrated on making each individual look serene.

Now she'd set the dolls free, and they all watched her. "They look happier, don't you think, Dottie?" This time, the bulldog didn't bother to sigh.

With forty minutes to wait before calling him, Sarah swing-stepped into the master bedroom and took apart the matryoshka on the dresser top. She turned the figures so they looked away from the bed. The realization that the largest doll, a matron holding a pie, had watched her and Joe have sex for the past few months made her nauseated again.

In the den, Joe's most recent award, a Cossack, sat on a table. Not a politically correct thing to give a Jew, now that she thought about it. It loomed over his antique toy banks, which flung coins through space and caught them every time, tin windups, and hand-cranked whirligigs. Sarah freed the family swallowed by the Cossack and set the dolls randomly amongst Joe's collection. In the center, surrounded, she placed the one so small it only bore "M.E." in gold. The figurine looked so pitiful and helpless among the massive toys, it made her mad for some reason. She gave it an angry flick of her finger, sending it skittering and crashing among the other objects. Then she felt ashamed and set it apart.

On every wall and covering the many bookshelves and trophy cases, Joe had displayed her ballet souvenirs and kept them dust-free. Bronzed toe shoes perched sur les pointes beside the last pair she wore on stage, which she'd happened to toss inside her gym bag instead of the trashcan. The peach-colored satin was as battered and bloody as a brawler's fists. On another shelf sat her first ballet slippers, seeming too small even for an eight-year-old. The pink ribbons her mother had sewn on twenty years before had faded to the porcelain hue of her right foot, now bare and un-partnered on the wood floor.

Framed performance photographs showed Sarah in color and monochrome, from prepubescent ballet school productions to center stage with the Atlanta Ballet: the body always rail-thin, long hair done up in a high bun, her face radiant. Most often, she'd danced as part of a corps de ballet, but she also partnered with intense, sculpted men and enjoyed some solo work, too. There she was, captured in the mid-flight of a grand jeté. She had indeed flown, soaring like that sparrow escaping over the wall. In another, she held an arabesque pose with her legs at a right angle, her grounded left foot en pointe, and an arm extended, fingers angled as if to display a beautiful ring. Phantom pressure in her absent left foot reminded her of that amazing trick: balancing her entire body on a few abused toes.

Joe had left plenty of room among the ballet artifacts for the paintings and sculpture she'd promised him and herself that she would complete. Sarah imagined the frames end to end and corner to corner: still-lives, abstracts, landscapes, portraits, street scenes, dancers, nudes. She had watched and memorized hundreds of online classes: brushwork, knife-painting, splattering, blowing, dropping, flinging, kicking, and rolling in it, for God's sake. Plus sculpture of all kinds, from classical busts to thrown pots to welded abstractions. She would master it all. Someday. Maybe starting tomorrow.

The other words returned, always lurking and waiting for an opening. Fraud. Failure. The den was filled with past glory, the old Sarah, a has-been at twenty-eight. About the only thing she'd achieved since the accident was record weight gain. Well, that and champion-caliber insomnia. If not for Joe's passionate attention, she'd have no happy memories from the past nine months.

Phones throughout the house rang, including one at hand, but she didn't want to stay in the den any longer. She hurried on crutches to the master bedroom and sat on Joe's side of the mattress, within reach of the phone on his nightstand. He'd be calling back to tell her stories and make her feel loved. No wonder her mother adored him. He excelled at everything, including relationships.

She thumbed the Talk button, desperate to hear from the only man who had ever treated her with such care. His minor deception about the food was easy to forgive. She'd rationalized his broken promise to throw it all away by the time she said hello.

Joe spent long minutes describing the banquet and the after-dinner speeches. Despite the mundane topics, his voice soothed her, and she stretched out with her head on his pillow.

He said, "I give my seminar twice on Monday and twice again on Tuesday. Everything's in place. I checked out the ballroom to make sure the hotel projector works with my laptop. I can't believe the size of the space they gave me. It seats two hundred."

The last time she'd danced on stage with the Atlanta Ballet, almost two thousand people, including Joe, attended—the smallest house during a long run. Still, he sounded nervous and proud, and she appreciated how he smothered her masochistic thoughts. She said, "Wow, that's a lot. How did you feel standing in front of all those empty chairs?"

"Lonely. We haven't spent a night apart since I almost got you killed."

"That was my fault, not yours," she said for the umpteenth time since the car wreck. She'd said it so often, the words no longer registered in her brain. Nor would they relieve his terrible guilt, she knew. Still, they had to be said. If she unfairly blamed him for one moment—"Look what you did to me!"—she believed that he would curl up and die. Thinking how good it would feel to have him spooning behind her, she said, "I miss you so much."

"You got my message?"

"Sorry I didn't pick up. I was...indisposed."

"'Indisposed' means slightly ill. Also unwilling. Are you OK?"

Damn, she couldn't slip anything past him. "Mom always used it to mean going to the bathroom. Anyway, I've been fine." Bile crept up her throat as her lies mounted, but she didn't want to panic him with the story of her concussion. He'd insist she call an ambulance or dial 911 himself. She'd be fine, nothing a little sleep wouldn't cure.

"How was dinner?" he asked.

"Listen to you, fishing for compliments." She made the zinging sound of a reel spinning out a long cast. "You know that everything you make is perfect."

"Sorry I didn't have time to fix some side dishes."

"I'm afraid you fixed more than enough."

"Eat only what you want—it'll keep. You sound tense. Is everything all right?"

She put a cheerier tone in her voice. "As right as rain."

"I hate to let you go, but you should get some rest."

"Yeah, I need every minute of that so-called 'beauty sleep' I can manage."

"Now who's fishing?" He paused and said, "I know you can't sleep without my help. Want to try something?"

Sarah caught the lustful huskiness in his voice. "What did you have in mind?"

"The only good thing about being apart is that we finally get to have phone sex."

She stared at the ceiling, stifling a groan. The scent of his skin and hair helped her conjure his physicality, but, with the night she'd had, it was impossible to get in the mood. She had never faked it with Joe, and feared this would be the first time.

God knew she'd had plenty of experience convincing past boyfriends of their studliness. Still, she opened her robe and promised herself she would try.

Chapter 6

SARAH MANAGED TO GET A FEW HOURS OF SLEEP despite a stiff neck from cradling the phone receiver to her shoulder until she and Joe had finally said goodnight. Apparently, he'd experienced nearly as much trouble pulling the trigger as she did. It had been a guilty relief when he'd finally gasped so she could add cries of fraudulent ecstasy to his voice. Even worse was lingering on the line afterward, pretending she was sated but looking forward to doing it again the next night. Most troubling, the deception had been second nature.

Lying awake in the dark, she summed up the experience: do what the man wants, pretend it's the best experience any woman ever had, then curse yourself for being a pushover while you deceive the guy you love. Way to go, girl. You really are a mess.

After the chastisement had run its course, she spent the time until daylight thinking about her decision to be an artist, the blank walls and empty shelves in their den, and how grateful she was to Joe for giving her the opportunity she had squandered so far, in addition to abusing his trust. Promises to start on new projects, to resume an exercise program, to stay on her diet, and to be a better wife, daughter, sister, and friend, looped in her mind in an endless mantra of recrimination and self-improvement.

In the morning, smudges beneath her eyes looked darker than the bruise on her forehead. Make-up concealed both flaws. After only eating an orange and some raw almonds for breakfast despite her hunger pains, she felt flush with penitential fervor.

Endless clothing choices gave her a temporary setback. After leaning on her crutches inside the closet for what seemed like an hour, she dressed in practical gear: T-shirt, jeans, cotton underwear, and sneakers. The cut of her denims accommodated Fred, and she locked in her stump with three grudging clicks. Only a vague outline of the socket rim at knee-level ruined the illusion of normalcy.

The clothes were more comfortable than those she usually wore. Having made her own clothing decision for the first time in months, she wondered why she allowed Joe to dress her like a mannequin in an upscale boutique.

That thought haunted her later in the morning. When the intercom buzzed repeatedly from the front gate, she wished she had chosen the kind of outfit he would've selected for her.

Dorothy heard the summons first. The bulldog dashed from the art studio toward the kitchen, barking at the insistent beehive of noise. Sarah sighed and pushed out of the chair beside her drawing board. Even after a mere hour of sitting, the first five steps always produced an all-around ache in her residual limb, a reminder that walking on an artificial leg was not natural. She focused on her gait, the swing of the prosthetic foot. Smooth and steady, smooth and steady. Meanwhile, the buzzer and bulldog vied to create the loudest, most annoying clamor. At the open studio doors, Sarah paused to look back at her painting-area and the fresh sheet of 200-pound watercolor paper she'd just soaked and stretched atop her board. Mastering her art would have to wait. She yawned cavernously and hurried down the hall.

A console set into the kitchen wall near the garage door held a black-and-white monitor, speaker, microphone, and push-button control for the gate. A senior woman, perhaps seventy-five years old, put her face close enough to the camera lens to sniff it, and poked the intercom buzzer again. She had rabbit-like features—beady eyes, a small nose, a trembling mouth—and wore her hair up, almost as high as Marge Simpson's.

Sarah guessed the woman smelled like talcum powder and gingerbread and loved to read cute stories to her great-grandchildren. She shushed the bulldog, thumbed the microphone, and said in her friendliest voice, "Good morning, ma'am. Can I help you?"

The woman talked without making any sound until Sarah coaxed her through the process of holding down the microphone button to speak. "I am Mrs. Robert O'Malley," the woman said in an accent much closer to South Philly than South Carolina. "Your neighbor? I guess you can't see my house over the Great Wall of China here."

Sarah admitted to herself she couldn't remember what the house next door looked like. From the yard, she only could glimpse black-shingled rooftops beyond Joe's eight-foot-high fence. She stammered, her underarms dampening from nervousness. "The, uh, the privacy fence is pretty high, I'm afraid."

"There's nothing pretty about it." Mrs. O'Malley mashed the microphone button again and said, "Are you going be neighborly and come out, or what? I've been waiting months for you to make your appearance and couldn't take it anymore. In my day, the lady of the house behaved like a lady." She brandished a dark, rectangular shape in both hands, as if bringing it down on some poor schmuck's head. "I even made you a present."

So much for first impressions. Sarah swallowed hard and, feeling like the poor schmuck about to get brained, replied, "Um, sure, sorry. You're our first visitor."

"We could've visited lots of times over the fence if you had a normal-sized one. This sucker would've kept in King Kong."

"I think my husband, Joe, meant for it to keep *out* King Kong."

Mrs. O'Malley continued to yell into the microphone, as if she were ordering at a drive-through. "Well it sure as shooting works on harmless little old ladies."

"Right. I'll meet you on the driveway, ma'am." Sarah pressed the button that opened the gate, and went through the garage, pinching her side in punishment for her weakness. Getting bullied by a biddy—what a wuss.

As the overhead door ratcheted above Sarah's head, Mrs. O'Malley shouted from the end of the driveway, "You've got gates sliding one way, folding up another. Do I have to watch out for trapdoors under my feet?" She glared through rose-tinted spectacles at the concrete beneath her lavender shoes, which matched the orchids on her dress. Despite the mid-summer heat, she wore a periwinkle cardigan sweater. Clutched in her hands was a foot-long glass dish covered with foil.

"No trapdoors, ma'am," Sarah said. She made steady eye contact with her guest and focused on keeping her left-side gait the same as her right, two tricks Dr. Ramos had taught her so she wouldn't give the appearance of limping. Up close, Sarah noted her neighbor smelled of fried shrimp and Lubriderm, near enough to her initial guesses to boost her confidence. "No landmines or attack dogs either," she added, indicating Dorothy, who merely fogged a living room window with a panting canine smile. "She's a French bulldog; they're bred to be sweet little pets."

"All those French hate us," Mrs. O'Malley said, looking Sarah over. "You a frog, too?"

"American through and through." Sarah noticed that her voice had relaxed into a languid drawl as she tried to put the elderly woman at ease. "Southern as sweet tea," she added.

"Well I hope you won't mind blueberry crumble from a damn Yankee." She thrust the glass dish at Sarah, who barely got her hands under it before the woman let go.

Sarah said, "Thank you—I appreciate this." Her diet was suffering one assault after another. If you want to make God laugh, her mother had told her, plan something. "And some of my best damn friends are damn Yankees," she added.

"Those must be them Facebook friends," her neighbor said, "because I haven't seen anybody coming and going but your husband."

Great, now we're under surveillance. Rather than pursue that conversational gambit with the dessert-wielding stakeout maven, she replied, "Sorry I didn't introduce myself earlier. I'm Sarah Lyn Gordon. I'd offer you my hand, but—" She wiggled the dish.

"You don't go by one of them modern double last-names?"

"When I danced in Atlanta—" Mrs. O'Malley's eyes widened and her brows rocketed toward her hairline. Sarah amended, "As a professional ballerina, I mean, not a, you know, like a stripper or anything. Um—" she fought down the urge to throw the dish at the old lady and retreat inside "—anyway when I danced I kept my own last name, which is Berger." She flinched at the woman's sour expression and plowed on, "But now that I'm here, I decided to go by my married name."

The old woman said, "I figured you was one of them." She pursed her thin lips and hugged her arms. "You don't strike me as a housewife, Mrs. Gordon. Did you win a ton from some lottery and quit the ballet, or are you in Federal Witness Protection?"

Though only ten a.m., the humidity was high, and the covered dish seemed to weigh ten pounds. Sweat began to stain the short-sleeved shirt across Sarah's back and chest. She said, "I'm sorry, ma'am, I didn't catch your full name."

"My Christian name is Helen. I have Grandma's name as my middle one, and I took my husband Robert's family name to honor him from the beginning, as a good wife should: Helen Grace O'Malley."

"It's a pleasure to meet you." Sarah's smiling mouth began to ache from the forced gaiety she struggled to maintain.

"I asked you whether you was rich or hiding out."

"Neither, ma'am." She didn't count her statement as a lie. Though Joe had lots of money from a trust fund, she never considered it community property. "I work at home. I'm an artist." As if saying it would make it true.

"I hope you don't make pornography or drop crucifixes in potty water or some God-forsaken thing."

"No, ma'am," she said. "I don't like that mess any more than you."

Mrs. O'Malley grunted. "You oughta know that I protested you putting up this fortress. Your husband approached the homeowners association about a waiver to the covenants. I said no right off, but the other six board members went against me."

"Joe can be very persuasive." Sarah wondered if the six others voted in Joe's favor to spite the old bat. Suddenly, she was grateful for the gigantic barrier.

"At first I thought y'all were drug dealers setting up one of them whatchacallits. Compounds."

"One day I hope to sell my art, but that's the only thing I'll be dealing from here." She had to set down the glass dish soon, before she dropped it on her foot—and with her luck it would land on the real one. "Would you like to come inside? I can get you some hot tea or something. You look like you're cold."

The woman stopped hugging herself. "I got poor circulation. My hands are palsied, too. See?" She held out trembling fingers. "I got heart problems, a leaky bladder, and God-knows-what-all. You probably saw my bad limp when I came up the drive."

Sarah didn't recall seeing the woman struggle at all, and Mrs. O'Malley's hands had stopped shaking when she began to mention her other ailments. "Some sweet tea then?"

"Thank you, no, Mrs. Gordon. I'll take a rain check." Mrs. O'Malley rubbed her elbow. Despite the cloudless sky, she said, "Rain's coming. My poor joints are just aching from a storm heading this way."

The woman looked back at the gate, and Sarah seized on the opportunity. "Please visit any time, and thank you for the dessert. I hope to see you again real soon."

"I'm counting on it—I need that dish back." The woman walked down the drive. Halfway to the gate, she began to shuffle with a severe limp.

ↄ

Barricaded once more behind closed gate, shut garage, and locked kitchen door, Sarah paced in the kitchen, trying not to nibble at the blueberry crumble she had uncovered and placed on the counter as a test of her willpower. As with Mrs. O'Malley's elbow, the end of Sarah's residual left leg now ached, causing her to hobble a little.

Thank God for that fence. It certainly kept out the Mrs. O'Malleys of the world. Anti-Semitic, anti-feminist, nosy old crone. Too bad there was a camera and microphone at the gate. No way she could've heard her if that high-haired bitch had been forced to knock.

Sarah wondered if a victim-vibe radiated from her the way the stink of her sweat did. Maybe aggressive types such as Mrs. O'Malley sensed it and took advantage. Maybe that's what Joe saw in her, even a year and a half ago. Rather than kick her though, his impulse was to take care of her.

Dorothy resumed her vigil for Joe at the front windows, while Sarah paused in her limping circuit around the room to stare at the berry crumble. A little sample wasn't going to kill her, unless that was her neighbor's idea. Her stomach rumbled, having long since digested the tiny breakfast of fruit and nuts. She was starving. One look down at the stranger's body, though, reminded her she needed to starve for a long, long time. Hell, she deserved to, for having lost such control. She pivoted away and resumed her walk through the long kitchen.

The room grew dimmer. Sarah watched through the front window as a fast-moving storm swallowed the daylight. Towering cumulonimbus clouds surged across the sky, shadowed in Payne's gray with a faint tinge of cadmium yellow sunshine at the edges. A minute later, raindrops whacked the glass. Mrs. O'Malley wasn't a complete nut after all. Or maybe her elbow was the only thing to be trusted.

Phones rang, and she retrieved the cordless mounted on a kitchen wall. Joe's number showed on the display. He said, "Hey, how's my artist extraordinaire?"

"Not producing anything extraordinary, I'm afraid." Hell, not producing anything, period. "How's my super-PiMP?" she asked, referring to his longstanding Project Management Professional certification.

"There's lots of competition for that title here."

"Well it is 'Hotlanta': Hookers for every taste, Sodom-on-the-piedmont."

"I mean at the conference," he said, over background chatter. "These people know their business. Are you eating lunch?"

"Not yet, but I will. I promise. By the way, it's raining here."

"You're getting caught by the storm that cooled off Hotlanta last night. Those same clouds rained on my rooftop, too, while we were, uh, talking. I think that's kind of romantic."

"I wish you'd ridden back to Aiken on those clouds."

Hearty female laughter and other crowd noises came over

the line. Joe excused himself and sounded like he was making his way to a quieter spot. Finally, he asked, "Are you all right, Sare?"

She could name a dozen things that made her not all right, but she said, "Fine, just missing you." Turning to resume her pacing, she glimpsed the glass dish of Sweet Death on the counter. "I had a close encounter this morning with one of our neighbors, Mrs. Robert O'Malley. 'Helen Grace' is what she considers her lesser, female name."

The crowd he had stepped away from seemed to have followed him. She barely made out his next question: "You went for a walk?"

Due to the background clamor, she couldn't decide if he sounded facetious, alarmed, or merely curious. "No, she came to visit and to tell me that she hates our fence."

"Good fences make good neighbors."

Sarah snorted. "That's exactly what I was thinking."

The voices grew even louder, and Joe excused himself again. When he next spoke, no one competed with him. "Anyway, I had a full house for my talk and got laughs in all the right places. There was lots of applause at the end."

How selfish, forgetting about his big presentation. Here she was fretting about her little problems while he was handling real responsibilities with ease. She said, "Sorry, I meant to ask how it went."

"God, what a heady feeling. You remember what that was like, from your old days in ballet?"

She winced at the verbal sucker-punch, hoping it was accidental. "Yeah, Joe, I'm afraid I do."

Chapter 7

RAIN FELL FOR MOST OF THE AFTERNOON, AND Sarah coaxed the bulldog into her studio for silent, baleful company. While Dorothy kept watch through the glass wall, she stared at her blank canvas. The storm turned her outside world—the enclosed yard—into watercolor washes, but she failed to get inspired. "I love the rain," she told Dorothy. "Why doesn't it give me the kick in the butt I need?"

The bulldog made no response, not a look, not even a sigh.

Joe called again after his second seminar, riding high on adrenaline and approbation. She told him how pleased she was. His "old days in ballet" comment still stung, though he was right. She was a has-been and probably should count herself lucky for having as long a run as she did, given the brutality of ballet.

Right before Joe came on the scene, her mother had provided a typically candid summary of Sarah's failings when she confessed to her parents about nagging injuries and waking some mornings almost paralyzed with pain: "The ballet never paid you much, but I figured you'd at least learn how to stay in shape. I'll send you an article from today's paper on stretching, to share with your teachers. If you don't take better care of yourself now, you'll be sorry when you're my age, Feygela. And find a nice Jewish boy you won't be ashamed to bring home."

The nice Jewish boy she'd found, Joseph Gordon, called again at bedtime. A grudging need for sleep had dragged Sarah down all evening. Somehow she couldn't give in, but nor could she focus on anything. She'd watched the same video five times but couldn't recall the first thing about pastel underpainting in mixed-media scenarios. Dinner was a half-can of tuna fish, straight from the tin. Mrs. O'Malley's dessert lay in several layers of foil at the bottom of the kitchen garbage bag. Sarah had been proud of not tasting even one morsel while scraping out the dish.

Joe told her about the evening activities organized for conference members. His voice soothed her so much, she found herself struggling to stay alert. She placed the landline phone against her hip and stroked her underfed belly, imagining it had become less flaccid, that her breasts and buttocks were tauter. Her last conscious thought was that, one day, she would be trim enough to sail like the house sparrow over the towering wall, leaping—soaring—in a truly grand jeté.

In a dream, she soloed on two strong legs before an empty theater, hitting her marks under dimmed house lights. The theme was rebirth. Piano music, a modern jazz score with a complex melody, played in her head rather than from speakers or the orchestra pit. Appearing as slender as in her old days in ballet, she danced well. She danced for herself.

The phone rang, waking her. It rested against her hip with such steady pressure that she thought Joe had come to bed. Then she remembered his call the night before and feared she'd hung up on him. She wiped saliva from her cheek and chin, and felt a large drool stain on the pillow. She yawned, "Hello?"

"Hey, my love," Joe said. "How long did you sleep?"

"When…what time is it?" Gray light edged between the blinds.

"It's 7:41. You mean…oh no, Sare, did I wake you? I'm so sorry, I'll let you go."

She murmured the same thing she'd said after their first full night together, when he apologized for holding her until morning: "Don't ever let me go. Please."

"No, not like that, never. But, do you realize you slept nine hours and we didn't even…I mean…Get back to sleep. I'll talk to you soon."

He left Sarah wide awake. She had slept hard; her muscles ached and the bones in her right foot felt abused. Even after rubbing the tips of her toes, they remained numb, as if she had done hours of pointe work on them. Her dream touched the surface of her consciousness a few times, like a fish nipping at food atop the water. When she tried to recapture memories of leaps and landings, though, they darted away, disappearing into the murky depths.

Rain tapped on the house again, casting the bedroom in gloom. When Sarah went to use the bathroom, she discovered that the latest storm had knocked out the electricity. Only their landline phones still operated, but everything else was dead. The dreary morning illuminated a window of glass blocks beside the vanity, sufficient for her to notice the battery-operated bathroom scale as she sat on the toilet. She hoped she wouldn't have to work on her painting in the near-dark; she had no idea where Joe kept the candles and flashlights.

The scale indicated she had dropped a pound since Sunday. Her stomach moaned, a sound that pleased her, and the hunger pains were exquisite. She remembered her first ballet instructor's advice to the chubby girls in class: "Grace in movement is a series of lines, not curves. Some of you are all curves. To be thin—a perfect line!—is to be beautiful. Oh, don't starve yourselves, certainly, but remain hungry, girls. To feel hunger is to feel control over your body. Ballet is about grace…lines…control."

Some dancers used diuretics and others chose bulimia. Sarah's willowy build gave her an advantage, so she only had to starve a little. She experienced irregular periods, anemia, and constipation during her years as a borderline anorexic, but nothing she couldn't handle. Mostly she had reveled in the control that lately deserted her.

"No," she told herself as she stared at the scale, "the control I gave up." She could, she *would*, get it back.

She sat on the plastic stool and washed herself in the darkness of the expansive walk-in shower. Pain from knotted muscles and tendons felt good—familiar—as she massaged them under the hot spray. The water heater used natural gas, so she didn't have to worry about a sudden blast of cold. Deciding to stretch, she stood and held the handicap bars for balance. She couldn't bend over as far as she used to. At her peak of flexibility, she could put her head between her knees and view her own hard-muscled butt. Trying to stretch as she'd done in the old days, a sudden tightness grabbed the back of her right leg, the hamstring seizing up. She heeded the warning. Take it slow.

When she did, babying herself but daring to stretch farther and farther, the resulting satisfaction made her want more. "Dottie," she called as she dried herself, "screw the rain. We're going for a long walk this morning."

Across the bedroom, the bulldog roused from a deep, snoring slumber. Dorothy stretched and cocked her head at Sarah, who said, "What? Didn't you realize Mommy knew about exercise? I used to live on it instead of food."

Moist heat from the shower had fogged the large vanity mirror. She wiped it clear and evaluated the stranger's naked form, touching the countertop for balance as she turned one way and then another, peering over her shoulder, sucking in, lifting and separating, ultimately wishing that she had left the damned glass steamy. The bruise on her forehead had faded to a muddy purple-gray that resembled her palette when she would blend too many watercolors.

She prepared for a long, damp walk, wrapping Fred mummy-like in cellophane. Manufacturers produced special beach and shower prostheses, but most models offered mere water resistance, not waterproofing. During prolonged exposure, moisture could seep past the hosiery; the foam would absorb it and make the artificial leg stink.

Clothing decisions were easier today. After donning underwear and a T-shirt, she tied her still-damp hair into a lank ponytail and pulled on an old nylon tracksuit. The last time she'd worn the crimson outfit, she went for a run alone through the sunny Atlanta streets and Piedmont Park and returned to find Joe waiting with a marriage proposal. He did it right, on bended knee. The diamond ring fit perfectly, since he'd once measured her finger while she slept. Overwhelmed by Joe's earnestness and the bright three-stone cluster on a platinum band, she gave her assent, laughing and crying. She apologized for the reek of her sweat, so he bathed her before carrying her to bed. Afterward, their mingled perspiration had smelled sweet.

Now, in the bedroom, she pulled up the zipper of her crimson jacket, and the water-resistant material stretched across her chest. Already the pants had wedged between her buttocks. The synthetic encasement made her overheat. She called to Dorothy again and trotted down the long hall, eager to sweat from exertion rather than mere existence. Her athletic shoes squeaked as she corrected the left leg's gait.

The bulldog consented to eat some of the special-formula dog chow Joe ordered in bulk, while Sarah nibbled a banana and a half-cup of yogurt. She retrieved one of Joe's red-billed Atlanta Braves baseball caps to shield her head from the steady drizzle, and tucked her ponytail over the adjustable strap in the back. Taking the house key, she exited through the front door with a black leash and collar. Warm, thick air enveloped her like a living thing.

Dorothy raced to the gate and hopped around in the puddles, as if she expected Joe to drive up. Sarah fought to secure the plastic clips of the collar while the thick-necked bulldog struggled to break free. With the leash finally in place, Dorothy gave an exasperated sigh, and Sarah gripped the nylon loop at the other end of the tether.

She wiped rainwater and perspiration from her eyes and stared at the gate mechanism. The electricity was still off, but there had to be a manual release. Her gaze took in the black metal gear-works, scanning for an emergency pull similar to the plastic rope that dangled from the inside of the garage door. The wet, ebony drive-train remained inscrutable, immovable, as she grasped and prodded with her free hand and cussed aloud.

Though only an eighteen-pound lapdog, Dorothy tugged Sarah's arm with surprising strength. Yelling, "Quit that, dammit," she jerked the three-foot leash toward her. Sarah stopped cold as the bulldog began to cough and hack. The flat, masked face drooped toward the grass. She thought she'd crushed the dog's windpipe, but, after a final retch, Dorothy raised an impudent chin, furrowed her already-wrinkled brows, and stared Sarah down. Rain glistened on the bulldog's muzzle like tears, making her appear more doleful than ever.

"Look, I'm sorry, OK?" Sarah squatted close to Dorothy's

level, grimacing at the tightness in her hamstrings. Stitches popped in the seat of the tracksuit. "I'm afraid I'm the one in charge when Daddy's not home."

The bulldog blinked her opalescent eyes and streaked away. When the nylon leash yanked free, it seared Sarah's right hand with a wide, deep burn. Dorothy fled around the corner of the house, the leash trailing across the lawn like a captured flag. Rubbing her inflamed palm, Sarah cursed some more and kicked the confounding mechanism that kept her locked inside the eight-foot-high walls. Fred supported her weight just fine, so she kicked the gears again.

Rain quickened, slapping her shoulders and Joe's cap. With a sigh, she gave in and returned to the house. Dorothy could stay in the rain for a while, she decided, acknowledging her childish reaction to the painful welt across her hand. A yelp from the backyard changed her mind.

Dorothy regarded her again, with chin raised but eyes panicked. The leash had snared a tomato cage, which she had yanked from the wet garden soil before trapping herself in a towering forest of other cages. Pale, fuzzy green limbs, leaves, and ripening tomatoes poked at her from all sides. The dog's tawny fur had turned dismal with rain and mud. She tugged within her confining collar and whined.

"I know the feeling," Sarah said as she trotted to the garden plot. She whispered encouragement, hoping to soothe the dog's fears as she freed her. When she opened the collar, Dorothy sprinted to the gate once more. By the time Sarah had set the tomato cages upright and tossed the broken limbs and lost fruit onto the compost pile, the dog had settled in the soggy Bermuda grass to watch her.

"Open sesame!" Her shout startled Dorothy, but got nowhere with the gate. "Oseh shalom?" Again, nothing. She hefted the struggling bulldog and slogged back toward the front door. A mottled sparrow took wing and disappeared beyond the fence. Goddamn lucky bird.

ɞ

Her damp clothes and ball cap chilled her, and rain-speckled cellophane trailed behind her as it unraveled from Fred's bare mannequin foot. After she cleaned Dorothy and the muddy tracks they'd made indoors, she noticed the message light and soft chirp of the answering machine. It ran on the fresh batteries Joe had installed, since the household power still was off. He'd called to check on her.

Near the phone, a plastic bag floated in a crystal bowl. She had forgotten about her discarded, leaky ice pack from Sunday night.

While she dried the bowl in the kitchen, the ice bag brought to mind her still-bruised forehead, the huge servings of unwanted food, and how pissed off she'd felt about everything. She returned the bowl to the end-table and lifted the receiver on the landline to call Joe. Then she decided she didn't feel like talking. She was in the mood for a joyous ache.

Sarah rewrapped the artificial foot, tied on her white sneakers, and went back outside to run laps around the house. She wished she could go barefoot, but the risk to Fred was too great, and running with one foot bare and the prosthesis covered would ruin her hip alignment. In contrast with Joe, who almost always wore shoes or slippers, she loved the raw, gritty contact with the earth. Spending much of her early childhood in Savannah outdoors in bare feet and then graduating to thin-soled pointe shoes had left her with the need to feel contours of the ground. Now even that was denied to her.

Outdoors, she picked up a stone to help keep track of laps— left hand for odd numbers, right hand for even—and stretched her leg muscles again before beginning a slow jog in the steady rain. The prosthetic foot flexed and pushed off, responding to the additional pressure. In her stump and left knee, pain ebbed as the limb seemed to accept the increased abuse. Bermuda grass scrunched beneath her, and grit from the sandy Aiken soil dirtied the pristine sneaker toes. Other than a few islands of young azaleas and saplings dotting the wide lawn, she had little to look at except the sprawling ranch house, Joe's garden in back, and his fence. Eight vertical feet of wet ivory panels in every direction, with the occasional security floodlight on top.

After one circuit around the house, she stepped up her pace, breathing harder, sweating freely inside the tracksuit. The high-tech leg didn't falter when she demanded more, and the grip of the gel liner kept her leg from pistoning against the socket. If not for the voracious mosquitoes, and the need to protect Fred, she would've stripped naked. Down to bra and panties, she amended, as her breasts thudded against her ribcage in spite of firm support, and the excess layers on her rump rippled whenever she struck the ground. With all of that baggage, there was no way she could do five miles anymore.

She figured that eight laps would approximate a mile. If she could do sixteen circuits—burn maybe a couple hundred calories—she would declare victory. Rain dripped from the red bill of the waterlogged cap and weighted down her blond ponytail against the nape of her neck. Heedless of puddles, she spattered her shoes and leggings with mud. She caught sight of Dorothy gazing out from a front window and, miracle of miracles, the dog actually seemed to be watching for her.

Around and around Sarah ran, wondering what a bird overhead would make of the sopping woman inside a huge rectangle doing laps around the long box-like house. Each time she passed the north corner, she glanced at her darkened studio. Behind rain-studded glass like a curtain of beads, she saw shadows of her art supplies. Clay and canvas existed to record inspiration; in the absence of the artist, they seemed as forlorn as an untouched piano, unworn toe shoes. Before she could return to them, though, she needed to begin remaking herself.

"That's eight," she called. "Now do another eight."

Confidence in her body grew, even as strength began to fail her. Every breath burned as blood throbbed in her face and hands. The joyous ache of exercise gave way to the pain of overtaxed lungs and laboring muscles.

Come on, she thought as she began her fifteenth circuit, switching the stone to her left hand. Go for breakdown.

Breakdown, or "The Point of No Return" as one ballet mistress called it, was the limit of physical endurance. By repeatedly taking her body to that frontier over the years, Sarah had stretched the envelope of complete collapse.

"Do five more, an even twenty. Keep moving!"

She and her peers in dance class had speculated whether they could extend the boundary infinitely, or would die trying. Twice-daily performances of *The Nutcracker* each December had made death seem preferable. Having demanded so little of herself lately, Sarah knew she now asked for too much.

On the seventeenth lap, a catch in her left hamstring forced her to shorten her strides, to slow her pace. Each breath seared her throat. The walls of her chest ached from the incessant bounce of her breasts. "Think you can take it, Fred?" she groaned. "Think I'll quit first?" Every muscle quivered.

Still, she continued to jog.

Before she completed her eighteenth time around, her legs began to spasm, and she had to settle for walking. Her stride soon devolved into a lurching gait, and then a painful limp as blisters erupted across her stump. She staggered but stayed upright. Hands balled on hips, shoulders slumped within her tracksuit soaked to the color of clotted blood, Sarah kept moving.

In the backyard, before she could complete her twentieth lap, she stumbled and fell. Ignoring the sanctuary offered by the dining room doors, she continued on hands and knees. Rain struck her back with the frenetic pace of a typist's fingertips.

She had to use her forearms to crawl along the side of the garage. Her overworked, jelly-like legs dragged behind. Squeezing the stone within her right fist, where the leash-burn had swollen into a four-inch welt, she summoned fresh pain to keep her mind focused. Finish what you started, damn you. Finish it!

On bruised, abraded elbows, she pulled herself across the wide driveway. She winced every time her left knee failed to stay bent and the artificial leg scraped the concrete. The cosmetic hose beneath its meager protection could tear and stain almost as easily as regular stockings.

When Sarah touched the grass on the other side, she shouted, "Winner!"

She lay face down in the yard, laughing and crying, the

elation and agony of "breakdown" now more than a memory from her old days in ballet. The visor of the baseball cap pressed against the soggy ground like a beak. Sweet scents of wet grass and earth filled her nose once she stopped gasping for air. In her darkened tracksuit, she imagined appearing to that circling bird as a body with every inch of skin flayed off. She felt stripped in both extremes: utterly raw and entirely new.

Chapter 8

UNDER DOROTHY'S INSCRUTABLE GAZE, SARAH left the prosthesis with its muddy wrappings in the foyer and shucked off her soaked clothes during a triumphal crawl to the bedroom. After the longest shower of her life, she applied gel strips to her blisters and then dripped dry on the bathroom tiles. She awoke atop the towel she'd stretched out, long after promising herself only a few minutes of shut-eye. For the second time in three days, she had passed out on the floor.

The bathroom fan whirred and banks of lights around the huge vanity mirror blazed. Beyond the glass-block window, the sky had darkened further. When she consulted a battery-operated clock on the countertop, she saw she had lost most of the day.

Still, she decided there was time to rest a little longer before dinner. Hunger pains reinforced that desire to wait. Every muscle ached as she crawled across the lush carpet toward bed. The stub of her left leg smarted. What she had not abused while running, she'd made sore by sleeping on ceramic tile for six hours. Curiously, Joe hadn't called. She felt certain that ringing phones would've roused her. She groaned as she tried to haul herself onto the bed, a real effort since she had no leverage with either her amputated left leg or her weakened right. "So this is what they mean," she gasped, "by not having a leg to stand on."

Dorothy trotted up the hallway, nails clicking on the hardwood, and peered in. Lying naked atop the covers, Sarah said, "Oh, Dottie, this is what my old days in ballet felt like. How wonderfully awful and awfully-fucking-wonderful."

The bulldog sighed and returned to the living room windows.

Running her fingers through stiff, unruly hair, Sarah considered how much energy she needed to muster to let the dog out and then fix something to eat. Maybe a smoothie and a hard-boiled egg or…hmmm.

She heard her name and, focusing her eyes, recognized all the elements of an erotic dream: gorgeous Joe held her bare shoulders, his collar unbuttoned and Windsor knot askew. There was a desperate look in his left eye—the black triangular patch with its slim headband covered his right, making him appear vulnerable and dangerous at the same time. So sexy. His grip was insistent, possessive.

His tie flicked like a silken tongue across her stomach. She willed it lower, but it continued to tease her navel. She touched his trousers, searching along the inside of his thigh, disappointed he wasn't erect. The fantasy puzzled her since she didn't get excited by obstacles and frustration.

"Sare!" Joe took her questing hand. "You're OK?"

Dorothy barked beside him and pawed his leg. Sarah blinked and said, "Huh? I thought…What time—wait—what day is it?"

"Tuesday night. Quarter after nine."

Still sleepy, she paused to admire Joe's wherewithal. He didn't even need to look at a clock to know the time. So in-tune with the world, so— "Your conference! Did something happen? You weren't supposed to be home until tomorrow."

"I left. I did my second seminar at three, and the line here was still busy, so I waited another hour while I tried to reach you." At his feet, Dorothy whined for attention.

"We lost power for a while," she said, in the midst of a long yawn.

"That only affects the cordless phones. The landlines should still work. And the answering machine can operate on batteries. I had all kinds of terrible thoughts: someone breaking in, knocking the phone off the hook so you couldn't call out, trapping you."

She came more fully awake, surprising herself with the vehemence in her voice. "I was trapped. Your goddamned gate wouldn't open." Then the sight of the black patch struck her. Behind it, his right eye would've turned outward, the iris and pupil edging into the far corner of his eye socket. Stress had overwhelmed him—just as it had at the hospital—and she was to blame. Again.

"All I could think about was some maniac in here," he continued, ignoring her. "So I cut out at six and got here as fast as I could. The Georgia State Patrol stopped me for doing ninety-three outside of Augusta, otherwise I would've been here sooner."

Her eyes widened. "You never go even five miles over the speed limit."

"I never had a wife being attacked by a homicidal rapist before, though I couldn't convince the cops of that. So I finally got here and ran through the house, shouting your name. I saw that leg and a trail of filthy clothes on the floor leading this way." He gulped and went on, "And here you are, sprawled naked, with a bruise on your forehead and your hair a mess, and I thought it was all true and—"

Sarah put her fingers over his mouth to calm him. "The bruise is self-inflicted. Like everything else wrong with me." She covered herself with a blanket, uneasy now as he stared down and the whole melodrama became clear. "You mean to say that a problem with the phones sent you racing here all the way from Atlanta?"

He said, "I had to know you were safe." He finally petted Dorothy, quieting the dog's pleas.

"And your eye: that's from stressing out, right?"

"I was worried sick, scared I hadn't protected you."

"You might try locking me in Fort Knox next time. You'd think that I could get away from this place if I wanted to."

"There's a manual release on the gate. Wait a minute—'get away'? What's wrong with this place that you need to escape from it?"

She touched her now-throbbing forehead. "I didn't mean that. I only wanted to take Dorothy for a walk. Is that too much to ask?"

"All I want is to take care of you, to make sure you're safe and secure."

"You do, but...never mind." As he continued to loom over

her, she looked around, wanting to shift his focus. She pointed to the phone on his nightstand and said, "It's still not working?"

Joe crossed to the other side of the bed and held the silent receiver toward her. "No dial tone. I'll check the others and put the house back in order, the way I left it."

As soon as he went down the hall with Dorothy in tow, Sarah grabbed her crutches and, still naked, hobbled to the bathroom. The leash-burn across her right palm brought fresh bursts of stinging pain.

With her supports propped against the wall, she wanted to ease the door closed, but in her haste she slammed it shut before turning the lock on the knob. She sat on the cold toilet lid, picked a large, clammy towel off the floor, and wrapped it around her shoulders and knees. Shaking, she fought an irrational urge to cry as she tried to figure out what was disturbing her so much.

In a few minutes, knuckles tapped on the door. Joe said, "Are you OK, Sare?"

She tucked the towel closed beneath her armpit. The overtaxed muscles in her right leg trembled as she hopped to the door. She unlocked and opened it—and screamed.

Joe dropped the muddy tracksuit that, lying across his arms, had looked for an instant like a flayed, mutilated corpse. He adjusted his eye patch and asked, "What's wrong with you?"

Chills spread over her exposed skin as she quailed. "Nothing," she stammered. "I'm afraid I'm not myself."

"I'm glad you said it first. Do I need to get you a prescription?"

"I don't need doping. You scared me, is all. It looked like… Shit, I wore that thing when I took a run outside, around the prison yard."

He picked up her outfit. "'Prison yard?' Ouch."

"Sorry. That was uncalled for."

"When did you start running again?"

Sarah leaned against the doorjamb. Balancing on her sore right leg had become a chore. "Today was the first time. I had to get a little exercise before I did something crazy."

"So you ran in the pouring rain on a prosthesis you'd said hurt to even walk on? Nothing crazy there."

"It didn't hurt any worse running on it, and it sure beat sitting on my fat ass."

In a louder voice, he asked, "Are you mad at me for being concerned? For expressing an interest in your well-being?"

"No, of course not." She grabbed her crutches for additional support and tucked the foam pads under her armpits. The towel began to slip, threatening to expose her. "But you're so concerned that you race all the way back from Atlanta 'cause you can't get me on the damn phone? That makes me sad."

"If you hadn't set the receiver down wrong in the living room, this wouldn't have happened. It wasn't seated in its cradle. Didn't you hear the annoying off-hook signal?"

Sarah shook her head. "I must've gone out to run right after I hung up."

"Well, then we both made a mistake."

She swing-stepped past him to her closet. The towel gaped in front but shielded her back. In the bunker of her closet, surrounded by clothes and shoes on three sides, she sat on a bar stool and dressed in fleecy sweats. No doubt she'd soon overheat, but uneasiness made her seek the armor of thick clothing. After rolling up the left leg of the baggy pants over her stump, she emerged on crutches again. Joe had remained in place by the bathroom. "OK, I'm afraid I screwed up," she said, "but I can't believe you were so worried. Really, Joe, that's not normal."

"You mean 'normal' like wearing sweats in July?"

"I mean you're so overprotective. Nothing else bad is going to happen to me. I can take care of myself. I'm not some agoraphobic shut-in, like Monica." She looked away as heat rose in her face and perspiration clawed her ribs. Joe was touchy about his sister, who still lived in Virginia with their father. Though Monica was Sarah's age, she'd never held a job or gone out on a date. Joe phoned her at least once a week.

"Monica's had a traumatic life," he said. "She was only six when Mom died."

"I'm not picking on her. And I don't want to argue with you." He folded his arms and leaned against the bathroom doorjamb, clutching her soiled outfit in one large hand. "Isn't that what 'normal' couples do?"

"Why are you spoiling for a fight?"

"Maybe because I'm feeling unappreciated. Would a 'normal' husband even attempt all that I do for you: make a good living, take care of the house, and see to your every need? No. Would a 'normal' husband come to your aid as I did? Never. He'd blow it off, go to the hotel bar, and check out the hotties in town for the conference." She tried to interrupt, but he plowed ahead. "I realize it was a false alarm and that I look ridiculous, but how could I have known that?" He yanked off the black patch, revealing his right eye.

The upper and lower eyelid twitched, squinting in the bright bedroom light, but she could still make out the slick expanse of bloodshot whiteness. The brown iris and shrinking pupil had edged into the outer corner, like a frightened animal trying to make itself very small. He pointed at it and yelled, "I care enough to risk my life to make sure you're safe. I'll be damned if I ever put you in danger again."

Sarah swing-stepped over to him, leaned her crutches against the wall, and put her arms around his waist. She pressed her cheek against his silk tie and waited, holding her breath. Only after he hugged her back did she relax. "Forgive me?" she murmured. "I'm a stupid ass."

"Stop that. I know you've been sad about me being away. It's made you jittery." Joe stroked her back in a soothing circle. "Would you tell me about the bruise?"

"I banged my head leaning over the sink."

He rested his chin against the part in her hair. She felt his jaw bob as he said, "And the welt on your hand?"

"Dorothy yanked the leash free." She sighed. "Maybe I can't take care of myself."

"That's why you have me. What I'd really like to know is, why were you playing with my matryoshkas?"

His smile warmed the top of her head. She nuzzled his chest and said, "I'll answer you, but only if you explain how you know about the hotties at the Sheraton bar."

Even pressed tight against him, she couldn't hide a mournful wail from her empty stomach. He punned, "Looks like we were both saved by the knell." When she groaned in response, he added, "I'll warm up dinner for us."

She knew he'd soon discover the missing lasagna, so she rehearsed her story while changing from sweats into her robe. With the patch resettled over his right eye, Joe led the way to the kitchen. She trailed him down the hall, his house shoes thumping in counterpoint with the firm placement of her crutches and pat of her bare foot. Dorothy met them in the dining room and fell in behind Joe. Sarah brought up the rear of the procession.

"It might take a while to heat something," she said. "I had an accident with the lasagna."

At the word "accident," his shoulder blades flexed as if an arrow had struck him in the back. Still, he kept walking, and replied with his stiff-upper-lip British imitation: "Were many lives lost, dear woman?"

"Just the entrée's, Prince Joseph."

He didn't pursue the matter, but his pace quickened to the refrigerator, perhaps to inventory other casualties. After unwrapping the fudge pie, he said, "Hmm, since the portions have multiplied, let's splurge and each have two."

Before she could speak, her stomach trumpeted its assent.

He also reheated two portions of the frozen sausage bake, after making a show of cutting her piece "extra small, like the pie wedges." They ate at the tiger-maple dining table under chandelier lights adjusted to romantic dimness. The grease-and-sage flavor of the warm sausage contrasted well with the mild cheese and egg mixture that held the casserole together; buttery breading on top yielded a hint of his homegrown rosemary as she savored and swallowed. The food acted like a narcotic, flooding her with a desire for more. She coveted his large portion even as she cursed her gluttony.

Between bites, she said, "Sorry I was such a bitch when you got home. Play hooky from work tomorrow, and I'll make it up to you. Your manager doesn't expect you back until Thursday anyway."

"It's just as well I came back tonight. I can't afford to miss another day. Those engineers get distracted so easily when I'm not applying the lash." He hefted a big forkful into his mouth and made a pleased humming sound.

"Oh, the lash." She gave him a peek inside her robe and continued to flirt while they ate. When she next glanced down, most of her meal had vanished. She had virtually inhaled it. Using a favorite trick from her ballerina days, she cut the remaining portion into tiny pieces and pushed them around her plate so she could count them. Sixteen. She would save half of them and chew the other morsels fifty times each: eight scraps then would seem like plenty.

His uncovered left eye stared at her deft work with the fork. "Did I make it too hot? Will it cool faster that way?"

"You've never seen me play with my food?"

"Sure, when we first met. But since we got married, you matured into someone who appreciates it."

"Like a hog at a trough, I'm afraid."

"Stop it. You said I'm the one spoiling for a fight? Here." Joe carved away a hunk of steaming casserole and speared the cluster of beige, white, and gold with the fork tines. "Enjoy." He guided the food to her waiting mouth.

Chapter 9

SARAH HAD HELPED HIM FINISH HIS DINNER AND both plates of dessert before realizing she'd undone her small dieting achievement. She let Joe shower and get ready for bed first. As he slid naked between the sheets, she told him, "Don't start without me, lover." His splendid body had responded to her continual flirting, but his expression remained guarded. Time to make up for the rotten homecoming and change that pout into a smile.

But first things first. She locked the bathroom door and left the noisy overhead fan running. Propping her crutches beside the toilet, she wondered how best to make herself throw up.

Bulimia had never appealed to her before, but now she saw it as a way to undo her mistake, to regain control. And administer the punishment she deserved. She raised the lid and seat without a sound. Down on her sore knees, with the robe providing a cushion against the tile floor, Sarah held back her hair. Her silhouette wavered in the commode water. She inched a tentative finger into her mouth and touched the tender wetness at the back. The base of her throat constricted in a gag reflex. Just this once, and never again. Her short fingernail prodded the soft tissue. Tears sprang to her eyes as she pressed harder.

A convulsive wave began in her abdomen and surged upward. It curved her spine and rolled her shoulders. Aching muscles tensed for the anticipated vomiting. When her finger hesitated, the fist that held back her hair pushed down until her throat was impaled. Her body shuddered, wracked by the irresistible momentum of purging. She wanted the release but feared it, too.

The next time would be easier, a voice inside told her—and there would be a next time and a time after that. Now she understood. Oh God!

She stopped herself, a braking process that seized every part of her, more painful than anything she'd felt that day. The initial retching knotted her stomach, and dry heaves buckled her diaphragm. Chills shook her sweat-glazed body, and self-disgust made her cry out. A hiccup of grief and pain ricocheted off the cold pool of commode water, creating ripples, sounding like an angry bellow as it echoed past her ears. Only a trace of saliva dampened her fingertip, though she wouldn't have been surprised to see a clot of blood. She braced for Joe's knuckles tapping on the door, tensed for his voice that would be full of concern, eager to comfort. Tears slid off her cheeks and sprinkled the water— she would give in to no more than that.

He didn't check on her. After flushing the toilet and washing her hands and face, she edged open the door. Joe slept on his back. He had given up on her. Even in sleep, his down-turned mouth displayed disappointment.

She cried anew.

ᥴ᧞

Sarah spent a sleepless night in the den, watching artists' videos and reading how-to websites. Originally, she intended to clean up her mess in the foyer, but Joe had already done it. Mud no longer streaked the floor, and he had put her leg somewhere, but she couldn't find it. As she memorized the techniques on display, she couldn't resist swallowing over and over. Thinking she would soothe her irritated throat, instead she kept it inflamed and continued to relive her sorry episode.

Early the following morning, she swing-stepped to the bedroom on her sore leg. The welt still caused discomfort as her right hand gripped its crutch, and the blisters on her knee throbbed beneath the gel strips. Frequent yawning had made her jaws ache. The outer corners of her eyes pinched together, as if stitched closed by exhaustion.

Joe always got up at 5:30 on weekdays so he could hit the gym for an hour or more before doing a full day's work. She made sure to arrive at his bedside before his clock-radio sounded. Unable to read its settings in the dimness, she flipped a few switches in hopes of disabling the alarm.

Despite her pains, she really wanted to do something for him—to erase his disappointment and alleviate her guilt about the dramas of the previous night. She imagined easing down alongside his naked body, resisting the urge to touch him with her mouth until she reached his midsection. Then she would take him. So much better than a bony index finger in the throat. But with her luck, she thought, Joe would jerk awake and gag her, and she would puke all over him. The bulimic fellatrix.

Still, he might like to wake up to something special, instead of hearing that alarm blare. She lowered the crutches, eased onto her knees, and searched for the edge of the covers. The radio roared with the static of a tuner between stations.

Joe turned off the alarm—he never hit Snooze. He stared at the clock-radio and then peered down at Sarah. "What are you doing down there?"

"Um, hoping to surprise you." She gestured at the clock-radio. "Surprise!"

"You're as hoarse as a heavy smoker." He eased past her and went to his closet, his scrumptious body supremely un-aroused. "Are you coming down with something?"

"Just a sore throat. I'm probably dehydrated."

"And tell me again why you're on the floor," he said, pulling on his robe.

"Looking for a cure?" When he didn't laugh, she collected her crutches and pushed upright onto her foot, ignoring his offer of help. Squaring her shoulders, she said, "Your eye looks better. How many blowzy blondes do you see?"

"I see one gorgeous woman—and if you look around for her, I'll kick out your crutches." The sharpness of his tone caught her by surprise. Perhaps he'd shocked himself as well, because he added in a much gentler voice, "Sorry, I hate it when you insult yourself."

Some pent-up frustration of her own leaked out. "I'd stand on two feet—but you hid Fred the Wonder Leg."

"It's beside the stationary tub in the garage, where I washed the sock and liner. The sneakers are drying, too. I didn't hide them; I merely cleaned up your mess."

She'd forgotten to check the garage; except to exit the house, she never used that space. If she had a car, some freedom, she might've thought to look there, but she surrendered instead of pursuing another fight. "I'll do better."

"To keep the house clean, would you please wear separate shoes indoors? If you're going to keep running." Joe kissed her bruised forehead, making her wince.

He reset the switches on his clock-radio and headed to the bathroom. She called after him, "I'm glad you're home. Sorry about last night. This morning, too."

"Nothing to be sorry about. Tonight, we'll get back to normal." She didn't detect any irony in his voice. He closed the bathroom door behind him, leaving her alone with that contentious word she'd hurt him with the night before.

☙

The scale reported 138.3 pounds, not as low as Sarah had hoped for, but it reassured her that she didn't need to vomit to lose weight. She knew she couldn't afford to screw up again though. In the shower, she recited the words of her first ballet teacher like a mantra: "Remain hungry."

Behind the bathroom door, Joe had set out wide-legged verdigris slacks with a sleeveless earthen tunic and beige underwear, dangling on hangers above low-heeled shoes the pale-brown of a hermit thrush. He'd placed a trouser sock and the left shoe on her clean prosthesis, and set the dressings in a neat row on the vanity, along with a tube of diaper-rash ointment Dr. Ramos had recommended to prevent abrasions on her kneecap. When she emerged from the steamy room, assuring herself she could endure the painful blisters aggravated by the socket, the house was quiet. Joe had left for the gym and work. He had departed without a kiss or even saying goodbye.

On the breakfast tray, however, he'd left a segmented orange arranged like a blooming flower on a magnolia-white plate. Walnut halves and whole almonds nestled in the center of the fruit like exotic stamens and pistils. A second plate contained two pieces of buttery pound cake Joe had thawed and broiled to perfection before slicing them diagonally and arranging them as a pinwheel. He had leaned a note against a slender glass filled with pale yellow juice. Tasting the sweet pineapple nectar, she read his copperplate printing: "The sum of these flavors reminds me of you."

Somehow, he had divined her breakfast regimen of late, and added his own high-calorie twist. She wondered if he'd noted some missing groceries or went through the trash counting rinds. According to the logic of his note, eating all of it meant she would consume herself. Then would there be more of her or less? Or more of what she was and less of the woman she wanted to be?

On the dresser, the largest matryoshka stood alone, surveying the whole room including the bed again. It looked fatter than before. Joe merely had re-nested four characters inside the figurine. However, Sarah could imagine it had devoured the others.

She knew he wasn't acting intentionally creepy but only performing his usual compulsive rituals. Nevertheless, chills raked her spine like icy finger-bones. She turned the matryoshka to face to the wall.

The pound cake, she decided, would go down the garbage disposal.

౭ఎ

Sarah stood on the flagstone patio and inhaled the smells of moist earth and mid-summer vegetation. She lifted her face to the sun while Dorothy selected places to mark in the backyard. The bulldog behaved with Joe's deliberateness. Only when a bird landed in her line of sight was she impulsive, kicking up tufts of Bermuda grass as she charged the invaders.

Sometimes the birds resettled on the privacy fence. A mockingbird tilted its head and twittered at the dog. Sarah said, "That's right, you tell her." She contemplated her new idea, a self-portrait. Since her car wreck, her sense of who she was had ebbed away. She'd lost more of her identity the more weight she put on, as if she were hiding from herself. The intense scrutiny of a self-portrait might help to restore her wholeness.

Considering a setting for her work, a landscape background appealed to her—despite the amount of time she'd spent in ballet studios and on stages, she thought of herself as the outdoorsy type. She wished there were some mature hardwoods in the yard. However, the builders had bulldozed every living thing and then planted the lawn, a few sapling redbuds, crepe myrtles, and one young Japanese maple. None of those would do for a background unless she planned to paint herself as that sprite dancing on top of the phallic mushroom.

A clamor of phones summoned her indoors to the kitchen. Calling from work, Joe asked, "How was breakfast?"

"All of it was delicious, thank you." Fibbing about food hardly counted. She wasn't covering up anything serious, and she spared his feelings. Still, she wondered if the ease with which she told him yet another lie signaled something worse to come. Was she intent on ruining the only good thing in her life? Her fingers jittered as she raked them through her hair. She told him, "You always show your love so completely."

His tone brightened. "I'll bring home all kinds of proof, including that hair coloring I promised, and a new cell phone for you. We'll keep it charged so you won't have to worry again about getting in touch with me."

"I wasn't the one who drove home from Atlanta at ninety-three miles an hour because of a busy signal." Hearing the tone in her voice, she tried to turn this into a joke: "When I had my Miata, I never drove faster than eighty-five."

"You would've...I mean that car would've killed you if given another chance. I'm glad there won't be a next time."

A panicked bark sounded from the French doors in the dining room. Claws scrabbled on the glass.

Sarah returned to the dining room to let Dorothy inside, dissecting Joe's comment. She knew he wouldn't answer affirmatively, but still she had to ask: "Was I really that bad a driver?"

Joe said, "No, it's sports cars in general: they're inherently dangerous."

"I don't need a sports car. A safe, reliable sedan like yours would be fine."

He paused for a moment. "You want to start driving again?"

"See! You do think I'm a terrible driver."

"No, not really. It's just that it sort of runs in your family. You've told me about some real crack-ups your dad's been in." He paused, then said, "And there was Michael, of course."

Though her younger brother had died almost ten years earlier, electric tears still burned beneath her eyelids at the mention of his name. Michael's hotrod had left a Georgia back road at high speed and rolled several times. It broke apart in the moonlit woods, killing him at age seventeen. Wiping her nose, she said, "I need to be able to get away…to go places, I mean. What if something happened to Dorothy and I had to race her to the vet?"

"I'm fifteen minutes away, less than half that if I drive like I did yesterday. You won't do Dorothy any good if you wind up needing another surgeon." His voice changed from lecturing mode to an intimate murmur. "I didn't mean to upset you about Mike. Did I really make you cry? I'll set up a doctor's appointment, Sare—you need some help relaxing."

"No, I don't want to spend any more days in a fog." She took a deep breath, blinked several times, and gave in to the embrace offered by his voice. "Never mind about the car. I'll call you if I need help."

"Now you're talking—don't be afraid to lean on me."

"I bet you say that to all the one-legged girls."

"Not funny. I think you got your dad's sense of humor. Your mom's jokes are much lighter."

Something else to add to her ever-growing list of self-improvement projects.

When she didn't reply, he asked, "Are you painting this morning?"

"I stretched a new canvas the other day."

"What do you have in mind?"

She said, "It's a secret, a present for you. Something to remind you of me."

"'Remind'? I don't need reminding, Sare. I think about you all the time."

Sarah thanked him and ended the call, telling him she needed to use the bathroom. Another lie. On the way to her studio, she wondered exactly what he thought about her.

❧

Seated at her drawing table, she considered preliminary sketches for her self-portrait. Recalling the name of their gated community—Eagle's Lair—she contemplated a rugged mountain niche as the setting for her picture. She imagined herself perched there, eyes damp and cheeks ruddy from cold gusts, and dyed-blond hair whipped up to make the wind corporeal. There had to be some logic as to how she got to the eagle's lair, however; she couldn't have materialized alone on a cliff face. In her mind's eye, she painted suggestions of coiled rope over one shoulder. After all, she put herself in that spot, and she needed some way to get out.

The idea of her picture progressed to a consideration of wardrobe. First she mentally dressed her likeness in a khaki safari-style shirt, shorts, and ankle boots, but then she debated whether to show her legs at all. Maybe the bottom of the canvas should include her knees but nothing lower, and Joe could decide whether she was whole…The thought made her grimace. Her swollen bust and broad hips dramatized a similar issue—would it be a portrait of the once and future Sarah Lyn Berger Gordon, or the way she really was at present?

"Present" reminded her she now had promised the painting as a gift for Joe, who adored her current figure, big boobs in particular. So, a compromise: she would give him cleavage, but only show herself from the waist up. She mused about working a Satanic deal like Dorian Gray's, except she'd be thin forever and her portrait would keep getting fatter. "A Jew making a bargain with the Devil," she muttered. "Feh."

Ringing phones interrupted her musings. It was too soon for Joe to check in again, and Mom never called early on weekdays, so Sarah tried to ignore the noise. After all, she hadn't done any actual drawing yet, just her usual schtick of thinking about art instead of making it. But who could it be? She grabbed the cordless before the answering machine picked up. Caller ID displayed a 919 area code and "Square Deal Auto Center," a pun on the historic squares in Savannah: her older brother's garage.

After she answered, Nathan said, "How you doing, Sara H?" When she was six and Nathan was thirteen, he kidded her about the construction-paper letters she'd taped to her bedroom door, with the orange H mounted too far from the S-A-R-A in other colors. He never let anything go. Maybe it was a family trait.

In response to The Question, she told Nate what he would want to hear, what everyone wanted to hear. "I'm fine, natty Nat-E" Since teasing remained his primary mode of communication, she gave it back to him: "Gosh, a call from my big brother. What's the occasion, dude?"

"Ugh, I'm hurt. You just put a bullet in my heart." In the background, air wrenches whined and pneumatic lifts hummed. "Actually, it bounced off. When wife-number-two skedaddled, I had it packed in Kevlar."

She set her blank drawing pad aside and settled onto her sofa. "Your balls, too?"

"Naw, she took 'em with her." A distant clatter of metal and lyrical shouting by Hispanic men muffled his next comment. Nathan yelled something in Spanish and got back on the line. "Sorry. The new guy is still figuring out that hot metal is *caliente*, but I guess I burned my fingers plenty of times, too, starting out. Everybody's gotta learn the hard way."

"It's so funny to hear you speak Spanish. You used to complain all the time when you were taking it in high school."

"Damn-sight more useful than all those years of Hebrew School. Not too many guys like me are lining up to be grease monkeys."

"I'll bet some of your female customers like the novelty, though."

"Of course," Nat said. "You wouldn't believe how many of them want to shtup high up on the pneumatic lift, in the backseat of their Volvos. I keep an extension ladder handy. Speaking of romance, how's your endless honeymoon with Mom's favorite son?"

"Son-in-law, you mean."

"Naw, I hear she's gonna adopt Joe. I won't be the oldest anymore and you'll be committing incest, but Mom will have her golden boy at last." He changed his voice to a dead-on impression of their mother: "Your mouth to God's ear, Nathan."

Sarah loved hearing that her marriage and husband were considered perfect by her family, that she had finally made the right choice. She circled her mouth with one hand, making a megaphone. "Bitter, party of one. Now seating Mr. Bitter."

"Damn right I'm bitter. I was cruising, racking up points with Mom. She was jazzed when I started wasting my weekends playing golf with Dad and hanging out with him and the other altekakers at the J." Sarah smirked at his nickname for the Jewish version of the YMCA. He clicked a lighter and blew into the mouthpiece. When he spoke again, he sounded as if he'd clamped a cigarette in one corner of his mouth. "Then you go and marry the Stepford Husband. Now all she talks about is how wonderful Joe is, meaning Dad and me are farshtunkn. You know how she does. What'd Mike call her 'technique'?"

"The kamikaze kugel." At first she smiled at the memory of her little brother riffing in the family room when their parents were out of earshot. Then she reflected on how seldom she thought about Mike anymore or anyone else but herself.

Nate said, "Yeah, looks as sweet as pie and then hits you like a bomb. She wants me to ask Joe for pointers on how to keep girls happy, like I was sixteen."

"It'll kill you to know that Joe doesn't need a pneumatic lift. Or an extension ladder."

"I hate that guy." The speaker whooshed as Nat apparently blew more smoke at his phone.

Sarah made her tone more serious. "Are you really looking for the next Ms. Wrong?"

"Always. Not too many Volvos in the shop lately, if you know what I mean. At this point, the babushkas down at the J are looking pretty good. Maybe I can bag a rich one and get set up like you."

Sarah balled her fist around the phone. "I wasn't looking for that when I dated Joe, any more than he wanted to get rich from his mother dying when he was sixteen. She was killed in a plane crash, and the airline was at fault."

Nathan said, "Oh shit, is that how he got his money?"

"His dad invested the life insurance and lawsuit payouts in trust funds for Joe and his sister, Monica."

"I guess I can't hate him anymore—thanks for ruining that for me. Is he still treating you like a goddess?"

Despite her recent frustrations with Joe, Nate deserved some more retaliation instead of the bald truth. She purred, "I'm afraid he is. We celebrated our one-year anniversary last week, but modesty forbids me from telling you how."

He shot back, "You know, I can always tell when he's talked to Mom. You're not the only one creaming over him."

"Gross! Don't tell me that."

"Oh yeah," he said, obviously seizing on her disgust. "I go over to their place for dinner and, if he's talked to her any time that day, her eyes are shining and she kinda glides around. All me and Dad hear at the table is Joe said this, Joe did that. I swear she smokes a cigarette after every one of his calls."

Sarah slid lengthwise across her couch, turned on her side, and then pulled her knees toward her chest. "You're saying he's calling her during the day?"

"Two, three times a week at least. Does that bother you, Sara H?"

"Why should it? It's a free country." She flicked some lint

from the cushion, and tried to sound casual. "What do they talk about?"

"Oh, look who's going fishing!" He made the zinging reel-cast sound she had picked up from him long ago. "Are you jealous?"

"Of course not. I'm thrilled that he loves Mom."

"Don't worry, he only says good things about you: how proud he is that you're doing your art, what a trooper you've been since...Well, he says what a fine wife you are, and how thrilled he is to be a small part of our happy goddamned family. He touches all the bases, pushes all the right buttons, and Mom goes limp."

She grumbled, "I'm glad they get along so well."

"Yeah, I can hear it in your voice. They're as thick as thieves, Sara H. It's actually the reason I'm calling." A loud bang from the garage preceded more yelling in Spanish. "Joe just talked to Mom about an idea that knocked her on her tuchus. She called me here, and I want your take on it."

Sarah leaned forward, staring at the endless blackness of the rubber-mat floor, her new project forgotten. "I talked to him a short while ago. Why didn't he tell me about it?"

"Maybe it's a surprise, in which case, you didn't hear it from me. Joe said that we should do a memorial to Michael in a few months, on the tenth anniversary of his...you know. He said he'd take care of the expense for a large granite monument at the cemetery, with an outdoor Mourner's Kaddish and all. What do you think?"

It was a sweet notion, but she was hearing it from the wrong guy. Tears burned her eyes, but she couldn't decide if they were because of Joe's gesture toward her family or his insensitivity toward her. She blinked a few times and said, "It's a nice idea. He mentioned Mike to me, so I guess it came to him after we hung up."

"Well, act surprised, OK? The last thing I need is Mr. Perfect on my case. I'm all for it. You got yourself a class act, sis, even if he does make the rest of us look so bad."

She cleared her throat. "Thanks for calling. Time to get back to 'doing my art.'"

"Must be nice, Ms. Homebody. That what you do all day?"
"Oh," she replied, "sometimes I just run around the house."

Chapter 10

SARAH MADE SOME SKETCHES OF HER SELF-portrait ideas, but didn't feel confident about beginning work on the canvas. The facial expression looked all wrong. What she drew always came out more somber than it should. In fact, the woman in the sketch looked pissed. She'd considered using acrylics and doing the work alla prima, finishing the painting on the first try to capture the essence of the scene, but her conversation with Nathan echoed, and the impressions she sought to capture kept changing.

She said to Dorothy and the blank canvas, "What the hell am I gonna do, yell at Joe for talking to Mom? Bust him for planning to surprise me?"

He kept her so off-balance lately. While Sarah stripped off her smock, she concluded that, a year into their marriage, the only thing she knew for sure about her husband was that he loved her to death. That notion brought to mind his thoughtful tribute to Michael, still the family favorite, and circled her back to Nathan's comments.

Time to stop being a homebody, get moving again, and see what lay beyond Joe's fence. She changed into the athletic shoes she had worn for her rainy jog, and led Dorothy outside. The bulldog raced across the front lawn toward the gate Sarah had opened from the control panel, and she had to run to keep up.

Sunlight leaped off Joe's walls and blazed overhead. Blinking hard, she couldn't tell where she put the prosthetic foot as she sprinted, so she just had to trust Fred to do his job.

As her eyes grew accustomed to the glare, she ran harder on

muscle-sore legs, creating slack in the leash as she caught up to Dorothy. When they dashed outside the monochromatic fence, she imagined emerging on the yellow-brick road in the full-color Land of Oz.

Instead, she found herself at the terminus of Tangletree Drive, a dead-end street. "A street with no outlet," Joe had corrected her on the day of their walk-through. To Sarah, though, "no outlet" sounded like being bottled up forever. At least with a dead-end, she could turn around and leave the way she'd come.

Mrs. O'Malley's Georgian-style manor next door reflected sunlight from its many windows. The old woman could probably watch the street from nearly every room in her house. Her mailbox was situated near Sarah and Joe's, where only anonymous fliers collected. A post office box Joe rented received the bills, catalogs, and the occasional item forwarded from their old Atlanta address. He received all mail-order packages at his office.

Across Tangletree was the thicket that likely had inspired the street name. Skinny pine trunks crowded together and gnarled branches jostled high above. While Dorothy led her toward those woods, Sarah glanced back at her home. She saw only the pale concrete strip leading to the garage, and the procession of tall ivory posts and solid tongue-and-groove joints that enclosed the yard.

A grape-colored Cadillac Fleetwood with five Masonic badges affixed to the trunk backed down Mrs. O'Malley's driveway. The car turned into the street and revealed its severely damaged passenger-side: a crumpled front fender and a wheel well that someone had beaten back into the semblance of an arch to accommodate a new white-wall tire. Cadmium red paint streaked the dents like fresh blood.

Sarah waved out of politeness, and the passenger window buzzed down. Over a fierce blowing sound inside the car, Mrs. O'Malley called out, "I've never seen you outside Fort Apache, Mrs. Gordon." Her tower of gray hair swayed in the windstorm. She had exchanged her rose-colored spectacles for mirrored aviator glasses.

When Sarah halted, the bulldog pulled the leash taut in her

blistered hand. Her shoulder popped in its socket. Massaging the aggravated muscles, she said, "That's about to change, ma'am. I'm afraid I've been cooped up with my art too long."

"I was going to say, I know shut-ins that get out more often. Watch those bare arms of yours don't get scorched. You're as fair as my daughter Suzy—she burns like a marshmallow in a campfire."

To short-circuit the lecture, Sarah asked, "How many children do you have?"

"Just one. Suzy's plenty, believe-you-me. You remind me of her in lots of ways. Neither of you return my cookware."

Sarah winced. "I've washed up the dish and can bring it by later. The crumble is delicious, thanks again. Um, it's half-gone already."

Her neighbor looked her over. "That I can believe. Suzy can sock away the food, too. You'd almost fit into the clothes she's left here.

Sarah caught herself clenching her fists and thinking about putting a few more dents in the woman's quarter-panel. She told herself to relax. Her neighbor was a rude nutcase, that was all. Heeding her mother's instructions about congeniality, she tried a new tack. She pointed at the body damage on the car and asked, "When did you get hit, ma'am?"

"Six months ago—I keep it as a reminder. Come out of the sun a minute." She punched a switch and the doors unlocked. "But leave that French dog in the road."

Sarah fantasized about telling her to go to hell, but she was determined to stay polite. Still, she gave her arm a pinch for being manipulated so easily. The dented passenger door produced a metallic groan of protest when she opened it. She sat and pulled in her legs; her left sneaker dragged across the padded door interior until she raised her knee higher. The long verdigris slacks and a calf-high sock hid the prosthesis. However, with the polyester-blend stretched tight over her knees, she had to cover the socket outline with her left hand.

Dorothy continued to tug the leash, rocking Sarah against the white leather upholstery. The frigid wind that blew from the vents soon raised goose bumps on her arms. She said over the air-conditioned roar, "The damage reminds you about something, ma'am?"

"It's a reminder that you can't trust nobody no more. Everybody's got secrets." The sunglasses cloaked Mrs. O'Malley's gaze, so Sarah couldn't see where the woman was looking. Her neighbor wore a short-sleeved, knee-length lavender dress with beige hose. For their first meeting, she'd huddled inside a cardigan despite the hot sunshine. Now she didn't appear to be chilled, though the high-output fan blew on her thin arms and swirled Medusan strands of gray hair away from her beehive and over the headrest. Mrs. O'Malley said, "You better listen to what I say. Like my Suzy, you strike me as the kind that even friends take advantage of."

Sarah squeezed the cup of the prosthesis as she absorbed the latest insult. "A friend did this to your car?"

"No, I'd never seen the gal before. But she looked well-to-do, drove a pretty red convertible. One of those sporty things. A Miasma."

"Miata," Sarah mumbled, loosening her grip on the leash as she recalled her own roadster. Dorothy pulled again with bulldog willpower, and Sarah had to plant her right foot on the pavement to keep from getting yanked out of the car.

"Right," Mrs. O'Malley said, "one of them. You'd naturally think that she'd have tons of insurance, but she didn't have any. Of course I didn't know that when I put myself in her way."

"Excuse me, ma'am—you wanted her to hit you?"

"Damn straight. She looked like she was loaded." Mrs. O'Malley reached into a purse that sat between them, pulled out a lethal-looking nail file, and skimmed it rapidly above her fingertips. "I did good over the years, picking out drivers that looked rich and careless, blabbing on their cell phones. I'd ease into their blind spots and sometimes they'd bang into me. You never seen anybody do a better whiplash." She stopped filing, seized the back of her neck, and wailed.

Even the bulldog stopped tugging and stared wide-eyed. Sarah's shoulder and neck muscles tightened, and she shuddered from remembered pain. She asked, "You're a...how do I put it, an intentional accident victim?" Maybe Joe was right: she'd be safer staying off the roads.

"A lady's gotta have a hobby. My Robert never made much, so I did what I could while I ran my errands."

"What happened with the woman in the red convertible?"

"Why, that teeny car got squashed like a bug against my fender. It happened near the Aiken Tech exit on I-20. I did the whole routine, crying for her to call 911 and all that. The state troopers hauled her away for not having insurance or even a damn license. She had a ton of unpaid tickets, too."

Sarah said, "So you couldn't get your car repaired."

"Of course I could. Hell, I could buy a new one today if I wanted, but I need the reminder so I won't do a dumb thing like that again."

"If you don't mind my asking, can you make a lot of money that way?"

"Over the years, the settlements gave us enough for a hefty down-payment on this house, but Mr. O'Malley's life insurance policy took care of the rest and then some. I lost him last August. He understood the value of good coverage, believe-you-me."

Sarah eyed the senior citizen, imagining Mrs. O'Malley spending decades watching Robert for some careless behavior that would one day result in a plausible, fatal accident. She fought back a desire to flee behind her high walls.

Mrs. O'Malley reversed the nail file in her hand and clutched it like a dagger. Before Sarah could react, the old woman leaned over and jabbed the calf of Sarah's left leg, saying, "Oops!"

Sarah failed to react until she realized Mrs. O'Malley had deduced her secret. Despite her anger, the sheer brazenness of the act stunned her. She merely patted the leg, but couldn't feel a hole in her slacks. The woman dropped the file into her purse with a nod, apparently satisfied with the result of her experiment.

When Sarah found her voice, she said, "I wasn't hiding anything from you, ma'am; it's a private thing."

"Just like my 'hobby,' Mrs. Gordon. That's how friendships form: we share some of our personal business, our stories. I'm guessing that, like my daughter, you don't have many friends. And I've outlived all of mine. I could use a new one—I'm a people person." Her mirrored shades flashed as she gave a toothy grin.

Sarah wondered if she were being set up for an accident of her own. She replied, "I can honestly say I've never had a friend like you."

"Yeah, I do make a mean berry crumble. So, what happened to your leg?"

After Sarah told her the details, Mrs. O'Malley shook her head and said, "I hope you sued somebody's pants off."

"The police called it a no-fault accident."

"You see how unfair it's getting? If I'm ever in another crash, it'll have to be just for the fun of it."

☙

Sarah lugged Dorothy back inside. Her arms ached as if she'd done a hundred pushups, and her lower back throbbed. Sweat drenched her skin, hair, and every stitch of clothing. The bulldog, panting frantically from the heat, had refused to take another step when they were a mile away from the house. As soon as she set Dorothy down, the animal recovered mobility and raced for the water dish in the kitchen.

On the answering machine, Joe had left two messages. His first one conveyed the tone of an adult humoring a headstrong child: "Just checking in. I hope you're not out in this terrible heat." His second recording sounded more concerned.

Despite her need to recover, she called his office immediately. When his recorded voice said he was away from his desk, she told him, "Please don't rush home. I'm safe and secure." She left the same message on his cell phone, and then went to clean up and rest her aching body. A nap eluded her, though, because she feared she'd awake with Joe looming over her. They definitely needed to talk.

Late that afternoon, Dorothy announced his return. The excited yelps and scrabbling claws on hardwood echoed up the hallway. Sarah left her studio with no progress made on her self-portrait and followed the sounds of canine joy toward the kitchen.

Near the door that led into the garage, Joe played with Dorothy. He wore a gray suit and yellow-print tie and crouched above the bulldog like a *GQ* baseball catcher. Dorothy flopped onto her back and kicked at his sleeves with all four paws while he scratched her belly. Plastic grocery sacks and a small shopping bag from a cell phone store sat beside him, along with the mail he'd retrieved from their post office box. He sang out, "Hey there, beautiful," when Sarah's shoes squeaked on the dining room floor and gave her away.

He looked yummy, no denying it, and he was focused on her. Her stomach flipped as it used to do. Intentions to lay out her concerns and complaints began to dissolve like paint being lifted off a canvas. By the time she reached the kitchen, only a vague uneasiness remained, along with hunger pains. She said, "You've got your hands full with that grizzly bear. I'll put the groceries away."

"Grisly is right. She's got bits of straw in her coat and pine sap between her toes." He lowered his face to the bulldog and crooned, "Where's baby bear been bounding?" Dorothy mouthed the tip of his nose and kicked at him again. Her rapid breathing sounded like laughter.

Joe took hold of Sarah's wrist as she stooped to gather the grocery bags. He said, "Don't bother with those. You're probably tired from your walk."

"Busted," she said. "I guess Dorothy's fur gave me away."

"That, and the hideous sunburn on your arms and face. Over dinner, I'll give you my famous lecture on melanoma."

"And then you can spread Solarcaine all over me," she cooed.

"First, you get to hear my talk about safety." He held fast to her wrist. "You left the gate open."

"Come on, I'm trying to be funny." She attempted to pull away, but his grip tightened. When she relented, he did, too, but he didn't let her go. To break the mounting tension, she kissed his mouth. Its hard line felt like the Rodin statue she had bussed on a dare from some high school friends on a field trip. Joe didn't respond any more than the bronze man in the museum had. Covering her concern, she said, "OK, more flirty than funny. Either way, I'm afraid I blew it, since you're not laughing and your pants are still on." When she tried to smile, her lower lip trembled.

He released her and snatched up some of the grocery sacks. "That gate is there for a reason."

"I forgot to close it, is all. Anyway, I thought we lived in a secure neighborhood. There's that guard at the entrance."

"He'll let in almost anybody."

They grabbed for the cell phone bag at the same time, and their foreheads knocked together. Cussing, she dropped onto her rump, and he settled on his knees. Dorothy scurried away and barked at them from a safe distance, while Sarah's ears rang and tears stung her eyes. She touched the tender spot between her brows. "This thing is never gonna heal."

"Sorry. I guess I'm a little stressed." He kept his eyes closed and hung his head.

"Double-vision?"

"If I don't open my eyes, I won't have to find out, will I?"

She asked, "What are you really so worried about?"

His head still down, he looked at her with his right eye closed, like he was sighting down a rifle barrel. "I really am worried about the gate. We both know it takes less than a minute for your life to change forever. For the worse. Someone or something can wreck it just that fast, believe me."

While he could've been referring to her accident, or his mother's death or Michael's, she sensed something more immediate disturbed him. She whispered, "Who would want to do that, Joe?"

"You'd be surprised; someone you least expect." He set the bag on the table and began to sort cans, boxes, and produce. His right eye looked fine.

Trying to lighten the mood, she said, "It could be Mrs. O'Malley, our neighbor. I think she's got an insurance policy on me, or maybe both of us." By the time she explained herself, they had put the groceries away, her headache had eased, and Joe seemed to have calmed down. He even hummed as he reorganized the goods she had placed at random on the pantry shelves.

Only a box of hair coloring and the cell phone remained on the kitchen table. He showed her how to operate the smart phone, wrote down its number for her, and then plugged it in to charge the battery. "Keep it on, so I can always reach you."

"No more worried messages or risking your life because of a busy signal?"

"I worry about you because I love you." He took her hand, his grip gentle this time, and made his voice a husky whisper. "And because I care, I'm going to take you into the bathroom and touch up your dark roots."

Sarah snorted. "What every woman longs to hear."

"Most wives hear, 'What's for dinner?' I'll handle that, too, while the color sets."

"Is that really what most wives still hear?"

"According to the ones at the office. Along with, 'How much money did you spend today?' and 'Is once a week too much to ask?'" He squeezed her fingers and said, "See how lucky you are?"

Chapter 11

THE FIRST TIME SARAH HAD COMPLAINED ABOUT the dull burnt-sienna color of her hair and its yard-long limpness, Joe seized upon the notion of remaking her hairstyle. Her discontent had rumbled up a few weeks after the car wreck, when she was fighting her addiction to painkillers and nothing seemed right. He studied, got the best tools, including a mannequin head and wigs to practice on, and even bought a stylist's apron on which he had printed "Homicide Blonde—Dyed By My Own Hands." She was a natural blonde as a little girl, so her mother raved when Joe drove Sarah to Savannah and presented the new, improved version, with shoulder-length waves. It provided a distraction from her limping around on the foam-covered pylon and rubber foot of her preparatory prosthesis. She'd been grateful to Joe for giving her family something more appealing to gawk at.

Now, in a latex-gloved hand, he held up a bottle of the coloring that would keep Sarah a blonde for the next month. She sat on a wooden chair with her back to him, a towel protecting her shoulders and neck. They both looked in the vanity mirror at the slick, shiny hair he'd piled and fastened atop her head with plastic clips. Waving away the lingering ammonia odor, he continued to amuse her with his faux-British accent. "And we have enough left over to highlight Madame's nether region."

She clamped her thighs together, rippling her brows in exaggerated distress. "Won't it burn my private parts?"

"Pray, do not be pusillanimous, Madame. I would apply it to each follicle with the utmost care."

"You're talking about a lot of follicles. Though it probably won't itch as much as when I had to keep it all shaved off to avoid a lumpy leotard."

The phones rang. Joe raised an eyebrow, and Sarah sighed. "Better answer it, Jeeves," she said. "My nether region can wait."

By the time Joe had stripped off his gloves and strode into the bedroom, the answering machine in the living room came on. A woman's voice emanated from its speaker. Sarah couldn't make out any words as they echoed down the hall and reached her in the master bath. Joe hurried to his bedside, and silenced the machine and the voice when he picked up the phone. He listened for a second and dropped the receiver back in its cradle. With his back to her, he said, "Only a telemarketer. I thought your mom might be calling."

He still hadn't turned around. Sarah went to the bathroom doorway and asked, "What's she selling?"

"Your mom?" Finally, he glanced her way.

Sarah rolled her eyes. "The telemarketer, Mister Ee-vay-sive."

"I didn't ask. If you respond to those people, you can't get rid—" The phones pealed again, and he snatched up the receiver and dropped it back in place. After a couple seconds, another call came through, and this time he said into the mouthpiece, "You misunderstood…No…I'm sorry about that. Don't call me again." He hung up and loomed over the phone, as if daring it to ring. When it didn't, he headed for the hallway.

"Joe," she said. "What's going on?"

"Everything's under control."

"Dammit, you sit and talk to me." Her commanding tone seemed to surprise him, and he halted.

When she sat on the bed and waited for him, though, he said, "The coloring might get on the blanket." Head down, he lumbered into the bathroom. She was forced to follow, wondering what he would tell her. Maybe it was better not to know.

He took a seat on the toilet lid, and she perched on her chair. "I messed up in Atlanta," he said. His platinum wedding band glimmered against the paleness of his fist. "At the welcome banquet, everyone at my table was so friendly. We exchanged business cards and promised to keep in touch."

Her scalp began to itch, and something irritated the back of her throat. She wanted to blame the hair coloring, but knew better. The more she swallowed, the more choked she felt. Despite her growing anxiety, she told herself to remain forceful. "So one of the 'hotties' from the Sheraton bar is calling you?"

"Jeez, you don't forget a thing. She was at the table, not the bar. Her name's Christie Palmer, and she works for a high-tech company in Colorado."

"And she's calling you at home to discuss project management, right?"

"Were you always this sarcastic?" He rubbed his hands across his knees, glowering at her. "When we dated, you were always sweet."

"Maybe I was being ironic and you missed it." She took a deep breath, eyes closed. In a calmer voice, she asked, "Will you tell me what happened with this Christie Palmer and why she's calling our house?"

"I'm trying! We talked about work and our families. She's got a little boy. I guess I was too nice. She's having problems at home—her husband's a real jerk—so I offered some advice. Isn't that what 'normal' guys do? Try to fix problems?"

"Why did she tag you as the solution?"

Joe frowned, probably annoyed that she had cut to the chase. "I think I was the first person in a long time who listened to her. We chatted on and off, and I thought that was the end of it. But she called the office today and then left messages on my cell phone. I guess she got our home number online. I'll get it changed to an unlisted one."

"I'll bet she came to all your seminars."

He grimaced. "After the second one on Tuesday, when I was trying to reach you and all I got was the damned busy signal, she said a bunch of people were meeting for drinks at the bar before dinner."

"'A bunch of people' meaning just the two of you." Sarah blinked at him, dry-eyed, scowling.

"I honestly don't know. I went back to my room to pack and

keep trying the number here, and then I checked out and sped home. Because I love you. Because it's you I want to be with."

She balled her fingers to keep from dragging them through her dye-covered hair. "That gate you're so fond of isn't going to do much good," she said, "if you welcome stalkers into our lives. I was worried about our neighbor, but this woman could be the real psycho."

"I said I was sorry!"

"You didn't, actually. You apologized to her. Not to me."

"Oh God, Sare," he moaned, his face descending into his hands, "I am so sorry." He yanked at his eyebrows with trembling fingers. "I didn't sleep with her, I swear. Still…what a goddamned shit-headed fuckup you married." Tears welled as he jerked out more of the tender hairs. His right eye moved outward, and exposed glistening whiteness.

She seized his arms, but he continued to rip at his brows with merciless precision. "Stop, Joe, stop," she yelled. "You're hurting yourself!"

He allowed her to pull his hands away. "I can't feel a thing." Squinting in the brightness, he stood and shuffled machinelike past her and into the bedroom where he took his patch from the nightstand. In a hollow voice, he murmured, "I'll fix dinner. Your hair color needs to set another twenty-three minutes."

"To hell with dinner," she called to his back, but he plodded down the hallway and into the dining room. Dorothy raced across the floor to join him, and then the back door opened and closed. Sarah stood at the bedroom window and watched him plod around his garden and harvest only the most perfect vegetables for their meal.

Dorothy nipped at his trouser cuffs and pawed at him until he acknowledged her. He squatted down, took her wrinkled, black-masked face between his hands, and talked to the bulldog until she demanded a belly rub. When the line of his mouth softened into a brittle smile, Sarah hugged her sides and wandered down the hallway. The stub of her left leg throbbed with the panicked pace of her heart.

In the living room, she noticed the faint chirp and the message light blinking on the answering machine. Caller ID displayed a number and a name—Nick Palmer—and reported that the individual had called three times within a minute. She assumed Christie Palmer had phoned from home and the number was in her husband's name, as Joe had put their account in his.

Her index finger paused above the Delete button on the answering machine. Joe had explained everything. She might hear the first thought Christie expressed, but nothing she needed to know. Listening to the words, capturing the Palmer woman's voice, would only add to the bad memories of the past few minutes.

Joe's self-destructive remorse showed her how much he regretted talking to the conventioneer from Colorado. All Sarah wanted from him was a simple apology for not being up front with her, for the telemarketer charade, for being careless. Thinking about her own deceptions of late, she would apologize, too, so he wouldn't be the only one confessing.

A whisper of doubt halted her finger against the cool dome of the Delete button. The woman could have been calling to thank Joe for a glorious night in bed, or warning him about some disease he might have contracted from inside her—something he would expose Sarah to the first chance he got. He could've made up everything and now was faced with an affair gone awry, a vindictive mistress, a maniac.

As more fantastical, horrible notions occurred to her, she jabbed hard at the Delete button but the electronic voice did not report that it had cleared out the message. Then she remembered: to prevent accidental erasure, the machine required a message to be played before it could be deleted. Her fingertip now poised atop the larger, oval Play button. She still could walk away. Joe would remember the message soon enough. He could listen then delete it and wipe the caller ID information, too. If she hit Play, the message light wouldn't blink anymore, the chirp wouldn't sound. He'd know she had listened, and he'd believe she no longer trusted him.

But if I let him delete it, I'll never know for sure.

The door leading outside opened in the dining room, closed

again, and Joe's footsteps approached. She considered trotting around the opposite side of the enormous stacked-stone hearth that separated the rooms, but knew such an action would look guilty if he caught her. Instead, she stood in place, gazing at their wedding portrait and the re-nested matryoshka doll. All three pairs of eyes stared back at her.

Joe rushed around the corner of the fireplace, his eye patch still in place. He carried the food harvested for dinner in a wicker basket. When he saw her, he stopped in place.

His momentum swung the carryall toward her, and a plump tomato careened onto the hardwood floor. The bright red fruit split on impact. It rolled, leaking translucent juice and yellow seeds. Setting down his burden, he said, "Sorry about that. I know I can't say it enough times."

"Stop beating yourself up." She picked up the large, dripping tomato, and cupped it in one open palm to contain the spillage. It still radiated the summer heat. Her heart, ripped from her chest, would feel that heavy and hot.

"Go ahead and play it," he said.

"What do you mean?"

"Play the message. That's why we're both in here. Let's hear what she had to say." He stalked toward her, and she backed away, but then he stooped and wiped up tomato juice and seeds with his starched handkerchief. Balling up the pink-stained cloth, he said, "Push Play. It won't bite you, I promise."

Tomato juice oozed through the spaces between her fingers, and blood-warm drops slid down her wrist. She was clenching her fists. To relieve her growing anxiety, she raked her free hand against her scalp, coating her fingers with slick dye. Plastic clips snagged and yanked out hair by the roots.

Overwhelmed by stress and cussing out loud from the pain, she ran to the kitchen and threw the tomato into the sink. She scrubbed her hands, head down, eyes closed. Over the sound of running water, she thought she heard a woman's voice and then silence.

She took her time drying her hands while Joe let Dorothy inside. It was done—the message she had tried to delete was gone. Other than some hair roots, one fresh tomato, and her husband's expectation that she believed and trusted him, she had lost nothing.

Her vision blurred as she strode out of the kitchen to attempt to repair the damage for which she now felt partially responsible. They met in the dining room, pink-stained kerchief still gripped in his hand as if to stanch a wound. He enfolded Sarah and pulled her against him. Tears that had amassed against her eyelids flowed all at once. She pressed her face to his chest and gave in to the tumultuous feeling while he apologized over and over, telling her exactly what she wanted to hear, and saying, "I promised never to hurt you."

When her crying subsided, he led her to the living room sofa. Dorothy glared at her from the dog bed beside a tall front window. The hair color from Sarah's head had blotted the Homicide Blonde motto on his apron. He used the towel still slung around her shoulders to wipe dye smears from her skin. Grimacing at his blotched apron, Joe said, "I guess I've made it a complete nightmare now."

She shook her head, not trusting her voice yet, and accepted his juice-damp kerchief. It smelled of balmy mornings and green tomato vines as she wiped her runny nose.

"I came to get you," he said, "because you need to hear the message. Afterward, you can still consult a divorce lawyer if you want to."

"Stop it," she croaked. After clearing her throat, she tried again. "I would never leave you."

His shoulders relaxed, and he gave her a faint smile. "I'll try not to give you any more reasons to do so." He pushed the Play button.

The machine announced the day and time of the recording and then the woman's voice invaded their home again: "This call is for Joe Gordon. It's Christie Palmer. Can you please call me at 303—" She started to give the same number displayed by caller ID, but the message cut off when the bedroom phone-receiver had been lifted.

Of course. A would-be mistress calling the home of a married man wouldn't say anything lascivious or damning. Not that the Palmer woman had cause to, Sarah reminded herself. Exhausted, she wanted to flop back against the sofa and sleep forever, but held herself erect. Her dye-covered hair would be toxic to the upholstery—the last thing she needed was Joe going ballistic over that.

He asked, "Do you want to hear it again?"

"No. I want to wash out this crap that's bleaching my brain."

"Two minutes to go, I think." He checked his watch and nodded.

Heat rose in her face, but she wedged a curse behind her teeth before it could fly at him. The phones rang, and they stared at each other. His face didn't show any signs of guilt or anger, only raised eyebrows of curiosity. However, when he checked the caller ID box, his posture eased.

"Your mom," he said. "Do you want to talk to her?"

She'd forgotten about Joe's many calls to her mother—"thick as thieves," Nathan had said—as well as his plan for a tenth-anniversary memorial for Michael. The new conflicting emotions churned with her present kaleidoscope of feelings.

Joe studied her face, and probably heard her teeth creak from clamping her jaws together. He lifted the receiver. "Hello, Mom. May we call you back later? Great. Love you."

He hung up, glanced at his watch again, and said to Sarah, "Those were sixty seconds of tension I don't care to repeat. Let's go."

After he pulled on his coloring gloves and rinsed and conditioned Sarah's hair, he blew it dry while she sat before the mirror again. The loud activities didn't permit conversation short of yelling. With their jangled nerves, she knew both of them would mistake their raised volume for anger. The silence between them continued, however, as he brushed and curled her blond locks. Every time he opened his mouth to speak, she squeezed her eyes shut. His hands began to quiver against her head as he arranged her bangs.

Finally, she stopped punishing him. "Sorry," she said. "I'm behaving like an ass while you try to make me look perfect."

He stared at her reflection and let his hands fall to his sides. "A mirror," he told her in a strained voice, "shows exactly the opposite of what's true. You were perfect until I came along." He turned on a heel and walked out.

From the kitchen came the sounds of vegetables chopped with such harsh blows that she feared he would whack off his fingers. Recalling his earlier, terrifying self-destructiveness, Sarah slid onto her knees. She licked her fingertips and pressed them to the cold floor tiles. With utmost care, she lifted the dark hairs he had yanked from his eyebrows. They crisscrossed her damp skin like tiny scars.

Chapter 12

AT THE DINING ROOM TABLE, SARAH RAISED HER glass of sweet tea toward Joe. "A truce. No! I mean a pledge," she said, giving him a quavering smile. "No more tears or bad feelings. No more guilt, no more blame. And, unless that Palmer woman shows up here, no more hair-pulling."

He closed his eyes and nodded. Raising his tumbler as well, he stopped short of clinking it against hers. "No more self-abuse," he said. "Unless it's phone sex." Their glasses touched.

"Here, here." She forced her smile wider and tried not to stare at his eyebrows, which remained inflamed. The tiny hairs he yanked out had gone down the drain. Initially, she had considered keeping them, since they were a tender part of Joe, but she recalled Mrs. O'Malley leaving her Cadillac dented as a reminder that "you can't trust nobody no more." That was a memento Sarah did not want.

Beef stock with translucent ovals of fat surrounded the stir-fried vegetables and meat she nibbled. She tapped a wedge of potato against the plate, trying to knock off the oily broth, and found herself laboring to think of things to say. His own attempts at small talk— "Where did you walk today? Does your sunburn itch?"— failed to inspire her. What she'd hoped would be a poignant reconciliation dinner took on the aura of a dismal final date.

As conversation waned, she focused more on the greasy food, keeping her mouth full to avoid repartee. That brought forth another silent bout of self-criticism: she was violating her personal goal to remain hungry. No more trying to puke away mistakes.

Her spirits brightened when she remembered the need to return her mother's call. Setting down her fork, she said, "I better call Mom back before she gets worried."

"At least finish your meal."

She dropped her paper napkin over the food she hadn't eaten, concealing it too late. "It was delish, but I'm stuffed. Leave everything, and I'll clean up later." She retreated to her studio, limping slightly in her haste, before he could tempt her with dessert.

Running away like a scaredy cat instead of laying out the changes they absolutely had to make. Shit. Ever since she began to assert her needs even a little bit, they'd experienced nothing but conflict and chaos.

Sarah dropped onto the couch and picked up the cordless phone. She speed-dialed her parents' number. At the sound of her mother's voice, she said, "I'm sorry, Mom," instead of identifying herself. "I'm afraid I'm interrupting dinner."

"Feygela, nothing is as important as my darling children. How are you?"

Sarah gave her automatic response to the rote question. "I'm fine, thank you."

"Is Joe on the line?" Mom asked huskily. "Make sure you get that incredible son of mine on the phone."

Nathan had been right. Blinking with dèjá vu, Sarah said, "So, you've adopted him? You called Joe 'son'."

"It's my right—that's how I feel about him."

"Should I become the daughter-in-law, just to keep our marriage legal?"

"Feh, you're always picking a fight. Would you get him, please? Afterward, you can stab at me like a serpent's tooth, to your thankless heart's content."

She snorted. "Oh, you've been to the theater again. That was *King Lear* as written by who, Billy Shakestein?"

"Mock all you want." The Borsht Belt accent gave way to a steely, quit-screwing-around tone. "Just get Joe on the phone."

Sarah pushed her fingers through her hair, wrecking Joe's careful arrangement. "I'll get him." Wondering what fresh horror awaited her, she cracked open the studio doors and called for Joe to pick up a phone. She returned to the couch and waited.

A click preceded Joe's voice in her ear: "I'm here."

She glanced at her closed, windowless double doors. Not knowing how near he was made the hairs on the back of her neck stand up for some reason. What the hell was wrong with her? She started to give her thigh a vicious pinch, but then remembered Joe savaging his eyebrows and the terror she'd felt watching him.

Aren't I guilty of the same masochism, time and again? Why do I keep punishing myself?

She flexed her fingers and forced them to lie flat on her lap.

Her mother said, "Joe?"

"Yes, ma'am, at your beck and call."

"Have you told Sarah about your plan for the memorial?"

"No, ma'am," Joe said. "I haven't had a chance, what with work and errands and styling your beautiful daughter's hair and trying to care for her as she deserves."

"That's so sweet. I'm certain you made her look perfect."

"You brought her into the world that way, Mom. I only hope I didn't mess her up too much."

Sarah assumed the mutual-admiration society could congratulate each other the rest of the night, so she said during the pause, "Pardon me, but what memorial, Joe?"

"You gave me the idea this morning, when we were talking about Michael."

In her recollection, they'd actually discussed her poor driving, his relief that she didn't drive anymore, and his suggestion that wrecking cars was endemic to the Berger family, possibly genetic. However, she appreciated the effect he had on Mom—who sounded positively awestruck—and the compliments he wafted her own way soothed some of the nervous tension in her chest. She didn't argue with him, but said instead, "Tell me everything."

He proposed the same plan Nathan had described, but furnished many embellishments—"a respectful granite obelisk," "a memory box displaying photographs"—that caused her mother to exclaim tearfully. Sarah had to admit he'd hit a home run.

When he asked Sarah what she thought of his ideas, Mom broke in with, "You're such a mensch, Joe. Michael's feeling so honored and so proud of the gentleman, and gentle man, his sister brought into our family."

"Mom's right, Joe," Sarah said. "It's a lovely idea."

"I know what tragedy feels like," he replied. "I know how it haunts you like a shadow that's always falling across your face, no matter which way you turn. Maybe this will let some sunlight in."

༄

Joe had gone to sleep before she could join him in bed. She watched him for a while, his body within reach but his inner self far removed. His poetic words haunted her, and she ached just to hold him and be held. Of course, getting laid would've been nice, too. Chastity-as-penance really sucked. So to speak.

Retreating to her studio, she glowered at the neglected canvas and discarded sketchbook. The three glass walls reflected back her scowl and zaftig shape, a trio of horrors there was no way she wanted to capture in a self-portrait.

She flicked off the lights, extinguishing the mirror-like effect of the windows. Instead of seeing herself in three directions, she now created the illusion that the walls had disappeared and she'd become invisible. She imagined jogging out onto the moist Bermuda grass, the roofline security lights failing to capture her as she danced beside the privacy fence. The gate would open at her command, and she would take flight…

Hoping this inspiration would lead to something creative, she decided to lie on the couch and, as her mother advised, go with the flow. She thought about Joe's words concerning tragedy and shadows and sunshine. The man kept revealing new facets of himself, some poignant, some frustrating, and others bordering on scary. Maybe that's what marriage was all about—discovering new things to love about your mate while deciding what you also could endure. What new things was Joe loving about her, if any? And how much more was he willing to put up with? She hugged her arms, despite the sunburn, and drew up her knees. Without intending to, she fell asleep in the dark.

The squeak of the studio doors startled her awake in the morning. Pale blue dawn silhouetted Joe as he looked down at her. "Separate beds," he said. "I really am in trouble."

"You're not in trouble. I'm afraid I dropped off." Sarah cringed at the phantom pain in her left leg that now seemed to extend all the way up to her hip. "And not all of me is awake yet." She sat up and braced the prosthetic foot on the floor. With a push of the release button, she came out of the socket. After edging up the leg of her slacks, she stripped off the dressings and then massaged feeling back into her knee and the rounded end of muscle below it. The skin felt wrinkled and waxy, as if it had soaked in water too long.

Joe asked if he could lend a hand, and she declined his offer, regretting it the instant she waved him away. Refusals of assistance would not help her restore harmony.

Fresh hurt rattled in his voice as he groused, "Lately you're getting more sleep without my help than with it."

"Sorry for waking up grumpy. I can always use a hand." When she rolled her neck, some vertebrae popped. Touching a sore spot between her shoulders, she said, "Here, for instance."

He came toward her, dressed for the gym in gray T-shirt, thigh-hugging shorts, crew socks, and sneakers. His office clothes would be on hangers in his car. "Roll onto your chest and get comfortable," he said, rubbing his hands together.

"That's not as easy as it used to be." Her breasts compressed like overstuffed pillows and pushed against her ribcage when she followed his instruction. Without warning, he straddled her buttocks. His familiar weight relaxed her so much she groaned.

Huge, warm hands slid inside her tank top and along her spine. Deft fingers unclipped her brassiere. "A bra shouldn't mark you like this," he said, rubbing the skin gouged by elastic straps.

She understood his implication, that he would start purchasing an even bigger size to accommodate the even bigger her. "All the more reason to diet," she asserted. "Like with Fred's socket, I don't need a larger size, I need a smaller me."

His thighs gripped hard around her as he leaned forward, and his crotch ground against her tailbone. Sultry breath swirled the hair beside her ear as he whispered, "This is nice. Don't mess it up." He leaned back again and relaxed the hold on her legs, the Marlboro Man on his filly.

Her tank top rode higher as he sought the soreness between her shoulder blades and above. Strong fingers moved in unison, executing a perfect rhythm that made her moan. Heat spread into her neck and face, across her back, and down into her chest. It rolled in waves through her abdomen and crotch and along her arms and legs until her whole body pulsed.

He said in a low, hypnotic cadence. "Imagine the tension leaving your body through the tips of your fingers and toes. Through every strand of hair. It doesn't rush out, it flows—in time with your heartbeat. No hurry. Your body knows the right pace. Trust your body."

His hands continued to work on her upper back and neck. Whenever he lifted his palms, it felt as if he'd removed life support and left her even more crippled. The relief of his hands returning to her skin brought forth deep sighs. "Call in sick today," she said and bucked against him. "At least skip the gym. Please?"

"You know how important my routines are to me." He leaned into her lower back, and his fingers worked down to her butt. "It'll be a busy day. In fact, I might have to come home late. The car has two hundred thousand miles on it now, so I need to take it for another servicing."

"I'm all for servicing. I think I'm a quart low—where's that dipstick?"

He scooted backward along her slacks and muttered, "We're getting carried away." Touching the faded scar that arced across the end of her stump, so unafraid and accepting that even this gentle act became erotic, he asked if her leg were still asleep.

"It's wide awake now. All of me is wide-fucking-awake." She groped blindly behind her, trying to seize his shorts.

Joe eased off her legs, stepping backward toward the doors. "Tonight," he said. "I promise. We'll go right to bed. No stalkers, no tears. We'll get back to normal."

"There's that word again." Sarah sat up and flexed her shoulders, tense once more. With a nod at his distended shorts, she said, "I can help you with that."

"Tonight."

"Now." She pulled off the tank top and discarded her bra. Her breasts felt hot all over, the nipples thick and hard.

His gaze dropped to her bosom and lingered. Backing farther away, he said, "But I can do so much more for you when we have time."

Sarah tried to lift her butt and yank down her slacks and panties, but she couldn't get much leverage with only her right foot to plant on the floor. After a brief struggle, she fell back against the cushions and resorted to pleading, "Stop treating every orgasm like a goddamn merit badge. Won't you just do me?"

"That cheapens both of us. Feel this tension? How badly we want each other? Let it smolder until tonight."

He retreated to the exit, and she cried, "C'mon, Joe, it's only making love."

"For me, it's making art. It's the only way I know how to create something beautiful. And you of all people should understand that." The doors closed behind him.

Chapter 13

"I ALWAYS THOUGHT ARTISTS MAKE BETTER ART when they're miserable." Sarah pushed away the amateurish sketches on her drawing table and said to the fresh rainstorm and Dorothy, "Maybe I'm not unhappy enough. Maybe I'm not an artist. Maybe I'm in a period where I have to be totally despondent to move forward."

Cloaked in her robe, she swallowed another aspirin and chased it with bottled water. "And speaking of periods, there's no maybe about this one." As she'd gained weight, her monthly menses worsened. During her years in ballet, she carried so little body fat that if a light period drifted through at all, it merely skimmed her insides. Now cramps thudded like a Wagnerian hammer every twenty-eight days, and she didn't just bleed, she hemorrhaged. Worse, the latest cycle began a day early, ruining her chances for any action that night and throughout the next week.

Joe hated the messiness of intercourse during menstruation. He'd even postponed the first time they had sex, putting her off for three days after her cycle "just in case." Though he would still kiss and hold her, the vagina was verboten. Sarah snapped her drawing pencil in half and threw the pieces against the half-baked ideas for her self-portrait.

He'd left a summer-weight dress, lacy underwear, and low heels for her, but she hadn't bathed yet, except to cleanse her left leg. According to the scale, she had dropped another half-pound, but the good news failed to cheer her. She'd rejected Fred in favor of her crutches, and ate a wedge of fudge pie after devouring the slow-cooked grits, bacon, and toast Joe had prepared.

She opened her robe, sucked in her stomach, and stared down at the stranger's body, cursing the protruding tampon string that now added to her woes. The phones rang. Even without a watch, she knew the time. Ten a.m. Like clockwork, Joe was checking in. She cinched the robe belt and swing-stepped to the cordless unit. Sure enough, caller ID reported Matryoshka Engineering and Joe's office number. She dropped onto the couch and clicked Talk.

After an exchange of greetings, he said, "I hope you're still smoldering."

"No, the fire's out. Dead," she reported, putting an extra dose of gloom in her voice. "My period started."

"Jeez! According to your birth-control pills, we should've had tonight at least."

She allowed herself a rueful smile at the remorse in his voice. "A bird in the hand, Joe…you should have jumped in this bush when you had the chance."

"I know, I know. God, it's been the week from hell, hasn't it? Still, it's not the end of the world, Sare."

"But it's the icing on the cake, if you'll pardon the disgusting imagery."

His volume sunk to a concerned whisper. "Are you still angry at me about those calls?"

"I wasn't really so mad at you about that—it was your cover-up that pissed me off. You apologized, and we kissed and made up. Let's move on."

"We never did kiss."

She conceded the point and added in a weary voice, "And the making-up part's hit a snag, too. Shit."

"Maybe I'll start coming home at lunch, to give us more time together."

"Fine," she replied, hating the way she bit off the word. She took a diaphragmatic breath, let it out, and affirmed, "Dorothy would be excited to see you. I would, too."

"Thanks for the addendum. I wish I could start today, but the garage has my car."

She almost asked how he liked it, not having the freedom

to drive around, but, in an effort to restore harmony, she made small-talk: "Did they give you a ride back to work?"

"No, one of my friends here picked me up and offered to take me back."

"That's nice of him." She began considering other conversational gambits.

"Uh, 'her' actually: a woman named Rita Bolivar. I've mentioned her before. The product manager who negotiates the specs for our work."

It would've been easier, and understandable, for Joe to have fibbed. Sarah reinstated some of the points for honesty and forthrightness she'd deducted the day before. She tried to match Rita's name with a half-remembered group photo he'd shown her. One of the women pictured stood out: a tall, athletic-looking brunette whose short skirt and bright, scoop-neck top complemented luscious brown skin. However, asking about looks—"The leggy one with the perfect boobs?"—would sound distrustful. She said, "Give me another hint."

"The one from the Caribbean. She's won eight of those Russian nesting dolls."

"Now I remember. She named them Snow White and the Seven Babushkas." Of course—it had to be the one with the great body and a sense of humor. Marvelous. Maybe Joe had a wandering eye figuratively as well as literally.

She never used to get jealous. Half the men she'd dated were hard-bodied danseurs, who spent their days and nights cradling other, more elegant women in body stockings. Maybe once she knew Rita Bolivar, she could stop fretting. "Invite her over for dinner sometime," she suggested, "to pay her back."

After a pause, he said, "I thought you liked your privacy."

Sarah snorted. "During my 'old days in ballet,' I shared a dressing room with up to a dozen other women. One company had a unisex wardrobe closet we all had to cluster inside. I've even had to strip naked backstage to do a quick-change, with the crew standing around. No, as far as I'm concerned, every day's an open house. Bring her on!"

He said, "You're smiling. I hear it in your voice."

"I guess I am. God, those were insane, wonderful days. In real life, I've never been as grotesque or angelic as I was in ballet."

"Oh, I wouldn't say that."

She laughed and exclaimed, "You're grinning, too. Which have I been lately?"

He made the zinging reel-cast sound. "Going fishing for a compliment?"

"Or a smack-down. Which is it? Please tell me."

"We're smoldering again, Sare. I'll check in later and give you another stoking."

He hung up, but the afterglow of his smile remained in her imagination. Seconds later, a cramp knotted her insides. She leaned hard on her crutches as she swung over to the table with the aspirin, and had to sit down to free her hands. By the time she swallowed another pill, his smile and her good feelings had disappeared. The relief they'd shared over a lighthearted moment made them forget her period. When he next called, she would have to bring him down all over again.

She held her head, elbows braced on the tabletop, until claws scratched against the chair leg. Dorothy gazed up, furry skin folds framing opalescent eyes. The bulldog's jet-black jaws opened and closed, revealing a charming under-bite as the animal pleaded for something.

Sarah lowered her hand, offering fingers for the dog to sniff, but Dorothy batted at them instead. Fawn-colored hindquarters wriggled in time with a series of soft barks. Never before had the bulldog approached her. She asked, "Do you need to go out?"

Dorothy froze except to tilt her head and prick her bat-like ears. Then Sarah considered the past few days and asked, "You wanna go for a walk in the rain?" The dog became a wiggling, dancing dervish, and barked louder. "OK, OK, you'll have to wait a minute. Mommy has to attach her leg. I'll bet not too many dogs hear that excuse."

In the bedroom, Dorothy sat on the carpet while Sarah put on the tracksuit Joe had washed. She cleaned the socket, prepared her leg, joined them with three solid clicks, and managed to cram in a fourth. A firmer fit than before, but still not where she needed to be. Athletic socks and tennis shoes soon covered Fred's foot and her own. Standing before the hall-tree mirror with her sunburned arms and face on display, she draped a thin belt around her middle to confirm hip alignment. She thought she saw a little progress around her waistline. Were those her hipbones? "Shalom, y'all," she said. "Welcome back, old friends."

In her mind, she heard a piano echoing—recorded rehearsal music, major chords in four-four time—and pictured a large, brightly lit room with mirrors along one wall. Polished wood underfoot, almost as springy as the bedroom carpet, was stained a lighter hue than the barre, which was positioned midway between shoulder and waist. An unseen ballet mistress clapped her hands, and said, "Plié."

Sarah turned out her right foot, planting the heel and sliding the toe-box of her sneaker clockwise ninety degrees. Perfect. "Both feet, Miss Berger," the disembodied voice scolded in a French accent that made Sarah's last name sound like "Booger." The voice went on, "Or have you sent your left leg to the jazz and tap class in the basement?" Unseen girls giggled, trilling in minor keys below the piano accompaniment.

Bearing down on the left heel, Sarah pressed her cocked right foot snug against it, as if to demonstrate "three o'clock." Her left hip rotated, which initiated the turnout of the prosthetic foot. Keep the knee straight, she told herself. The piano maintained its metronomic beats. As the toe of the tennis shoe swung counterclockwise, she imagined turning back time.

The torque absorbers inside Fred allowed for a maximum turnout of forty-five degrees. Instead of showing "quarter to three" on a clock face, with her feet opposed to each other in a straight line, she had to be satisfied with "eight minutes till." The invisible instructor accepted that limitation. "Bend at the first beat, Miss Berger. Now!"

A C-chord resounded, and Sarah flexed her knees, descending in time with the music: back straight, bottom in line beneath it, diaphragm solid. Knees bending over feet, arms rounded, fingers loose. Tuck those thumbs in over the palms. The part of her mind that judged with the ballet mistress' eyes watched everything: lines, breathing, vibrancy.

"Chin higher, Miss Berger, parallel with the floor. If you fear that it's weak, you may wear the Nutcracker's beard." More giggles, an arpeggio that faded as the music continued. Sarah counted beats and rose with the start of a new measure. Mirroring the smooth, slow motion of a flamingo rising from a crouch, her knees straightened and legs came together, elevating her with fluid grace.

"Again, Miss Berger." The ballet mistress never complimented. Silence equaled success. Other than voicing an instruction, any comment from her indicated failure.

While Sarah watched her movements, she recalled an old ballet quip: your reflection was the only proof of your existence. She rose from her fourth plié, enjoying the burn in her thighs, when Dorothy barked at her. Piano music stopped abruptly and class ended. The dance school evaporated, but not before she glimpsed a ballerina in the mirror returning her gaze.

The French voice resumed lecturing while Sarah dressed in wet-weather gear. "It's in the muscles, Miss Berger. Every plié, tour jeté, and pas de bourrée is locked inside. Your muscles know the steps. The brains are in your feet, yes?"

Sarah couldn't resist replying, "With one foot lost, do I now have only half a mind?"

"No, Miss Berger. Now you must redouble your efforts—and do twice as much with what remains."

⁂

Later, she sat at her drawing table again, depleted bottle of aspirin at her elbow, and tensed as her insides clenched. Instead of gut-twisting pain, she felt her empty stomach contract. It groaned. She'd long-since digested the puny lunch of apple slices and a small salad after a sodden hour-long walk that morning. Dorothy slept beside her foot—another first. Sarah guessed the bulldog had exhausted herself more from shaking off rain every few minutes than from making the three-mile loop around Eagle's Lair.

Their walk through the exclusive neighborhood of well-tended landscapes and sprawling houses inspired her to re-conceive her gift to Joe. Instead of depicting herself as the focus of attention, she would describe an eagle, magnificent in its power and grace, returning to a fortified lair with wings flared as it prepared to land. Her face would hover in the crisp sky, like a mirage, watching the homecoming with an expression of contentment.

Outside, faint daylight pressed through the heavy cloud cover and spread late-afternoon shadows across the west side of her studio. Joe was late. Contrary to her prediction, he'd remained upbeat about their evening plans when he placed his usual check-in call at two. His only complaint regarded the garage manager's incompetence. Poor planning had resulted in a backlog of work, so there was a chance the technicians wouldn't get to his car until the next day. As a Project Management Professional, Joe could not abide poor planning.

Intending to keep his spirits buoyed throughout the evening, she wore the clothes he'd set out that morning: the pewter-colored frock, lacy underwear, and slip-ons. To his ensemble, she'd added thigh-high hose, which made the color of her leg and the prosthesis appear identical, and she cinched them with garters to give him a thrill. Now, with time on her hands, Sarah considered her latest sketches and added a few penciled details, quick strokes with the point and sidelong swirls like a charcoal rubbing. The contented look of her self-portrait still eluded capture.

Dorothy's snores changed to panic barks in one startling instant. The bulldog charged the western glass wall and hit it with her forepaws. Standing on her hind legs, ears forward, she yapped at the closed gate. Then her fierce noises changed to the triumphal yowls she reserved for Joe's arrival. The intercom buzzed, prompting Dorothy to rocket down the hallway.

The bulldog panted at a living room window while Sarah walked to the kitchen and wondered why Joe didn't open the gate with the remote control in his car. He stood before the camera lens in his business suit, looking good even in monochrome. Past his left shoulder, an Acura SUV idled near the curb, its driver-side window lowered.

A woman sat behind the wheel. Despite the overcast day, she wore narrow sunglasses with stems that disappeared into very dark, wavy hair. The longest tresses curled across collarbones sculptured in bas relief against her dark skin. With the door blocking Sarah's view, she couldn't tell how much else the woman's low-cut top revealed. Rita Bolivar, very much in the flesh.

Sarah reminded herself not to condemn Rita before she got to know her, nor to upbraid Joe for having a beautiful friend. Keying the microphone, she said, "Hey, Joe. Are they holding your car hostage?"

"It was still on the lift at closing time. They'd promised it would be ready, but I guess it'll stay up there all night. Rita offered to give me another ride in the morning."

Sarah bristled at the imagery that "ride" conjured, then cursed her dirty, suspicious mind. She revised plans for the evening, figuring that she'd learn more about the Rita woman by talking to her, instead of quizzing Joe and then probably second-guessing every nuance in his voice and body language. The best way to kill jealousy and distrust was to meet the enemy and discover a regular, unthreatening person there. For all she knew, the woman had a husband and kids. She asked, "Did you invite her for dinner?"

"Not yet. We'll have her over next week. Will you let me in, or do I need to say a magic word?"

The power to open the gate or deny him admittance made her bold. "Let's thaw out the rest of your sausage bake," she said, "and there's salad fixings and dessert."

Glancing over his shoulder, he signaled Rita to stay put. The woman smiled, perhaps responding to his expression, which Sarah couldn't see. After he turned back to the camera, stone-faced, he murmured, "We can't serve leftovers to a guest."

"It's a casserole; once you spoon it on a plate, you can't tell leftover from fresh." Before he could try to dissuade her, she asserted, "Wave her inside, and I'll be right out."

"I really think we can do better than that—next week." He

stared at the lens, waiting for her reply. When she did not, he sighed and beckoned Rita to enter.

Beaming with victory, Sarah opened the gate for them with the press of a button. Triumph turned to concern, however, as she checked her reflection before a gilt-edged mirror in the dining room. The sunburn on her face had begun to peel, especially along the bridge of her nose. Rubbing her lips together while she sketched had worn the coral gloss thin, and beads of mascara clumped on her eyelashes. She'd left herself no time to apply fresh make-up.

"Shit."

She took a dozen careful steps to assure herself she walked without a limp. To make an elegant exit from the house, she decided to glide out the front rather than duck beneath a clattering garage door. Dorothy darted around her and raced across the wet grass to Joe, who met the French bulldog on the driveway. As the gold SUV parked behind him, he crouched and murmured baby talk to Dorothy, keeping her at arm's length to avoid soiling his navy blue suit and shined shoes.

Sarah bent over to welcome Joe home with a mannered kiss—no open mouths in front of their guest—but added an affectionate rub across his shoulders. Like a concierge, she went to open the driver door. Even before she realized it, she'd fallen back on her mother's lessons in exaggerated courtesy and subservience. Too late now. She gave a big "howdy" smile to the woman, who looked even more stunning up close.

Though Rita had not yet removed her sunglasses, Sarah guessed that chestnut eyes complemented her luscious brown complexion and black hair. Silver touched the woman's skin in many places: hoop earrings that would've appeared too big against a less swanlike neck, bracelets and a delicate watch clasping her wrists, rings on every finger, and a coiled necklace of many strands that cascaded onto her pushed-up bust. An anklet also—the next thing Sarah noticed when she opened the door. The circle of silver shone like a halo above a four-inch viridian-colored pump as Rita set down her leg, which was bare and toned.

Gleaming lips curved together into a smile as Rita brushed

down the hem of her short jade skirt. She offered her manicured hand before Sarah could extend a graphite-smudged one, which would've prompted Mom to deduct the earlier points awarded for good hostess manners. Having failed in deportment, Sarah could see she had few other possible advantages over Rita Bolivar, who stood six inches taller and obviously exercised as much as Joe.

Worse, the woman introduced herself in a melodiously accented contralto, like a spokesmodel for the British Virgin Islands. "Thank you ever so much for inviting me to dine in your home. It's so old-fashioned—everyone else wants to go out to restaurants."

Joe sometimes commented on how sexy he found Sarah's voice, but she knew she sounded like a Semitic redneck compared to the Caribbean Carmen. The inspiration for the British accent he sometimes imitated was clear. Sarah shortened her vowels and focused on proper grammar even more than usual. "You are most welcome. Dinner at home suits us. We're an old-fashioned couple, Joe and I. Just a couple of homebodies."

Rita removed her sunglasses, revealing another surprise: irises even greener than her dress. Faint lines beside Rita's eyes bolstered the authority she exuded in her posture and speech, and placed her age at thirty-five or so. "Joe told me you married a year ago," the woman said. "But there's no baby yet, my dear—that's not very old-fashioned. Especially for homebodies." She gave a throaty laugh.

The sudden switch of topics, from their quaint dining habits to procreation—with a possible implication of frigidity—made the sunburn pulse on Sarah's face. Joe came over and rubbed the small of her back in a tight spiral. Despite his private gesture, she couldn't shake her suspicion and jealousy. She wanted to be friendly to their guest, or at least civil, but couldn't let Rita's insinuation go unchallenged. "We practice a lot, believe me. A whole helluva lot." She took the twang out of her voice, adding flatly, "When the time is right, we'll know just what to do."

While Dorothy barked at Joe's legs, he asked, "What are we talking about?"

Rita smiled wider, flashing chalk-white teeth. "The blessings of being a happy couple."

"The secret to that," Joe said, "is for one person to be the gardener and the other to be the flower he takes care of."

Rita pursed her lips. "I see. And can a gardener remain satisfied tending to one lone bloom? Would he not desire a whole flowerbed?"

Stammering, he said, "Not this one." He ducked behind Sarah and tried to quiet the bulldog.

"And once the flower is planted where the gardener chooses," Rita continued, "it must stay put, regardless of the treatment it receives."

Joe grumbled, "I didn't know you held such strong opinions about horticulture."

"In the months you've known me, have I ever been timid on any subject?"

"No, you're not what I'd call a shrinking violet," he punned. Excusing himself, he returned to paying full attention to the insistent bulldog.

Sarah had never seen him in full retreat before. She edged closer to Rita and said, "I'm afraid this wasn't a good idea. I thought y'all—the two of you—were friends."

"Indeed we are, but someone has to take up for the poor flower. And remind the gardener of his responsibilities to it."

Unsure what to make of the woman, Sarah gave her a bewildered smile and invited her indoors. When she led Rita up the driveway, Dorothy barked a few times at the guest and fled across the lawn. From a safe distance, the French bulldog yapped some more.

Joe scolded their pet while Sarah apologized, but Rita said, "I'm not bothered in the least." She leaned forward, hands on knees, and sang Dorothy's name until the animal stopped barking. The slender necklace swung against the ends of her hair. While the woman compelled the bulldog to take a few uneasy steps closer, Sarah watched Joe. He stood ahead of Rita, such that a glance backward would've allowed him to peer through the oval of silver necklace and straight down her bodice. Instead, he gazed at Dorothy's tentative approach, and, when he did look back, it was to smile at Sarah.

It was more self-control than she could exercise. Indulging in voyeurism—every ballerina's secret vice—she studied the lines and evident musculature of Rita's legs, haunches, and torso. The dancer and artist in Sarah compelled her to focus on physicality. She didn't know the woman at all, but soon would be able to draw her with anatomical precision.

And without mercy she contrasted every perfect feature with her own. She named each one in her head like swinging a hammer against a spike, driving her spirits lower.

A chickadee swooped off the fence and touched down behind Dorothy, who spun and darted after it, breaking Rita's spell. The bird flew off, and Joe told her, "There's an old Southern saying, 'You could talk the birds right out of the trees.' I swear, you talked that guy right off the fence."

When his gaze finally strayed to her chest, she straightened. Pulling down the hem of her short skirt, she said, "Fence? This wall is taller than some of the trees around Nanny Cay. On Tortola, where I was born, we'd call this place a stronghold." Her teasing, combined with the lilting accent, made Sarah smile despite herself.

"It's just a fence," Joe said. "We like our privacy."

"But see how easy it is to surmount, my dear? All you need are wings."

Oncoming dusk brought a swarm of mosquitoes. One landed on Rita's forearm, and she shooed it off. Sarah raised her hand to splatter a bloodsucker on her own wrist, but Rita said, "God made them, too."

With reluctance, Sarah waved at the pest, and Rita gave her a victorious smile. Sarah couldn't decide if the grin indicated approval or something else. She brushed away others, saying, "Let's go inside before God sends a biblical plague of them."

Joe led Rita and Sarah to the front door and ushered them inside. He hustled the bulldog into the foyer, shut the door, and dried her paws with a towel he retrieved from the coat closet. With a flick of the terrycloth, he whacked a mosquito that had come in with Dorothy. "I know," he told Rita, cleaning the gray smudge off the wall, "but God made many, many more." He wiped the dead pest from the floor and carried the towel toward the laundry room. Dorothy stayed close on his heels. "Sare," he called behind him, "give Rita the five-cent tour, and I'll get dinner ready."

The woman had walked over to the wedding portrait above the living room mantle. She looked over Sarah, who joined her in front of the fireplace, and then gazed again at the large photograph. Sarah read Rita's expression as "sympathetic." While she might indulge in self-pity, she hated for others to feel sorry for her. Putting more gaiety in her voice than she felt, Sarah quipped, "People say my likeness to his first wife is uncanny, but I'm afraid it's not exactly *Rebecca*, is it?"

"Do you mean—"

"I'm joking. That's me up there. I've put on a little weight since then."

Rita said, "Your hair is quite different."

"Joe thought I needed a dramatic change. I was going through a bad spell."

The woman nodded, as if she had fit in a puzzle piece. "After your accident."

Realizing that Joe had betrayed her secret, Sarah blinked hard in anger. She wondered what else he'd told their guest. So much for "We like our privacy." With arms crossed, she said, "So you heard about that?"

"Joe said you lost your leg, and that you used to dance professionally in ballet."

"Did he also tell you that, during my bad spell, I spent a month getting over a love affair with morphine, while a bunch of antidepressants had me fercockt? Did he share that I once cried for fourteen hours straight?"

"I—"

Losing control, her head buzzing like a jar full of bees, Sarah stepped very close and said, "Did he mention I went 'round-the-bend, totally ape-shit, for two days?"

Rita backed away, holding her palms out. "He didn't, and I would never—"

"Except for aspirin, I'm totally drug-free, but Joe probably told you that he likes me better when I'm sedated."

The woman stopped her retreat. In fact, she took a step forward, as if preparing to charge. "Sarah, this is not at all old-fashioned, assaulting a guest in your home."

Sarah took in a full measure of air, trying to relax and resume her role as the gracious hostess, if that were even possible. "You're right," she said, hanging her head. "I'm sorry." She breathed deeply once more. "When there's something wrong with you, you want to keep it a secret. You play a game to see if you can hide it from strangers."

"Nonsense—I'm sure there's nothing wrong with you. And I need not be a stranger." Rita offered her hand again.

Sarah shook it with reluctance, but sincerity shone in the woman's expression and confident grip. A flood of gratitude surprised Sarah and relaxed her all at once.

Rita said with a mischievous lilt, "Stay clean now. I do insist on drug-free friends."

"You have to draw the line somewhere," Sarah agreed. "I know all about drawing lines; I'm an artist."

"Um, Joe told me." Rita's smile changed from playful to chagrined.

He appeared around the corner of the stacked-stone hearth, coming up behind Rita. "I thought I heard my name. What are we talking about?"

Rita rotated halfway around and included both Joe and Sarah with her body language. "Dinner," she purred. "What is Joe preparing for dinner?"

"Sausage casserole," he said, "with a salad, and brownie sundaes for dessert."

"Sausage? Oh dear me, I'm a vegetarian."

Joe gave Sarah an up-from-under glower. Instead of responding to him, she told Rita, "I used to be a vegetarian."

"Now that I didn't know. Why ever did you quit?"

"I always hated cooking, so Joe started doing it for me. He said I'd feel stronger and dance better with animal protein in my diet."

Rita slapped the air in front of Joe's nose. "Bollocks! Two garden salads for the ladies, Mr. Gordon. If you do a proper job of it, we might deign to sample the dessert." She took Sarah's arm and led her to the sofa, where they sat together.

Joe said, "Sorry, Rita. How was I to know that you don't eat meat?"

"If you went out with the others at Matryoshka, instead of lunching at your desk every day, you would have known." In unison, she and Sarah said, "Workaholic," and smiled at each other.

Chin raised, Joe strode into the kitchen. The driveway gate slid shut, following his command.

Rita indicated his privacy fence that dominated the view beyond the windows. "'Something there is,'" she quoted, "'that doesn't love a wall.'"

"That sounds familiar. What is it from?"

"Why, from your Robert Frost of course: 'Mending Wall.'"

"I'm afraid I don't love that wall myself," Sarah said, "but good fences can keep out bad neighbors."

Rita patted her arm. "It need not keep in good people, however. What say we make a date for a poetry reading at the library or some other sojourn into town?"

Sarah contemplated a little time away from home, away from the fences and walls of the neighborhood. The chance to make friends with such a self-assured woman was irresistible, and it beat the hell out of hanging out with Mrs. O'Malley. She said, "That's an offer I can't refuse."

Chapter 14

SARAH EXAMINED HER DRAWING OF RITA BOLIVAR, portrayed relaxing on the living room sofa. Adding more details—rings on the fingers, the anklet curving around the best-looking leg she'd seen outside the Atlanta Ballet—she finally started to feel at home working at her drawing table.

In addition to being a sexpot and gifted with a gorgeous voice, Rita had a pedigree, too: she was related to Simón Bolivar, the great liberator of South America, from which her people had emigrated, ending up in the West Indies. Sarah had decided Rita could liberate her from her self-imposed exile from the world. Using her as a role model, she also would get in shape again and have a template for self-confidence. Her new motto would be WWRD: What Would Rita Do? She always performed best when she had a high-achieving woman to emulate.

It was just like her to pick Miss British Virgin Islands as her standard. Mom always said she aimed too high and set herself up for disappointment. Not this time.

Sarah smiled as she touched up the cheekbones on her study of the BV Islander and drew in thicker bangs. Thinking about her mother's theory of cleavage power, she extended the crease that emerged above the neckline and deepened the shadows under the bust.

The woman had left an hour before, with a promise to pick up Joe early the next morning; they went to the same gym. He had been sulky during dinner, and Rita seemed to enjoy tweaking him. She'd given him such a lecture at dinner about slaughterhouses and the evils of animal fat he couldn't finish his sausage casserole.

It had pleased Sarah to see him under fire. She'd found it hard to forgive him for telling her secret to Rita. The only thing that helped was realizing he'd spared her from having to listen to the usual pity and other shmontses.

She returned to touching up the face, trying to get Rita's expression right. The woman had looked so comfortable, self-assured. Now how would that feel? When she tried to conjure that state of mind, she needed to go all the way back to the last time she danced on stage.

Thinking about the Babe from BVI and how much she'd enjoyed her company, Sarah let her left hand flick across the page without conscious thought. She added more shape to a cheekbone, touched the outer edge of the eyes with wisdom lines. A slight smile reshaped Rita's mouth, and Sarah recognized the contentment she sought for her own likeness, the look that had eluded her.

It was the look of a woman who did what she wanted and didn't take any crap. She thought about her increasingly tumultuous relationship with Joe and how much she missed their intimacy and closeness. So, girl, WWRD?

She found Joe at the kitchen table, suit jacket and tie slung on the chair back, with Dorothy lying near his feet. His laptop sat near his elbow along with the paper checkbook he kept as a backup when paying the bills. In the dishwasher, water sluiced with the steadiness of waves tumbling on shore. Apparently finished with keeping the household in order, he jiggled an antique Cracker Jack game between his thumbs and forefingers. The click of BBs against the walls of the maze sounded like shells in the surf.

The sounds reminded her of strolling on the beach, holding Joe's hand during their honeymoon. She waited until he looked up and said, "Remember our last night in Bermuda, when we realized we hadn't made love on the beach yet?"

"Sure." He set down the game. "The sand got everywhere before long; you told me it felt like ground-up glass inside you. Are you saying I'm hurting you again?"

She thrust out the palm of her hand like a traffic cop. "That's not where I'm going with this. Remember how we washed off in that little cove? After you bathed me, I knelt in the water and finished you." She grinned and added, "You tasted like the sea."

He turned his chair to face her, his expression softening. Dorothy resettled under the table with a sigh. "Moonlight made the droplets in your hair sparkle," he said. "Every time we moved, the water phosphoresced. You want to go back to Bermuda?"

"No, I want a taste of the sea." Sarah stepped so close that he had to part his legs so she wouldn't trod on his feet.

She stroked his face, and Joe took hold of her hips, pressing the skirt against her. He ran his long fingers over her buttocks and his thumbs grazed her thighs as he whispered, "But what can I do for you? With your bleeding…"

"You can sit back and enjoy it. Take what I want to give you."

"Did you ever have sex with your clothes on?" She shook her head. Oblivious to her mounting aggravation, he continued to stroke her.

She stepped back out of reach. "Why can't I focus on you and get pleasure from that? I used to do it all the…" She snapped her fingers. "Oh, but not since my accident. Damn it to hell, that's it—you don't wanna feel like you're taking advantage of the poor crippled girl, right?"

"Stop it. I never think of you that way. Why are you spoiling this?" He pushed out of his chair, prompting a frightened bark from the bulldog. "We could've had a fun, romantic evening, but instead you made me invite Rita in so the two of you could tag-team me. Now you're saying that I only screw you out of pity."

Sarah fought to control her voice. "What I want is so simple: sometimes I'd like to do things for you, to you. All I want in return is your satisfaction."

"And all I'm saying is why should I be selfish? Why can't I satisfy you, too, so we'll be equal?"

She hugged her sides as a menstrual cramp twisted her gut. Her eyes moistened, but she didn't know which thing, or how many things, to blame for the sob that forced its way out with an anguished yelp. "We're not equal," she cried, bending over. "You decide everything."

"Oh God, is that what this is about?" He reached her in one long stride and held her arms as pain and sorrow kept her bowed. "Sare, look at me. Come on."

Ashamed of how fast she'd lost command of the situation, she resisted straightening. He finally coaxed her upright and drew her against him, pressing her cheek to his cold, starched dress shirt. His embrace used to comfort her, but Sarah now felt imprisoned and adrift at the same time. She couldn't summon her wits.

He said, "You're wrong, I don't call the shots. I'm only responding to your needs." He stroked her hair. It felt like he was returning flyaway strands to their proper place. "Sometimes I think you're not aware of the signals you send, what your body tells me."

When she responded, her voice sounded hoarse and, she feared, defeated. "It's not about sex."

"I know exactly what it's about. I've done this dance before. My last girlfriend said I smothered her. 'Suffocated,' was the exact word she used. Probably like I'm suffocating you now against my shirt." If he wanted her to laugh, he'd wasted his effort; she still was fighting for two calm breaths in a row. "Most of my girlfriends didn't stick around long enough for me to smother them. Sometimes it was my orderliness, other times my eye. I was the 'neat freak' or just a plain old 'freak.'"

With a few more shuddering breaths, she finally regained her composure. So much for WWRD. Right now, what Rita would've done is kick her in the keister. "I'm sorry they hurt you, Joe. I'd never say that."

"But I am smothering you, right?"

Sarah leaned back and rubbed her face. Make-up streaked her fingers and his shirt. When she met his gaze, she was disappointed his right eye hadn't turned outward. She wished Joe cared so much about her grief that the stress of it almost blinded him. Because she hadn't caused him sufficient concern, and couldn't muster the strength to try a new approach, she quickly gave in. "No," she said, "you're not." She took a deep breath. "I thought I would do something you'd like, is all. I'm afraid I've made a scene over nothing. Sorry."

His eyes narrowed, and he pursed his lips in skepticism. "Are you still upset about that woman calling here and the stupid way I tried to smooth it over? Do you think I'm a cheat?"

"No, you're not hiding anything from me; I can see that in your eyes." She wanted to free herself from his grip, so she said, "I need to wash my face." When she eased backward, he wouldn't yield, so she tried a diversion. "Sorry about your dress shirt. My make-up ruined it."

He let her go and pulled at the stained fabric, inspecting it. "I'll put it with my 'Homicide Blonde' apron. Hopefully they're the last casualties from this crazy week." She didn't echo his smile, so he continued, now with bitterness, "So what happens next? We've yelled at each other more in the last few days than in eighteen months combined, and you're as emotional as you were after the accident. Except you're also completely unpredictable. Are we starting over yet again?"

"No," she repeated, weak with exhaustion. "We're OK. Let's call it a night. I'm beat."

"And unhappy, too. Am I doing everything wrong now? You used to brag about how perfect our marriage was."

"No more questions, Joe. I'm so tired, I don't know what I'll say next."

He straightened the cuffs of his ruined shirt. "Your first words at dinner last night were dead on: you're calling a truce."

"No, I'm surrendering outright, and I'm going to bed." She turned around and trudged toward the doorway.

"Bed used to be our favorite place to meet," he mused behind her. "What is it now?"

She refused to respond.

Chapter 15

MATTERS DID NOT IMPROVE IN THE WEEK THAT followed. One brief argument ensued after Sarah put laundry in the washing machine and bits of shredded tissue from a wad she'd stuffed in her pants pocket flecked everything in the load.

Rather than risk more conflict, Sarah relinquished all household duties once more and stayed quiet much of the time around Joe. He responded with sullen silences that loomed between fits of excessive politeness. Despite the increased tension, he continued his routines. He even fixed smaller, vegetarian meals to suit her when she began pushing any meat off to the side, but he displayed none of his usual enthusiasm. While they didn't fight, they engaged in a campaign of aloofness, a very cold war.

"Time is longer than a rope." Rita Bolivar had used that proverb from the British Virgin Islands during her visit. It perfectly captured Sarah's week of cramps and bleeding and weary melancholy.

A few days after her period ended, she finished the sketch of her self-portrait on the canvas and pushed her chair back to study it. Faint lines like spider silk merely hinted at the overall design. The contented set of the mouth seemed false to her, as if she'd taped it over a far-less attractive expression. In fact, unable to conjure the look a second time, she had copied it directly from her drawing of Rita. It would have to do.

As a reward for completing another small step, she took a break to do ballet exercises and Pilates in the master bedroom. In place of the low heels Joe had matched with her mahogany slacks and beige tunic, she pulled on athletic shoes. The hall-tree mirror displayed her trimmer figure; the clothes Joe had purchased lately no longer fit as well. That morning, the scale had reported a weight of 130.5. Jogging a few miles every other day and taking Dorothy for long walks had added a patina of peach to her complexion, as close as she ever got to a suntan. An appetite that continued to decline with the mood in the household also contributed to the ten pounds she'd lost.

Exercise had become easier now that the stub of her leg fit with greater comfort in Fred's socket. She never used her crutches anymore except to wander the house late at night, when she didn't want to risk fumbling in the dark with the artificial leg. If she woke Joe, she would have to deal with his petulance. Lately, she could only relax around him when he slept.

She settled into her imaginary ballet class. An invisible pianist began the four-four tempo she'd made her standard score over the past week. "Plié." The ballet mistress always began dance exercises the same way. Forcing out thoughts of what now passed for life-as-normal with Joe, Sarah moved like a marionette under water, all fluid grace and control. Every pivot or bend, every new line she created, countered resistance with momentum.

One, two, three, four. *One*, two, three—The phone rang, halting the illusory class. Joe still checked in with perfunctory calls twice a day, but never at noon. On the line, a man identified himself as the security guard at the Eagle's Lair front gate and said a woman wanted to see her: "A Miss Bo-li-var."

Rita had promised a poetry-reading date and even mentioned getting together again for dinner, but Sarah had expected some notice. She also assumed Joe would negotiate all the details far in advance. An instinct told her that he didn't know about the un-chaperoned visit.

Sarah asked the guard to admit her surprise guest. She changed back into slip-ons and headed to the bathroom to apply cosmetics with much more confidence than she felt with watercolors and acrylics. Hiding behind a painted mask was easy; revealing the truth with paints continued to plague her.

She squeezed in eye drops, flinching with each cold splash. The liquid stung at first, but soon removed the angry red streaks that had limned the whites. Muddy smudges beneath her eyes required more concealer than ever. Her insomnia had returned with a vengeance. If Joe didn't extend his usual remedy to her soon—or leave town again on another trip—she feared she would never sleep soundly again.

"So what good is slimming down when everything else is dreck?" She frowned at her reflection and added more blush, recalling other make-up sessions that took place minutes before the curtain rose. While painting her face after an ugly breakup with an ill-chosen boyfriend, she'd speculated that if a scientist offered her suspended animation between ballets, a dreamless void to take the place of living, she would've seized the opportunity. Now if that scientist showed up on her doorstep, she would tell him, "Only wake me when you've invented a time machine, so I can go backward. I hate today and dread tomorrow."

In the kitchen, she pushed the button to open the gate. Dorothy ran to a living room window and stood on hind legs, whining as her front paws clawed the molding. "It's not who you think it is," Sarah said as she walked to the front door. She unlocked it with the key she now kept with her at all times, and waited on the stoop. Though sunny again, an earlier line of rainstorms had darkened the concrete to the color of her blouse and left the air sticky. In the front yard, a dozen birds hopped around and harvested worms from the soggy earth.

Rita pulled up and parked the gold SUV in the driveway. Sparrows and robins fled over the walls at her approach. She lowered the tinted window, and watched them from behind her sunglasses. Waving to Sarah, she called in that melodious West Indian accent, "Would you care to join them?"

Sarah's gaze followed the last sparrow as it disappeared into the pine trees across the road. She approached the driver side. "Forever?" she asked.

"Today, for lunch. Tomorrow, who knows?" She laughed in a descending scale. "Though I had in mind a place that serves vegetarian fare instead of earthworms."

"I would love to go out to eat. I can't remember the last time I did."

"Ah, a workaholic—just like your husband."

The real reasons were too numerous and complicated to go into. While the bulldog yowled from the window at Rita's Acura, Sarah returned to the front door to lock it. Her cell phone, she remembered, was still on the kitchen table. She'd overcome her fear of leaving the gate open while she jogged or took Dorothy for a walk—Joe had said he would order an additional remote control since she was "determined to be out and about"—but she always took the phone he'd given her. He called that number during some of his check-in times, as if to make sure she kept it at hand. At night, he always charged the battery. She hollered, "Give me a minute," and retrieved it before locking up again. Dorothy pawed the window and barked, obviously not happy to be left alone.

Sarah settled against the leather passenger seat. The interior smelled new. Though Rita had learned her secret already, she still placed a hand over her left knee, where the slacks revealed outlines of the prosthetic socket. The vent blew tepid air around. The dashboard showed the thermostat set at seventy-eight. Her bottom and the back of her thighs had heated up by the time she strapped on the seatbelt.

Sporting a more modest neckline than before, Rita wore a lemon blouse beneath a tailored royal blue pantsuit. Familiar silver jewelry—rings, bracelets, necklace—gleamed against her skin. She raised her window and said, "I hope I'm not interrupting anything," and indicated the cell phone Sarah had retrieved. The slim sunglasses reflected distorted images of Sarah's face. "We can do this another time."

"No, this is fine. Joe likes to be able to reach me, is all."

Rita nodded. "I recall he walled us in when I came for dinner. Do you have a way to close the gate?"

"I'm afraid not, but it's OK." Perspiration dotted Sarah's upper lip and trickled along her ribs like molasses. The heat began to irritate her, loosening the cap on her bottled-up anger. "Do you pick on him all the time with those kinds of comments?"

"No, only when he needs it." The smile of contentment stayed put, as if she would've liked nothing more than to parry hostile questions all afternoon.

Sarah wiped sweat and make-up from her chin. "What I might need is a little more air conditioning. Mom says Southern girls are supposed to 'glow' or get 'dewy' when they're too warm. I schvitz like a sumo wrestler in a steam bath."

"'Schvitz'?" Rita clapped softly. "A marvelous term, but I do apologize for the lack of hospitality." She lowered the thermostat to seventy, but then bumped it two more degrees while Sarah dabbed at her forehead with a wadded tissue. "I never outgrew the steady warmth of Tortola. It keeps the pores open and reminds you how alive you are."

As cold air rushed over them, Rita backed down the driveway and onto the street. Instead of facing the Acura forward, though, she accelerated in reverse up Tangletree Drive. The video display from a rear-mounted camera showed nothing but gleaming wet pavement behind them.

The sensation of speeding backward reminded Sarah too much of her wreck. She gripped the leather armrest and stared at the side-view mirror with its warning about objects being closer than they appeared. Even with cold air gushing on her, panic-sweat soaked her armpits. "Have you, uh, lived here long?"

"Oh, for many years. I don't get back to BVI nearly often enough." Rita glanced at her mirrors and the display. "Did you travel much while dancing?"

"Some tours. Around the U.S. One time in Europe." Joe's fence shrank from view. The reversing SUV neared the intersection, and they shot past a sign that warned "No Through Street." She thought for a second it applied to the crossroad behind her, that there was no escape from the dead end. They might be racing toward a wall even higher than Joe's.

With a quick glance around, Rita continued backward into the intersecting boulevard. She halted and shifted into drive. Tires squealed as they shot forward. A grin emphasized her sculpted cheekbones as she said, "Wasn't that splendid?"

Relief only came to Sarah when the car began to cruise forward. "Awesome. Like a ride at Six Flags." Her heartbeat steadied as they sailed ahead, passing the estates she saw when she walked and jogged. After two miles of winding roads, and speed humps on the straight-aways, Rita drove through the exit of Eagle's Lair, and Sarah's heart accelerated again. The guard waved from his booth, and a wrought-iron gate hummed back into place behind them. For some reason, the dramatic end of an overture played in Sarah's head, and her stomach clenched as she anticipated the start of Act I.

They turned onto Pine Log Road to head into town. Rita gestured at Sarah's right leg and asked, "Is that a tendu, my dear?"

Sarah had extended it under the dashboard with her foot pointed, creating one long line from hip to toes. "Wow, you know ballet-speak, too." Her muscles quivered while she struggled to maintain yardstick-like straightness. "As we were waiting for the gate to open just now, I thought about standing in the wings and stretching, getting ready to leap onto the stage when I heard my cue." She relaxed her right leg at last, and tried to extend her left. Even with the shoe pushed up beneath the dashboard, she couldn't flex the artificial foot. "Do you dance?"

"I studied for a few years only, not at all as seriously—or successfully—as you. So leaving your neighborhood felt like jumping onstage?"

"For some reason, I've got the same butterflies in my stomach." They passed modest ranch homes built along the roadside among slender pines. Sarah guessed that they'd been there long before Pine Log had become a major traffic artery. Side streets led to newer, grander communities with names promising nautical adventure, natural paradise, or sanctuary.

Rita said, "You're looking around quite as if you don't recognize anything."

"I don't. Both times Joe drove me through Aiken, I was in a funk. The first time, I still wore my preparatory prosthesis. It's a clunky thing with a crude rubber foot. Morphine was only a fond memory, but I ate Demerol and codeine like candy." Staring out the window, she marveled at how far from home Rita already had taken her. "We did a walk-through of the house back then, in January, and he told me about all the remodeling he planned."

"Why leave Atlanta?" Wet pavement hissed under the tires as Rita scooted her SUV around a slow-moving sedan.

"Our condo had a lot of stairs," Sarah answered. "We wanted to move anyway." The woman looked unconvinced, so she confessed, "Joe thought that living in a charming town with a slower pace would help me heal. And forget."

"And what did you think?" Residences gave way to commercial zoning. Pine Log merged into Silver Bluff Road and the traffic became denser, with small businesses and strip malls stacked up on both sides. Rita expertly wove among the cars and trucks, never braking.

"At the time, thinking wasn't something I did real well. He's a smart, caring man, so I left it up to him."

"Oh, by all means, leave it up to the man." Rita gunned the engine and the Acura flew through the busy intersection with Hitchcock Parkway. "So your second visit to charming, slow-paced Aiken was on moving day?"

Sarah had returned to gripping the leather armrest. It occurred to her that she might leave the impressions of her fingertips as Joe had done in her Miata. She answered, "About four months after the walk-through." Anticipating the follow-up question, she said, "I'd graduated to this prosthesis, but I stayed in a kind of fog. My doctor had taken me off the painkillers that'd helped me sleep—"

"Your insomnia remains, correct?" At the next light, finally forced to stop, Rita signaled a left turn onto Whiskey Road. "You've yawned five times thus far, and you look…fatigued."

"Uh-oh. You've been my friend only since last week, but you're already starting to mince words." Sarah had no recollection of yawning. The cold air relaxed her. She closed her eyes for a moment.

"—missing it." Rita's voice rose in a singsong warning.

Sarah blinked awake and followed the woman's pointing finger. On the left side of the road, a serpentine brick wall undulated along a sidewalk. Behind the ribbon of red and mortar-gray, huge live oaks towered. A wrought-iron gate gave her a glimpse of their lowest branches, which arced almost to the ground like massive parental arms bending to cradle the children who toddled nearby.

"Hopelands Gardens," Rita informed her. "They have a tiny

amphitheater with summer concerts, and there are fountains and walking paths. You must see inside."

"Today?"

"No, our mission today is to dine and share some stories. I wonder if yours is *The Sleeping Beauty*." On both sides of Whiskey Road, brick walls protected grand Victorian manors that sported deep balconies and sleeping porches and reminded Sarah of the architecture in Savannah. According to Rita, the locals called them "cottages." She said, "Notice the side-streets made of dirt? Here in the so-called 'Winter Colony,' that's not due to poverty."

The next traffic light switched to red, and a horse crossed the paved highway, commanded by a woman rider resplendent in black and white equestrian attire. While the palomino stallion clopped along, it nodded toward the halted cars, and the woman saluted, touching the brim of her helmet with a leather crop. When the pair reached the other side, she patted the horse's silver-blond mane and nudged its massive ribs with her boots. Together they cantered down a clay track still damp enough not to yield any dust.

The light turned green and Rita accelerated, saying, "You dozed past the polo field and country clubs."

"I had no idea all this existed," Sarah said. "It's beautiful."

Rita indicated one intersection, where Easy Street joined Whiskey Road. "There's a wry—or should I say 'r-y-e'—sense of humor on display, too."

They stopped in a left-turn lane. To their right, the wide boulevard of South Boundary Avenue seemed to go on forever. Huge live oaks on both sides intertwined their uppermost branches far above the road, creating a tunnel of green for those who passed beneath. Sarah said, "Imagine riding in an open carriage under those leaves, or walking hand-in-hand."

Traffic started again, and the cathedral-like aisle swept away from Sarah's view. "Clearly you enjoy nature," Rita said. "Do you and Joe go for many walks?"

"I'm afraid it makes him uneasy when I leave the house, like something even worse than my car wreck could happen to me."

"And he would assume blame for that as well."

Sarah wanted to ask exactly how much about their lives Joe had shared, but the woman had resumed her guided tour. To the left, a serpentine wall of whitewashed bricks bordered a mansion converted into the county historical museum. Ahead the pavement gave way to a sandy lane that tires, feet, and horseshoes had made lumpy. Rita said, "That's an entrance into Hitchcock Woods, the largest urban park in the U.S. Some two thousand acres. Even with a trail map it's easy to get lost in there."

"That doesn't sound so bad," Sarah mused, "disappearing for a while."

"Indeed. As long as you don't hide from yourself."

The road veered to the right, becoming Laurens Street. After they crossed a bridge that spanned a railroad track, the central part of the city began to show itself. Ornate fountains and greenswards landscaped with pistachio trees separated the north and southbound lanes of the broad street, with diagonal-to-the-curb parking. Chinese elms shaded the sidewalks, and many of the brick-fronted and clapboard businesses sported awnings. Rita wedged her SUV into the only available space, between a full-size pickup and an open-top sports car.

Sarah peered down into a Miata nearly identical to the one she'd destroyed. The leather interior was tan, and the black hood gleamed. She knew just where the bucket seat would meet her back and haunches. Imagining the silver gear-shift knob under the fingers of her right hand, her wrist flexed with the short throws to progress from first to fifth, as clear in her muscle-memory as the five positions in ballet. Her left leg sought a clutch pedal to facilitate the gear changes, tapping down the artificial foot. Her right foot moved in counterpoint; it pressed and released an invisible accelerator while she recalled the roar of the engine. When she at last became aware of her shoes thumping the Acura floorboard in two-four time, the pain of all she'd lost threatened to overwhelm her again.

"May I give you a hand?" Rita called from the sidewalk.

Sarah flushed, unsure of how long she'd stared at the convertible. Her phantom left leg had begun to throb. She opened her door and said, "I'm fine, thanks." Her voice sounded brittle in her ears. "I used to have a roadster like this one." She stepped down and, unable to resist, touched the leather headrest on the driver's side. A very long strand of hair clung there. She couldn't tell whether the hair was brown or blond.

Rita engaged the locks and alarm and dropped her keychain into a leather purse. "Are you quite all right? You're limping."

"You've heard of amputees who feel pain in a long-gone limb? The nerves higher up don't know there's nothing down below. Believe me, it can hurt like a mother."

"Peculiar expression, that."

Though she could tell Rita a thing or two about the hurt a mother could cause, she said, "I'm sparing you the ugly version."

"Ah, that one I do know." She led Sarah up the wide, elm-lined sidewalk, past antique stores, collectibles shops, and clothing boutiques. "Have you noticed that women—and mothers in particular—bear the brunt of profanity? To insult a man, you need only insult his mother: son of a bitch."

"I'd never thought about it that way before."

"Why do you think men have settled on those terms as the ultimate insults? Why is a female dog so much worse than a male *canis*? Furthermore, why don't you ever hear someone called a 'fatherfucker'?"

Women and men dressed in office attire and leisurewear stared as they walked past. If they were Southerners, Sarah knew they would remain polite and not comment on Rita's language until out of earshot, but her face and neck heated up nonetheless. She looked at the concrete beneath her feet and murmured her answer like a pupil in Sex Education class. "The women-must-be-pure thing? A double-standard?"

"Nonsense. If men have yelled the b-word at you, it was because you were exerting power, dominance, control. When you did as they wanted, they had no complaint, correct?"

"But to call someone a—" she lowered her voice even more "—mother-effer…"

"Who in our culture, other than a prisoner, has less power than a mother? Even a child has more laws and social agencies on its side than dear old mum. Society says that a chap would have to be very low indeed to shag such a miserable creature."

Sarah acknowledged Rita's point, but, hoping to avoid further spectacle, she attempted to divert her. "I admire your outspokenness."

Rita plowed on, exclaiming, "And the colloquialism for that? Why, it's 'ballsy,' of course. In business, they compliment a woman by giving her such male attributes. As soon as she crosses an invisible, ever-shifting line, however, she's a bitch. See how language can control perception and thought?"

"Joe told me once that if you control your language, it can help you control your life."

"True. He could control another's life by the same means. Men have tried to do this to women from the start."

With no one around them now as they strode along the sidewalk, Sarah indulged herself, pointing out, "On the other hand, only men insult each other with 'cocksucker.'"

Rita had a ready answer. "Solely because men decided that women—and men who act like women—are the only ones degraded enough to enjoy...tasting that delicacy. Speaking of which," she whisked open a glass door and ushered Sarah inside, "you'll love the food here."

Chapter 16

AFTER THEY CROSSED A CHILLY, CARPETED ROOM lit by wall sconces, and were seated in the only unoccupied booth, Sarah leaned across the table and said, "I'm confused. When you used the term 'delicacy,' were you being ironic?"

Rita put away her sunglasses and pinned Sarah with a bright green-eyed gaze. "Absolutely not. I adore the male body."

"But I'd begun to think you hated men."

"One can do both, I assure you. However, I only hate some men. Others, I quite enjoy." She flashed a broad smile and picked up the menu, a single sheet of heavy parchment. "I recommend the peanut sauce, used as a salad dressing, mixed in the Thai stir-fry, or slathered upon the manhood of your choice."

"Even as cold as it is in here, I'll catch fire if you make me blush any harder."

"Too ballsy?"

Sarah muttered, "I'm afraid we could offend someone, is all."

"In that case, I shall reign in my tumescent candor. How embarrassing for me, after all, if I were forced to deliver your smoldering remains to Joe. 'So sorry, chap, but disreputable dialog did in your dearly departed.'"

Snorting, Sarah reached for her water glass. Mindful of appearing too enthralled by her new friend—she feared that Rita would perceive her as the clingy type—she glanced around at the well-dressed customers, the elegant arrangements of food, and the subdued wallpaper and wainscoting that enfolded the interior.

A waiter approached with the wine Rita had ordered for them. Sarah turned her attention to the menu. Someone with excellent calligraphy skills had described fifteen entrees and appetizers with poetic brevity. When she noticed the prices, hot blood resurged in her cheeks. "Oh, shit! I didn't bring any money. What an idiot—I'm so out of practice."

Rita beamed as the waiter set down two glasses of white merlot without any slip in his neutral expression. "This is my treat; I invited you out, my dear. Sorry, Dylan," she said to the waiter, "you shan't have extra hands for the dishwashing, or whatever special humiliation you reserve for destitute ladies."

Dylan dipped his head but couldn't hide the smile that lit his handsome face. He looked up again, composure restored, and asked if they would like to order.

Rita fixed her elbows on the table and peered at him over steepled fingers. "Not merely order, my dear. I intend to rule."

"As ever, your command is all we wish for, Miss Bolivar." Dylan bowed, and his tie edged out of the black suit jacket. The silk hung down, long and dark.

"Then bring the Thai stir-fry, and make it extra spicy. Though exposing yourself has already opened my pores aplenty."

Dylan corralled his tie, blushing furiously, and Sarah wondered if Rita had that same effect on everyone. She said, "For me, also, but mild, please."

The waiter replied, "A splendid choice. Miss Bolivar likes it too hot in my opinion."

"My dear Dylan, perspiration is healthy, and especially welcomed in this icehouse." Before he could respond, Rita said, "Please let me introduce you to Sarah Gordon. Sarah, this is Dylan Moorcock, a lovely name for a lovely man."

Dylan bowed once more, this time pressing the tie against his shirt. "A pleasure, Ms. Gordon. We hope to see more of you."

Sarah smirked and said, "That depends on how much wine I have." While Dylan headed for the kitchen, edging the shirt collar from his neck as if to let the steam out, she and Rita burst out laughing. "You're a bad influence! I haven't flirted with a waiter since I was twenty."

"Nonsense. He's no mere waiter—he's Dylan." Rita tasted the merlot. "One of the men I quite enjoy."

"You mean you two…"

"Tonight, I've decided."

Sarah asked, "Doesn't he get a say?" She sipped the fragrant wine and sighed as the slow burn descended to her stomach.

"There it is again. Why should I leave such an important decision to a man?"

"And there you go. You do hate them."

"Perhaps I'm sensitized to how thoroughly they'll control a woman's life, if permitted. Let me tell you a story." Rita set her glass aside and leaned forward, hands clasped on the tablecloth. "A good friend of mine named Linda spent the better part of ten years—or should I say the worst—married to a very controlling fellow. He never beat her, never insulted her, but nor would he let her leave their house. Linda didn't have keys to the deadbolts he threw each day when leaving for work. The windows stayed locked shut as well. She was in love with him nonetheless. He catered to her every need, other than granting her freedom."

Sarah took a gulp of wine to hide her annoyance at the woman's righteous tone. At last, the point of the lunch date: to tear down both Joe and their marriage. Out of politeness, she said, "Oh my. How did Linda spend her days?"

"She cleaned the house and fixed his meals. He went home at noon each day to check on her. Sometimes he made surprise visits to ensure that she was 'safe.'"

"That sucks." Sarah concealed a yawn and traced crosshatches on the tablecloth with her fork. "Did they have children?"

"No, he controlled contraception as well, ensuring she swallowed her pill each day. To make certain that Linda had no unsupervised encounters, he used a post office drop instead of a mailbox, and took all parcel deliveries at his office. He also put up a forebidding wall that kept out the neighbors." She drank some water and pursed her lips. "Whenever he left the house, he first unplugged their phone and took it with him."

Sarah hugged her arms, surprised at the gooseflesh. The last detail sounded too creepy to be an invention. When the tale began, she'd assumed Rita exaggerated a relationship-from-hell story from her own life. Now, a sense of foreboding told her

Linda was a real person in danger. She asked, "What happened to her?"

"Altogether stir-crazy, she broke out a window one day, but cut herself quite severely climbing through. The husband found her sprawled on the lawn; in hospital, they had to give her two pints of blood. He then affixed bars over the glass, 'in case of burglars.'"

Sarah could imagine arriving home to find her own windows barred, her glass-enclosed studio walled up, and Joe saying how worried he was about her and how important it was to keep their home safe. With rising fear, she asked, "How did it end?"

"Hoping for rescue, Linda smashed out every window and then set fire to the back of the house: a calculated risk with disastrous results. Firefighters found her dying of smoke inhalation when they broke down the front door. After an extended stay in hospital, she lived in a sanitarium for even longer."

"Where is she now?"

"She found herself a flat and got a job, but the poor dear didn't know who she was anymore. Linda was dead inside. Now she's trapped with some other man. I haven't heard from her in months."

Sarah shook her head, rejecting the possibility. "Why would she do that?"

"Why does a woman go from one drunk to the next, one wife-beater to another?" Rita sipped more water. "I told you, Mum introduced me to poetry. I started with nursery rhymes, of course. One of them always chilled me, and now it reminds me ever so much of dear Linda: 'Peter, Peter, pumpkin eater,/Had a wife and couldn't keep her;/He put her in a pumpkin shell/And there he kept her very well.'"

Sarah said, "I'm afraid you think that Joe's keeping me a prisoner. He'd never do that—unlike the maniac in your story, Joe really does love me. There are some parallels, sure, but here I am, free to roam around."

"And the cell phone at your waist? You took it so you would play by his rules, is that not so? You're afraid to do otherwise."

"I am not." Sarah gulped her wine.

"'Afraid' is a word you use quite often. You're afraid of disappointing Joe, afraid of offending strangers, afraid of setting the terms of your own life."

Sarah pushed out of the booth and threw her napkin on the table. "How dare you lecture me?"

Many of the diners stopped their conversations; Rita watched her with an identical look of detached curiosity. The kitchen door swung outward, and Dylan approached with their meals on a tray. What was she going to do—walk home?

She eased back into her seat and spread the napkin on her lap. They remained silent as Dylan served her first, saying, "One chilled Thai stir-fry, for Ms. Gordon, mild but still packed with surprises." With a smile, he glanced at both of them, and then served Rita without comment or expression. Backing away, Dylan asked, "More wine? No?" He retreated with a promise to check on them soon.

"Sorry," Sarah mumbled.

"Why apologize, my dear? You should be furious. No one likes to have their fears laid bare. These are the misgivings you ponder at night, in lieu of sleep, correct?"

"I'm changing things. For months, I'm afr—um, I never even left the yard. Now I jog around the neighborhood or take a long walk every day. I'm losing weight, doing ballet and Pilates—"

"You're productive in your artistry?"

A lie would've been easy, except she hesitated and knew Rita noticed her pause. She prolonged it by forking up a few golden noodles, a sliver of red bell pepper, and a triangle of braised tofu. Chewing the chilled food with deliberate slowness, she savored the sweet, nutty sauce, the tang of ginger, and pungent garlic. The remainder of white merlot chased it all down with cold, liquid fire. She said, "May I have another?"

Rita signaled Dylan and pointed at their wine glasses. To Sarah, she said, "Your art?"

"I'm making a lot of progress," she said, justifying the exaggeration.

"What do you think about most often?"

The question surprised Sarah, and she answered without

planning her response. "The way we used to be, the way I used to be."

"How did you used to be?"

"Whole." She stabbed a bamboo shoot and nodded thanks as Dylan brought them fresh glasses of wine and removed the first round. "I mean that in many ways."

The woman pursed her lips skeptically. She asked, "And you and Joe?"

"Happy. No fights, no cold shoulders. Sex out the wazoo. On the weekends when I wasn't dancing, we'd do it six times, plus Friday nights and Monday mornings."

Rita raised her eyebrows and said, "That's quite a resilient wazoo you have."

"Bet your ass it is." Sarah held Rita's gaze until she realized how ridiculous they sounded. A loud snort escaped her, and then they both started to laugh, heedless of the attention they attracted. Wiping her eyes, she said between giggles, "Resilient wazoo! God, it sounds like the name of a James Bond heroine. Pussy Galore's kid sister." That started them hooting all over again.

With the release in tension, Sarah could concentrate on her meal. "I'm glad I didn't storm out of here," she said between bites. "I doubt that I could've made it home on one and a half legs."

"Nonsense. You can do far more than you realize." Rita pushed her remaining stir-fry aside. "Speaking of mobility, did you replace your Miata?"

"No, my adventures with roadsters are over. I'm afraid—there's that word again—I couldn't handle an automatic, let alone a sports car with a stick-shift."

"So what do you have parked in that enormous garage beside Joe's old sedan?"

"A riding lawnmower," Sarah said. "If I get desperate, I'll take a spin on that."

"Surely you have enough money—"

"Joe has plenty. He bailed me out of a huge debt. After that, we cut up my credit cards, except one with a puny limit that's for emergencies. I'm not saying he won't buy me what I want—"

"But he doesn't want you to drive," Rita finished for her.

The woman knew her so well, knew so much about her life with Joe. Sarah ate a few more bites in silence and then set down her fork. The wine gave her throat a fruity burn, but no more pleasure. Still, she drained her second glass of it, feeling reckless. Steepling her hands as Rita had done, elbows planted on the table, she sighted over her fingertips and said, "On the way here, you said Joe would blame himself again if I got injured a second time. How do you know that?"

"He so much as told me, my dear. During his first month at Matryoshka, he related the story of your accident and confessed to feeling terribly guilty. He sent you on an errand or some such?"

"It was bad luck, is all. I've told him that. What did he say about it?"

The woman shrugged. "He accepts responsibility for the incident and never wants to repeat what he sees as a tragic mistake. In meetings, I've witnessed his habit of taking blame for events far beyond his control. Who knows where that comes from?"

"I figured you'd know, if anybody."

"And why is that?"

"You two have grown really close in a few short months," Sarah said, cheeks and neck warming with an alcoholic flush. Her hand trembled on the rim of her empty glass. She wished she could have one more drink, but decided to plunge ahead. "Are you in love with my—"

Rita clasped Sarah's wrist with a light touch that surrounded her like a bracelet. "Merely exerting force is not the same as taking control of a situation. You're becoming aggressive but you're giving up your wit and grace, which is never a good tradeoff."

She released Sarah and sipped some wine. Swirling the rosy liquid that remained in her glass, she said, "This is control: measured cause with predictable effect. It's like making love, which is most satisfying when you allow power to shift between you and your partner. Back and forth, each tasting the thrill of dominance and the pleasure of yielding. Don't act like a loose cannon, my dear. Be a lover in control."

Sarah took a breath that lifted her chest and straightened her spine. Her shoulders relaxed as she settled into ballet alignment. If not for her shoes pressing into the carpet, she felt as if she would float out of the booth. Grateful for the surge of confidence Rita had given her, she allowed jealousy to subside. Her suspicion, however, did not. "Why are you doing this—challenging me, lecturing me, getting my goat one minute and then stroking me the next? What's this all about?"

"This is a rescue. I see a woman struggling to save herself, and I can't help but do my bit however I can. Do you object to my motives or my modus operandi?"

Shaking her head, Sarah said, "You're like a blend of Gloria Steinem, Dr. Phil, and Obi Wan Kenobi."

Rita applauded as she chuckled. "Let's do add a BV Islander to that stew, say Eugenia O'Neal, and make it a proper callaloo. Nonetheless, I'm highly flattered." She signaled to Dylan for the check. "Also, I'm rather late. The Commissars at Matryoshka expect a report from me this afternoon, or it's off to the gulag."

"Seriously," Sarah said. "What do you want from me?"

"I only want you to be happy."

"You mean, like before my accident?"

Rita shook her head. "Don't sell yourself short. I mean for you to achieve a far superior happiness, which comes from tranquility, self-determination, and dignity."

"And if I alienate Joe in the process?"

"Then he isn't worthy of you."

But what if I still love him? How can I remake him, too?

Sarah clawed through her hair with both hands, shocked by the rapid switch from exhilaration at the woman's words to a deflating sense of hopelessness. She wanted to curl up in the booth and sleep off the two glasses of wine and the endorphins Rita had whipped up.

Dylan delivered a slim leather folder that bore the restaurant name. With a nod to the half-full plates, he said, "I'm afraid our fare wasn't worthy of you ladies."

Sarah seized on the word, becoming alert again. "Don't be

afraid," she said. "It tasted too good to finish in one sitting, is all. Could you box mine up?"

Dylan asked Rita if she wanted a box, too, and she replied, "Thank you, no. I'll return here tonight."

"Did either of you save room for dessert?"

Rita gazed at him. "That is why I'm coming back, dear Dylan."

He grinned and cleared the table. After checking the bill, Rita withdrew from her pocketbook a credit card and two of her business cards. Sarah recognized the Matryoshka Engineering logo on the latter, a silhouette of a half-opened nesting doll. She thanked Rita for lunch as the woman wrote her cell phone number on the card and passed it over.

When Rita repeated the process and put that business card along with her Visa in the folder, Sarah said, "Aha! Now you'll keep your phone nearby, waiting for the man to call or text."

"Simple courtesy, my dear." Rita reached behind the bill and withdrew a small gray rectangle embossed with "Dylan Moorcock, Actor and Playwright" and his phone number and e-mail address. She said, "The man blinked first."

Dylan didn't allude to finding Rita's card. All business, he delivered Sarah's boxed meal and Rita's credit card with receipts and wished them a good day. Sarah watched him check on the other diners in his section. "He's a good actor."

"I hope I don't reach the same conclusion," Rita replied. She wrote down a tip and a total and signed the restaurant copy.

Sarah asked, "Does your aggressiveness scare off most men?"

"You'd be surprised at the number of them who worship a powerful woman. They're tired of being in charge, scared of making decisions. They want someone to take the reins."

"So those are the ones you date?"

"No, I don't have any patience for their neediness. I go for the 'real men,' those who think they're in control." Rita brushed her cheek with Dylan's card. "And when they yield to me—when I see that surrender in their eyes—good heavens, it's a heady rush."

"I'll bet. What happens after they yield?"

"Why, I tire of them, of course. You're giving me a disdainful look, but should men alone enjoy the conquest, the thrill of convincing others to override their better judgment? Case in point…" Rita dangled her keys in front of Sarah. "Ms. Gordon, what say you drive us back?"

Chapter 17

THE KEYCHAIN SAT LIKE A HUNK OF LEAD IN
Sarah's palm while she eyed Rita's SUV, which looked huge
parked beside the squat black roadster. She said, "What if I get
pulled over or hit someone? I'm not even carrying my old Georgia
license, and I've had two glasses of wine."

Rita took Sarah's plastic box of food. "Nonsense. I won't
allow you to fail. Press the unlock switch to open the doors."
When Sarah hesitated, the woman asked, "Are you afraid?"

Sarah aimed the remote at the windshield and jabbed the
button as instructed.

The sun hadn't quite dried the pavement, but it left the
interior of the SUV stifling. Once behind the steering wheel
with the engine switched on, Sarah found the roar of the air
conditioner distracting. She needed to hear everything she could.

At her request, Rita raised the thermostat. Nodding with
approval at the higher temperature, the woman slipped on the
narrow sunglasses she favored. "Proceed," she said.

Sarah's beige tunic stuck to her back and ribs. After repeatedly
checking the mirrors, looking out every window, and monitoring
the screen that displayed Laurens Street behind them when she
shifted the Acura into reverse, Sarah felt like her head would
twist off. She managed to still her left leg after a futile search
for a nonexistent clutch pedal. Her right foot quivered against
the brake while she backed out of the parking space, making the
SUV buck as if water had leaked into the fuel line. Shifting into
drive with deliberateness, she apologized for her nerves.

Rita said, "You know how to do this. Relax and have fun."

"In a sports car, your butt's almost on the ground. I haven't been this high up since I drove a rental van from Savannah to Atlanta." She signaled and pulled into a U-turn lane.

"Were you going off to college?"

"No, I've never been to college." The vehicle coasted as she drove with her right foot hovering above the brake, knuckles white over the steering wheel. "I went from high school into full-time dance classes and pretty soon landed an audition with the Atlanta Ballet."

A car fell in behind her and followed too close. She pressed the accelerator. The Acura surged forward, and she took her foot off again, rocking them in their seats until she relearned how to do it smoothly. "I nailed that tryout. Everything I did was perfect. It was like I was being controlled by a higher power." Whenever she accelerated or slowed, her right hand came off the wheel to touch the gear shift, an unthinking reflex as she struggled to get comfortable with the automatic transmission. She blamed it on the merlot. An intersection up ahead displayed the Whiskey Road sign. "Right turn at the light?"

Rita complimented her sense of direction and asked, "So you don't take one bit of credit for your performance?"

"Of course it was me dancing. I'd just never danced so completely in The Zone." She slowed the SUV with steady braking and glided to a halt behind other drivers waiting for the light to change. Sweat trickled from her hairline. She wiped it away and dried her hand against her pant leg, leaving a streak of make-up on the mahogany slacks. "You've heard athletes talk about The Zone?"

"I'm not a fan of sports." Rita nudged the thermostat lower. "I'm very physical, as you might have surmised, but I lose all interest if I'm not the one at the center of the action."

Sarah snorted, and she eased off the brake as traffic proceeded. "Well, it's a genuine phenomenon, and that was the only time I've ever experienced it. Like it was fate or something."

"There you go, giving up control again. You cannot even take credit for an exemplary display of your talent."

She knew Rita kept her talking only so she'd relax behind the wheel. Still, the woman sure made her feel defensive. "OK, it was me, but it was every part of me working in sync." She unclenched her fists on the steering wheel.

"And how did that feel?"

"Oh, big-time naches, totally."

"Nach—" Rita emphasized the harsh "heh" sound in the back of her throat "—es?"

"Sorry, it's Yiddish: happiness, joy. My parents' slang slips out when I'm excited or tense." When she glanced at her rearview mirror, a burst of adrenaline jolted her. Following close behind the Acura was a police car. "Oh fuck!"

"Now that one I do know, but I didn't realize it was Yiddish."

"No, I mean, 'Oh fuck, there's a cop following us.'"

Questions screamed in her mind. How long had he been there? What was the speed limit? The alcoholic buzz evaporated. Whiskey Road wouldn't widen into four lanes for a while yet. The nearest intersection was a block away, so she said, "Um, maybe I'll pull off and let him go past."

"Nonsense. You're doing fine. Keep your speed at forty."

"That's the posted limit?"

"It's thirty-five, but you'll annoy the officer if you make him go that slow."

Sarah frowned at Rita, and eased down the accelerator pedal until the speedometer showed thirty-seven miles per hour. "This feels like a slow-motion chase." Sweat blurred her vision and seeped through the armpits and back of her blouse.

"No one's chasing you, my dear." Rita adjusted the thermostat downward again. "Tell me more about Joe's past. Contrary to your belief, I hardly know the man."

Rita sounded amused rather than hurt, but Sarah still regretted her unseemly accusation over lunch. She said, "He had a rough time as a teenager, I'm afr…sorry to say." Her gaze flicked to the rearview mirror so often her eye muscles hurt. She tensed for the sound of the siren or the flash of strobe lights. "His mother died in a plane that crashed because of shoddy maintenance."

Checking her speed yet again, and adjusting the wheel to re-center the SUV in her lane, she said, "Joe's mom was going to a realty convention to receive a national award. He told me how much she deserved that honor. What a nightmare."

"How did her death affect him, do you think?"

The police car remained so close behind, Sarah could see the young officer's immature mustache. Up ahead, the road widened, with a passing lane on the left. "At the time of the crash," she said, relaxing a bit, "he was sixteen, playing football in high school, trying to score with cheerleaders, the usual teenage-boy stuff. After she died, his dad was fermisht—sorry, totally shaken up—so Joe took on his mom's duties around the house. He quit the after-school things and did the cooking, cleaning, and gardening."

Rita said, "Making up for his mother's loss."

"I guess he wanted to take care of the family like she did, maybe so they'd miss her less. That cop's still behind me." Despite the extra lane, the cruiser dogged her.

"Your turn's coming up. Take a right onto Silver Bluff."

Sarah signaled and checked her mirror again. He followed. "So, um, his sister, who was six at the time, went into her shell and hasn't come out. Monica reminds me of Boo Radley, you know, from *To Kill a Mock*—"

"I know the story well. Do you think I would learn Robert Frost but miss Harper Lee?"

"Anyway, she's fish-belly white from never going outside, withdrawn, and really skittish." She squeezed her fists tighter on the wheel so her fingers would stop trembling. Her voice quavered a little as she said, "Joe tries to get her on the phone every week to coax a few words out of her, but she mostly stares at the TV day and night."

"And their father?"

"A workaholic, never remarried. Except for pursuing the wrongful-death lawsuit and setting up the trust fund, Mr. Gordon hasn't done right by Joe. They had a falling out, so Joe went away to college, and then he moved to Atlanta—" Emergency lights burst on across the front and top of the police car. A second later, the siren cut loose with a staccato burst.

Cursing in English and Yiddish, Sarah pulled over. Since Silver Bluff Road didn't have a shoulder or curbing at that point, she stopped on a sandy front yard. With no ID or license, she assumed she would be arrested. She'd have to call Joe from jail. Rita reassured her and began to remove laminated cards from a pocketbook. Between the frantic chatter in Sarah's mind, her thudding heart, and the racket from the siren, she couldn't register the woman's words.

The police cruiser shot past, took a hard right onto Hitchcock Parkway, and disappeared from view. Its wailing siren faded away. "Well, shit," Sarah said. She leaned back against the leather upholstery. Adrenaline subsided, leaving her ears ringing and skin prickly. Her mouth tasted like an old penny. Cars drove past, much faster now that the policeman had gone, but she felt no urge to join them. The phone pealed and vibrated in her pocket, jerking her upright again.

She removed the slender device and recognized Joe's cell number on the screen. The clock showed 1:17, about forty-five minutes prior to his usual afternoon call. "It's Joe," she told Rita. "Does he know you came to see me?"

"It wasn't his business to know."

Sarah answered the call, and Joe said, "I give up, Sare—which street are you jogging on? I've looked everywhere."

"You're home?"

"I was. Now I'm driving around the neighborhood looking for you. I thought I'd surprise you for lunch."

In the story about her friend, Rita had said that sometimes Linda's husband made surprise visits. Sarah chewed the inside of her cheek while she decided how to respond. "I'm, uh, having lunch with Rita. She took me out to eat."

"Did she? Well, you picked the better deal. I was only offering myself and a salad."

"It was the only deal I had at the time. She surprised me first." Rita watched her through the narrow sunglasses with the same expression Sarah's ballet teachers wore during her performances: evaluating, rooting, willing her not to screw up.

A rotund man in his sixties charged out of his front door in a stained T-shirt and canvas pants held up with red suspenders. He yelled at Sarah to clear out of his yard.

Sarah asked, "Joe, can I call you later?"

"I'll wait around. When is Rita dropping you back here?"

She would have to switch seats with Rita. Otherwise, Joe would pounce on her for getting behind the wheel, and when he found out she drove without her license his disapproval would rain down. "We'll be a while yet. Come home tomorrow at lunch and I promise to act surprised."

The man stormed across his sparse grass, shaking his fist and threatening to call the police. Sarah checked her mirrors and told Joe, "Gotta go, lunch is here. Talk to you soon." She switched off the power and dropped the phone in her lap. Sand spurted beneath the tires as she jammed down the gas pedal and steered the Acura back onto the road. A car horn blared behind her, causing her to swerve a bit before getting the SUV under control.

Rita quipped, "That was fun."

"Will you have to answer to Joe for this?"

"I believe you're the one married to him, not I. He knows what he'll get if he demands an explanation from me." When Sarah prompted her, Rita said, "He'll get wit and grace and control. Not aggression. Just as he'll get from you, correct?"

Sarah sped through the intersection with Hitchcock Parkway as the light changed from yellow to red. "Correct," she replied. Settling back in the seat, hands looser on the steering wheel, she said, "You can turn down the A.C. Thanks. I feel better."

A quarter-mile from the Eagle's Lair turnoff, she recognized Joe's white Camry heading toward them. It was twenty years old—a car he'd bought used as a teenager and the only one he'd ever owned. Her first instinct was to duck behind the dashboard, and that started her laughing. When she explained herself to Rita, the woman joined her in a few more chuckles. Sarah considered honking and waving as the distance narrowed between the SUV and Joe's car, but that would display aggression, not wit or grace. No point in taunting him; he only wanted to take care of her. Instead, she sat up straight, in plain view.

He wore a distracted frown, the look of the preoccupied. They passed one another in a flash, his speed well over the posted limit. She checked her mirror to see if his brake lights flared, but he hadn't noticed her. A pang of guilt spoiled her mood—she knew she was driving him crazy.

She said, "He's probably racing back to work."

"It occurs to me that if I return there minutes behind him, I'll expose your lie. You told him lunch had only just arrived."

"Ay-yay-yay, you need to get back to make your report. I'm so sorry."

She continued to apologize, but Rita shushed her. "Thirty additional minutes won't matter."

"Then come inside for a while. I promise not to close the gate—you won't get walled in like before."

"No, that would have you playing hostess, and I can be a tiresome guest. Drive on. Tooling around the countryside is more comfortable for both of us, don't you think?"

"Correct," Sarah replied, imitating Rita's accent, enjoying herself again. "Do you really think I look comfortable behind the wheel?"

Rita said, "You look quite content, a powerful woman commanding a powerful machine."

Sarah drove them past Eagle's Lair and continued heading south. "I hope I didn't sound too chicken when you offered me the keys."

"Not at all. I tend to dismiss those who show bravado but no ability. There's a BV Islander proverb: 'Willing is a good man— or woman—but able is a better one.'"

"I like it," Sarah said, piloting the Acura with a light touch as the road curved past other neighborhoods. Shoulders down, chest out, she settled without effort into proper ballet alignment. "Ms. Bolivar, if you're still willing, I believe we'll make an able woman out of me yet."

Chapter 18

THE EXCITEMENT FROM PULLING INTO HER OWN driveway lingered even after Sarah had clambered out. With her box of leftovers in hand, she squinted in the dazzling sunlight and waved goodbye to Rita. Her new friend backed into the street and, as before, reversed up Tangletree Drive at a daring clip. "Friends with the West Indian Wonder Woman," Sarah marveled out loud.

Claws scratched at a window pane. Dorothy whined and batted the glass, her bulldog face lit by a wrinkly harlequin grin. The animal had never before expressed happiness at Sarah's arrival and that gave her a lift as well.

Dorothy shifted her focus to the open gate, perking up her ears and panting.

"Mrs. Gordon." Mrs. O'Malley hobbled up the drive in a tailored violet-colored suit. She continued, "I'm here to complain about that woman driving so recklessly. Is she a friend of yours?"

Sarah reminded herself to be powerful, balanced, and in control. She replied, "I'll talk to her about it, ma'am. Rita's high-spirited, is all. It's her way of having fun."

"She'll have a hard time satisfying the police with that excuse after she backs over some poor old lady fetching the mail. Because we're on friendly terms now, I wanted to warn you that the next time I see her flying up the road backward, I'll call the damn cops."

She was the second person who had threatened to do that in the last half-hour. Joe would say such things came from abandoning the safety and security of home. He was right, but now that she'd taken steps toward regaining her independence, Sarah couldn't let the risks scare her. She said, "Rita's a lovely person who wouldn't intentionally put anyone at risk. I can't imagine you ever needing to file charges—or an insurance claim—against her."

"You can't ever know for sure about people." Mrs. O'Malley peered at the clear plastic box in Sarah's hand and shook her head. "That might be the ugliest dessert I ever seen."

"It's a Thai stir-fry. It would've gone well with your berry crumble, but I'm afra—I mean, your dessert is now just a sweet memory."

"So can I get my dish back anytime soon? You're tying up my glass."

"Absolutely." Though the woman made her nervous, Sarah asked out of politeness, "Would you like to get out of the heat while I fetch it?"

"No thanks. I never go into other people's homes. Don't you pay attention to those stories on TV about axe murderers who live next door?"

Sarah snorted. Unable to restrain herself, she asked, "Do you always accuse your new friends of being serial killers?"

"Oh, I don't mean you, of course. Anyone can see you're harmless. Those arms don't look like they'd manage even a tiny hatchet."

Sarah's lower lip pushed out as she evaluated the soft flesh of her biceps. Time to add pushups to her exercise routine. She gave herself permission to take offense, and decided that one new friend—Rita—was enough for the moment. "Please give me one minute, and I'll get your dish."

She unlocked the front door and fast-walked to the kitchen, having to stutter-step around Dorothy, who barked and capered underfoot. It was hard to keep the bulldog from bursting outside when she exited again, glass in hand.

Mrs. O'Malley was glowering at the fence, and turned the look on Sarah as she approached. "No need to have washed it, Mrs. Gordon," she said, snatching the cookware away. "I was planning to clean it properly."

To hell with this, Sarah decided. She recalled the woman's question during their first meeting about whether she made offensive art. "If I can't convince you to stay," she said, "then please excuse me. I had a lot to drink at lunch, so I plan to piss all over some religious symbols, and then I need to try out a new dildo for my latest porn film."

Mrs. O'Malley turned the same rosy hue as her glasses. Without another word, she retreated at a vigorous pace, while Sarah strode inside to the control panel in the kitchen. She jabbed the button to shut the gate, forcing the woman to scurry through the narrowing gap. On the closed-circuit monitor, Sarah watched her neighbor scamper toward home.

"Mom and Dad raised me better than that," she said to Dorothy, who hopped at her feet in a canine jig. "And Rita wouldn't give me any points for wit and grace, but damn that felt good."

After letting the bulldog out to potty, she wanted to share her admittedly petty and immature victory with someone who would appreciate it, and thought of Nathan. From her studio couch, she called Square Deal Auto Center, but her older brother was "helping a customer" according to the man who answered. She pictured a Volvo rocking atop a lift. Hope you're having fun, dude.

She couldn't go into any details with Mom, of course, but Sarah decided to call anyway. The last few times they'd talked, she'd been prickly around her mother. Time to make it up to her, while she was in a good mood.

Mom picked up after a few rings. She hollered away from the phone, "Al, I said I would get it. Knock it off with the kvetching—who ever calls for you?" After a pause, she continued yelling, "Well, maybe if you stopped giving them money they'd stop calling, and then when the phone rings, we would all know it's for me." Into the receiver she said, "Hello?"

"Hi, Mom," Sarah said. "I'm calling on behalf of the Fraternal Order of Police."

"Oy gevalt, that man is going to put me in an early grave. How many of those FOP stickers does he have on his back window already? You can hardly see out. It's like he's trying to ward off the evil eye along with the traffic tickets."

Sarah snorted. "I'm glad nothing ever changes at home."

"And you would think those big goyim with their guns would call themselves something more manly than 'fops.' Don't get me started. I appreciate your call, Feygela. I spend my days lingering by the phone, hoping a child of my body will remember me."

"I think of you all the time, Mom."

"Then a call more often would be nice, with me lingering and all."

"Well, I did call, and I want to tell you things are looking up."

"You and Joe are having a baby?" Again hollering away from the phone, "Al, such news. Guess what our Feygela—"

"Mom! No, calm down. There's no baby."

"Al, never mind, go back to your crossword. OK, OK, so it's Sudoku." Her mother said into the receiver, "I've been informed that, in no uncertain terms, it's Sudoku. So what's looking up? There's been some progress on the self-pity wallow? No more suicidal depression? I know, you're not as big as a house—maybe just a duplex now, yes?"

Sarah relaxed against the cushions and said with a laugh, "I knew I got my memory from someone in the family. Do you ever forget anything I say?"

"Of course not. If I'm floating too high, I should plotz with one poke of those serpent's teeth Mr. Shakespeare mentioned. If I'm full of tsuris, I dredge up some nice, or at least vaguely pleasant, thing a child of mine once uttered, however long ago. When you *finally* have children, you'll understand."

Again with the tatellah shtick. Maybe it was not such a great idea to call.

Trying again, she kept the smile in her voice. "Well, I'm improving with all three. I've lost a little weight, and I'm feeling better about myself and my art."

"And with Joe how are things?"

"They're fine."

The playfulness vanished from Mom's tone. "Oh, Sarah Lyn, what did you do?"

Suddenly she became a kid again, flush with dread as the guilt hammer was about to swing down. "What do you mean? I haven't done anything wrong."

"'Fine' is what a wife says forty years into a marriage, when the most romantic thing she's done for her husband lately is to trim his nose hairs. You've been married what, twelve months and change, and things are only 'fine'? What did you do?"

"Mom, we're good. Really. Why wouldn't we be?"

"Your track record with men isn't what I'd call sterling. Not to say it's always been your fault, though you're the one who welcomed them into your life each time."

"So I'm to blame even when I'm not to blame?"

"Did I say that? I just mean I wouldn't put it past you to ruin the easiest marriage God ever conceived. Exactly what does Joe ask of you? You earn no paycheck, you don't do housekeeping or cook or run errands. As far as I can tell, you have just one wifely responsibility, which you have managed to shirk."

Sarah cringed, so sorry she'd called, but then she got angry. "Wait, how do you know all this?"

"Ah ha," her mother said, as fast as a trap being sprung, "so it's not just chazerei."

"In some alternate dimension I guess it's true, mostly, but how do you know?" She gripped the phone tighter as the answer came to her. "Nate said Joe's been calling you. Do y'all talk about me?"

"I ask about things, and he tells me. Reports have been glowing until lately. He's such a good man, but you've got him twisted in knots with stress and worry."

"I can't believe he's telling you our personal business."

"Not in any detail—don't get meshugga. But when you called with good news, I thought you'd finally come to your senses, and God had rewarded you."

"I have come to my senses." She pushed to her feet and began to pace within the glass-walled box.

"So how is it that you're making Joe so crazy?"

"Not that I owe you an explanation for anything, but you have no idea what it's been like for me."

"Yes, since the unfortunate event."

"For God's sake, Mom, an 'unfortunate event' is when you lose your keys. Say it for once. Please? I lost my goddamned leg." Sarah took a breath and bellowed, "I lost my goddamned leg when it tore off below the knee in a gory trans-tibial amputation, because firemen had to yank me—unconscious and in shock—away from what was left of the fiery wreck of my car."

She steadied herself against the drawing table. "Come on, Mom, it happened just that way, and we all have to deal with it. You know from Michael's death that refusing to say the words won't undo anything."

Her mother's voice sounded brittle as she muttered, "Since you lost your goddamned leg. There, happy?"

"No, I'm really pissed that you and Joe talk about me behind my back."

"Well, don't take it out on him. You can beat up your mother all you want." She chuckled ruefully. "It's part of the bargain women make with God so we can have resentful ingrates for children. But Joe doesn't deserve it."

Wit and grace and control. Remember: WWRD. "Mom, I love you and I love Joe, but I'm finally starting to see what I've allowed to happen with my life. I'm totally responsible for it, and I'm not blaming anyone. But it's way past the time when I need to make changes."

"And if these changes alienate Joe?"

Rita's words came back to her. "Then he's not right for me." As Mom began to sputter, Sarah said, "Listen now, just hear me out. I've allowed him to take care of me—and I gladly took his care—far too long. I need to start being responsible for myself and face whatever happens."

"What if you find yourself divorced, with no college degree, no job prospects, and, please excuse me, barely a leg to stand on? What will you do then?"

"I'll get by. I always have."

"No, Sarah Lyn, you never have." Her mother's voice was

a dagger of ice in Sarah's ear. "Who paid your sky-high rent in Atlanta and all the extra ballet classes and the shoes and the shmata, while you danced for what amounted to grocery money? Your father and me. Who bailed you out of the debts you hid from us, with the car payments and credit card bills? Joe."

Mom continued stabbing at her, "You've told everybody you're not interested in his money, so I don't know how much alimony you can bank on, especially after the lawyers takes their cut. You're certainly not welcome to come back home and filch off of our retirement savings, and you won't survive a week as a homeless person. It seems to me that you only have one option: make your marriage work."

While Sarah tried to formulate a reply, her mother said, "Better get busy. Joe might already have one foot out the door," and hung up.

Chapter 19

SARAH DECIDED MOM WAS RIGHT, BUT FOR THE wrong reason. She wouldn't make her marriage work because she'd be ruined without it. Rather, she'd do it because she still loved Joe. She'd been with cruel and hurtful men; Joe certainly wasn't one. She hated that he talked about her and their life to Mom and Rita and God only knew who else, but he didn't do it to hurt her, only to help him figure her out. If she could make just a few adjustments in the way he thought about things—or at least in the way he behaved—they would have a relationship that worked for both of them.

She had to stop living her life in fear of what *could* happen. Lightning could strike her, she could lose her other leg in an accident, a million things could occur. But it was clear what *would* happen if she didn't keep pushing herself and Joe in a better direction.

He arrived home ninety minutes late that afternoon, bearing groceries and two summer-weight dresses with a matching pair of shoes for each outfit. Not the actions of a man with one foot out the door, unless continuing to pamper her was a smokescreen to camouflage his true intentions. Sarah watched him for clues. It was so easy to overanalyze people, but taking them at face value also had been disastrous in the past.

As usual, he'd chosen somber earth tones for her: pumice and chestnut. He preferred muted colors for himself as well, having dressed that day in a suit of battleship gray with a maroon tie. Dorothy wiggled her rump for him in the kitchen. He crouched and obliged her with a rub while he asked, "How was lunch with Rita?"

Sarah held out the chestnut-colored dress at arm's length. "It was nice. I brought home leftovers if you want to try some. It does have tofu."

"Ah, the vegetarians' attempt to sublimate their craving for meat."

"Wanting protein isn't the same thing as craving meat." Listening to her tone of voice, she reminded herself not to argue. They needed to break that cycle and rediscover the affection they used to show all the time. She draped the outfit against her, which covered the beige tunic and mahogany slacks he'd set out for her that morning. The dress was too big, but she wanted Joe to notice it rather than point out his mistake. "What do you think?" Holding the top of the sleeves to her shoulders, her elbows jutted like wingtips.

Joe pressed the waistline of the dress against her, and spread the material past her hips. He pulled the outfit aside, as if looking behind a curtain, and peered at her midsection. "You moved in a notch on your belt." His fingertips stroked her cheek and chin. "Your face is losing its shape, too."

He didn't sound happy for her, but she smiled nonetheless. "Slimmer" also was a shape. "Thanks for thinking of me anyway. The store will take them back."

With the dresses and shoes shoved back inside the shopping bag, he said, "I don't want you starving to death, but as long as you're comfortable—"

"You're happy, I know. Are you happy now?"

"Sure." He took a jug of whole milk from a grocery sack and put it in the refrigerator.

"Come on, look at me." Wit and grace and control, she reminded herself. "A confession of happiness is usually accompanied by a smile. In some cultures, happy people have even been known to grin."

"I'm happy," he said. "Really." He showed his teeth, more Cheshire cat than ecstatic newlywed, and deposited fruit into designated ceramic bowls on the granite counter. Beyond his mouth, his face betrayed nothing.

He reached into some more plastic bags, and she took hold

of his wrists. "Tell me when you knew you wanted to marry me, when you didn't want to be with anyone else."

"The romantic thing would be to say, 'From the moment I first saw you,' and I wish it were true." She let him go, and he put his arms around her. His hands explored her waist and hips and squeezed her backside. "I won't lie to you. I had my doubts. Even after we began living together, I kept waiting for you to find something wrong with me."

A lie would've cast him in a better light, so she had to congratulate Joe for honesty. Though he probably fondled her in part to determine her new size, she still thrilled at his touch and delighted in putting her hands on him again. If they could get reacquainted physically, maybe they could soon reunite in every other way.

Through his suit jacket, Joe's shoulders were broader, the muscles encasing his ribs harder. He'd added another layer of armor during the time she stripped away some of her protection. His glutes, now more pronounced, tightened against her palms. She joked, "So you proposed because I failed to reject you?"

"No, because at last I knew I could make you happy and take good care of you."

Sarah ached to press herself against him. Though she wanted to be a lover in control, she knew she'd soon give in and let him focus on her, just to get them rolling again. She asked in her huskiest voice, "But what did I do for you?"

"It's what you still do: make me feel manly and desirable and—" He kissed her. The slow, deep kiss she longed for changed from soft to insistent. His breath blew hot against her cheek. He eased her against a row of windows. Rectangles of molding boxed-in her back while he covered her front. His lips finally slid away. "Needed," he murmured. "You make me feel needed."

"I need you. Right now."

"You want dinner in bed afterward?"

"Fuck dinner." She put her tongue in his mouth.

After another kiss, he said, "I could take that many ways."

"Take me in many ways." She groped at his pleated trousers. "I can't make it to the bedroom."

"We might scare Dorothy. She's already hiding under the table. How about—"

The cell phone trilled on his hip. His hand went to it immediately. She whispered, "Leave it for now. For me."

He said, "It might be trouble. No one ever calls after work." The ringing stopped. Backing away, he thumbed a few buttons on the phone and told her his father in Virginia had tried to reach him. "I'm really sorry, Sare, but this probably is important."

The rapid chimes of a speed-dialed number soon followed. "Dad? Pick up, it's me." He rolled his eyes. "You called fifteen seconds ago. Well, if you need—Hey, Monica, it's me. Did Dad…oh, you did? That's a first. What—" His brows furrowed. He seemed to look through Sarah before focusing on her. He mouthed, "Dad. Heart attack." After that, he stared at his black lace-ups and made "mm-hm" noises as his sister talked.

Sarah touched his arm to show she understood. The heat they'd generated together fled from her. Again she'd have to wait for her turn. Embarrassed by her selfish thoughts, she gave Joe a gentle hug. She remained there against him, her cheek pressed to his gray suit lapel.

He hung one arm around her. His fingers idly patted her shoulder as he said, "No. I need to be here. Call me back tomorrow and let me know how he's doing. Better yet, give me the hospital number." He disengaged from Sarah, decoupling and turning away with such grace that she imagined pirouetting one revolution on her right foot. Her arms floated out to him. The end of a pas-de-deux.

After taking a pen and small notebook from his breast pocket, he jotted down the information Monica recited. Sarah could only stare at his back and worry along with him. She dropped her hands; the choreographer had left her on stage with nothing to do, a dancer without steps.

When Joe hung up, she asked the necessary questions, resuming her role as concerned wife, and he answered, "He's in the ICU. His secretary found him in his office, slumped over his desk. If he wasn't late for a meeting, she wouldn't have stuck her head in. She has no idea how long he'd been like that, so there'll probably be some brain damage. The woman did CPR and called Monica after the paramedics got there."

"She saved his life."

"For the moment at least—he's in a coma. The secretary's giving Monica updates since my sister won't talk to strangers. You mind if I call the hospital? I need to tell them I'm next of kin. Then we can go to bed, I promise."

"God, Joe, forget about bed. We need to start packing for Virginia. We'll have to kennel Dorothy. If we can get a flight tonight—"

"Like I told Monica, I need to stay here. I remember what happened with you the last time I took a trip."

Sarah ran her fingers through her hair. "This is crazy. Your dad could be dying. What happened last time hardly involved me: you raced home because of a busy signal—but not before getting mixed up with some slut from Colorado." Damn, she hadn't meant to bring up Christie Palmer. Rita definitely wouldn't have done that.

"I didn't get mixed up with her. We talked and she misunderstood. I knew you didn't—" Dorothy emerged from beneath the table and barked at him. He glared at the bulldog and said, "Hey, quit that!"

The animal backed under the table again, head down, and Sarah yelled at Joe for shouting at Dorothy. She balled her fingers into fists, closed her eyes for a moment, and fought for control. "Joe, we need to go see your father."

"If he comes out of his coma, he won't want to see me. You know we don't get along."

"You need to go to him before it's too late."

He took the key ring from his pocket and strode toward the French doors in the dining room. Unlocking the deadbolt, he said, "It's been too late since Mom got killed. Dorothy, let's go out."

The bulldog still cowered under the table. Sarah knelt and gave Dorothy a big smile. "Come on, Dottie. You wanna go out? That's it. There's a good girl." She kept in step with Dorothy's rapid gait, heading straight for Joe. "I'll see to her. Why don't you start packing?"

He opened the door and moved out of the way. Staying in between him and Dorothy, Sarah led the dog to the backyard. The door closed behind them. She tapped the house key in her pocket, even though she realized that he only shut it to keep out the mosquitoes.

The humid evening air smelled like rain. Her stump throbbed in its socket with a confirmation of the forecast. Waving insects away, thinking about how quickly passion had turned into pathos, she watched Dorothy select two spots to mark in the thick Bermuda grass. While the lawn and garden continued to thrive during the wet summer, Joe's chest-high compost pile had suffered, soaking up the frequent rains like a sponge. Instead of transforming into a steaming, fertile compound, it hulked in a matted mound, cold and sopping at its core.

If my father had suffered heart failure, I'd damn sure catch the next flight, or drive if I could get there quicker. I'd even steal a car if I had to, but there was Joe, as cold as his dead compost heap.

Not daring to look back at the house, she counted the late-feeding sparrows in the yard. If she saw him standing there still, her efforts to rein in her temper would fail, and she would explode.

Dorothy trotted to the house, but Sarah still faced away. She braced for the sound of the latch. When claws scratched at the base of the door and the bulldog begged to get inside, Sarah relaxed. Joe must've become rational again and left the room to pack.

She headed for the bedroom, but then heard a knife chopping vegetables in the kitchen. Joe had taken off his suit jacket and tie and rolled up his sleeves. He had arranged a neat line of produce on the kitchen island. Olive oil heated in two large skillets above hissing blue flames. After slicing one of the zucchinis into disks, he said, "I thought I'd do ratatouille. One vegetarian, one omnivore."

"Why are you being like this?"

"Like what?" He started to chop again. Green-edged coins fell away in identical thicknesses.

"So damned bullheaded. Your father is dying, and you're making dinner. Explain to me why you hate him so much."

Joe set down his knife. "I've never hated him. But I can't do anything for him either. I can do things here. For you."

"I don't need things done for me. I can do for myself. Can't you see that?"

"Fine." He pushed the cutting board toward her along the granite countertop. "You fix dinner."

"To hell with dinner. We need to get packed and get Dorothy to the vet before they close. Where's their number?"

She started to lift the phone, but he covered her hand with his. "No vet. I don't want her getting kennel cough or something. She was cooped up in an animal shelter for months—I won't put her in a cage again."

"A friend from work then? Would Rita or someone else take her? Do you want to drive to Virginia and bring her with us?"

"None of the above. We're staying put."

Sarah yanked her hand free and switched off the burners beneath the simmering olive oil. The bitter stink of gas lingered. "You'll regret not saying goodbye to him. I hate that I was rehearsing a ballet the night Michael got killed. I can't even remember the last thing I said to him. Probably some joke about him racing off again to see his hot date." She took hold of his wrists. "Didn't you feel bad for not knowing you should say all the important things, the last time you saw your mom?"

"Of course. We didn't talk much on the drive to the airport." He backed away from her and crossed his arms. The starched dress shirt strained over his muscles. "Mostly, she fretted about us having to go home in a snowstorm, while she was headed to sunny Florida."

"Why set yourself up for more regret? This time, you know you need to say those things. You have to say goodbye forever, just in case."

His eyes moistened, but he held his tears in check. "You know I said goodbye to you in the hospital? The nurses told me you'd be fine, the surgeon said so, too. I didn't believe them. I held your hand and apologized over and over and wished it were me in that bed, and I told you goodbye. But I got another chance with you."

"You might not get that with your dad." She pointed at the clock above the stove. "Time's slipping away…Let's go tonight; I can help with the driving."

"You haven't driven a car for almost a year."

Instead of revealing her experience with Rita's SUV, she said, "The last time I didn't drive for that long, it nearly killed me. I can't afford to get rusty again. Any time I make you nervous, you're free to criticize." She headed for the bedroom, and Dorothy followed her.

Joe called, "I have the only set of car keys. We're not going."

Sarah stopped on the other side of the dining room. She swung around, pivoting on her right foot so fast that the bulldog had to scramble out of her way. "We're driving to Virginia, Joseph. Tonight. I know he didn't show you much love, but he's your father. Now stop acting like a petulant asshole and come pack your fucking bags."

Real smooth, she thought, turning again to march toward their bedroom. Wit and grace and control in abundance. Totally.

Chapter 20

JOE REFUSED TO GO. HE CALLED THE HOSPITAL and learned his father remained in a coma. When he told Sarah his decision was final, she abandoned the half-filled suitcases on their bed and stormed into her studio. In a fury, she barricaded the doors.

A minute later, she pulled the couch aside to let in Dorothy, who scratched at the varnished wood like a cat. The sun set in a somber pool of yellow, as pale as a hardboiled egg yolk. She flicked on the overhead lights and roamed the room, her stump throbbing. Her phantom left foot seemed to be on fire.

Sick of wringing her hands in frustration, Sarah stopped pacing near her prepared canvas. Without another thought, she raised the easel to standing height and uncapped tubes of acrylics. Neglecting to don a smock or shoe covers, she shoved her ergonomic chair aside and squeezed gobs of paint like liquid jewels into separate trays. She wetted a synthetic No. 4 flat brush and loaded it with cobalt blue.

Instead of underpainting to block in primary shapes, as countless videos had taught her, she ignored the spider silk of graphite lines she'd traced earlier and slashed the canvas with rapid brushstrokes, following her instincts. The alla prima approach suited her aggressive mood. She applied banners of pure color in thick curves with nothing blended or diluted. Synthetic brushes piled up on the oilcloth-covered table as she used each one for a single color only. Tempering her fury with a limited palette, she fused the primaries and secondaries and juxtaposed them to create brilliant hues.

Her beige blouse collected splatters of yellow ocher and vermilion. Cobalt violet streaked one forearm, and flecks of viridian stippled her knuckles. Her mahogany slacks bore the marks from leaning against the discarded brushes still loaded with bright paint. A sprinkling of every hue made the rubber mat tacky underfoot; her dress shoes glittered as if pasted with sequins.

Rediscovering the act of creation became a sensual experience. The fingers of her left hand, slick on the brushes, slid along the wood shafts past the seamless metal ferrules, and nestled in the chisel shapes and round bristle heads. She gripped the canvas edges with her right hand and smeared her palm across the liquid sky that emerged with each stroke. Her nails and fingertips amassed a thick impasto of colors, and she took to smearing her hands across her chest, thighs, and bottom as she worked. The acrylics would never wash out of her clothing, which had become a second canvas molded to the contours of her body.

The studio doors bumped against the couch, waking Dorothy. The bulldog had been snoring on a cushion. Joe said, "Sare, are you OK? Come out and have dinner with me. Let's talk about this."

"I'm working." She blinked just in time as the follow-through of her slashing brush peppered her cheek and brow with ultramarine. Her lips were sticky with it, and she licked them. The acrylic tasted faintly of oil and cream, reminiscent of the craft glue she had eaten in grade school. Her art was inside her now, across her tongue and down her throat. Blood would carry ultramarine throughout her body. She imagined painting Joe with it when she took him inside her again. When, not if. She was determined to pull them through their latest setback.

Sarah tossed the brush aside and grabbed for a clean one from her dwindling stock. She touched the tip in distilled water; droplets clung to the pale bristles like tears on blond eyelashes. Paint trays, palettes, mixing cups, and the oilcloth bore a bright array of jewel tones. Scattered among them, equally colorful tubes of acrylics, uncapped and all squeezed in the middle, just as she did with the toothpaste despite Joe's reminders. She swung around to the canvas again, unsure of which color to add. Maybe it was a sign she was done.

Realizing how dehydrated she'd become, Sarah put the clean, wet brush in her mouth and sucked off the water while she stared at her canvas. The main shapes had remained the same, a heroic eagle, its lair, and her face hovering in the sky. However, the theme had transformed entirely. The eagle, in streamlined bands of crimson and violet and ocher, soared as purposeful as an arrow *from* its mountain niche, rather than to it, flying toward the fresh light of dawn. Poised in the morning sky like a golden goddess, her self-portrait didn't look merely content but radiated joy. She took up a No. 1 brush, dipped the ultra-fine tip in a button of titanium white, and signed her work "JL Berger." As an afterthought, she added a hyphenated "Gordon." There was just enough room for it.

Joe knocked hard, prompting Dorothy to bark a few times and hop off the couch, no doubt coloring the pads of her paws. Only Joe remained untouched by the art. He knocked again and said, "You talked about crazy earlier. This is crazy. What's got into you? It's my father, so it's my decision."

The doors moved inward and pushed the couch ahead of them. Sarah looked for something to wedge through the handles. Then she realized she'd never turn their marriage around if she kept him shut out of her most private place. Wiping her hands on the seat of her slacks, she said, "Don't strain yourself. I'll move this out of the way."

The pressure on the doors eased, and she pulled the couch away with some difficulty. Its stubby wooden legs gouged the rubber mat. Joe leaned into the studio and frowned at her. "What happened to you?"

She admired her acrylic-encrusted fingers. "You should see the other guy."

"First you storm out of the bedroom and then you barricade yourself in here and slap on paint like a Maori."

"That's just it. I painted. For the first time ever, I really feel like an artist." She blocked his line of sight to the easel. "I can't let you see it though, until I get it framed. It's your gift."

He edged inside with repeated glances at the floor, as if he might step in something awful. "After all the yelling and cussing, you made me a present?"

"The creation part was a gift to myself. The result is yours."

"You're getting stranger by the minute, Sare. You're also a mess." He waved for her to come with him. "Let's get you cleaned up. Your rings need soaking, and I'll have to cut that stuff out of your hair."

She peeled a gob of swirled colors off her fingernail and flicked it at him. "Were you always this condescending? When we dated, you were always sweet. Unquote."

Holding up his hands in surrender, he said, "Look, I'm concerned about the paint all over your skin. Can't you get blood poisoning from that stuff?"

"Acrylics are mostly fatal to clothing."

"So why didn't you wear your smock and shoe covers?"

"There wasn't time. I had to get started before I exploded again over this business with your dad." She went to the western side of the studio, wetted a clean towel at the stationary tub, and returned to where Dorothy huddled under the paint-strewn table. Wiping the bulldog's paws with firm strokes, she murmured, "Good girl."

"And tell me why you care so much that I see him."

After wrapping a clean towel around the bulldog's middle to protect the fur from her paint-covered hands, she carried Dorothy past Joe and set the bulldog in the hallway. She faced him again, the towel loose in her grip. "Because you're cheating yourself out of what's literally a once-in-a-lifetime opportunity. You're also denying me a chance to help you through it. But I don't want to fight about this."

"Seems like that's all we do lately."

"Only because my needs are different now. How can I help you see that?"

"I do see it," he said. "I see you don't need me anymore."

He walked the length of the house to the kitchen. It was a straight shot from the hallway, and Sarah watched him the whole way, recalling the Hitchcockian vertigo she'd felt before. This time though, she knew her balance wouldn't fail her.

℃⅁

She skipped dinner that night, cleaned up her studio, and got ready for bed only after confirming Joe had gone to sleep. He'd unpacked and put away the suitcases she abandoned earlier on the bed. Having rejected the idea of going into one of the guest bedrooms for the night, she perched on the mattress, trying to quiet her rumbling stomach and make herself weightless while she removed the prosthesis. Her paint-smeared clothes and dress shoes would have to be relegated to the artist-wear portion of her closet. For now, she left them piled on the carpet.

Exhaustion overtook her. She managed to switch off the overhead light before she descended into a kaleidoscope of confusing dreams.

When she awoke, gray daylight seeped through the blinds. Joe had risen before his alarm sounded, and left without going through his normal routines. She had a sense of déjà vu: rain pelting the house, her husband gone, and no food prepared for her or clothes set out.

Her paint-stained clothes and shoes had disappeared from the carpet. Joe had probably thrown them away. His final words of the previous night—"You don't need me anymore"— resounded in her memory. She knew he intended to punish her by not making breakfast or choosing that day's outfit for her. While saddened by his vindictiveness, she found she preferred to help herself. Instead of being daunted by the extensive choice of clothing, she now reveled in it. She bypassed the dull colors that Joe liked in favor of an older turquoise blouse and brilliant white slacks.

The top was a little snug through the bust, but looked as though she chose to display her figure rather than simply put on a shirt she'd outgrown. Her slacks were tight across the hips and through the seat, but manageable. Five clicks resounded when she locked the liner into the socket. She weighed 125.4 without any fudging—at last, she could remove her rings and see her true weight.

She hoped to have a calmer discussion with Joe about taking

the Virginia trip while his father still lived, but his usual morning call did not come. No doubt he had resumed fighting their cold war, so she decided not to call him either. In light of his now-familiar sullenness, a mere jog wouldn't satisfy her need to get away for a while. She retrieved Rita's business card from her purse and dialed the woman's office number.

"Hello, my dear. I didn't expect to hear from you so soon."

"How about lunch today? My treat. If there's time, I'd like to run an errand afterward."

"Not ten minutes ago, Joe asked me if you and I had another date planned."

Sarah asked, "How did he seem to you?"

"A mite frazzled. At first I thought you'd had as ripping good a time with him last night as I did with Dylan. Then I decided perhaps not."

"Definitely not. Can you pick me up again?"

They agreed on a time, and Sarah took Dorothy out for a walk. A light drizzle still fell, so she propped an open umbrella on her shoulder. Having one hand tethered to the bulldog and the other occupied with the wooden handle called to mind a modern dance number she'd performed at a recital in Savannah. A long sash linked the hands of slicker-clad dancers in bright yellow pairs, with red parasols on opposite shoulders. Sarah reenacted some of the steps when Dorothy stopped to smell a manicured boxwood hedge. Swinging the leash low, she bounded over it, spinning in midair with her umbrella held high so she wouldn't get twisted in the nylon tether.

When she landed, the artificial leg supported her weight with a mild bump between socket and limb. She'd become so accustomed to Fred she'd forgotten to touch down on her right foot. However, the commotion alarmed Dorothy, who blinked up at her in the drizzle, ears flattened. Sarah confined further moves to promenades and adagios.

The rain had ended by the time Rita appeared. Dorothy carried on as usual when Sarah opened the gate from the kitchen control panel and the gold Acura pulled up the driveway. The bulldog barked with a ferocity she seemed to reserve for Rita alone. Before Sarah exited through the front door, she changed into white slip-ons with low heels, shouldered her purse, and lifted the canvas she'd propped in the foyer. She hadn't scrutinized her work until late that morning, hoping to evaluate it with more objectivity than she could've mustered the night before.

Her painting seemed to have improved with time. Subtle details she'd overlooked—a glint of sunlight on the eagle's beak, the sharp edges of the cliff side, gold flecking the brilliant viridian of her self-portrait's eyes—now gave her hope she actually had some talent she could develop further. Love of her creation made her selfish and possessive. Instead of giving it to Joe, she considered hanging it in her studio.

She carried the canvas out to the SUV and held it up to the driver's side window. The bright colors reflected in Rita's sunglasses. Sarah said, "I'd like to get it framed."

The woman reached out toward the thick impasto of colors, silver bracelets jingling on her bare arm. "It's lovely. When did you do this?"

"Last night. I was pissed at Joe, but he did fire me up enough to paint this. I'd thought I would call it 'Eagle's Lair' for him, but now I want a title that suits me."

Rita said, "Its name is 'Freedom.' Without a doubt." She disengaged the hatchback lock so Sarah could store the picture in the cargo hold.

As they reversed up Tangletree Drive, Rita's lime-green skirt rode high on her bare legs. She pressed down on the accelerator with a high heel that complemented the watermelon hue of her revealing top. "I approve of the color choices in your outfit as well as your painting. You look as if you're ready to sail off to BVI."

Sarah thanked her, looking downward to avoid motion sickness. She plucked the blouse a little more from her slacks so her stomach wouldn't show as much. "But brights don't look nearly as good on me as someone with your coloring."

"Nonsense. The women who pull it off simply have a more powerful inner glow."

"Well, yours is formidable, I'll give you that. Speaking of

flashy colors, be careful of the 'blue-light special'—my neighbor said she'd call the police if we sailed up the street like this again. She thinks it's dangerous."

"I concur, my dear. But that doesn't mean it's not fun." Rita executed a controlled skid into the main thoroughfare, and the SUV shot forward.

Chapter 21

SARAH TREATED RITA TO LUNCH IN A NARROW lane off Laurens Street called The Alley. They sat in a booth of the pub-like restaurant, ordered Chardonnay, and Rita expounded on her steamy rendezvous with waiter, thespian, and playwright Dylan Moorcock. When Sarah asked if he was indeed a good actor, Rita claimed, "I have physical evidence that he did not fake anything."

Their laughter helped Sarah relax. She detailed the latest upset with Joe, even confessing that they hadn't made love since his trip to Atlanta. Rita said, "No wonder Joe looks frazzled."

"Promise you'll keep these things secret."

"By all means. I'm Joe's friend, but the bonds between women are so much more important." She clinked her wineglass against Sarah's.

After Sarah paid with her credit card—the first purchase she'd made in Aiken—they retrieved her painting and walked to a nearby art boutique that advertised custom framing. From behind a long counter, a skinny woman in a black pantsuit took several long looks at the picture and enthused, "My stars, such vibrancy and energy." She peeled a half-dozen frame samples from the Velcro-covered wall behind her. Fitting different options against each corner of the canvas, she asked, "Where ever did you buy it?"

Rita grinned and poked an elbow at Sarah, who said, "It's just something I painted last night."

"Hey, I painted last night, too, but I might as well have been touching up my baseboards compared to this. Where do you show?"

Sarah's face flushed with heat. She hadn't received a better compliment in a long time. Even Joe rhapsodizing about her, before their recent troubles, had failed to rouse such happiness. "It's only a hobby so far," she said. "I mean I'm just starting out."

The woman took a business card from beneath the counter. "Call me when you're ready to start selling it. After we agree on pricing, you keep fifty percent of the net sales."

"Seventy-five," Rita said. "Gross."

The proprietress smirked. "So, you don't show—yet—but you brought your agent along?" They agreed on sixty-five percent gross and picked out a frame.

Pressing the wide copper-tinged border flush against the corner of the canvas concealed the end of Sarah's signature. The proprietress said, "This one's the best of the bunch, but you'll lose the 'Gordon.'"

Sarah replied, "That's all right. I know it's there." Glancing at her ring finger, she saw that she'd forgotten to slip her wedding set back on that morning. She smiled at the coincidence; these absences didn't stop her from knowing who she was.

The woman promised to have the framing completed in a week, and asked Sarah to bring in her work for consignment any time. On the way back down Laurens, Sarah twirled a few times along the wide, rain-darkened sidewalk. "This calls for a drink!"

Rita congratulated her and said, "Only one, if you're going to drive us back."

"I'm too psyched to drive—I think I'll fly home." They headed back to the restaurant, but Sarah spotted a bicycle shop at the opposite end of The Alley. "Make that 'pedal home.' After our champagne, I need to treat myself to a present."

With four ounces of Moët White Star warming her insides, she and Rita perused the dizzying selection of bicycles arrayed in rows on the floor of the shop and set along the walls. Rita twice glanced at her watch, and Sarah said, "You go on. I'll ride back."

"Nonsense. The streets are still wet and grimy—those white slacks will look keelhauled by the time you get home. And would you really want to pedal all that way in those shoes?"

"When I was a kid, I pedaled in bare feet—that'd be a sight

these days." She hadn't ridden a bike in years, but it would give her the freedom to travel around Aiken while providing another form of exercise, something an automobile couldn't do.

The store owner allowed her to take a twenty-one speed, nickel-colored and very light, into The Alley to try it out. A well-kept lane with no parking allowed and a low speed limit, it provided a safe place for a test ride. Fortunately no traffic was present.

She was grateful to be wearing slacks, but the cotton-Lycra blend stretched tight across her thighs when she straddled the bike frame, and wedged beneath her the moment she perched on the spring saddle. Balanced on the artificial leg and tilting to her left, she put her right foot on the rubberized pedal and pushed down. The bicycle rolled forward. Now listing to the right, she raised her other knee and glanced down to position Fred on the rotating pedal since she couldn't do it by feel. The prosthetic foot flexed when she put her weight on it, and the slender tires continued to turn.

Her instincts took over. She sat up straight and pumped again with her right foot and then the left. With greater speed came more balance and confidence. Finally, she released the handlebars and stuck her arms straight out from the shoulders. Her fingers curved up like the wingtips of the eagle in her painting. Looking back at Rita, who stood in the shop doorway, she grinned like a kid, and the woman smiled back even wider.

Ahead of Sarah, a Popsicle-orange Corvette turned into the narrow path and moved in her direction shockingly fast. The driver's stereo propelled throbbing waves of percussion that crashed over Sarah. An insistent bass line vibrated the air and made her fingers quiver.

Her heart rate quickened to match it. She grabbed the handlebars, eased over to her right, and squeezed the brake. With the tires inches from the curb, she put out her right leg and halted, propping herself up. She'd forgotten to request a helmet. What would Joe do if she ended up brain-damaged in a coma, like his father? Would he visit every day? How soon would he stop? She gave the young man in the approaching sports car a nervous smile. Hopefully he saw her and wouldn't want to endanger the flawless paint job on his car just for the novelty of running over a one-legged cyclist.

The Corvette slowed and cruised past, windows down and a heavy metal song thumping. Looking her over, the driver nodded his approval. Awesome, she thought, a noted authority thinks I'm a babe. Look all you want, dude; just don't flatten me.

She turned in behind the orange car and practiced speeding up and then braking by counter-rotating the pedals. Fred responded well to every demand she made. While she gained more confidence in the prosthesis, the driver stared at her in the rearview mirror. Then he turned up his stereo even louder and sped away with a sharp squeal of rubber. His spinning tires hurled a hundred tiny bits of glass and gravel at her.

She averted her face, flinching as the debris stung her knees and knuckles. It occurred to her then she needed more than just a helmet. Rita cursed the driver as he skidded around the corner. With the rush of endorphins, Sarah felt like she could catch up to the punk, but she practiced self-control and coasted to a halt beside a muttering Rita.

The bicycle shop owner totaled Sarah's purchases, and, with less than two hundred dollars remaining on her credit card, she slung her purse over a handlebar and rolled her bike out the shop door. In one arm, she cradled a smooth-shelled white helmet with large front vents and a ponytail port; inside she'd nestled fingerless gloves and knee and elbow pads. Rita walked alongside her and talked about cycling in the rural mountaintop area above Road Town in BVI. "It was lovely following Ridge Road, like balancing along the green spine of Tortola. Azure water in every direction, stretching forever. To a little tyke with skinned knees, it was the top of the world."

"That sounds beautiful." The chain clicked a steady rhythm— four-four time—as the wheels rotated.

"Only if you have money. I was fortunate. Dad and Mum could take me and my sibs over to Virgin Gorda to visit the Baths, these miraculous labyrinthine grottos filled with pools of water and amazing little fish, pale palometas and yellow-and-black-striped sergeant majors." She thumbed her remote to unlock the doors. "Then we'd sail around, gorging on conch consommé and pepperpot. For those who must do without, though, an island is a prison."

Sarah opened the rear hatch of the SUV, and then inspected the back seats for a release mechanism to fold them down. With the purchase of her bicycle, home seemed less and less like a prison. However, she made up her mind not to tell Joe about the bike until they were on their way to Virginia. In the meantime, she'd hide it in her studio, under a tarp. No need to upset him with yet one more change to absorb.

They maneuvered the bicycle inside the Acura without difficulty. An old blanket in the back protected the leather upholstery. Sarah thanked Rita and apologized for making her late. "The Commissars at Matryoshka might be waiting in your office with a one-way ticket to the gulag."

"Nonsense. I have my cell phone if they need me."

Sarah patted her belt and then looked down and around her and in her purse. "Shit, did I leave mine in the restaurant? Did it fall out?"

"You weren't wearing it or carrying it when you locked up your home," Rita said, wiping her hands before she climbed in the passenger side. While Sarah slid behind the wheel, her friend continued, "I didn't point out such a thing because, even if it wasn't intentional, it constitutes a major victory. You've shed the leash and collar."

"Hey, thanks for the dog metaphor. I told you I carry it out of courtesy, is all. But I guess since Joe didn't call the house this morning, he won't try my cell phone either." She took the keys Rita offered and started the engine. The adrenaline rush from her encounter with the Corvette had blown away the mellowing effects of the champagne, and left her tired and edgy. Backing out of the diagonal space into the street required too many stuttering taps of the brake for her liking, but she eased into a confident smoothness while she drove home.

⌘

Joe had shut the gate—no doubt out of spite when he found the house empty again at lunchtime. Sarah cruised down Tangletree, staring at the ivory expanse that blocked her driveway. "How do you like that? Now I'm gonna have to break into my own damn home."

Rita tipped her sunglasses down her nose and asked, "How shall we do it?"

"We? *We* will become a battering ram." Sarah gunned the engine and roared down the street toward the gate. Noting with satisfaction that Rita seized the armrest, she took her foot off the accelerator. "I'm only kidding. Hell, I guess I could borrow a ladder and a sheet from Mrs. O'Malley or some other neighbor." It occurred to her that she didn't know anyone else, and Mrs. O'Malley probably never would forgive her for her filthy parting remarks. When Rita asked about the sheet, she replied, "Haven't you ever seen a prison-break movie? They knot the sheet at intervals and use it to climb down. After I scale the ladder, I'll break into the prison rather than out of it." Only fifteen minutes had passed since she'd decided never to think of home that way again. Why did every victory have to be so short-lived? She parked in front of the gate, working her jaws as her anger at Joe blazed hotter.

Rita clasped Sarah's wrist with gentle pressure. "Control, my dear. You're throttling my steering wheel."

"It was such a petty, obnoxious thing for him to do."

"Then we'll summon the guilty party and call him to account." Rita took out her cell phone, speed-dialed a number, and said, "Hello. Your lovely wife and I are poised outside your castle... The invitation to lunch came from her after you consulted with me. She is allowed to make such decisions, isn't she? Well then, would you return home, blessed king, and lower your drawbridge?" She glanced at Sarah. "In that case, look out any west-facing window and you'll see our dilemma."

Sarah exited the car in a fury and stomped to the kiosk beside the gatepost. Staring into the camera lens, she leaned on the buzzer and thumbed the microphone. "Dammit, Joe, are you in the house? Come on, this isn't funny. Open the gate." In fact, a dispassionate voice in her mind did find it ironic, if not funny, since she'd put Joe in the same position: locked outside the gate, with Rita waiting in the SUV.

His voice came through the speaker grille in a scratchy monotone. "I don't remember closing it. When I arrived, I couldn't find you. You kept saying you had to get away, and I thought maybe you'd left me."

"Why would I do that? I went to lunch with Rita, is all. Won't you please open the gate?"

"Of course. Sorry."

The gate slid back on its rail. While Dorothy panted at a living room window, Joe emerged from the garage, ducking beneath the wide door ratcheting above his head. The high walls and long, crouching house appeared ominous. Sarah recalled Mrs. O'Malley checking underfoot for trap doors on her first visit and finally understood how the old woman had felt.

She'd never seen her husband look so bad. He seemed drunk, even though she knew Joe never imbibed. With the black patch in place, only his puffy and red-rimmed left eye showed. His tie hung crooked and his dress shirt bagged around his waist. He had rolled up one sleeve; the other extended to his wrist but the cuff dangled unbuttoned and the sleeve showed accordion-like wrinkles.

He looked past her and said in the same deadened cadence, "Why didn't you stop by my desk and tell me you two were going out?"

Rita leaned against a front fender of her Acura, arms and legs crossed. "Do I also need your permission to eat lunch?"

"No, of course not. It's just that I don't know what to expect anymore." The loose shirt cuff dangled against his wrist like a flap of skin. He showed Sarah the cell phone clutched in his hand. "You left this on the kitchen table. I thought you did it on purpose, so I couldn't reach you."

"I'm afraid—no, I'm not afraid. I simply forgot it. What happened to you?" She sniffed in his direction. He smelled of cold sweat, not liquor.

Joe wouldn't meet her gaze. "He's dead."

"Oh my God, I'm so sorry." She hugged him, and his arms draped around her.

He spoke above her head, jaw bobbing against her scalp. "The hospital called an hour ago. Heart failure. Failure of the heart—somehow, my heart's failed you, too."

"You didn't fail me. Everything will be all right." He already had too much to cope with, so she decided to send Rita away with the bike and collect it another time. Turning out of Joe's arms, she said to her friend, "Please excuse us. Thanks for the outing—I'll call you later about our shopping spree. I've kept you from work long enough."

"Nonsense. We need to get your bicycle out."

Joe blinked at them both, and Sarah, containing her annoyance, told him, "Rita's shown me what a beautiful city you chose for us. I thought I'd pedal around Aiken to see all of it. You use a stationary bike at the gym, so you know what good exercise it is."

"Cyclists with two good legs get run down all the time."

"We don't have to talk about this right now. There are more important—"

Rita opened the SUV hatchback. "Don't worry; she purchased every safety item short of body armor."

"You encouraged Sarah to do this, didn't you?"

"It was her idea entirely, and a ripping good one. I might get the identical thing myself. Would you deny me such an acquisition? No. Then why would you forbid her?"

He squeezed Sarah's cell phone in a tight fist. "Sare, I almost lost you once. I can't let that happen again."

"You're wiped out because of your dad. Go inside. I'll be there in a minute." She worked with Rita to remove the twenty-one speed. Half inside the SUV, she hissed, "Couldn't this have waited?"

From the back, Rita replied, "No. You're through with hiding, my dear."

Joe appeared behind Sarah. "What can I do to help?"

She put the helmet in his hands and piled the other safety gear into it, as if filling a bowl. "Thanks. Really, Joe, please go in and rest. I'm coming right behind you."

After closing the hatchback, Rita said, "I'm sorry about your father; we all hoped he'd pull through. Shall I tell your manager and the project team?"

"I've e-mailed everyone already."

"How long will you be away?"

"I don't know. There's the cremation to coordinate. No funeral or memorial service, but he did name me executor of his will, and there are other issues." He glanced at Sarah. "I have a lot to sort out."

Chapter 22

AFTER RITA DROVE OFF, REVERSING UP Tangletree as usual, Sarah rolled her bike into the garage. She put down the kickstand on the spotless concrete near his ancient white Camry, flawless despite its age. Joe set the helmet on the saddle, draped her pads over the frame, and put the gloves on the handlebars, switching them once to make sure he put each glove on the proper side. "Go ahead," he said. "Say you told me so."

"I won't do that. What kind of person do you think I am?"

"An unhappy one—unhappy with me." He jabbed the button on the wall to close the garage door.

It took a few seconds for Sarah's eyes to adjust from the glare of daylight to the gloom of a few bulbs far overhead. By that time, Joe had gone inside. She followed him into the kitchen. "Your father just died. Please let me help you through this."

Standing before the control panel, his eye patch jet-black against the pallor of his face, he closed the gate with another sharp poke of his index finger. "Like you wanted to help me drive to Virginia last night? Here comes the 'I told you so.'" He spun around and banged her cell phone on the table. Dorothy yelped. Ears back, the bulldog scampered away.

Sarah knew his rage stemmed from grief and regret, so she held her temper. "I'm sorry you didn't get to say goodbye to him."

"I have to pack. The next flight's in four hours. I got a one-way ticket."

He headed into the dining room. To continue the conversation, Sarah was forced to trail him, walking double-time. She said, "What about me?"

"I'll be busy up there." Joe continued his long strides to the hallway. "Running around, settling everything."

"Last night, you said you didn't want to be apart from me."

"I don't want you cooped up with Monica, especially since you can't stand her."

"Nonsense—"

"One of Rita's favorite words." He stopped and turned. Sarah had to sidestep into the den to avoid a collision. "I guess I have her to thank for your sudden aggressiveness," he said. "From ballerina to ball-breaker." He resumed his march.

"Don't do this, Joe." She followed him into the master bedroom. "You're grieving and hurt. I don't know what it's like to lose one parent, let alone both, but it can't be too different from losing a part of yourself. That I do know about."

He took two suitcases from his walk-in closet and tossed them on the bed. After un-zipping them, he walked to the dresser and said, "Because of me."

Sarah's first impulse was to beat him with something heavy until he became reasonable. Instead, she watched him pack his underwear.

He purchased a one-way ticket. Will I ever see him again?

In as calm a voice as she could manage, she said, "I had an accident. You didn't destroy my leg any more than you killed your own parents."

"Oh, but I did kill them."

She grasped the door jamb to steady herself. "What?"

Joe lined up tri-folded dress socks and undershirts in tidy rows within the suitcase. "I made a choice that ultimately killed two birds with one stone." He adjusted the patch over his right eye. "My mom didn't want to go to Florida that day. Despite the national award she was getting, she hated the thought of us driving to the airport and back home in a snowstorm. She said she'd rather stay put."

"What happened?" Her fingers ached from her tight grip on the molding.

"My dad said she shouldn't miss such a big honor. Monica was scared and against it all the way, but she was only six and already neurotic, so she really didn't count. I was the oldest, practically a man. So they gave me the deciding vote."

"Oh God." Fighting down a choking sob, Sarah ran around the bed to him. She rubbed his chest in an effort to soothe his heart.

His head drooped. He appeared to stare at her hand, but perhaps he saw only the recollections from decades before. "The whole time I was growing up, I stayed close to my mom. Helped her raise Monica, learned how to cook from her. We were always in sync. Whenever my parents argued, I took her side. Not to play favorites, but because she was more sensible than Dad. To strike a balance, though, I hung out with him as much as I could. I played the same sports he did, we went to ballgames. I even asked him to rate my girlfriends." Joe shook his head. "He was as tough on them as he was on me."

His voice deadened and his expression blanked. "So, with snow piling up on the streets, I decided my mom needed to get that award in person, in front of a big crowd. She needed a break from everybody at home. I sided with Dad, and voted against her."

Sarah shut her eyes, too late to hold back the tears. "What did she say?"

"That she trusted her men to know best." His hands raced up and dug into his hair, revealing wet stains that had darkened the armpits of his shirt. White knuckled, he clawed his scalp and wept.

"No, Joe, don't. Please!" She pulled at his forearms but couldn't overcome his strength. His fingers sawed back and forth, making a sickening rasp.

She tugged and yelled at him to stop until he relaxed. Black hairs stuck to his hands, and blood limned three fingernails. "Look what you did," she cried. "Why do you hurt yourself like that?"

"I sentenced her to death." He swayed before Sarah. If not for her firm hold, she knew he would topple over. "I can't ever show her I'm sorry enough."

Still weeping, she said, "You didn't kill her."

"Dad tried to keep it inside, but every once in a while the blame came spitting out like fire."

"That's not fair." He seemed steadier, so she released him and wiped her face.

"Was Dad ever fair?"

"Sit," she whispered, "and I'll get something for your head."

Sarah soaked a washcloth in the bathroom, standing near the place where she'd lifted the hairs he yanked from his eyebrows weeks before. She used the cloth to cool her face and eyes and then hurried to Joe. He sat on the bed, head hanging, one eye closed and the other masked. His exotropia no doubt would linger for some time. He'd once said that it had almost never plagued him until his mother's death.

With the washcloth, she patted the furrows he'd carved into his scalp. The narrow gouges revealed little blood but considerable inflammation. Doctoring Joe rekindled the tender feelings for him she had craved.

Dorothy crept nearby and climbed into her dog bed. She curled in a tight ball and sighed. Joe echoed the sound. He said, "The plane crashed on takeoff, ending up in the river. We heard about it on the radio and fought our way back to the airport. Gridlock and blizzard all the way."

"There's no need to talk about it anymore." She turned the washcloth over and wiped his hands. The blood under his close-cropped nails resisted her efforts. While she rubbed the stains, water drizzled across her wrist and down her forearm. She told him, "Everything will be all right." The crying had left her throat raw.

"Five made it out, but not her. All we could do afterward was pray that she died on impact, instead of drowning in the freezing cold water." He considered the fingers she scrubbed clean and looked up at her. "Isn't that a wonderful thing to wish for?"

"Don't, Joe."

"Dad loved her so much, even if he didn't know how to show it. Losing her ate him up. I killed them both, Sare—it just took longer for him to die."

She said, "And my accident took your guilt, this terrible wound, and tore it open again." Her stomach knotted and tears coursed down her face once more. Against her will, she imagined what he might've done to himself every day as punishment while she recovered in the hospital. He'd suffered lasting scars, just as she did. Though none of his were on the surface anymore, they ran as deep as hers and also might never heal.

He staggered upright, out of her reach, and pulled shirts and slacks from his closet. "It's like a Greek myth, where some poor bastard is doomed to repeat the same mistake over and over. Killing everyone he loves."

"I love you." She wiped her eyes with the washcloth, but the tears kept streaming. "Please let me come with you."

He glanced at his watch and cursed. Muttering about his flight, he prepared his clothes for the suitcases: each pair of pants with cuffs married together and joined at the waistband and then folded in half, the dress shirts becoming smaller, uniform rectangles of cotton bisected by rows of buttons. The precision of the routine reinvigorated him; color returned to his cheeks, and his movements quickened.

All the while, Sarah watched helplessly. She repeated her request when he went into the bathroom and filled a shaving kit with toiletries. Ignored for a second time, her tears ended. She threw the wadded washcloth into the sink and said, "Why don't you want me to go?"

He closed the kit with a snap. His voice sounded strong again. "Like I said, I have a lot to sort out."

"Are you leaving me?" She gripped both sides of the doorframe, blocking his exit.

"I don't know. You rewrote all the rules we play by, and I can't figure out how to please you anymore. Now can I pass?"

"Do I please you?"

"I didn't think you still cared about that." He squared his shoulders and marched toward her.

She yielded, turning in profile. He brushed past, his elbow scraping her chest. "Of course I care," she said. "Ever since you got back from Atlanta, I've tried to figure out how we can make each other happy again."

"You used to let me take care of you. That made me happy."

"That was a one-way street, a gardener with his flower. You suffocated—"

"Ah, there it is, the magic word. The kiss of death." He finished packing and hefted his suitcases. "We both have a lot of thinking to do. If you still want me, ask yourself why you need me to be so different."

"Because I've changed, too."

"You're right," Joe replied. "I hardly recognize you."

In the kitchen, he set down his bags by the door leading to the garage. Sarah caught up to him. "If you're forbidding me to go, then I forbid you to take the car. Why should the airport charge you for parking while I'm stranded here?"

"You have your new bicycle…my dear," he added, mimicking Rita.

"I can't bike Dorothy to the vet if she needs to go. I can't haul a week's worth of groceries. You're leaving me with nothing."

"No, I'm not. Look on the cooking island. There's a thousand dollars in that envelope. I also left a spare ATM card in there with the PIN, in case you need more. There's enough money in my account for plenty of bikes."

"This is my decision, not yours," she said. "I'm taking the car against your wishes. If I get hurt or killed, you warned me and your conscience will be clear."

"And if I refuse?"

"Then whatever happens to me will be on your head forever." She held out an open palm. Joe stared at her, and she quoted, "'Cyclists with two good legs get run down all the time.'"

He removed the key ring from his pocket. After he unclipped the car key, she said, "Your P.O. box key, too, so I can get the mail. What's the number?"

Joe told her and placed the gold key in her palm as well. "Are you going to at least drive me to the airport?"

"Call a taxi. Better hurry."

☙

When the cab arrived, Sarah waited out back with Dorothy in the shade of the patio. Insects hummed in the late afternoon heat, and birds hopped through Joe's garden and pecked at the soil. The bulldog didn't exhibit her usual excitability while the gate slid open; she stayed close by and watched Sarah, who sighed, sounding like a mourning dove.

"Let's go say goodbye to your daddy." She led Dorothy around to the front. Her stump throbbed so much in its socket she limped.

Joe helped the driver load the suitcases in the trunk, and then got in the front passenger seat. He seemed to hurry, but when he met Sarah's gaze, he said something to the cabbie and climbed out. His eye patch remained in place. Crouching low in fresh slacks and a polo shirt, he called to Dorothy, who ducked her head and put her ears back as he scratched her. "Daddy's going to be gone for a while. Mind your mommy, OK? I'm sorry for scaring you. Daddy can be a great big ogre."

When he stood up, Sarah wrapped her arms around him and put her forehead against his chest. She said, "Mommy can, too. I was out back praying for your parents, and for your safe trip, and for us. I haven't talked to God this much since my accident." He didn't respond, so she said, "You're sure I can't help you get through this?"

"There's too much else going on between us—it's all knotted together. I'm usually good at organizing my thoughts, but now I'm only confused."

She asked, "What can I do for you while you're away?"

"Decide you want to be the girl I married."

"Can you stand being married to the woman I am now?"

He kissed her, fast and polite, as the cabbie watched them. "I need to go. The security line at Augusta might be long." He got in beside the driver again. His closed window reflected the towering ivory fence—she could barely see him.

She called, "I love you." Please say it, please say it, dear God please make him say it.

The passenger side window buzzed down. "Me, too," he replied. "I'll call you."

Chapter 23

HE DIDN'T CALL THAT EVENING OR THE NEXT morning. Sarah checked with the airline to confirm the Augusta flight had arrived safely in Richmond. On the pad of graph paper he kept on his nightstand, she noted the standard times of the two daily trips between the small airports, one at ten a.m. and the other at six in the evening. Her multiple calls to his cell phone went unanswered. After the first few tries, she stopped leaving messages.

She found his address book in a bureau drawer and dialed the Gordon residence in Petersburg, but no one answered or responded to her recorded pleas for a call-back. During her last attempt, she pictured Joe going over his father's will, ignoring her call, while hollow-eyed Monica huddled in a chair and stared at the ringing phone.

To distract herself, she cleaned out the refrigerator and freezer of every kind of food she wanted to avoid. She inventoried the garden to determine what would ripen over the next few days, and made a grocery list. During her two trips into town with Rita, she'd spotted supermarkets along the way. She couldn't carry a week's worth of food in her backpack, but she intended to go every few days as part of her expanded exercise program.

The sanitation and recycling trucks came late on Friday mornings, so she filled the plastic trashcan in the garage and opened that door as well as the gate. The recycling bin nested within the large green container, which she rolled out to the curb beneath a sky so hazy it looked white. A sundog shimmered in the southeast with a halo of colors. Shielding her eyes, she squinted at the circular rainbow in the cloud cover while, next door, Mrs. O'Malley backed her purple Cadillac down the drive.

Sarah felt sure the woman wouldn't even acknowledge her after their last conversation, but she waved nonetheless. The car stopped at the bottom of the driveway.

Mrs. O'Malley slid out from behind the steering wheel wearing a puce pantsuit. With her gray hair stacked high, she looked like a scrawny eggplant. "Mrs. Gordon," the woman said, chin held higher than usual. Her mirrored sunglasses reflected the white sky.

"Ma'am." Sarah pinched the bodice of her peach-colored tunic and rippled it to encourage ventilation. "It sure is a scorcher today."

Her neighbor removed two slender waste bins from the Cadillac trunk, and said, "It is." She set them against the curb and filled the containers with small white trash bags, each of which had been stuffed to bulging. "Be careful, you might dehydrate so much, you won't have any water to pass."

Sarah winced. "About the other day, I—"

The woman removed her sunglasses and fixed her beady brown eyes on Sarah. "Obviously you don't care about my friendship, Mrs. Gordon."

Behind the woman's offended glare, Sarah saw genuine pain. She'd wounded Mrs. O'Malley much as Joe had hurt her, with harsh words, carefully aimed and fired point-blank. Sarah replied, "I was wrong to say what I did." She approached, palms out. "Please, I won't make excuses, but I promise not to do it again."

"Nobody has ever spoken to me so hatefully or offensively."

Sarah considered all the awful things Mrs. O'Malley had said to her. Should the woman just get a pass on them?

Perhaps.

She decided to try forgiveness. In time, if she practiced it faithfully, she might be able to set aside blame and do it for Joe without misgivings. It was the only way she saw to resurrect some of what they once had. If he forgave himself, they could recover quicker. "I'm very sorry," she said. "I do value your friendship. I hope you'll forgive me."

"I lost sleep over it. At my age, I can't afford that. My hands won't quit their damn shaking." She displayed her trembling fingers.

"Please, ma'am. I'll never live it down, but I hope we can try again."

With suddenly steady hands, Mrs. O'Malley put her mirrored sunglasses back on. "I guess we could, though I suppose you haven't talked to that woman yet about her dangerous driving habits."

"I did, actually. Rita understands your concern."

"But she won't stop doing it. You should know I filed a report with the police. I hope they come down on her like a ton of bricks."

"Rita's doing the best she can. I guess the same can be said for all of us."

"No, Mrs. Gordon, most of us can always do better."

❧

Forgiveness would only enable her to set aside blame. To work toward a better marriage, Sarah decided, she needed professional help. She knew she shouldn't have rejected the counseling recommended by her doctor following the amputation. Had she given herself permission to whine and cry and scream and finally learn to cope under the guidance of a decent therapist, she doubted her marriage would've taken so many awful turns. Joe would have to develop new relationship skills as well, but maybe she could give them a flying start.

She went online and searched for marriage counselors in Aiken. After checking out a half-dozen websites, one caught her attention because it seemed less somber and melodramatic than the others. Esther Teraphim, Ph.D., psychotherapist and relationship counselor, had an office on Park Avenue, which intersected Laurens Street. While going to lunch with Rita, she'd passed that spot. The tone of the site was serious, but it avoided the pandering, staged photos of attractive couples having a meaningful discussion under the gaze of the wise psychologist or the "do this or you'll have an expensive, soul-crushing divorce" fear tactics of the other sites.

With her hand on the phone, Sarah had to silence every excuse her imagination could muster. Finally, she overcame her most primeval argument—"I'm afraid"—by owning up to it. I am afraid, she told herself. So what? She lifted the receiver and punched in Dr. Teraphim's number.

A recorded voice asked her to leave a message. At the tone, Sarah said, "My name is Sarah Berger, um, Gordon. I'd like to make an appointment for marriage counseling." She took a breath. "My husband Joe is out of town. I don't know when he'll be back, but I'm free any time. Thank you, doctor. Here are the numbers where you can reach me." She left her home and cell numbers. After she hung up, her calmness surprised her.

As a reward for taking such a proactive step, she went back online to look for dance clothing and supplies. She wanted new tights and leotards for ballet exercising. Another search, dancing instruction, revealed a local school for children called Ballet with Barbara. The thought of young girls introduced to the art form—warm-up exercises at the barre, holding the basic positions, moving with proper alignment like marionettes on the ocean floor—made her smile. She hoped Barbara went easy on the girls with curves.

Before the day heated up further, Sarah took her first long ride on the new bike. She'd changed into jeans and a black, short-sleeved top, which would hide sweat stains and conceal her bra better than light-colored fabrics, and she coated her exposed skin with sunscreen. With her bicycle helmet and pads in place, a backpack containing water bottles and an apple, the cell phone at her waist, and credit card in her pocket, she set out.

As before, she had to carefully place her prosthetic foot on the pedal, but she soon trusted that when her left knee moved, Fred would respond. Effective use of the artificial limb was a matter of confidence. She scooted around the gate at the entrance to Eagle's Lair and turned onto Pine Log Road, heading for town. No hills challenged her, but neither could she coast for very long as she tried different gears. In no time, sweat streamed from her face and soaked her clothes. She pined for a stiff breeze. Passing traffic soon granted her wish.

Only a few inches of asphalt shoulder separated her from the cars and trucks whipping by. A minivan streaked past with a wind gust that forced tears from her eyes. Soon after, a passing eighteen-wheeler created a vortex of air that knocked her sideways, almost flipping her onto the sandy soil before she regained control.

With the front wheel still wobbly, she tried holding her arms looser instead of tighter, and her ride smoothed out. Physics could be counterintuitive. For more stability, go faster, not slower; to keep from getting knocked over by the wind, try to go as rapidly as the traffic generating it. She put thoughts of Joe aside, pumped her legs, and lost herself in the creation of speed.

As she neared the grocery store parking lot, she realized that she'd forgotten to purchase a U-bar lock to secure her bike. Aiken seemed safe enough, but she doubted that a brand new, unprotected twenty-one speed would remain hers for very long.

The store roofline provided deep shade, so she rested there and guzzled water before resuming her journey. By the time she cruised down Whiskey Road, perspiration had dried on her shirt in salty rings, and her ponytail hung limp and sopping from its helmet port. Her lips stretched in a smile that only faltered when she let herself think about Joe.

She pedaled by the undulating brick wall that protected Hopelands Gardens, and planned a future outing there. Each day she would explore something new. No bike lane existed on Whiskey Road for her safe travel, so she was delighted when traffic thinned at South Boundary Avenue. Instead of going into town immediately, she leaned into a right turn and glided beneath the mammoth live oaks. The cathedral ceiling of green leaves couldn't block the humidity, but it provided a welcome respite from the white glare of sky.

Grand Victorians and sprawling clapboard mansions gave way to modest, less picturesque homes, so she reversed course and headed for the bike shop. When she dismounted in The Alley, she staggered against a brick wall, only then realizing how saddle-sore she had become. Bruises throbbed across and underneath her rump, and abrasions plagued the insides of her thighs. She'd overdone her workout again, and still had to get back home.

A bell above the door tinkled when she entered the shop. The owner glanced up from custom-taping a set of handlebars, and said, "I haven't seen such a bowlegged walk since the last Augusta futurity and rodeo."

For another eighty dollars, he sold her a bike lock and an ergonomic saddle, which featured a scooped-out indentation for each buttock and a shortened front end to eliminate the constant rubbing against her thighs. He agreed to install the new seat for her, so she had a half-hour to rest.

Sarah hobbled out of The Alley and around the corner to Newberry Street, where wind-blown spray from an elaborate fountain and umbrella-shaded tables along a promenade welcomed her. She packed away her gear and sat down to eat. The apple she brought had become warm and soft; it had a mealy taste she washed down with hot bottled water, but it managed to soothe her grumbling stomach.

Newberry Street provided shade and respite, but few other diversions. If she didn't smell like a Tour de France competitor, she would've hung out in a restaurant or shop. With Park Avenue only a half-block to the south, she decided that walking on sore legs would hurt less than remaining seated on her tender behind. She adopted an unhurried gait and eased down the promenade.

At the intersection she headed west, looking for Dr. Teraphim's address, but had to backtrack along another block of offices to find it. Brocaded curtains in the front window shielded the interior. Mindful that she'd sweated through her clothes and her hair was in disarray, she still wanted a look inside the place where she ultimately might find marital salvation or conclude all was lost.

She finger-combed loose strands, retied her damp ponytail, and opened the door. The curtains shut out most of the sunshine, but bronze-colored sconces provided mellow lighting for the small, unoccupied anteroom. Cool air drew her inside, where Romantic-era piano music played softly. The waiting area featured a padded banquette along one wall and two upholstered chairs, separated by a table, along the other. Opposite her stood another door where a small card stated In Session.

On the table sat a stack of Dr. Teraphim's business cards and a placard inviting visitors to call for an appointment. She took one of them and entered the number in her cell phone. Reassured by the setting—what felt like a sanctuary for reflection and healing—she eased outside as reverently as she would have exited a temple.

With time left before her bike would be ready, she followed Park Avenue to Laurens Street and waited for traffic to pass. She crossed the thoroughfare to the other side, which she had not yet explored with Rita. On the second floor of one clapboard building, she saw movement behind a long row of plate glass. A quick blur of small girls in black and white piqued her curiosity. She had found the dance school, Ballet with Barbara.

A storefront on the ground floor displayed used sporting goods. One doorway at street level led inside the shop, and another, half-opened, revealed a staircase. An auburn-haired girl in white tights and a black leotard pressed her fingers to the inside of the second-floor window and looked over bustling Laurens Street. As if someone had called her name, the young student spun around and trotted away from the glass. The chance to glimpse the serene beauty of a children's ballet class compelled Sarah to climb the steep wooden stairs despite the soreness in her legs.

The loose handrail rattled under her hand as she ascended. A narrow wedge of sunshine from the street entrance and two low-wattage bulbs lit the brick stairwell. She could barely see where to set down the keel of Fred's foot. A pockmarked sign mounted above the landing advertised Ballet with Barbara. Beside it, a Plexiglas holder for brochures was empty except for two crushed cigarette butts.

Glass set in the door showed a studio with a ballet barre, tumbling mats strewn across the scuffed wood floor, a miniature trampoline, and a cheap portable stereo. Floor-to-ceiling windows and dozens of fluorescent tubes overhead bombarded the room with light. The dozen eight-year-old girls at the barre cast very small shadows. Few tried to mimic the instructor's demonstration of battement tendus, the extension of one leg and fluid return of it to fifth position, right foot turned out in front. Instead, most of them echoed each other's yawns while they practiced Rockette-style kicks.

Mirrors lining one long wall exaggerated the chaos. The ballet mistress, a stout woman with black hair cut in a bob, clapped her hands and drawled, "Unh-uh, that's all wrong."

The one student who'd performed it flawlessly, a petite girl with white-blond hair, jolted as if the barre had become electrified. Her brows arched in a surge of panic, and she examined her form for mistakes. The worried expression only changed to relief when the teacher addressed some other students. Another perfectionist. Having been that girl, Sarah empathized, knowing that the earnest youngster would always accuse herself whenever the teacher halted the class to correct someone.

"Come on in." The instructor waved to Sarah. "Mothers are always welcome."

"I'm only a visitor," she replied, easing her head into the room. She inhaled the familiar odors of chalky talc and sweaty feet, and held the door handle tighter as memories swept over her. "Can I watch anyway?"

"Sure. The more the merrier. I'm Miss Barbara."

A few chairs lined the wall beside the door. Sarah introduced herself to the teacher and put her backpack on one of the seats. Mindful of her sore rump, she remained standing.

Barbara pushed a button on the CD player, and, as the *Swan Lake* overture began, she said, "OK, you Dixie pixies, dazzle Miss Sarah. First position."

Sarah couldn't help but do it along with the class. Heels together, her feet as turned out from one another as the prosthesis would allow, she held in her bottom and lowered her shoulders. This had the effect of pushing her chest out while flattening her spine. Round the arms, level the chin, and keep the knees unbent. Along with a few of the others, she picked out a spot just over head-high on which to focus her attention. The wall behind Barbara displayed tattered Degas posters overlapping vintage ads for Capezio toe shoes. Perfect. Tucking in her thumbs and keeping her fingers alive and separated, she could imagine how daunting, and ultimately boring, ballet must've been to many of the girls. So much to remember, and they hadn't even taken a step.

She glanced over the class. The perfectionist she noticed earlier had frozen in textbook first position. Most of the others could get there with the proper corrections. A few should've been outdoors climbing live oaks in Hopelands Gardens or sharing secrets behind a curtain of willow limbs; they didn't suffer stoically. The auburn-haired girl who had looked down from the window groused, "Miss Barbara, can we, like, move or something?"

"Before you can move the right way, Wendy, you have to learn how to be still."

"Booooring," the girl replied. "I'm not a statue, you know. Like, hello-o."

The other students laughed, except for the perfectionist. Though the girl wore a mask of serenity, Sarah knew she was taking inventory, head to toe, over and over, to ensure everything remained in the proper position. Never satisfied, always dreading a mistake.

Barbara clapped her hands again over the giggles and spontaneous chatter. "The rest of us are working on first position, Wendy. If you don't want to join us, you can sit by Miss Sarah."

Wendy and many of her peers stared at Sarah, who could see herself in the mirror across the room still holding first position in her sweaty clothes and matted hair. She looked like she had cooties. In her early years of ballet classes, many of the girls attended not because they wanted to dance but because their mothers were determined to infuse them, against their will, with poise and femininity. The restless ones, much like Wendy and her cohorts, had spoiled it for the more eager pupils and ruined a chance to discover what their own bodies could do.

Sarah cleared her throat. "Excuse me, Miss Barbara," she said, using the official ballet-mistress address for the benefit of the students. Everyone, including the perfectionist, now watched her. "I used to dance a little. If you'd like, I could show Wendy and her friends how to turn. Help them burn up some of their nervous energy."

Barbara folded her arms and pursed her lips, the look of someone pretending to consider a proposition. Wendy and three other girls wandered to the window, where they pointed toward the street and whispered. The woman said, "You know your first position, but I got these rascals under control. Thanks all the same."

Any instructor, even a poor one, wouldn't want a stranger to try to take over. However, for the sake of the perfectionist, and even for Wendy, Sarah appealed to the teacher's mounting frustration with her unruly charges. "I'll make them so dizzy all they'll want to do is hold still in first position."

Barbara tried to summon the girls at the window. When they didn't respond, she tossed up her hands. "I wouldn't mind seeing that, I sure wouldn't. If you take the posse this one time, it's all right with me. Y'all can work in the far corner." She pointed to a convergence of the window and the wall, and, with a shout that startled everyone in the room, ordered Wendy and the three others to go there. Barbara added in a quieter voice, "What do you say to Miss Sarah for helping you, girls?"

They said in singsong unison, "Thank you, Miss Sarah."

In actuality, Sarah wanted to work with the perfectionist, but she knew the ballet mistress never would part with such a cooperative, talented student. Maybe she would open "Sissonne with Sarah" one day. "Sauté with Sarah" would be easier for people to say, but they'd think "cooking" not "jumping."

While the rest of the class returned to the beginning of *Swan Lake* and first position, Sarah spaced her assigned girls a few feet apart. She whispered, "I've got a secret. You won't get dizzy at all when you turn, if you learn to do what we call spotting."

Wendy rolled her eyes. "Yeah, like I don't know how to spin already."

"Well, I don't want to waste your time," Sarah said. "So show us."

Wendy whirled around, her arms like a propeller. Before the girl stopped, Sarah said, "Again." She repeated the command during the second spin. "Again. Again. Again." Before Wendy completed her sixth rotation, she staggered into some of her friends who pushed her into the wall a few feet away.

The girl slid to a sitting position, eyes glazed. In a minute, she staggered onto unsteady feet and said, "I did, like, eight or nine. How many can *you* do, Miss Sarah?"

"I don't know. Somebody count for me." She wanted ballet shoes for proper turning, but her sneakers would have to do. "Watch how I hold my arms, still rounded in first position, and notice what I do with my head." She assumed the proper stance and focused on the back of the perfectionist's motionless white-blond head. For confidence in balancing, she would pivot on her right leg and use Fred to push off.

"I've picked my spot—locked my eyes on a stationary target— and I'll return to it each time." She anticipated an upcoming measure in the overture, counted beats, and said, "Go!" Her shoulders and hips rotated while she kept her head still and neck loose. Halfway through the turn, she snapped her head around faster than her body and found her spot again as she completed the spin. Her left knee lowered, and she thumped the wood floor with the artificial foot. Eyes focused on her spot, she was turning again. As she whipped her head around, she imagined its momentum pulling her body through the rest of the turn. Then she did it over and over again, the pains in her legs forgotten.

The four girls, including Wendy, chanted, "Fifteen, sixteen, seventeen…"

After twenty, Sarah stopped because her spot had moved. The perfectionist now watched her with a wide grin. Sarah nodded to the girl and apologized to Barbara for the disruption as the teacher gaped at her. Leaning in toward her four pupils, Sarah said, "Anyone interested in learning how to do that?"

Chapter 24

SHE TRANSFERRED GROCERIES FROM HER backpack to the refrigerator, and took Dorothy out into the sweltering heat of the backyard so the bulldog could sniff around. In the shade of the patio, Sarah stretched aching leg muscles. While the new bike seat helped with comfort, it didn't make the effort of pedaling any easier. Fresh sweat had soaked through her clothes, and the stifling humidity kept her moist and hot. She was relieved when she called to Dorothy and the bulldog responded the first time to join her inside.

On a hunch, she went to the living room to check messages. Joe had called twice while she was away from home. He hadn't tried her cell phone. How would they ever make things better if he kept playing games? Taking a deep breath, she pushed the Play button and listened to his lovely voice, which no longer said the affirming words she longed to hear.

"Sorry I missed your calls," he began. "I'm getting some things done up here. The crematorium retrieved Dad's body from the hospital. They'll have his ashes ready within a week, and I'll stay plenty busy until then. Dad's will provided for people to look in on Monica, but it won't get through probate court for months. I'm hiring the same company in the meantime, and have a meeting with them tomorrow to discuss her needs.

"Monica's not taking his death well. She stopped eating, and she's more aggressive than I've ever seen her. But I guess I'm used to all of that." A series of tones followed as he punched phone buttons. He said, "Sorry, I can't remember the code to erase and re-record a message. Forget that last part. I didn't mean it." He tried one more combination and the message quit.

A half-minute later, he'd called back. "Gee, I guess you're still out." He chuckled, sounding self-conscious. "About my last message, I suppose a shrink would say I'm passive-aggressive, whining something like, 'I'm used to that.' Mostly I think I'm confused, and it's making me lash out. I don't know how you want me to be anymore. All I know is, you seem to dislike everything about me that you used to love." He paused long enough for Sarah to wonder if he'd set down the phone. "The problem with these machines," he continued, talking faster, "is that they don't respond, so I keep babbling on and on. I know you'll have some kind of response when we talk next. I hope you'll tell me it's all been a terrible misunderstanding. I really do love you. I wouldn't try to mend things otherwise."

Caller ID indicated he'd phoned both times from the Petersburg house, so she called there. After three rings, the machine answered. Joe had replaced his father's lengthy monologue with a simple invitation to leave a name and number.

She hung up and tried his cell phone but with no better result. At the tone, she said, "It's Sarah. I got your messages, but I wonder why you didn't try the cell phone you so badly wanted me to keep at my side. Yes, I did forget to carry it yesterday, but that won't happen again. Try it and you'll see." She took a breath, disliking the rising hostility in her voice. In a more sympathetic tone, she said, "You told me Monica isn't doing well, but not how you're handling your father's death. It must be hard, and I'm here for you. Please call me back."

Words continued to tumble out. "I think the problems between us really are a terrible misunderstanding. Not because I'm mistaken, though. It's because you're choosing not to understand my needs. Is the 'terrible' part that I have different needs than I did before? I appreciate you're trying to mend things between us…but what I see is a mending wall, like the Frost poem Rita loves to quote. I see a barrier going higher and higher between us. It turns out good fences don't make good neighbors or a good marriage. Help me knock it down, Joe, and we'll meet in the middle. I love you. I really mean that, too."

She'd considered, but rejected, telling him about the appointment she made with Dr. Teraphim, who had called her cell phone while she biked home. Joe would likely view such a step as an admission of failure. One of the therapist's clients had relocated, freeing up a Monday morning timeslot, and Sarah had agreed to meet then before she could talk herself out of it. She decided to embrace the hurt she knew would come during the counseling sessions, much as she accepted the pain of exercising. Each new ache meant she'd reached another milestone in taking control of her life.

Barbara had offered her a job assisting with the ballet classes, which contributed to Sarah's eagerness to pursue therapy. She could cry and rant for fifty minutes every Monday with Dr. Teraphim, and thunder up the stairs five days a week to dance away her blues with the ballet students. When she showed Barbara the prosthesis, lifting her pant leg and unrolling her sock, the woman had said, "Shoot, you dance better on one and a half legs than I ever did on two. These kids are too young to be messing with pointe work anyway, so you won't need to be all that surefoot—uh, nimble. If we can teach them the basic posture and steps, their folks won't have wasted their tuition money." They had shaken hands and agreed on a starting wage of twelve dollars an hour, in cash.

Though she needed to shower, a jumble of emotions—from frustration with Joe to elation over the proactive steps she'd taken that day—prompted her to pick up the living room phone to share her news. She called Rita's office number at Matryoshka.

Following the exchange of greetings, Rita asked, "What do you hear from Joe?"

"I'm playing phone tag with him. All that fuss about me not carrying my cell phone, and then he goes and leaves two messages on the machine here." Sarah summarized the calls and her return message.

"It sounds as if he's avoiding you, my dear. He knows you go out every day now; this is his way of getting his say without prompting an argument. That happened in the final stage of my last relationship."

Her new friend always gave voice to Sarah's darkest thoughts. "Why would he do that if he wants things to improve?"

Instead of responding to her question, Rita asked, "Does he have any old girlfriends around Petersburg or Richmond?"

"God, I don't know! What a question to ask." Sarah plopped into an armchair, not caring if she ruined the upholstery with her sweat and odor. A headache began to throb behind her eyes. She massaged the closed lids with her thumb and index finger, and said, "Isn't there a more likely explanation than he's hooking up with someone? Doesn't the first thing you said, about him trying to avoid an argument, make more sense?"

"Of course. I apologize. I'm afraid—to take up your discarded phrase—that you're only going to continue to get hurt. I would hate to see that."

"But what's the alternative?" Sarah rubbed her forehead, wishing she hadn't asked.

"You know the answer to that, my dear. I need not voice it. However, you didn't call to hear Cassandra foretell of some tragedy. What may I do for you?"

Dorothy ambled over and lay down with her small black-furred chin on Sarah's left shoe. Leaning over to scratch behind the dog's ears, she took no pleasure in the fact that now she could do so without grunting with effort, that her stomach no longer scrunched in as many folds. Divorce—had it really come to that? She said, "I thought I had good news, but you might not agree. I made an appointment with a marriage counselor for Monday."

"Was that part of your message to Joe?"

"No, and please don't tell him if he calls you."

"Everything you say I hold in strictest confidence." Rita's response sounded cross.

Sarah leaned back into the cushions, the pain undiminished behind her eyes. "My turn to apologize. I'm not sure how he'll take it, is all, and I know how secrets can get revealed by mistake when friends talk. Have you heard from him?"

"He called to ensure that Matryoshka didn't close up as tight as a nesting doll due to his absence of twenty-four hours."

"How did he sound to you?"

"Harried," Rita said, and she sighed. Sarah wasn't sure if her friend sounded wistful or resigned. Rita continued, "Perhaps your therapist can help you. In any case, I admire your willingness to try. How else have you spent your day?"

"I helped out a ballet class. There's this school on Laurens Street. It's kind of shabby and the teacher isn't much, but maybe we can make it into something better."

"Just as you're trying to recreate your marriage. Hear, hear!"

The enthusiasm sounded sincere, and it cheered her. She said, "Thanks, I really appreciate that. Do you have plans with Dylan for the weekend?"

"Goodness no. We're not a couple, after all. Here's another saying from BVI: 'Come see me' and 'Come live with me' are two very different things." She laughed in a descending scale. "Haven't you ever shagged a fellow without embroiling yourself in a relationship?"

"A few times, but it was always their choice, not mine. I guess I'm old-fashioned: falling in love before sleeping with someone and now trying to save a floundering marriage instead of kicking it to the curb and looking for someone else."

"I didn't criticize you for those things. I'm the very model of support."

Sarah thanked her again, and contemplated a sudden vision in her imagination: Rita as a model, her regal features molded with clay, her lovely face replicated in sculpture. Sarah had studied plenty of videos and practiced, but she hadn't felt inspired yet to create art from the rich gray earth stored in her studio. Now, her fingers itched to knead and shape. She said, "So are you free on Saturday, or do you have plans to corrupt another unsuspecting stud?"

"As a matter of fact, I am free. What shall we do?"

"I'd like to begin a sculpture of you. Have you ever sat for one?"

"I can't say I have, but why stay put when you're enjoying your freedom? Now where could we go gallivanting…would you like to see Charleston? It'll be as hot as the dickens, but lovely nonetheless."

Sarah replied, "I need to be here in case Joe calls, since he might not try my cell phone."

"Nonsense. You think you're trapping him by lying in wait, but he has you trapped. You're making yourself a prisoner, my dear, just like my friend Linda. Except in your case, you're doing it willingly."

Sarah stood, and Dorothy backed up in panic. "If I want to talk to him, what else can I do?" Despite her sore muscles, she paced in a small circle, coiling the phone cord around her body. The spiral of plastic sheathing against her arms felt as cold and dry as snakeskin. "Am I supposed to leave a threatening message like, 'Call me or else'?"

"Is there an 'or else'?"

Sarah turned in the opposite direction, unraveling the cord. "No. I never wanted to hurt him or ruin what we had." Her anger rose. "All I wanted was to feel better about myself."

"I'm sorry I pushed so hard," Rita said. "When do you want me to come over?"

"Maybe it's not a good idea. I don't want you to feel like you're cooped up with a prisoner."

"None of that, now. I'll arrive at the noon hour with provisions for lunch. I'm sure Dylan will put in something extra-special for you, if not for me. You're an amazing person, Sarah—not only painting but sculpture, too?"

❧

Sarah took a cordless phone into the bathroom while she cleaned up, and listened the entire time for a call from Joe that didn't come. On a whim, she'd set out some old casual clothes on the vanity—a cotton top and khaki shorts—alongside underwear Joe had purchased for her only a month before, and received two pleasant surprises: the outer clothing fit her with less binding than she expected, and the bra and panties were too loose. The scale showed her weight as 124.8, down more than fifteen pounds from her all-time high. Though she knew some of the drop was due to temporary water loss from so much exertion, she still cheered.

With her mood lifted for the moment, she put aside her sadness over Joe. She attached the cordless phone to the waistband of her shorts, and, on her other hip, she wore the cell phone. To Dorothy, who sat near the bathroom doorway, she joked, "I'm a gunslinger with mismatched six-shooters, to go with my mismatched legs."

The sight of the prosthesis and nylon dressings that came to mid-thigh no longer shocked her. In fact, she considered stripping off the cosmetic cover and foam "musculature" underneath to take Fred down to his robotic endoskeleton, giving her a *Terminator* look. She then could paint designs on a nylon sleeve that would stretch over her socket and the sock and liner above. Rather than resign herself to Fred's artificiality, she could celebrate him as art. Hmm, something to think about.

Inspired to create again and try new things, Sarah took a garden salad into her studio and prepared the north end for sculpture. She readied the equipment. From study, she knew her most important tools for shaping were her thumbs, and to a lesser extent, her fingers and palms; however, once she had the large masses of clay assembled, she also would turn to her slender paddle, boxwood blades, scrapers, smooth wire-end tools, and wire-wrapped scratchers, to block out the primary facial planes and features. She set them on the oilcloth-covered table like surgical instruments.

Some of the cylinders of clay she'd packed away had remained damp and pliable. After adding fired and crushed clay called grog and a handful of sand and pumice to a sample portion, she kneaded and beat the cool, timeless material against the thick plaster surface of her wedging table. It took a number of test combinations until she created what she thought was the right consistency. "Plasticity," the online instructors called that quality of workable clay: stiff enough to hold any form, but with enough suppleness to record the grazing of her fingertips across its surface. Finally satisfied with her recipe, she prepared whole loaves of clay.

Then she replayed some videos in the den to help her make her most basic decision: whether to cast a hollowed-out sculpture, which she would then bisque-fire in a kiln to stoneware hardness, or create a solid clay portrait as the basis for a plaster bust. She had a variety of fillers to blend in prior to shaping and firing. By the maturing point of 2,300 degrees Fahrenheit, fiberglass would fuse and give the sculpture extra strength, while vermiculite or sawdust would burn up and leave air pockets and an open, grainy appearance to suggest classical antiquity.

On the other hand, bins beneath the table also held plenty of fine-grained casting plaster, which would capture Rita's ethereal beauty. Bisque-firing would require her to locate a college art department, brick company, or someplace else that would rent or give her space in a kiln, whereas she had everything needed to make a plaster bust at home, especially the time.

"Dottie," she said to the bulldog napping underfoot, "this is called 'casting' about for a decision, ha-ha."

She thought about the challenge of forming the metal structure that would support the weight of the clay bust, to do everything from scratch and learn as she went. It seemed like the way to go. She watched more videos to memorize the steps for building the armature and then went to work.

Sarah only bloodied three knuckles and split two fingernails as she bolted together the bare skeleton—a vertical steel pipe surrounded by a quartet of curved aluminum tubes—and mounted it on a heavy, shellacked pine-board plinth. She threaded the top of each aluminum curve with dangling wires and affixed to them some crossed pieces of wood called butterflies to help support the heaviest masses of clay. The armature was the size of a child's head; clay would fill and then surround it to produce a life-size adult bust. She sucked blood from her fingers and glanced around, noticing how dark the room had become.

The western wall of glass showed the sunset afterglow: an azure horizon topped by the ultramarine of nightfall. The North Star alone stood out in the sky, "the wishing star," her mother called it. Having prepared her studio and materials, there was nothing to do but practice with the clay until shaping it felt natural.

Sarah took up a cylinder she'd set aside for experimentation.

Her thumbs and fingers worked the cool, dense material. In ballet, the brains were in the feet; in sculpture, the hands took center stage. Giving herself over to the squeezing and pressing and stretching, she no longer could distract herself from thoughts of Joe. Her desires for reconciliation, for his acceptance of her, and for his own willingness to change made her wish obvious. It also felt naïve and impossible.

Chapter 25

SARAH SLEPT WELL THAT NIGHT, NEVER MOVING from what she thought of as her side of the bed. Her hand strayed to Joe's pillow, cold beneath her fingers. She wondered whether she always would sleep on the left side of the bed—even if he never returned—or someday migrate to the center. What would that feel like, the hypothetical evening when she decided the entire bed was hers alone?

Alone.

For the first time, her real leg hurt more than her phantom one, due to the cycling. However, her heart ached worst of all. She confirmed the cell phone remained on and both it and the cordless handset still had power. Sitting at the edge of the bed, she pulled on her robe, put a phone in each pocket, and gathered her crutches to swing-step to the bathroom.

When she returned to the bedroom to get dressed, she needed to add an extra, thicker sock over the usual one covering her locking liner, to get a secure fit within the socket. She'd succeeded in working her residual limb down toward its former trimness. Not there yet, but closer to her goal.

She chose comfort and practicality instead of dressing up as she usually did for Rita: roomy denim shorts, ankle socks, and a T-shirt she had bought in an Atlanta art-themed boutique with the silkscreened inscription "Sculptors Only Do It with the Rock-Hard." Its twin, another present she'd given herself declared "Painters Savor It with an Educated Pallet." As daring as the message was, her bare left leg with the sock and liner showing above the socket, and the prosthesis on display below it, made the real statement. This was who she was—she didn't need to hide herself any longer.

The sculptor joke stretched across her firmer bust as she tied her hair back in a ponytail. She speculated about whether or when she'd do it again with Joe—she'd certainly lost a little cleavage power. Imagining him naked and ready on the bed, she felt desire, but it was a cool fire now, banked and in control, instead of the "do me now" hunger that used to obsess her. If she didn't need him anymore, but still wanted him, was that a sign of growing maturity or the death of genuine passion? Maybe Rita would know.

She shared some of her cottage cheese breakfast with Dorothy. No longer did she think of the animal as Joe's pet—this was her dog now. Clearly she had moved to the head of the pack in Dorothy's mind as well. After securing Dorothy's leash, she took her bat-eared companion for a long walk as the day heated up. What a relief not to care if Mrs. O'Malley or anyone else saw the artificial leg with its foam-muscle camouflage. How her neighbor's eyes would pop if she witnessed the stripped-down *Terminator* look. Sarah wasn't ready to expose herself that much.

At five minutes to noon, the guard at the gate called to ask whether to admit Rita. Sarah granted permission, and waited for her in the narrow shade of the front step. She expected Rita to bare a lot of skin on such a blistering day, but her friend surprised her again.

Rita emerged from her SUV in black jeans, flats, and a white, short-sleeved dress shirt buttoned almost to her throat. She didn't wear any of her silver jewelry, nor her favorite sunglasses. Without the adornments, she looked far more naked than Sarah had envisioned. "I love your blouse," Rita said. "Is the saying true?"

"It is in my case. Or was anyway. I like your simple elegance."

"I didn't know what to wear. I thought the jewelry might be distracting." Rita removed a shopping bag laden with plastic containers from the backseat. "Shall we eat first or get a start on your masterpiece?"

Sarah took the bag from her, surprised by its heft. The

reinforced handles dug into her fingers. "God, did you order some of everything on the menu?" She led them toward the house, noting Rita had not remarked on her exposed prosthesis. Such a class act.

Her friend said, "I told Dylan to prepare a banquet for us. You can dine on the leftovers until Joe returns."

"You're not assuming his place, are you?" Sarah asked. "Becoming my caretaker while Joe's gone?"

"Perish the thought. I'm simply giving us both a treat. There are things Joe can do for you I never could." Maybe she meant the last comment to sound naughty, but it came out a little melancholy. Without her earrings, the holes in Rita's brown lobes made her look vulnerable.

Sarah set down the bag and gave Rita a big hug, grateful the woman didn't startle as she put her arms around her and held her a moment. Rita squeezed back. The simple human contact felt comforting, better than anything she'd gotten from Joe in ages. She stepped back and searched Rita's lovely green eyes. "Thank you for the meal and for spending the day with me. It means a lot."

"To me, too. Let's discover what treasures Dylan has heaped upon us."

Dorothy yapped as Rita entered the house and then retreated to the high-sided bed against the window. Sarah guided Rita around the hearth and into the dining room. "Sorry, I need to socialize her more. Anyway, I think I barked like that when we met."

"Not at all, my dear."

"I did so, over by the fireplace."

"Only because of your anger at Joe," Rita said. "The few times you've been agitated in my presence, we were inevitably discussing him."

"Let's declare a holiday from that. No men allowed today." Sarah had set two adjacent places at the dining room table and now unloaded the clear-topped plastic boxes, opening each one and gushing over how good everything looked and smelled. From the bottom of the bag, Rita produced a bottle of the white merlot

they'd enjoyed during their first lunch together, and Sarah found
a corkscrew and wine glasses.

Despite her minutes-old pledge, Sarah couldn't resist
mentioning Joe. "The first time you took me to lunch," she said,
spooning Thai stir-fry on Rita's plate and then her own, "we
discussed Joe's guilt about my amputation and other things that
go wrong beyond his control."

"I understood that no men would be joining our party today."

"Just this one thing and then I won't mention him again. You
said something like, 'Who knows where that guilt comes from,'
only more eloquently and with a far prettier accent—"

Rita forked a thick wedge of grilled shitake mushroom on
Sarah's plate. "I couldn't have expressed myself better than that,
nor with a lovelier cadence. If you Southerners were not such
egregious anglophiles, you'd realize how much more enchanting
you sound than Brits and BV Islanders."

"'Egregious anglophiles?'"

"Outstanding—but for undesirable qualities—and those
who fawn over all things English."

Besides a sumptuous meal, Rita even supplied words-of-the-
day. Come to think of it, Joe used to do that, too. Sarah said,
"Well, I learned before Joe left how that 'egregious' guilt was
born. He blames himself for his mother's death in that plane
crash I mentioned." Between bites of the succulent vegetarian
feast and sips of wine, she explained the choice his parents had
asked him to make and told her about Joe gouging his scalp.

Rita stared into her long-stemmed glass for a half-minute
after the story concluded. A constellation of ruby lights reflected
in her eyes. She finally asked, "Why do you think he chose that
moment to tell you? He kept it a secret for the first year of your
marriage and the entire time you dated. I doubt he's ever told
anyone."

"Because he wanted me to understand him," Sarah said.

"Nonsense. He wanted your sympathy, your pity. Drawing
blood, for heaven's sake! He's at that stage where his only hope is
that you'll feel sorry for him."

Sarah put down her fork. "What stage?"

"Oh dear, there goes Cassandra again, spouting her prophesies. I do apologize. How is your food?"

"It was delicious, thanks." Sarah pushed her plate aside. "I'm full now."

"But we've only just begun. Try one of those eggplant roll-ups."

"No," she replied, and drained her wine glass. "I've had enough."

Rita sighed. "Shall we defer our dessert?"

"We better do that." Sarah shut the containers within her reach. She carried an armload to the refrigerator, trying to ignore the dread that spread like burning oil through her chest and stomach.

Rita followed with the remaining plastic boxes and the wine. When Sarah nudged the refrigerator door closed, they bumped elbows and their apologies overlapped. Facing each other, they stopped talking. Then Sarah whispered, "I hate the thought of losing him."

"But you're finding yourself, and—as much as you love Joe—which is more important?"

Sarah trembled with grief, but she put her hands out as Rita leaned forward. "I know the answer, but everything I've done seems so selfish now."

"It has to be that way, my dear. If you devote your life to someone else, what remains when that person is no longer there?"

"I thought he'd devoted his life to me, too."

Rita squeezed Sarah's fingers and interlaced them with her own. "You know I'm friends with Joe, but it seems to me he devoted himself to shaping you, so that you'd fit with some ideal he fantasized about."

"So what do I do?"

"Become the shape of your destiny instead. And decide whether he fits alongside you." With a final squeeze, Rita stepped back. "Now then, I'm anxious to see how my likeness takes shape in your capable hands."

The compliment helped Sarah regain control. She took Rita to her studio. While her friend investigated the art supplies by touch, sight, and scent, Sarah beckoned Dorothy through the open doors. The bulldog slunk in and curled up on the dog bed beside the western glass wall, still eyeing the intruder.

Rita sat in the ergonomic chair at the short end of the worktable, close to the armature. Sarah confirmed she would be able to look from her subject to the sculpture without turning her head. She said, "Don't get your hopes up, Cassandra. I've never done this before."

"What should I expect?"

"It won't look like much for a while, and then it won't look flattering at all. According to the experts—or, anyway, the artists who put recordings of themselves on the Internet—sculpture takes its own time to grow and mature. Then, all of a sudden, it seems to finish itself."

Focusing on art allowed Sarah to set aside her agony over Joe. She sliced off the end of the nearest loaf of clay and handed the demitasse-sized tip of cool gray earth to Rita. "One of the instructors warned that as you shape the medium, it alters you in return. By the time you complete a work, you're a different person." As her friend pressed and pulled the clay, she added, "Apparently, the real fascination isn't always what you do with the raw material, but how it changes you."

Sarah took up the remaining length of clay and smacked it into her open palm, as she'd seen sculptors do in their videos. Following their lead, she squeezed, patted, and pinched it until every nerve in her hands had awakened. Despite the wine with lunch, and the ache that compressed her heart in a powerful grip whenever her thoughts strayed, her senses remained sharp. "Relax," she said, noting Rita's rigid posture. "I need to build up the core first."

She lumped clay around the vertical steel pipe of the armature and expanded from there. Encasing the dangling wood butterflies with the gray earth, she ensured a stable mass within the otherwise empty spaces as she worked outward to the aluminum tubing. After every dozen deposits along the front of the framework, she walked around Rita and built up more of the back and sides, getting used to the pattern of Rita's hair and the geometry of her head without the distraction of facial features. The figure gained form in the hunks of clay she continued to press together, the edges of each handful still discernable.

She recalled that building up a bust required definition of the skeleton first: the bones of the shoulder, the clavicles, vertebrae, and skull. One artist who was blind had a compelling approach, which Sarah decided to try. She washed and dried her hands at the stationary tub, and asked, "May I touch you? I want to feel the shapes."

"But of course." Rita glanced at the clay-covered armature. "I assume you want to start with my face, since your portrait doesn't even have a nose yet."

"Actually, I have to start at the base and get that right." She walked behind Rita and prodded with fingertips and thumbs cupped around each of her friend's shoulders. "Ballet mistresses said I had brains in my feet because I could remember so many dance steps. Well, this blind artist on the Internet said you can develop brains in your hands. Get the feel of the humerus and scapula, front and back and sides, and work inward to the collarbones, breastbone, and spine." She slid her fingers under Rita's collar points and then traced the gentle curve of the clavicles. Each sensation registered in her mind, creating an image of the core sculptural masses and planes.

"Don't worry," Sarah said, her fingers encircling Rita's neck, "I'm not strong enough to strangle you." The woman chuckled, but her hands gripped the armrests. Sarah continued to stand behind Rita as she felt the slopes along the back of the skull and followed the curves over the scalp. Her fingers eased through smooth black hair that tumbled across the backs of her hands in silky cascades. Sarah murmured, "Close your eyes so I don't poke them by mistake." She touched Rita's forehead, felt her brows and ears, and then examined the angles of the cheekbones.

The muscles in Rita's face tensed at the initial contact and remained rigid. Sarah wondered if her insistent touch made Rita uneasy or upset. A lifetime in ballet had meant instructors putting their hands all over Sarah, always adjusting and correcting. Dancers got used to it or they got out. However, she knew most people needed much larger personal space than ballerinas, so she didn't linger long in any area.

In her mind, she created the likeness of Rita, memorizing every detail, so she could refer back to that mental picture in the days and possibly weeks to come, when the real artistry would occur, or fail to. So far, she was operating on theory, imitating the work of others, and learning as she went. Hopefully she wasn't creating just a huge waste of time.

As her fingers edged along the curve of Rita's jaw, she wished she'd touched Joe so intently before he left, so she could summon the physical reality of him at will. Joe...her thoughts always circled back to him. "All done," she finally said. "Thank you. I'm sure that felt really weird."

She came around to face Rita, noting her dilated pupils, shallow breathing, and flushed skin. "Are you all right? Would you like to take a break?"

"I'm fine." Rita swallowed and took a deep breath. "It's such a...no one's ever touched me like that. But it's familiar nonetheless. Does that make sense?"

"It's your mother's touch," Sarah said, remembering the blind artist's words. "Maybe your father, too, but definitely your mother. I'll bet she felt you like that when you were a baby, memorizing the miracle of you with her hands." She lifted smaller clumps of clay and worked on growing the sculpture, talking as she went so she wouldn't judge everything she was doing. "The hardest thing to learn is seeing everything in three dimensions. I have to keep fighting the tendency to make an outline in clay and simply add to it." Instead, she focused on seeing a unified whole that swelled out at her from every vantage point. More instruction came to her, and she said, "Each object has a front, back, top, bottom, and sides. Eyes, ears, lips, everything. My challenge is to remember that."

She filled out the neck and defined the dimensions of the head, its width, length, and depth, using her paddle to block out the shape and then finessing it with her thumbs. Her confidence started to grow as she lost herself in the work. At the back, she gave form to the rest of the skull and paddled on what would become the thick fall of hair that draped across the shoulders.

Walking around front again, she squinted at the bust to isolate her gaze. The life-size figure still appeared to consist of individual lumps of clay, but it had gained solidity in the past few minutes. It had a "presence," in the words of one online artist.

The more she needed to clarify the shapes in three dimensions, the smaller was each application of clay. This became a process of discovery for her, as she undid as much as she accomplished, but even the mistakes felt like progress. She mostly used her thumbs and pea-sized pellets of earth as she built each feature toward herself. Establish the skeleton, add sinew, drape skin over that, add hair and suggest clothing. For a while, she explained each step to Rita as she undertook it, but they soon fell into a companionable silence.

Sarah asked her friend to gaze at some distant spot beyond the eastern glass wall. The woman's body relaxed in the chair, face serene. Sometimes, though, her brows furrowed or mouth twitched. Rita glanced over whenever that happened, and Sarah always said, "Do you want to take a break?" Rita would reply in the negative and again stare at a far-off point.

Standing for hours produced aches in Sarah's foot, her knees, and back. She finally declared a rest, directed Rita to the guest bathroom off the hallway, and relaxed in the den for a few minutes, scanning through videos to make sure she hadn't forgotten anything critical. Afterward, she took Dorothy outside, where clouds had thickened and settled low and gray overhead, making the humidity even more oppressive. She did pliés and stretching exercises on the flagstone patio until her muscles warmed and she had broken a sweat.

"It smells like rain again," Rita said, shutting the French door behind her.

"Yeah, my left leg aches; the stump is a great barometer."

"At times I forget you don't have use of two full legs. Even viewing you in shorts all afternoon, I forgot to notice. You move with such confidence, and you were fabulous on the bicycle."

Sarah snorted. "Totally. I hear Hollywood is about to cast me in a reality show about a simple but lovable cripple: *Fairest Gimp*."

"Bollocks. You look fetching and powerful. I hardly recognize the woman I met only a short while ago."

"You and my husband both. Joe said the same thing before he took a cab to the airport."

"He didn't drive himself?"

"I wouldn't let him have the car. Do you mind if we don't talk about that? If I focus on Dorothy chasing the birds or contemplate the sculpture—anything but him—I feel good."

"Of course," Rita said. "About the sculpture, I probably shouldn't have peeked at your work, but I must say I'm struck by the transformation. Only hours ago it looked like one ungainly mass atop another, whereas I now see the location of every feature. Even my ears."

"I'm still in the 'all thumbs' stage. It'll be a while before I pick up a scratching tool to pull the surfaces together or use the fine wire to smooth the features. I need to practice with them first. A number of artists have said sculpture is about patience, persistence, and faith." Sarah watched a female cardinal of soft brown and muted crimson fly an undulating route over the privacy fence followed by her garish mate. She added, "Maybe like marriage."

☙

The third time Sarah called for a break, night had darkened the yard and a soft rain fell. Her sculpture had progressed to the large-tool stage. A wedge-shaped scraper had defined Rita's strong cheekbones and the straight lines of her shirt collar, as well as the gentle curves of the nose and upper mouth. She had cut small bits of clay for the lips, eyelids, and the swirls of the inner ear that Rita's hairstyle didn't cover. Probably a hundred hours of work remained, but the sculpture actually bore a rough resemblance to her friend. Sarah always surprised herself when she showed a talent for something new.

Rita stretched and stood alongside Sarah to gaze at the clay portrait. "Will that expression change? I look rather dour."

"The classic busts are done this way, with the subject at

ease. Smiling uses muscles; people don't smile when they're fully relaxed," Sarah said. "You looked this way most of the day, probably like me."

"Not at all. You smiled, you frowned. You smirked and grinned. At other moments, you looked positively fierce." She paused as if to consider something and then added, "Often you looked ecstatic."

Sarah toweled off her hands and rubbed her cheeks with vigorous circular motions. "That explains why my face hurts. Let's get Dorothy outside again, and then dig into that chocolate cake you brought."

On the patio, she lifted her face to the misty rain drifting from the night sky. The security lights made each droplet glow like a lightning bug. Soon, the water glazed her skin and made her shirt cling. Time to get back inside before Fred absorbed the moisture.

She followed Dorothy into the kitchen, but didn't find Rita there. Maybe her best friend—time to start thinking of her that way—was back in the studio. Sarah headed up the hall but stopped at the doorway to her bedroom, where the overhead light was on. She caught a glimpse of long, brown legs. Bare. On her bed.

Entering the room, she found Rita reclined there on Joe's pillow, nude, one lean arm propping up her head to form a perfect triangle. In fact, as Sarah had guessed, everything about the woman was ideal. Breasts much firmer than her own, lean torso with great abs, a flare of hips that caught the light and framed another triangle, this one in black.

Rita said, "You're wrong, my dear. Mothers don't touch that way. Lovers do."

Sarah's heart leaped from first position to grand jeté. Lying there was a goddess who wanted her. She wasn't aroused, she told herself. Her instinct to tear off her T-shirt only was due to its wetness, not because the clinging made her so aware of her body. She just was feeling panic. How would she get this naked woman off her bed?

A traitorous part of her mind truncated the question: How

would she get this naked woman off? Joe was the expert at that; she'd only been on the receiving end. How in hell could she do what Joe did...or used to do?

He intentionally had avoided talking to her for days. Before that, every conversation turned into a fight. Clearly he'd stopped loving her. Maybe this was a new chapter in her life, with new explorations and discoveries about who she was. Or at least a way to lose herself for a while.

Rita watched her without another word, eyes done up to make the green even more luminous. Her free hand slid over Sarah's side of the bed, slender fingers making gentle circles as they smoothed the blanket.

During her old days in ballet, Sarah had been in close contact with hundreds of women. However, she only had examined them for comparison purposes, always find herself wanting but never wanting them. Something about Rita beyond her awesome body compelled Sarah toward the bed. The woman was powerful, confident, commanding, everything she wanted to become. Rita could teach her so much.

The fingers continued in a hypnotic rhythm, insistent but gentle, promising patience. Sarah climbed onto the covers and kneeled beside the goddess. Though perched much higher than Rita, she felt small and hid the prosthesis behind her. Practicalities sprang to mind. Would it be OK to leave Fred on? How awkward would it be to kick away shoes, to pull off shorts and panties?

She didn't know what she desired. Mostly she felt the urge to back off the bed and run from the room. However, the green gaze beckoned. The fingers traced slow, smooth circles. The lips glimmered. She told herself she still was deciding. Then her best friend's mouth curved into a knowing smile, and Sarah admitted what must've been obvious to Rita already. She had yielded.

Chapter 26

SARAH AWOKE ON SUNDAY MORNING TO AN EMPTY bed. She inventoried her aches and tender spots from head to foot and organized each into one of two categories: standing for hours while sculpting or lying for hours with Rita. Her hand slid over Joe's side of the bed, the sheets still rumpled but now cool and dry.

If her best friend had stayed, she could've helped Sarah remain in a guilt-free blur of new experiences. Instead, there were no distractions. Not even Dorothy's snores broke the stillness; the bulldog must've chosen another room in which to sleep. The vacuum demanded to be filled with a clamor of thoughts.

Oh my God, I have a mistress.

It wasn't Joe who was the cheat, it was her. But Joe deserved it for the cold way he'd acted, making her a prisoner in their home and then lashing out every time she fought for a little freedom. This was his fault—he drove her into Rita's arms.

Rationales…scapegoating…bullshit. She was the one with the wandering eye, the lax morals, the adulteress' excuses.

The worst part was that she hadn't been very good at the sex. If she'd discovered a natural talent there, as she'd done with painting and sculpting, she could've reveled in it and set aside the guilt indefinitely. As it was, she'd sensed Rita faking all night—every supposed climax looked and sounded the same. Poor woman, she'd probably gone home exhausted from acting as much as from giving her pleasure.

No surprise, Rita was far more talented. Gifted, in fact. Sarah's hands grazed her body as she remembered. Rita had even helped Sarah remove Fred and clean her stump before sending her to sleep with one more vigorous round of lovemaking, very much as Joe used to do. Still, she'd missed the physicality of Joe, the sheer size of him, the weight of brawny muscles. And the obvious equipment. As nimble as Rita had been, there was a deficit impossible to overcome. And, of course, the deficit that mattered most was she didn't love Rita. She still loved Joe, damn him.

Should she confess and get it over with? Joe, I love you and want to stay married to you, but I had an affair with a woman. And not just any woman, but someone you work with. And not just any colleague…

Would any defense be good enough? Could she say she was seduced? Plead low blood sugar?

Maybe there were degrees of infidelity. Sex with another man was forbidden, but she bet a lot of guys, if told their wives had slept with another woman, would say it was acceptable—if they could join in next time. Surely he thought Rita was hot, so maybe he'd consider this a misdemeanor rather than a felony.

A jangle of telephones disrupted her frantic thoughts. Likely it was Rita, calling to apologize for leaving, to assure her it wasn't a one-night stand, to make a date for later. The cordless unit was in the pocket of her shorts, which had been flung across the room. The landline on Joe's nightstand was closer. She leaned over and sprawled naked across the space where she'd been with Rita. Breasts, stomach, and thighs tingled as she slid to the phone.

What to tell her? Last night was great but we should be friend-friends, not friends with benefits. I want my husband, not a lover. I'm obviously not a lesbian, and I kinda sucked at being bi. Bad choice of words. Start over.

The phone rang again. She couldn't decide on the right tone of voice. Upbeat? No, don't want to lead her on. Regretful? OK, as long as there was no blaming. Of course, if it was Mom on the phone…Oy vey, just answer. "Hello?"

"It's me." Only two words, but his voice was unmistakable.

Her skin erupted in gooseflesh. Shivering, she yanked the covers over her shoulders. Shame and guilt mixed with relief at finally hearing from him again. "God, Joe," she said. "It's been so long. I've been worried sick." Don't rush. Ease into this and see where it goes. Maybe he's at the airport, about to catch a taxi home, ready to reconcile. Or maybe he's calling to demand a divorce. She asked, "Are you all right?"

"Everything's on schedule, so yes, I guess. I listened to your last message a number of times. I even looked up that Robert Frost poem, 'Mending Wall.'" He recited the title as if it were a curse she'd spat at him.

She said, "I—"

"I'm not the one who keeps building a higher wall, Sarah."

He hadn't used her real name since they dated. Hearing that instead of the diminutive pet name she'd grown used to felt like a slap against her cheek. She flinched, and then other reactions boiled up.

Wit and grace and control, Sarah reminded herself. What would Rita do? Some memories sprang up about what Rita had done. Not that—how would Rita handle this call? She said, "You're right. I'm totally changing our relationship." She considered dance terms he'd understand. "It's like we were stepping to a minuet and now I want to tango. The question is, do you still want to dance with me?"

"Haven't you found another partner?"

"What? Are you kidding?" She hunkered further under the covers. How could he know so soon? Had Rita confessed already? Did he have web-cameras in the house?

He said, "Right before my Atlanta trip, you started to rebel—as if my going away had given you the chance to go wild. Now you're completely different from the woman I married. You make all kinds of new demands; nothing I say or do is right. You're even different about sex: hyped up one minute but frigid the next."

"Frigid? I'm not the one—"

"If I were in a kidding mood, I'd ask if the devil ever possessed Jewish girls. Or maybe you're encouraging someone to get inside you."

Confessing infidelity was one thing, but being accused was something else entirely. Even if he'd guessed right. She fired back,

"This coming from the man who attracted a lovesick stalker in Atlanta?"

"I didn't try to attract her."

She slowed her breathing and the tempo of her thoughts. Making her voice low and calm, she said, "Joe, I'm sorry. You deserve a rational response, not cheap shots. I am not, repeat *not*, having an affair with some guy. I love no one but you." All true, no technicalities. Keep going. "I'm trying to make this work, but I need your help. You called to talk to me about this…situation of ours. So let's talk."

"I really don't want to discuss this 'situation' over the phone; I think I can deal with it better face-to-face."

"When will that be?"

"I don't know yet. There's still so much to do up here."

She waited for him to continue, but when he didn't, she asked, "So what else should we talk about?"

"I'm thinking about moving Monica in with us."

Sarah's first thought was she'd slept with the only other woman who'd entered their house. Maybe she was a sex maniac and needed to warn the twenty-something recluse. Then she had a vision of a true crazy person lurking around, skulking into their bedroom at night and staring down at them, taking up residence in her studio like a demented muse. She said, "We have enough problems without becoming her caretakers. She needs the psychiatric treatment and professional handling she's getting up there."

"Turns out she hasn't seen a therapist in years," he said. "She lied whenever I asked how her treatment was going. Dad lied to me, too. He caved in long ago when she said she wanted to stop. So there's nothing up here she'd miss."

"Except her house, which is everything to her. If you take that away, she'll curl up and die. Monica hasn't gone outside in over twenty years, right?" Sarah thought Joe might've had the same plan for her, to keep her safe from further harm, but it wouldn't help to bring that up.

He sighed and said, "I thought she was bluffing when she told me she'd die. She wants me to move back home; she says I can have the master suite, Dad's old room. Monica blames me for everything, but I'm still family."

"Well, what are her plans for me? Do I get to stay with you or is there a room for me in the basement? Or maybe she wants me to sleep with her. Um, bunk beds, I mean. Like sisters." Ay-yay-yay, where is my head? This is all turning to dreck.

"No basement, no bunk beds. I mentioned that we're having issues, so I guess she figured…"

Sarah pulled the covers over her head, hating the direction the conversation had taken. She said, "You're not seriously thinking about leaving me so you can move back in with your sister, are you?"

"I guess not, but she's so screwed up that being around her is making me crazy, too." He sounded exhausted, like a man surrendering after a long siege. Probably kept his eye patch on around the clock. "Sounds like another Greek tragedy. The survivors of my two worst decisions both claim me."

"Don't, Joe. You haven't wronged me or Monica. Those were accidents…bad luck…fate."

"If Monica moves in with us, I can provide for her, make amends in some small way." He grunted. "Then you can teach her about independence and how to break out of my 'prison.'"

"I'm not going there again—I already apologized for that. And I will not let her live here. That'll be the end of us."

"Then you can blame me for that, too, along with your leg."

"No. I'll never blame you for my wreck." The handset creaked in her tightened grip. "But if you bring her down here and throw away our marriage, Joseph, I will blame you forever." Having cheated on him, maybe she'd thrown it away already. Even if he was being a jerk, she still was the vow breaker, the adulteress.

His voice softened. "I don't want to ruin everything, Sare. But I feel like I'm trapped on a runaway train."

She took a breath and asked, "What do you really want? Don't answer me yet. Finish what you have to do up there, come home—alone!—and tell me. I'm not hanging up on you, or on us. I'm just giving you the space and time to think, because I love you and I know we still can have a beautiful life together. Think hard about this, Joe." There was silence at his end. She set the phone in its cradle.

Authoritative, affectionate, and dignified. A lover in control. Rita would have been proud. It was a good thing she was buried under blankets, because she wanted to punch a hole in the wall.

∽

Sarah finally forced herself from the bed, exhausted from analyzing every step of the conversation and deciding what she should've said, how she could've gotten a better result. She managed not to put her fist through any Sheetrock as she gathered her crutches and let Dorothy out to potty on the back lawn. Swing-stepping across the patio, she wondered whether she should call Rita or wait for her to phone. It had been over two years since she'd slept with someone new. What was the protocol again? Was it different when two women were involved?

She wanted to talk it out, so she figured Rita would, too. Back in her bedroom, she found her wadded shorts with her panties still inside: damning evidence of how eagerly she'd tossed aside her vows. She shrugged off her robe, dropped to her knees, and dug out the cell phone. In no time, she'd pulled up Rita's number.

Doing this bare-assed felt right; her body wasn't a stranger anymore. When she looked herself over, she saw potential. Sure, she'd have to keep working at it forever to get leaner and stronger, but she was headed in the right direction.

She'd buried herself under blankets when talking to Joe— if she'd spoken to him while exposed in every sense maybe she would've had a better attitude about herself and steered their conversation with more confidence. After all, Rita commanded respect with what she said and how she carried herself no matter what she wore. Her body projected that no-bullshit, woman-in-control authority better than any power suit. It was easy to imagine Rita conducting all her affairs in the nude.

Best not to think about that one. Focus!

Sarah rehearsed as she dialed and waited for her best friend to pick up. She certainly remembered those "You were wonderful last night, but it was a mistake" calls she'd made to boys when she was younger. The first part had never been true, of course. Then Joe came along, the perfect lover who became the perfect husband until everything suddenly went wrong.

What if Rita insisted they continue to explore their relationship, to see where it led? Sarah knew she'd have to ditch her altogether, which left Mrs. O'Malley as her only friend until she could meet new people. One good thing about her neighbor, though: there was zero chance of tumbling into bed with her.

Rita didn't answer. However, her luscious voice directed Sarah to leave a message, which she promised she would respond to at her earliest convenience.

"Hi, it's Sarah. Give me a call, OK? I really want to talk to you." Too encouraging, tone it down. "I mean, we need to talk about last night. You were amazing, and I'm so looking forward to working on your bust—the sculpture I mean—" Ay-yay-yay! "—but we really have to talk. I know I'm sounding meshugga, and I have no idea how to shut up. I'm hoping Dorothy will rip the phone out of my hand. OK, anyway, call me…OK?" She jabbed the hang-up icon and dropped face-first onto the carpet. What a disaster. Joe had been right about the problem with voicemail.

She wanted to retreat to her studio but knew an intense workout would do her good, even as sore as she was. After donning exercise clothes, she strapped on Fred and went for a five-mile run. The whole time, she replayed a highlight film of her day and night with Rita, interspersed with her recent conversations with Joe. The good, the bad, and the ugly.

Reminders of Rita were everywhere. For lunch she sampled leftovers of the takeout meal Rita had brought from the restaurant. Fortunately no more cake remained. They literally had dug into it around midnight, scooping out gooey handfuls and feeding them to each other while seated at the kitchen table. That had led to more hours of delirium and probably an incipient yeast infection.

After cleaning off the table and chairs, she decided to quit beating herself up with guilt and shame. Time to get lost in work on the sculpture. Even if she never wanted to sleep with Rita again, she would honor her for being an awesome mentor.

Unfortunately, the bust had not transformed itself overnight into a perfect likeness. She stroked and traced the blocky features. Every detail was crudely rendered, but the cool, moist clay held promise. The instructors on video warned at least a hundred hours of work would be needed just to get it ready for the plaster.

Standing behind the bust, Sarah drew a wire-wrapped scratching tool over the molded hair to add texture, and wiped clay from the tool after each stroke so the lines would remain clean. Whenever she gouged out too deep a chunk, she had to press in more clay and blend it with the surrounding textures.

Hours later, she shifted to one side of the bust and traced curves where the drape of hair overlapped an ear. At this rate, it would be Monday before she started to recreate Rita's bangs. Still, the effort felt worthwhile.

Meanwhile, the cell phone in her pocket stayed silent, no texts came in, and the house phones were mute as well. Maybe her best friend was running errands. It made sense—even very Southern, old-fashioned Aiken had plenty of stores open on Sunday afternoons. Maybe she still was deciding what to make of their night together. Maybe she was hooking up with Dylan again to get properly laid.

Chapter 27

THE HEAT AND HUMIDITY HAD EASED ON MONDAY morning, but Sarah still carried in her backpack a change of clothing, along with deodorant, a washcloth, and make-up to undo the effects of her bike ride into town. Although it made more sense to drive Joe's car, one look at her body in the bathroom mirror convinced her to keep working hard. Otherwise, the excuses would cascade until she had undone all her efforts.

After the seven-mile trip in gentle sunshine, she freshened up in the bathroom of a diner on Laurens, dressing in a short-sleeved blouse, slacks, and low heels. The kitchen prepared a special-order omelet of egg whites for her, which she chased with their fresh-squeezed orange juice. Five minutes early for her appointment, she locked her bike to a lamppost outside Dr. Teraphim's office and entered the dim, contemplative atmosphere of the waiting room.

The thin, androgynous therapist welcomed her at the appointed time with a smile and firm handshake. A coffee table separated them in a white-painted office lit with antique torch lamps and Scandinavian track lights. Dr. Teraphim sat across from her in an identical armchair with pen and pad.

Sarah had decided to focus on her problems with Joe; the affair with Rita was just a symptom. She launched into an explanation of Joe's guilt over her car wreck, their arguments, and her inability to get him to see her point of view on anything.

When she stopped to catch her breath, the therapist said in a soothing tone, "We'll get to all of that, I promise. Let's focus today's session on you. This is a marathon, not a sprint."

"I didn't run, I biked over." She lowered her face and sniffed herself. "Do I really smell that bad?"

"Certainly not," the woman said with a smile. "I was merely providing a metaphor. You mentioned your amputation. I'm impressed you can cycle."

"Sure, and I can jog and dance. I'll be teaching ballet after this. No pointe work, though." The woman asked more questions about living with the artificial leg and seemed genuinely interested, so Sarah finally removed her left shoe, took off her sock, and rolled up her pant leg. "Doctor, meet Fred."

Dr. Teraphim cocked her head. "It's interesting," she said, "that you've given your new limb a man's name."

"My prosthetist assured me that I'd partner with it like Ginger Rogers danced with Fred Astaire."

"So why not call your leg Ginger?"

Sarah turned her left knee, which rotated the shank and foot, and looked at the leg as she considered. "Maybe I saw myself as Ginger."

"So you were pretending to be someone else?"

"No, that's not it. Now I remember." Sarah crossed her legs, left over right, as she leaned forward in her chair. Cosmetic foam padding compressed against her right knee. She hadn't allowed the prosthesis to lie upon that leg even once before, but she wanted to run her hand down her residual limb and feel the transition over the socket to her artificial leg. "Joe started calling it 'Fred'—my new leg, this new part of me—and I just…ran with it."

Dr. Teraphim returned her smile and asked, "Would you consider giving the prosthesis a woman's name, like 'Ginger'?"

Sarah stroked her leg again: down the sock-and-liner-covered thigh to the knee, over the socket, and along the calf to the foot cover. "What if I say, 'My left leg,' instead?"

"That's a big step, if you'll pardon the expression, to suddenly accept it as your own. It's been 'Fred'—a different gender even— since January, and you've had only nine additional months to contemplate the loss of your natural leg."

"After nine months, maybe it's time to give birth to something new," Sarah said. "I've taken some big steps already." She tried it out: "This is my left leg. It's me. This is me." Her knuckles rapped the plastic socket. "It's my leg, and the only difference between mine and yours is I can take mine off below the knee whenever I want. It's an awesome feature, not a fault." Nodding, she said, "Yeah, I think I can work with that."

Dr. Teraphim pointed at her leg with her pen. "The big step is going from a plural to a singular. Do you see what I mean?"

"I think so. It's been me and the leg, me and Fred. Now it's just me." She stroked the foam-covered shank. It really didn't feel so bad propped over her right leg. Sort of comfortable. Then she thought of the reason she'd made the therapy appointment and shook her head. "Poor Joe," she said, "another change for him to adjust to. I've piled so much on him that he might insist on *us* going from plural to single again."

The therapist said, "My object is to give you the tools to manage those changes, so that you two become neither single again nor merely plural, but united. However, you can't determine how he chooses to react; you're only in charge of how you respond. Do you think he would accompany you here or even come on his own?"

"I don't know. I'm not even sure when I'll see him again. Or if I will."

∽

A few minutes before ten, Sarah left Dr. Teraphim's office with two pieces of homework: practicing new ways to express her feelings that could diffuse Joe's defensive reactions and a painting assignment to complete before the following Monday.

She headed down the street, reminding herself that she strode with her two legs, not one leg and Fred or Ginger or whatever. Both legs were hers.

Climbing the dim staircase to Barbara's ballet classroom, she found more than a dozen students slouched against the brick walls and perched on the steps. They told her the door was locked. One of the boisterous kids called out, "Miss Sarah, watch me spot and spin," and fought for room on the landing.

Some of the girls clapped when Sarah said she was their new assistant. The perfectionist traded nods with her and resumed her leg extensions, practicing tendus from a step in the exact middle of the stairwell.

Wendy, the auburn-haired leader of the noisy students, asked, "Why'd you want to, like, join this bunch of freaks and rejects?"

Fifty minutes of confession and frank discussion had left Sarah feeling bold. She said, "I'm different, too. Look at this." She stripped off her left shoe, sock, and even the mannequin-like foot cover, prompting some of the girls to yell, "Oh, gross." Revealing the J-shaped carbon foot produced even more exclamations. She performed a flawless tendu of her own and extended her left leg to let them gawk.

Wendy prodded the cosmetic foam on Sarah's calf, felt the keel of her foot behind the J, and declared her totally awesome. "So you're, like, one of the X-Men?"

The perfectionist had turned her white-blond head away, but couldn't hide her crying. When Sarah asked her why, she said, "You did everything right before. Why'd you have to show us that?"

"It's a part of me," Sarah said. "It's who I am. A dancer can't lie—our bodies always tell the truth." She tapped her carbon toe against the landing. "I can't do some of the things you can, and y'all need to know that. No matter how hard I try, I'll never be as good as you can be. If you don't work at it though," she said to Wendy and her minions, "I'll dance freaking circles around you."

Barbara swung open the door at street level and bounded up the stairs. Jangling a ring full of keys, she apologized for being late, but her pupils ignored her. Instead, they all looked at Sarah.

☙

Sarah got directions from Barbara so she could find the post office. She changed back into her sweaty cycling outfit and biked there before heading home. In addition to an electricity bill, some mutual fund statements, and catalogs, a small parcel sat in Joe's post office box. It was the spare remote control he'd ordered for the gate, so she wouldn't leave the property unprotected during her excursions. Redundant now that she'd commandeered his car.

His paranoia about safety now made her feel pity rather than anger: poor, trapped Joe, tearing at his body and mind for every unfortunate decision. Dr. Teraphim had warned her about the impulse to protect his feelings by reverting back to passivity, by trying to keep the peace. The therapist sounded a lot like her best friend. Pedaling past the open gate and up her driveway, Sarah gazed at the towering privacy fence and wondered if Joe had meant for it to shield not only her but protect them both.

After a wave to Dorothy, who batted the window in exaltation, she coasted into the huge, immaculate garage. Sweat dripped from her chin while she rolled up next to Joe's old Camry. She un-strapped her helmet, set it on the damp bike saddle, and let the backpack slide down her arms and onto the concrete pad.

Her cell phone pealed as she reached the door to enter the kitchen. She guessed it would be Rita this time and hoped they would have a laugh about their insane night together and her lame voicemail and then get back to normal. She missed talking to her. However, the screen showed her parents' number in Savannah.

She hadn't told her mother about the cell phone. A number of mental connections linked up as the phone clamored again for her attention. Joe must've given Mom the cell number one of the times he confided about their growing estrangement. Now Mom was calling to berate and skewer her again with guilt.

"Shit." Sarah wondered how soon the phone would quit ringing and record a message, but it cried out again and again, until she finally pressed the Talk icon. "Hello?"

"Sarah Lyn, this is your mother." No hint of the playful Borscht Belt accent. "It's my understanding that a mobile phone's purpose is to connect the caller with the intended party as rapidly as possible."

"Sorry, but my hands were full." Sarah took out her keys to go indoors. She had started with only the one for the house, but had since accumulated the Camry key and keys to the post box, her bike lock, and—that day—Barbara's ballet studio. The more complicated her life became, the more keys she acquired. Or vice versa.

Her mother said, "Why didn't you tell me about Joe's father passing?"

Sarah opened the door to the kitchen and stooped to rub the wiggling, grinning bulldog. "My fault again, Mom. It's been a little crazy around here." Dorothy batted with her forepaws and yapped for more attention.

"It sounds like you're running a kennel. Should I call back another time?"

"No, this is fine. I'll put Dorothy outside. Come on, girl." She closed the gate from the kitchen control panel and released the dog out back. Dorothy romped across the yard, scattering birds, while Sarah stood under a rush of cold air from a register in the dining room ceiling. She said, "Sorry for the interruption." Three apologies in less than three minutes. No more, she decided.

"If I have your undivided attention, can you please explain why your bereaved husband—that fine man I'd be honored to call 'son'—is grieving alone in Virginia while you're playing with your dog in South Carolina?"

Sarah raised her face toward the vent in hopes the chill would keep her calm. "It's simple: he didn't want me to go." Stretching her neck constricted her voice, which already sounded tight. She lowered her chin to her chest and said, "Isn't that what he told you?"

"He did, and get that tone out of your voice." She paused, and Sarah heard a knife chop through an onion. Whenever her mother was stressed, she cooked. "You know what I think about Nathan and his failed marriages. I could've happily murdered your father a hundred times over the years—" thwok went the knife "—but I never once considered a divorce."

"Don't worry, Mom, we're not that far gone. We've had a little setback, is all."

"You think? Joe was a little more blunt. I warned you before he might have one foot out the door. Now here he is in another state, dealing with all that chazerei, and he doesn't want you there to help." The knife cleaved something denser, maybe a potato. "Not good, Sarah Lyn. Not good at all."

Sarah felt the explosion rising within her. Then she recalled the positive-imagery technique Dr. Teraphim had recommended. She practiced a calm response, respectful but not pandering, to diffuse her mother's wrath. Not a Rita reply, but instead something with less bite and more of a chance for success.

Mom continued, "I said he deserved far better. And I told him not to be a stranger if you two parted."

"Wait, you want him to divorce me?" The air conditioning now felt too cold, and she retreated from the register shivering, her carefully prepared reply forgotten.

Angry chopping continued through the phone line. "I explained that I would understand the reasons for the failure and who was at fault. On behalf of our family, I apologized for the shameful treatment he's received." New background sounds, stirring things together in a bowl. Then a blender whirred. After a half-minute of noise, Mom said, "I'll never understand how you can be so unfeeling toward a man who's given you everything, especially a man in mourning who's already had terrible tragedies in his life."

Dorothy scratched at the lower panes of the French door and barked. Sarah had no idea how long the bulldog had been pleading to escape the afternoon heat. With Dorothy inside, she stepped outdoors and hurried across the shaded patio into the grass where sunlight beat down. Her sudden chills wouldn't go away.

She wished Dr. Teraphim sat in one of the wrought iron chairs, ready to advise her. From the whirlwind of her thoughts and emotions, she extracted another of the therapist's techniques, and said, "I feel sad that you told him that, Mom." No character assassination, only her feeling chosen from the four basic ones—mad, sad, glad, scared—in response to a specific, concrete action.

Mom's voice softened. "I don't expect you to approve, but surely you understand me."

"I understand that you've given up on us, but I haven't, and I won't." Sarah knew it was the wrong thing to say even before it left her mouth. It was meant to hurt and to put her above her mother. Just like that, she'd undone the effect of her earlier comment. She had to resist the urge to pinch herself.

"I haven't given up on you, child, but I'm preparing my heart for the worst." Small splashes were followed by sizzling, a familiar sound from childhood. Her mother was preparing her heart by making latkes.

Sarah watched a bird's flight over the south wall. Her gaze lingered on the peak of Mrs. O'Malley's roof. Her neighbor came off as mean-spirited and severe, but still felt pain and still reached out in friendship, doing the best she could with the mental baggage that encumbered her. Maybe that really was what most people did, her mother included.

Dr. Teraphim's lessons had been about ways to moderate conversations with Joe and diffuse his defensive reactions. Sarah realized she needed to apply those techniques to herself as well. Otherwise, she was just another part of the problem.

"I'm sorry for overreacting, Mom. I'm trying to make things better with Joe, I really am. I know it looks bad, but we'll work through this mishegoss and come out the other end as a stronger, happier couple. OK?"

"And if you don't, Feygela?" Fresh sizzling as she must've flipped over the potato pancakes. "What then?"

"Failure is not an option."

Her mother snorted. "Oy vey zmir. Man plans, God laughs."

"Maybe, but you know what happens when woman plans? God laughs with her, not at her."

"So what's your plan, Ms. Talmudic Scholar?"

"Step one is to make myself some latkes. They sound delish."

Chapter 28

NO CALLS CAME AFTER HER MOTHER'S, AND THE messages she left on Rita's cell phone went unreturned. The woman's "earliest convenience" wasn't soon enough for Sarah's liking, but she didn't make demands, only asked for a callback.

True to her word, she gave Joe space and time to think. She confirmed the flight schedules between Richmond, Virginia and Augusta, Georgia, the closest regional airport to Aiken. Each day at ten a.m. and six p.m., she wondered if he had arrived on the other side of the Savannah River and, if so, when a taxi would bring him home. So far, bupkes.

In her studio, she refined the bust of her best friend, using her most delicate wire tools to smooth the features, scraping off a hair's-width of clay with each careful stroke. The work proceeded faster than she'd thought—as promised, the sculpture seemed to be finishing itself.

She decided to split her artistic time between the bust and her homework for therapy. Her assignment was to depict herself full-length with as many colors as she wished. When planning the picture that had become "Freedom," she'd debated whether to portray anything below her waist, but now she painted her entire self in bright primary and secondary colors, her left leg the same red as her right.

Though she could stay busy working on her art and assisting Barbara's students, she also took early-morning walks with Dorothy, jogged alone through Eagle's Lair, and, after the ballet classes, cycled around Aiken. Each day, she picked a new direction to explore so that by Friday afternoon she'd traveled the four compass points and the main roads between them. Hopelands Gardens had provided a picturesque break during her travels, as had a few of the many sandy paths that crisscrossed Hitchcock Woods. When she wanted to paint landscapes, she'd have countless sources for inspiration.

She biked the south side of Aiken on Friday and followed Whiskey Road out of town, past the countless shopping centers and churches. After a stretch of open country, she spotted a development of low-slung office buildings on her right: the technology park that housed Matryoshka Engineering among other firms. On a whim, she pedaled through the parking lot, but didn't see Rita's SUV.

She arrived home in the middle of the afternoon, and rewarded herself with an extra-long shower after the bathroom scale reported her weight as 119.4 pounds. Closing in on 115. Maybe she'd set a new goal after that. Her legs still tingled from the bike ride, so she pampered them with a thorough shave and lots of coconut oil.

After cleaning the plastic socket, changing out the locking liner and compression socks, and reconnecting her leg with five solid clicks, she wandered into the kitchen to snack on a banana. Dorothy watched each mouthful, so Sarah nibbled off a morsel for her. The bulldog swallowed it, and then the tall ears stood up and her bony head swung in the direction of the living room. With a yelp, Dorothy bolted to the front windows where she barked and whined.

Sarah had closed the gate before letting Dorothy out earlier, so no one could've come up the drive. The monitor displayed Rita's Acura in shades of gray idling by the curb. Sunlight glared on the tinted windshield, obscuring Sarah's view of the interior. She thought she'd let her friend beg just a little before she admitted her, a small penalty for not responding to any of the messages.

Then the passenger door opened, and Joe stepped out.

He wore a wrinkled polo shirt and rumpled khakis. His black eye patch partially obscured his face. The early evening flight hadn't arrived in Augusta yet, but he could've taken a plane to

Columbia, two hours to the east. She'd neglected to look up flight schedules between the South Carolina and Virginia capitals.

It explained why she hadn't seen the gold SUV in the Matryoshka parking lot. Sarah caught herself fuming and practiced aloud, "I feel mad that you didn't call me when you planned to come home."

She dropped her half-eaten banana and its peel on the kitchen table, and watched Joe duck his head back into the vehicle. After a half-minute, he withdrew again, grimacing, and went around to the hatchback. The driver door remained closed with Rita inside. Sarah wondered if they were fighting. Perhaps her best friend once again had come to her defense and given Joe a tongue-lashing for his recent behavior.

He withdrew his suitcases from the back, the luggage tags still attached to them like the elongated outlines of teardrops. She was surprised she didn't feel the same relief and enthusiasm that had buoyed her during the first minutes of his Sunday phone call. Instead, using Dr. Teraphim's therapeutic vocabulary, she felt mad, sad, and, for some reason, scared.

Dorothy continued to howl from the living room, having heard or sensed Joe beyond the privacy fence. Sarah gave the bulldog some relief by opening the gate, which made him visible. She took a deep breath, stepped into the garage, and opened that door as well. While it slid overhead, she experienced the same butterflies she used to feel waiting in the wings, listening for her cue.

The opened gateway revealed Joe beside the rear of the SUV, his hand on the open hatchback, his eye patch dark against his pallor. Sarah trotted down the driveway in shorts and a V-neck top, noticing how he stared at her, as if checking out a stranger. Did he like what he saw? Was he shocked at how she exposed her left leg? Other questions overlapped in her mind as she considered the first thing she would say. With the suitcases at his feet, she could imagine him ready to leave home instead of just arriving, so she asked, "Are you here to stay?"

"I hope so. I left Monica well cared for." He looked her over again and said, "Your leg—"

"Your eye."

Wanting to start on a positive note, with a kiss and a hug, she reached for him. Joe ducked his head, cheeks reddening. She stopped and looked down as well. A breeze ruffled his black, wavy hair and the long tails of the luggage tags on which she read "AGS." He'd flown into Augusta, which meant he did so that morning at the very latest.

The air carried the hoppy odor of beer. Alcohol, he once said, made him lose control, so he never drank it. Now she had a reason to feel scared.

Her voice came out louder than she'd intended. "Oh, Joe, what did you do?"

Simultaneous clicks sounded from within the SUV—Rita had locked the doors. Questioning her now took priority. Joe swung the hatchback down, but Sarah caught the bottom edge and thrust it up again. She elbowed him aside, scrambled into the wide cargo area on her hands and knees, and closed the hatch, sealing herself in with Rita.

The woman turned in her seat, sunglasses hiding her eyes, and quickly faced forward again. She gripped the gear shift, and her thumb tapped the button that would engage the gears. After some apparent deliberation, she switched off the ignition.

Joe knocked on the rear window. "She's got nothing to do with this. It's me you're angry at."

Mad, sad, scared. Mostly mad. Fucking pissed, actually. Sarah climbed over the backseat without acknowledging him. Her left foot snagged on a seatbelt, but she'd watched for that and quickly extricated herself. With a secure grip on the seats up front, she hissed in Rita's ear, "We need to talk—my dear." She kicked feet-first into the forward cabin. Her sneakers thudded against the dashboard console, and she settled in the passenger seat.

Sarah said, "Hide behind those silly sunglasses all you want. I can stare you down regardless."

Rita set them on the dashboard, green eyes flashing. She wore a black miniskirt over bare legs, white high heels, and a matching tank top as snug as a leotard and just as revealing. The white blouse Sarah recalled from the sculpture session hung open over it, its collar upturned. All the silver jewelry was back in place; a chain curved over the tops of her breasts like beads of mercury. Rita said, "You're not acting in control, my…" She swallowed the word and cleared her throat. "This is your loose-cannon behavior come to the fore again."

"I see you wore black and white for both of us. Did you take this off for him, too?"

Joe tapped on Sarah's window and asked her to open the door, but she shook her head, not bothering to turn around. She would deal with him later. With the engine off and the sun blazing, the air became steamy. Her thighs made a moist tearing sound against the leather upholstery as she shifted to face Rita.

The woman hadn't been a mentor at all, merely a player. Rita had manipulated her from the very start, and she had been as impressionable as fresh clay. Like Dylan, she was just another conquest Rita had quickly tired of—overnight in fact. And then she'd seduced Joe to award herself bonus points.

Sarah said, "Whenever you knew we would get together, our first lunch date, modeling for me, you dressed in non-threatening outfits. No boobs on display, no bare legs in stilettos." She plucked at Rita's short skirt. "This is what you wear to get the men you want."

Rita lifted her chin. "I shan't discuss these matters when you're not in your right mind."

Sarah seized the woman's necklace and twisted her fist. Silver links dug into the skin of Rita's neck, and she tensed. "There comes a point," Sarah said, "when you gotta address the needs of the insane before someone gets hurt."

Joe pounded on the passenger window, shouting, "Don't, Sare. I'm the one to blame."

No, she thought, we all are, but to Rita she asked, "Is that true? Has Joe made a big mistake, or is this another unfortunate accident?"

Rita said nothing.

Sarah twisted further, pushing her knuckles against the base of Rita's throat. She leaned into the woman and trapped her left arm against the door while holding down Rita's right arm with

her free hand. The press of their sweaty bodies brought back
memories she tried to dismiss, but she had to admit that the
"mad" and "sad" she felt wasn't totally guilt-free. She also was the
cheat who had been cheated on, by her husband and her lover no
less. Rita gave both of us a tongue-lashing, she thought ruefully.

Joe came around to the driver side, calling her name. He tried
the door and beat his fists against the window. Sarah refused to
look at him. She told herself to focus on her former best friend.
That thought made her push in her fist harder, the links digging
deeper into her fingers as much as Rita's throat. Her knuckles
looked titanium white against the lustrous brown skin she'd
found so desirable.

Rita gasped. Tears clung to her lashes. "No, it's my fault," she
said, her voice a whisper. "He's so mixed up I could've coaxed
him into any sort of mischief."

"'Mischief'? I should strangle you for that." She gave her fist
a shake. "Did you always want him—for mischief?"

"At first I did."

"Of course. I remember what you'd said about your...tastes."
Joe had been the perfect fit all along: gorgeous, capable, and just
the sort of man who thought he was in control. Apparently her
taste in women ran to the complete opposite.

Joe yelled, "If you don't stop, Sare, I'll break a window."

Sarah kept her face inches from Rita's. "Will you talk to me,
or does he have to rescue you?" She shoved harder into her.

"I'll talk," Rita croaked.

Sarah leaned back and released the woman. To Joe she held
up her hands, as if in surrender. He gaped at her. "Go inside, Joe,"
she called. "We'll talk later." He didn't move, so she screamed,
"Goddammit, go."

He retreated around the SUV, grabbed his bags, and slunk up
the driveway. Rita had gone from massaging her neck to covering
her ears. She lowered her hands and asked, "Are going to keeping
yelling, or will you go back to throttling?"

"Count yourself lucky I don't take off my leg and fucking
beat you to death." Sarah stretched her fingers and rubbed her
hands together to restore circulation. "And speaking of fucking,

did you ever tag Joe before you seduced me, or was I so bad that you decided to shtup him out of revenge?"

Rita cleared her throat and touched it again. "He never gave me the chance until today. I'd made a number of plays for him, but he always deflected or demurred and talked about the importance of his wedding vows." She smirked. "You were *easy*, my dear."

She raised her hands defensively, but Sarah didn't feel like attacking her again—she wanted answers now, not blood. "He asked you to meet him at the airport this morning?"

"Joe called me every day this week, trying to sort out his feelings for you. He scattered his father's ashes yesterday in the Potomac, near where his mother died, and I talked him into flying home. He came back for me, not for you."

Even when talking crap, she sounded sure of herself. Sarah had to give her credit for that. There still was so much she could've learned from her. Such a waste. She said, "If he came back for you, he wouldn't be here. Y'all still would be shacked up in your favorite hot-sheet motel."

The SUV interior had become a greenhouse, the glass nearly opaque with condensation and the air stifling. Rita folded her arms and stared at the fogged windshield. She said, "Do you think I have so little class? I took him to lunch at the Partridge Inn in downtown Augusta. Beautiful old hotel with an elegant dining room—"

"Skip the menu." Sarah wiped sweat from her face and smeared her hands across the leather upholstery. "You poured beers into him, leaned across the table with those perfect tits, and said, 'Let me get you a room, my dear, so you can rest a while.'"

Rita grimaced. "Essentially. He needed me, someone who would listen to him without judging."

"What he needed was to come home to his wife, not stumble into an even worse screw-up." Sarah raked her fingers through her wet hair. "You know, the fact that my dog hates you should've told me something long ago."

Perspiration dappled Rita's skin. Rivulets traced meandering paths from her face, down her long neck, and left wet streaks on her chest. She said, "I don't know about you, but it's too hot in here even for me. How can you stand to be pent up for so long?"

"I'm used to it."

Rita started the ignition and turned the air conditioner to its highest setting. With a murmur barely audible above the roaring fan, she said, "Very well. Where were we?"

"You were just about to screw my husband."

"Heavens, you're relentless. I'm afraid—there's that phrase again, like a disease you've given me." Rita inhaled, wiped her upper lip, and tried again. "Unfortunately, I didn't know the alcohol would impair him so. His eye went haywire, and all he could do was blather about you."

"Is that all he could do?"

"Not quite." She stared at Sarah. "I finally got what I wanted, but he was displeased with his performance." A note of pride returned to her voice when she added, "That's not to say he didn't enjoy himself—if you'll recall, I do know a thing or two."

The last detail hurt the worst. Sarah hugged herself and folded into the leather seat. Frigid air blew on her wet, burning face. She asked, "Did you tell him about us?"

"Certainly not. I had enough trouble keeping him focused on the task at hand." Rita stroked her throat. "But rest assured I will now. If you're as incompetent with him as you were with me, it's a wonder he still wants to shag you."

"You are such a total bitch."

"Don't you recall my lesson about that word? Do you remember any of the treasures I shared?"

Sarah closed her eyes. "I remember everything, damn you. *Everything.* So I can't understand why you want to destroy me."

"'Destroy'? I created you! I took a girl going nowhere and made you into a self-assured, powerful woman. You think you could turn on me with such confidence if I hadn't believed in you first?"

"I was doing fine on my own. I'd taken the reins and headed in a new direction long before you showed up."

"You would've never reached this point without me. You'd still be running circles inside Joe's gated rat maze. In fact, I think you should return there now."

The electronic locks popped. Sarah's eyes opened as Rita collided against her. One of the woman's hands pushed the door wide and the other shoved Sarah out. She twisted and landed on her back. Her head bounced against the pavement, streaking her vision with a flash of light.

Rita dropped back into her seat, shoved the vehicle in reverse, and jammed down the accelerator. The squealing front tire drove over Sarah's left foot, making her knee torque in its socket and flare with pain. The open door passed inches above her face.

Behind her, the Acura continued its jackrabbit start and shot backward up the street, the door still ajar. A crash of metal on metal caused Sarah to roll over and blink until her eyesight had cleared. At the end of her neighbor's driveway, the rear of the Acura had crushed the back door and fender of Mrs. O'Malley's Cadillac.

Glass littered Tangletree Drive. A hubcap rolled in a slow death-spiral on the street. Its gyrations and noise quickened before it fell flat. In the front seat of the Cadillac, the old woman held her neck with both hands and shrieked. Despite the sounds of agony, her face looked radiant. Triumphant.

Rita curled her arms over the Acura steering wheel and laid her forehead against them. Sarah got to her knees, wincing at the fire that coursed through her left leg, and struggled to her feet. The tire had blackened her left shoe. She took an experimental step and thought something felt wobbly inside the foot cover, but she still could walk on it.

Hobbling toward the wreck, she wondered how long Mrs. O'Malley had waited with half of her car jutting into the road. Joe's shouting probably had gotten her attention, and she saw an opportunity. Despite the agonies of the past half-hour, Sarah smiled, imagining her cagey neighbor in court with a neck brace and every other piece of convalescent gear she could assemble. The police report the senior citizen already had filed about Rita's reckless driving would be Exhibit A.

Chapter 29

MRS. O'MALLEY CATERWAULED FROM THE Cadillac interior and continued to play her role long after Sarah had dialed 911 on her cell phone and told her neighbor the police and EMTs were on their way. Both times she passed the SUV, Rita refused to look up.

Joe wandered onto the driveway. He had showered, shaved, and changed into a clean, tight polo shirt and pressed slacks, looking like a sports model except for his eye patch.

She rehearsed the therapy script: I feel mad when you have sex—even bad sex—with another woman. And I feel sad and mad at myself because I had sex—albeit really good sex—with the same woman, even if she didn't think so. Not a helpful start. Hold it together now, with wit and grace and control. Not all of Rita's lessons were dreck.

Maybe she'd needed the woman once, to give her a kick-start, but not anymore. Limping despite her best efforts, she met Joe halfway and told him what had happened.

"She drove over your foot?" He looked down and pointed at the blackened shoe. "You mean Fred."

"I mean my foot. It's part of me."

Joe seemed to consider that and then nodded, his hands balling into fists. "I'll kill her," he said. He started toward the gate.

She seized his shoulder, which had gotten even more muscular, yet another layer of armor added. "Go inside. You hear those sirens?" She turned him to face her. "An ambulance and the police are coming. You're not going to kill her, and you'll end up having to stand there while she talks to the cops about how she spent her day and what brought her to our home. Do you really want that?"

"But Fred—your foot, I mean. She needs to be held accountable for that."

"I'll make a deal with her: she never mentions today to your boss or coworkers or anyone else, and I won't press charges."

"You'd protect me? Even after…" He looked away.

"Go inside, Joe. Let me handle this, and then we'll talk." So many biting comments had come to mind, but this seemed to be the best, if not the most satisfying, thing to say. She stepped past him, clenching her jaw at the pain in her knee, and headed back to the street.

Neighbors she'd never seen before had come outside to gawk at the wreck and crane their faces toward the sound of emergency vehicles making their way through the subdivision. She stopped beside Rita's window and waited. The woman glanced at her and finally buzzed it down a few inches.

Sarah said, "You might have felt a wee little bump as you made your getaway. That was your tire crushing my left foot." Rita's horrified cringe told her she was listening. "The problem is, I never want to see you again, on the street or in the courtroom. So here's the deal. You never speak of, write about, or otherwise communicate anything involving either Joe or me to *anyone*— meaning you don't tell Joe about you and me either—and I won't sue your ass for every dime you have or tell the cops what you did to me. Got it, my dear?"

Rita muttered, "Agreed," and returned her forehead to the steering wheel.

Again, there was so much more to stay. So many parting shots to take. But what was the point of motivating Rita to go back on her word? This way, Sarah thought, I can tell Joe about the affair on my own terms and in my own time. He would need to know someday, wouldn't he?

While emergency medical technicians attended to Mrs. O'Malley's many health complaints, the police talked briefly with Sarah. The officer's gaze kept straying to the socket and cup halfway up her left leg, until she told him, "I lost it in a car accident. I recognized the sounds of impact immediately—when Ms. Bolivar carelessly plowed into that sweet old lady."

Another officer took Mrs. O'Malley's tearful statement. The police then spent a long time interrogating Rita and writing tickets. Not once did she look at Sarah, who recalled another BV Islander proverb the woman once had told her: No matter how fast moonlight runs, daylight catches up.

Mrs. O'Malley beamed at Sarah when the EMTs returned to the ambulance. They hauled out a gurney to secure the senior for her ride to the hospital. Sarah made a mental note to bring a huge bouquet when she visited her neighbor there. Once the door to the hospital room had closed to witnesses, she would give the con artist a great big hug.

ℰↃ

After tow trucks had hauled away both vehicles, the ambulance had departed with Mrs. O'Malley, and the police had escorted Rita home, Sarah limped up the driveway. Having dealt with her former best friend, she wondered if she could summon the energy to step back into the ring for fifteen rounds with Joe.

Dorothy greeted her in the kitchen with yips and wiggles. The half-eaten banana was missing from the table, and Joe had tidied the rest of the kitchen as well. From the direction of the master bedroom, a vacuum cleaner whirred.

She decided that she couldn't talk to him yet. Not until he'd satisfied his compulsion to return the house to order, and she'd considered what she really wanted to say. The mad, sad, glad, scared stuff just didn't seem adequate. And when would she ever be glad again?

In the hallway, on the way to her studio, Joe ambushed her. He had switched off the vacuum and now blocked her path, no longer wearing the black patch. His gaze held hers with brown eyes that once had prompted fantasies about swimming naked in pools of chocolate. Now they merely looked flat, bloodshot, and weary.

Welcome to the fucking club. Probably not the best choice of words, since I joined the "fucking" club first. I definitely need more time to plan my speech.

He asked, "Did the cops haul her away?"

"Say her name."

"Rita, OK?"

"No, it's not OK," Sarah said. "And no, they didn't. Just took her home. Probably thought it was their lucky day, with the way she had dressed. For you." I feel mad, no, homicidal, when you stick your—

"Do you wish they could arrest me?"

"Look, I know you've sobered up, and now you're ready to confess and take your punishment. Well, I'm not ready. I need to think before we talk." She edged past, now slender and nimble enough to slide by without contact, even with her limp.

"You can't think on an empty stomach. Let me make you dinner."

"Dinner? Oh for God's sake, Joe." She shook her head in disgust, banged into the studio, and shut the doors behind her.

After Dorothy demanded entry, Sarah admitted her and then blocked the doors again with the couch. Rita waited for her on the worktable. The life-size clay bust bore a startling likeness to the woman. A few tweaks—details gleaned from long, close confinement with Rita that afternoon—and the work of art could've been flawless. Instead, Sarah hefted her mallet and aimed for a blow between the sightless eyes.

She didn't follow through.

"Shit." She chewed her lip and raised the mallet higher.

Again she couldn't bring herself to destroy the sculpture. Her emotions leaped between two extremes: enthrallment with the beauty of it and hatred of the person it depicted. In the end, she traded the mallet for a wire-end tool and set about refining the jaw line and the contours of the nose. She rehearsed the steps for plaster casting while her hands perfected the portrait. Beyond her studio, Joe resumed vacuuming.

The process of making a waste mold would ruin the clay sculpture, but could yield a sellable plaster bust. If the cast didn't come out well, she would have to be satisfied with obliterating every inch of it. A win-win situation.

When the image resembled Rita exactly, Sarah spread drop cloths and yellowed newsprint around her work area. From beneath her table, she removed porcelain pans and a bottle of bluing to color the innermost layer of the mold. Upon chipping down to blue plaster, she would know that the finished piece was less than an inch from her chisel.

She opened a bag of fine gypsum, fetched large bottles of distilled water from her paint area, and found her tin snips and large squares of aluminum. To section off the mold for easier assembly and extraction, she cut metal shims to press into the clay, the first step in the regrettable destruction of the sculpture.

Her memory reeled off the other items needed. If she lost herself in work, she would stop imagining Rita and Joe in the hotel room and also stop recalling herself and Rita in their bedroom and elsewhere. Self-righteous anger kept turning inward.

Joe knocked on the studio doors, prompting a startled bark from Dorothy on the couch. "Sare, we did this once already. I hear you banging around, and I know you're working on your art, but we need to talk. I want to get past this."

"I told you I can't do that right now." She wanted everything at hand before starting to work, so she also took out the items she'd need for washing the waste mold once she cleaved it from the clay bust: liquid green soap, her grandfather's old shaving brush with its wooden knob darkened from generations of use, and a softer brush for smoothing oil over every surface the fresh plaster would touch. Oil—she needed olive oil from the kitchen and would have to go through Joe to get it.

She set Dorothy on the floor and shoved the couch away from the doors. Joe pushed them open. He asked, "Does this mean you'll talk?"

"It means I need olive oil." She came around to him, closer than she wanted, to distract him from the sculpture. "Would you please get that for me?"

"Sure." He turned away, but then faced her again. "What's going on?"

She shrugged and said, "Just working. You used to be happy to help me. No more Mr. Nice Guy, huh?"

"What do you need olive oil for? Are you making a salad back here?" He scanned the studio. When he looked over her shoulder, his face fell. "God Almighty, it's like she's staring right at me. When did you make that?"

Sarah tried to block his line of sight, wishing she had thrown cheesecloth over the sculpture. "She modeled for me last Saturday, and I've worked on it all week. It's not some piece of voodoo I whipped up in the last hour."

"It's wrong to have that in the house." His fists clenched as he looked past her.

"It's wrong that you…Joe, I feel mad that you slept with her. Mad and sad and scared. I feel hurt and betrayed. Say you're sorry if it'll make you feel better, but I can't feel better right now. Right now, I need to work on my art."

"We have to destroy that thing, Sare." He marched around the end of the couch. "My memories are bad enough without—"

He moved fast. To head him off, she took two quick steps and vaulted over the couch, as much a hurdler as a ballerina executing a grand jeté. She landed hard on her left foot and heard it pop as she stumbled. Her leg shrieked with pain as Dorothy barked at them. Blocking Joe and blinking back tears, she thrust out her arms to keep him away from the sculpture. "It's art. Something that came from inside me."

Joe muttered, "We need to tear it apart." When he tried to race around her, she sidestepped with speed and grace despite being hobbled, old ballet moves coming back to her. She stood toe-to-toe with him again and glared, ready for anything.

Joe said, "I tried to wash her off me, to get clean. I'll even burn the clothes I wore." He dug his fingers into his scalp. "Then all that's left will be what's trapped in my mind and whatever she told you. But having that…that perfect likeness—"

"It's mine. I made it." She shoved him back a step. "It's not yours to destroy."

Joe stretched past her shoulder with a long reach. She tried to pivot, but something glued her in place. He was standing on her left foot.

She couldn't pull her shoe from under him. With his left arm, he pinned her against him in a desperate hug. Tears coursed down his face as his right hand flailed at the sculpture. Sarah yelled at him to stop and tried to move again, turning her left knee inward. The stub of her leg twisted in the socket and her knee ground against the unyielding shell. She screamed at the intensified pain and kept screaming when her forefoot snapped with a sharp bang.

Ruptured carbon fibers crackled, sounding like a sock full of straw. Joe stumbled back as she fought for balance. They both stared at her left foot. Any weight she put on it caused a rustling of splintered edges.

Dorothy retreated behind the couch as Joe sank to his knees. He whispered, "Oh God, Sare, what did I do to you?"

His exotropia had returned. When he tilted up his tearstained face at her, his right eye squinted at the sculpture of Rita, off to the side. He repeated the question to himself.

Sarah leaned back against the worktable for balance. For a hysterical instant, she thought bones in her left foot had broken. She too began to cry. Knives seemed to tear at her left leg from hip to stub. The agony soon distilled her whirling emotions into a single feeling, as focused as a laser.

Seizing the heavy mallet she'd discarded earlier, she said, "Here, damn you." She threw it in front of him. "You broke my body and my heart. Now take a whack out of my soul."

He hung his head. Trembling fingers balled into a fist. Fast and hard, he punched the mallet head. Once, twice, three times. The skin over his knuckles swelled.

Sarah shouted, "This isn't about your pain. Don't you dare make this about you." Joe cupped his injured hand, head still bowed. Using the table edge for support, the sculpture of Rita close behind her, she crossed her left leg over the right like a stork. She removed the shoe, pulled the sock free, and let them fall away. The foot cover and protective sheath came next. She slid them off to reveal the damage.

The fracture crossed her forefoot, just past the bolts that attached the heel to the J-frame. A jagged white line scarred the ebony finish across the top. Underneath, she felt the break where a thousand tiny splinters grated together. She threw the foot cover, hitting him squarely in the chest.

He pressed the sole of the hollow foot over his heart. His voice remained a whisper. "I'll leave a message for Dr. Ramos tonight, and Fed-Ex the…your leg to him tomorrow. God, look what I did. I can't believe how much I've hurt you."

"Believe it." She wiped her eyes. "You're always taking the blame for things that aren't your fault. Now, in one day, you've screwed up more than you have in your whole life."

"I'm so sorry, Sare."

"That's it? Do you expect me to forgive and forget?"

"Could you ever do that?" His wandering eye closed in the glare of the overhead lights.

"No, you've gone too far. If you were on fire right now, I think I'd let you burn."

Joe closed his other eye and nodded. He continued to kneel, the foot clutched against him, while she removed the prosthesis. She tossed it before him with a clatter. Instead of picking it up, he scrambled to his feet and rolled a chair to her. Rita had last sat in it while Sarah sculpted her. The woman's mark seemed to be everywhere. He said, "Sit here. Please. I'll get your crutches."

Reluctant to accept any kindness from him, she hesitated. It would be so easy to keep pouring on the acid comments and hateful looks, but what terrible things did he do that she hadn't done already? She'd cheated first. Her foot wouldn't have broken if Rita hadn't driven over it, which wouldn't have happened if she had stayed on guard. To blame him as the root cause for everything would be satisfying, but it wouldn't be right.

He stood at the ready, bracing the chair so it wouldn't move when she sat. She'd never seen a person look more contrite, more consumed with guilt and remorse. Sarah sat and removed the prosthetic stocking and the gel liner with its protruding ratchet pin, turning the sheath inside-out as she pulled it down her leg.

Joe left the room, carrying the shattered prosthesis. The

bulldog eased over and sniffed the discarded dressings. Sarah's right foot brushed the empty space under her bare left knee. She'd grown accustomed to touching her shoes together. With tears stinging her eyes again, she said, "Dorothy, I can't click my heels together anymore." There's no place like home? Yeah, right. There's no place like home for nonstop nightmares.

In a few minutes, Joe returned with his eye patch in place again, bearing her favorite crutches, which he propped against the worktable. He kept his face turned away from the sculpture as if the head of Medusa sat there, ready to turn him to stone. Crouching, with his face level to Sarah's, he said, "I moved some of my things into the guest bedroom and bath."

She didn't respond, so he continued, "I'll stay there as long as you want me to, or move out entirely. It's your decision alone." He stumbled on the last word, choking up. "Do you want that olive oil now?"

"No. Nothing else from the kitchen either."

He grimaced and nodded. "Is there anything I can take care of?"

"I think you've done enough for one day." She pressed the rubber tips of the crutches against the floor and levered herself upright, thankful he didn't touch her to lend support as the chair rolled backward. Sarah swing-stepped away from him, rounded the couch, and left her studio. She considered warning Joe not to touch the clay artwork, but decided that it didn't matter anymore. Did anything matter now?

Dorothy followed her into the master bedroom and settled in the dog bed against the wall with a sigh. Sarah echoed the bulldog's exhalation while she nudged the door closed with a crutch tip. She turned the lock on the brass knob. After a meditative shower, where she mostly let the water cascade over her shoulders and scalp, she propped her crutches against the hall tree by her side of the bed. According to Joe, the marriage bed now was hers alone.

Do I want it? Do I want anything here? Joe and Rita are everywhere. Would it be better just to take Dorothy and start over again somewhere new? Mom was right—I don't have anything of my own. But maybe that makes me free.

She shut off the light and slid under the sheets. Staring at the dark ceiling, she wondered what she needed more: the strength to stay or the courage to go.

✑

Phantom pains woke her late on Saturday morning. No epiphany had come to her during sleep, no clear direction. She wondered what she and Joe would do on Day One after his affair. And when would the calendar flip back to a new Day One, after she confessed her own affair? Remembering that definitely helped to keep her anger in check.

She put on an old blouse and running shorts from before she'd met Joe. Both were snug but provided good reminders to stick to her diet, since serious exercise would be difficult until her leg was repaired. She wouldn't be able to cycle to her Monday appointment with Dr. Teraphim And she'd be useless in the ballet class. Shit, shit, shit.

She chose not to wear her rings. Keeping her "mad" under wraps only went so far. If he felt sad and scared as a result, that was good—not feeling those things probably meant they were through.

In the studio, Joe had taken away her prosthetic accessories and returned the couch to its original place against the wall. He'd left the sculpture unscathed. Rita looked at Sarah with a frank gaze that reminded her of their faceoff in the Acura. Swing-stepping around the bust, she didn't see anything she would change. She decided to create the plaster portrait that day.

Sarah let Dorothy out back and stood for a minute in the sunshine, the flagstone patio already hot under her bare right foot. Joe opened the doors behind her. He'd dressed in jeans and a work shirt. His face was pale, the skin tight and dark around his eyes. "I didn't want to do any yard chores until you were up," he said, staring at the rounded stub of her leg. "The mower can make a racket."

Sarah nodded, lips pressed together. If she didn't speak to him on Day One, would Day Two be any easier between them?

Inhaling the humid air, she forced herself to look into his eyes and say, "That was considerate. Thank you."

"I'm glad you're sleeping well. I remember when the only thing…" He looked away from her, swallowed, and called to Dorothy, who ignored him. "She never minds me anymore," he said. Together, they watched the bulldog slowly stalk a dove. "What would she do if she ever caught one of them?"

"Kill it," Sarah replied. "It's an instinct."

"What does your instinct say to do?"

The dove made its rapid, distinctive peeping as it took off well ahead of the canine threat, and disappeared over the ivory privacy fence. She said, "It tells me not to get into this with you right now."

"I can't trust mine." Joe shaded his eyes as he gazed at his garden. "If I do the opposite of what my gut says, I'm forced to agree with you."

"'Forced'?" She turned on him and rebalanced with her crutches and foot. Discomfort caused by the hot flagstones added to her fury. Her instinct flipped. It told her to go to war.

She asked, "Have you been 'forced' to do any of the things you're regretting?"

"No." His voice remained somber but calm. "I'm sorry I broke Fred, I mean, your foot."

"You know damn well I'm not just talking about that."

"I admit that I've been making my decisions with something like tunnel vision."

"Sure," she said. "Looking straight through the tunnel of your dick."

He took a step back and held his hands up in surrender. "Nothing ever happened with anyone until now. And if I hadn't gotten drunk and out of control yesterday, all you'd be pissed about is me catching a lift home with Rita instead of you."

"No, screwing Rita is the biggest thing, but don't pretend it's the only thing. You'd already hurt me so much." Her eyes stung, but she refused to give in to tears. Dr. Teraphim's suggestions for productive discussions that avoided argument occurred to her much too late.

"Sare, I'm sorry. I was wrong and stupid. I can't bear to lose you."

"You mean you can't bear to let me get away."

Dorothy padded up to her, panting in a huge grin. Sarah ushered the bulldog through the doorway and preceded Joe into the house. He said, "Take your shots. I deserve it. Never wear your rings again; it doesn't matter. I still want us to be together."

She pivoted to face him. Leaning on her right crutch, she pointed the left one like a rifle. "Why? Why did you have sex with Rita?"

"Men always say their affairs have nothing to do with their wives. But this had everything to do with you."

"I'm not hearing an actual reason."

He said, "I thought you'd stopped loving me."

"And you thought this might help?" She set her crutch back in place and leaned hard against the foam pads, already exhausted by the argument. His logic and excuses seemed warped until she admitted she'd pretty much told herself the same thing before yielding to Rita.

"I didn't think you'd find out. I guess I have that in common with all the other cheaters. But I'd lost my confidence with you. I figured if I could please another woman, maybe I could find out how to make you happy again."

How could a smart man could act so dumb? "Rita told me she was not pleased. So you cheated on your spouse and disappointed your lover." Ditto for me, she told herself. God, this is complicated. She took a breath and asked, "Where does that leave you?"

"Begging for mercy and forgiveness."

"Did you really think I stopped loving you?"

"I did, until I saw how you attacked Rita. You wouldn't have been that ferocious if you didn't still care about me." His face betrayed his hopefulness.

"Caring is not the same as loving," she spat. "You taught me that."

So much for Day One.

Chapter 30

SARAH CRUTCHED INTO THE KITCHEN AND collected the olive oil for her plaster-casting. A receipt on the kitchen table showed a Federal Express shipment intended for Dr. Ramos in Atlanta, with delivery scheduled for Monday morning. True to his word, Joe had shipped her prosthesis for repairs.

The patio door closed and soon he slouched past the bank of windows, choosing to go all the way around to the garage rather than follow her into the kitchen. Soon, his riding lawnmower thundered to life, and he passed by again, his face now shaded with a baseball cap as he sat upright on the machine. Back and forth he drove across the Bermuda grass, the sight of him always preceded by the roar of the engine. Looking for signs and omens, she found them everywhere.

She scanned through a couple of videos in the study to make sure she understood the steps and had everything at hand. The incessant noise from Joe zipping past kept intruding on her concentration.

He'd completed the front yard by the time she was ready to mix the forty pounds of plaster she estimated that she would need. From her chair, she glanced outside to Joe's garden, which he approached carrying a pitchfork. He considered his stagnant compost heap for a moment and drove the tines into the thick mass he hadn't turned for many weeks. Sarah turned away, but looked back when she heard his sudden cry.

Joe scrambled toward the house as if someone had opened fire on him. He beat at his head so hard he knocked off his ball cap. Below his screams came the long, deadly bass note of a swarm.

Yellow jackets rose by the hundreds from the untended compost heap where they had made their nest. Joe flailed at his scalp and swiped at his shoulders and neck as he ran across the lawn, but the insects soon enveloped him.

Sarah quick-stepped down the hall, catching brief glimpses outdoors as she passed each room. So many of the creatures pounced on his skin and clothes that he began to disappear within a murderous cloud of black and gold. The same scream that had come from Joe now rose in Sarah's throat as she willed herself to go faster. Dorothy beat her to the French doors, which provided the only access to the backyard.

Doorknobs rattled in her grip as she tried to wrench them open. Joe had locked up as usual. Sarah sorted her keys in trembling hands and opened one in time to see him collapse facedown under the onslaught.

Screaming his name, she crutched across the patio. Sun-baked flagstones singed her bare foot. Even more yellow jackets rose from the skewered compost heap and added to the terrifying buzz. Their basso profundo droning and Joe's cries formed a nauseating chorus. It sounded like a song of death.

Curled on the ground, Joe continued to swat at his head and neck, but his movements had slowed. Yellow jackets covered his hands. She considered drowning them with the garden hose, but he kept it on a reel, stored in a large box. It would be impossible to handle quickly without the leverage of two legs. If she wanted to save him, she had to enter the swarm.

Yellow jackets zipped past and circled Sarah as she hobbled closer. Then they started to attack. Front mandibles bit hard and a straight stinger in the rear of each insect jabbed over and over. Unlike a bee's, it didn't tear loose. The bites hurt like skin pinched by tweezers, but the stings felt worse. Each one seared with the pain of a cigarette burn. Her face and neck and arms and legs caught fire.

Unable to fend off the relentless insects with her hands full, she cast the crutches aside and launched herself at Joe. His cries had become one long wail, and his movements had turned spastic. Either he'd given up or the venom was sending him into shock.

She narrowed her eyes for protection and brushed and slapped at the yellow jackets on her skin. Squashing a few increased the fury of the rest. Even after she'd smashed them, the burning, chewing sensations continued everywhere they had landed. Her whole body blazed, but she turned her hands to helping Joe. The buzzing reached a crescendo.

"Get up," Sarah shouted, and swiped yellow jackets from around her lips. The thought of them in her mouth and throat terrified her. "You have to run!"

She grabbed his shirt collar and the loops on the back of his jeans, crushing a dozen insects in her fists, and hauled him to his knees beside her. So many stings and bites had swollen his face it was unrecognizable. With her single foot planted, she shoved him upright and used his body for balance. Yellow jackets roared in her ears and crawled through her hair and inside her clothes.

Joe staggered toward the open door, slapping once more at his head. His hair was shiny with iridescent wings and jagged gold stripes. "Go on," she yelled, now clinging to him for support as she tried to hop alongside. She stubbed her toes on the flagstones and started to fall.

"Sare!" He encircled her waist and hauled her up against him. Together, they lurched toward the door. All the while, the yellow jackets attacked.

Sarah swatted at the creatures with her free hand while she maintained a hold around Joe's middle. Welts burned all over her, but they didn't compare to the hives that covered Joe. Between swollen lids, his exotropic eye wedged in its outer corner, looking at her.

They left a trail of crippled and pulverized insects on the patio. Dorothy snapped at low-flying yellow jackets until Sarah yelled at her to get inside. They followed the bulldog into the dining room, and she pushed the door shut.

Most of the swarm had regrouped around the compost heap, but dozens of the creatures still clung to them or zipped around the room. She said, "Cold shower, fast." They needed to ease their inflammation and drown the diehard monsters. Joe tried to carry her up the hallway, but he had weakened. His breath trailed out in thin wheezes, the sound of a man suffocating as his windpipe closed.

She used him for balance again as she hopped alongside and guided him to the guest bathroom he'd begun using the night before. They helped each other into the tub, and she turned on the shower. Cold water hit the top of her head like a giant icicle.

Sarah pulled Joe into the frigid stream. She held open her shirt and shorts to wash out the insects. Wherever she saw one, she slapped it dead, and when they were gone, she pried lumps of drowned and squashed creatures from his hair and then hers. Black and yellow bodies swirled around their knees and disappeared down the drain. The icy water reduced the swellings on her body, but Joe was too far gone. She stripped off his shirt, popping buttons, and gasped at the lumps that covered him.

Every crimson welt showed countless bites and stings. She cried, "Oh God, look what they did to you." An echo of his words from the night before.

"The burning." He dug at his scalp. His tongue had swelled, making his voice thick. "It's like they're still all over me."

"They're finished," she told him, feeling the lingering pains as well. "Stay in the cold water. I'll get something for the bites. Will you be all right?" He nodded, his swollen face as grotesque as a gargoyle. She crawled over the edge of the tub and used the doorknob to hoist herself. A few yellow jackets crouched on the walls, no longer aggressive without the swarm's protection. With flicks of a hand towel, she knocked each one down and killed them all.

Water drained from her hair and clothes. Blinking through the rivulets, she used the walls for balance and hopped to the master bathroom, her skin blazing with pain. She grabbed another set of crutches, her cell phone, and a box of allergy medicine and returned to Joe. He continued to kneel in the tub under the icy spray, no longer moving.

Perched on the tub edge, she forced antihistamines down his throat to combat his reaction to the venom and to further reduce the inflammations. She swallowed some of the pills, too, and chased them with a palm full of cold water. After dropping to her knees beside the tub, she turned on her cell phone and called for help.

The female 911 operator told her, "We'll have to send a unit from Augusta. Every EMT, firefighter, and officer in the area is responding to a big traffic pileup there in Aiken."

"There's no time. He won't be able to breathe much longer."

"Then the fastest way will be for you to drive him to Aiken Regional. I'll call them and make sure they're standing by."

Joe staggered to his feet and stripped out of his sodden jeans and boxers. He swayed beneath the showerhead, his body a mass of red eruptions. Across the pallor of his torso, pelvis, and legs, the relentless biting and stinging made him appear as if he'd been rolled naked in barbs. From the claws he made of his trembling hands, she knew he was forcing himself not to scratch. She struggled against the same impulse. Each bite and sting felt like a phantom yellow jacket would torture her forever. In comparison to his agonies, though, she'd suffered far less.

When she told him about the ambulance situation, he rasped from swollen lips, "Can't see. Can't drive."

"I'm driving you." She turned off the water and handed up a long towel. "I'll get your clothes, something that won't cling."

He patted his hair and flinched at the contact. "You can't."

"I've practiced, thanks to Rita of all people."

"I mean—"

"I'll explain later. We have to hurry—you look like you're going to pass out." She clambered upright, grabbed her crutches, and returned to the bedroom. When she peeled off her sopping clothes, a dozen yellow jackets tumbled out. They'd died against her body, smashed by her hands or drowned within the wet cotton. The clothing had concealed welts the size of boils.

After donning fresh underwear, a loose shirt, and baggy shorts, she slung her purse around her neck. The leather strap scraped against the bites and stings there, making her cry out. She tossed a shirt and slacks for Joe over one shoulder, stuffed his eye patch in her pocket, and managed to avoid Dorothy underfoot as she crutched back to the guest bathroom.

Joe had abandoned drying himself and swayed before the

mirror, gawking at the damage the yellow jackets had done. His white-knuckled fists told her of the torture he was undergoing.

"We better hurry," she said. "Do you need help dressing?"

He shook his head and took the eye patch from her. His movements were slow and uncoordinated, and his complexion was turning gray. He struggled to dress, so she set aside her crutches and took over, reassuring him that he would feel better in no time. Despite her words, she knew he would die if she didn't get him help soon.

When she told him they had to leave, he pointed at the crutches. "No good. Can't shift with that."

She'd forgotten his ancient car had a manual transmission—and she no longer had a left foot to press in the clutch. The look in his uncovered eye mirrored her thoughts: his mistakes have multiplied and compounded and are going to kill him, unless I do something really damn fast.

"Get to the car," she said. "I'll look around. Please, Joe, move! We need to go." With him lumbering down the hall, she returned to the bedroom and stared at the assortment of canes, imagining how hard it would be to force down the clutch pedal, shift with her other hand, and steer with her knees. Then she remembered her preparatory prosthesis.

During physical therapy, Dr. Ramos had advised Sarah to keep it for times when the definitive version needed adjustments or replacement. She found the three-pound leg in the back of her closet, still packed in the moving company box with Joe's copperplate lettering on the outside. Below the plastic socket, cosmetic foam covered an aluminum pylon, which connected to a beige rubber foot.

She sat on her stool, yanked two nylon socks over her stump, and folded back a neoprene brace over the socket. The thick compression sleeve rolled up to surround her knee and half of her thigh. Sarah tried to put her weight on the left leg as she rose, but the crude rubber foot couldn't flex. She stumbled backward and fell over the stool. The back of her head smacked the closet doorframe, and her vision whited out. It was like being pushed out of Rita's SUV all over again.

Coming to, Sarah pounded the carpet and imagined Joe dead in the passenger seat because she had failed. She rolled over, got to her knees, and used her right leg to lever upright. With no time to pull on shoes, she staggered barefooted into the bedroom.

The preparatory limb felt like a solid peg in comparison to the prosthesis she now thought of as her left leg. Her hip joints soon throbbed while she limped across the room. The new hurt helped distract her from the bites and stings. Dorothy followed close by, providing another challenge as Sarah had to avoid the bulldog. She used the wall for balance and made her way down the hall and into the dining room. Near the ceiling, a dozen yellow jackets circled or crawled across the walls. Eyeing them, she retrieved her keys from the lock and lurched into the kitchen, cursing the pain and her slowness.

She punched the button to open the gate and reassured Dorothy, uneasy about leaving the bulldog behind while yellow jackets still were alive in the house. In the garage, she jabbed the door opener before limping to the old Camry. Sunlight flooded in as she dropped beside Joe. He'd belted himself into the passenger seat, where he rocked with clenched hands and groaned in pain. His complexion had gone from dusty gray to the chalk white of the paintjob.

Sarah swung her legs in, mindful to lift the rubber foot clear of the doorframe. With the door closed, she raised her left knee, planted the foot hard on the clutch pedal, and started the engine. The shifting pattern differed from her Miata; another hurdle to overcome. She tried twice before figuring out how to put the car in reverse. Joe murmured something, possibly helpful advice, but he'd become inarticulate. She released the parking brake and shot backward down the driveway. The grooved accelerator pedal felt gritty beneath her bare right foot.

The engine roared as she got used to how high to lift her left knee before the rubber foot would come off the clutch pedal. On Tangletree Drive, she put the car into first gear and stalled the engine. Joe looked at her, the patch covering his right eye. Flushed with embarrassment, she said, "Don't worry, I can do this."

He spoke carefully and loud enough for her to hear. "I love you."

A drizzle of tears escaped before she could regain control. I feel scared when you're dying beside me, she thought, but said aloud, "I love you, too. You think I'd go through this chazerei for just anybody?" She found first gear and they darted forward. The allergy medicine was working; she couldn't feel any welts on her face when she wiped her cheeks.

They passed the spot where Rita had smashed into Mrs. O'Malley's car. With swollen, shaking fingers, Joe fumbled with the remotes on the visor that controlled the garage and gate. She threw the Camry into second and lowered his puffy hand to his lap. The neoprene brace pinched the back of her knee whenever she shifted. "Everything will be fine there. I'll get you home soon enough."

"Home. Together?"

"Listen to you fishing." She made the zinging sound of a long cast. The Camry placed her lower to the ground than Rita's SUV and handled turns more like her Miata, giving her the confidence to drive faster. If Joe objected to her speed, he didn't say. She tried to keep him talking. He responded to her questions first with phrases and then with single words. For a while, he moaned between answers. Then he fell silent.

During one of her bike rides, Sarah had spotted the hospital on the northwest side of town, so she decided to follow Hitchcock Parkway, the western loop around Aiken. She raced through intersections at top speed and crossed the double-line to swerve around tractor-trailers. She would allow nothing to delay her.

Ahead, at the major junction with Highway 1, the emergency lights of ambulances, police cruisers, and fire engines flashed. Officers directed a long line of cars and trucks down a side road. She'd blundered onto the accident scene, the reason Joe hadn't already reached the hospital.

A narrow lane caught her attention nearby. She'd gone down it once before on her bike to find an entrance into Hitchcock Woods. "Hold on," she said, hitting the brake pedal and clutch together and shifting from fifth down to third. Joe made no response. He had stopped rocking in place.

The Camry bounced twice as she cut the corner. A few other cars traveled that road. Hopefully they'd lead her back to the main highway—she couldn't afford to get lost. She could no longer hear Joe's wheezing breaths.

The Mustang in front of her bore a sticker advertising the University of South Carolina at Aiken. Sarah prayed that its pony-tailed driver was heading there for a Saturday class. She thought she remembered a street sign indicating the campus was on the same parkway as the hospital.

Following the Mustang through a series of rapid turns, they traveled ever-deeper into a neighborhood. Cussing to herself, she considered backtracking, but then the car turned once more and they emerged at an intersection with Highway 1. The driver took a hard left across a temporary gap in the east- and west-bound traffic. Sarah sucked in her breath. Her left leg throbbed from real and phantom pains.

With cars bearing down from both directions, she accelerated, shifted, and steered in perfect concert, a seated ballet of precise movements.

The Mustang swerved for a quick right onto University Parkway, and Sarah stayed on its tail. She flashed her lights to thank the driver and followed the signs to the hospital. Despite delivering Joe in record time, she feared she was too late.

Chapter 31

TRUE TO HER WORD, THE 911 OPERATOR HAD alerted Aiken Regional Medical Centers to prepare for their arrival. The emergency room staff was making preparations for the accident victims who had not yet arrived, but they admitted Joe immediately. Sarah followed him and a staff member to a curtained stall in one corner, wide enough for a hospital bed, a chair for her, and little else. IV bags hung at the ready.

A dark-skinned male nurse with the bulk of a football player clucked his tongue while he inspected the inside of Joe's elbow for a decent vein. Dehydration had left them flat. He cleaned the area with alcohol, jabbed, and apologized when a fuchsia bloom spread beneath Joe's skin. The needle had punched all the way through the weak channel.

While the nurse tried to find another vein in which to thread his needle, a harried, graying doctor in her fifties explained to Sarah, "We're treating your husband for allergic anaphylaxis. His blood pressure's way down and his airways are closing up tight, so we're giving him epinephrine—that's synthetic adrenaline—to speed up his heart rate. He'll get antihistamines, too, a stronger infusion of what you gave him already. But you delivered the most important dose by getting the pills into him so soon."

Joe winced, and the nurse announced, "Got it." He covered the needle in Joe's arm with a sterile pad and confirmed the smooth flow from the IV bag.

The doctor leaned close to Joe's swollen face, lifted the patch to study his right eye, and said, "You're a lucky man, Mr. Gordon. Your wife saved your life."

Joe nodded. Sarah took a gentle hold of his welt-covered hand. "When will he feel better?"

"Oh, he'll waltz out of here in a few hours, believe it or not. He'll be tired, but looking like the man you married. Are you doing OK?"

"The burning and itching have stopped." The swollen patches on her skin had diminished to small red spots. "I really hadn't noticed until now."

"Pain is mostly in the mind; you were so busy getting him here, you forgot how much you hurt. Same as your trans-tibial amputation, I'll bet." She nodded at the crude prosthesis. Sarah sat with her knees together, her bare right foot against the beige rubber one.

Joe squeezed Sarah's hand in a fierce grip as he jerked upright. His feet lifted off the bed as well. "It's the epinephrine, Mr. Gordon," the doctor explained. "It probably feels like an electric shock surging all the way to your fingers and toes. You'll get that jolt every minute or so for a while." Shouts from the emergency room entrance signaled the arrival of more accident victims. She asked the nurse to give her an update on Joe's blood pressure when she returned.

The male nurse slipped the curtain closed behind her. His baritone hinted at a colonial-British accent, with soft a's and r's. "How are you feeling, Mr. Gordon?"

"Electrocuted." Joe surged forward and his feet popped off the bed before he resettled again.

"That's real good. The epi's getting your blood pressure and heart rate up. Relaxing the airways, too. You're breathing easier, yes?"

"A little." He jolted and fell back with a groan. Sarah continued to hold his hand despite the crush of his fingers every sixty seconds when more adrenaline cycled through. His color had improved; the pallor was starting to give way to a healthier pink.

Beyond the curtain, the emergency room staff called instructions and requests to one another as sneakers squeaked, gurneys rolled past, and a few people cried out. In the next stall, a physician called for more units of blood.

Joe said, "I might've looked dead, but I took it all in. You're a good driver, Sare. And you lied to me earlier—you wouldn't let me burn."

The nurse smiled at Sarah. Sudden heat in her cheeks stimulated the insect bites and stings, making her want to scratch them again. "Of course I wouldn't, you putz." She explained to the man, "The yellow jackets interrupted a marital 'discussion,' let's say."

The nurse took Joe's blood pressure and opened a valve in the bicep cuff. Air escaped with a hiss. He said, "I know all about these 'discussions.' It's a good thing I'm a big man. Otherwise, my wife would've killed me long ago."

Sarah asked, "How long have you been married?"

"Twelve years this September. You?"

"About thirteen months. Where did y'all meet?"

"We met in Igbo," he said, pronouncing the village as "Eeboo." He paused while he took Joe's pulse and made another notation on his clipboard. "That's in eastern Nigeria. I fancied Safiya, but didn't know if she was the one for me. So I crossed the seven rivers and climbed the seven mountains to reach Alusi Ifunanya, the Goddess of Love."

Joe frowned. The swellings had retreated enough for his brows to contract and his forehead to wrinkle. He said, "You spoke to a goddess?"

"To an oracle. She stood me in the center of a chamber, and said to close my eyes. The answer to whether Safiya is my true love would then come, she told me, spoken in my mind by the goddess."

Sarah and Joe both asked, "What did she say?"

"She said yes. So I returned to Igbo and married Safiya. We have seven children, with an eighth on the way." He grinned, revealing several gold teeth. "You might believe it's pagan nonsense, but think about this. Anyone who manages to cross seven rivers and climb seven mountains—and know he would have to do it all again just to get home—is bound to discover that the person who inspired the journey is his true love. Or hers." He nodded at Sarah, who still held onto Joe as he endured the adrenaline surges. "I'll check on you soon, Mr. Gordon. It looks like you're in good hands."

He closed the curtain behind him. Next door, the physician continued to call instructions to the triage team, but in softer tones. The chaotic clamor had ebbed as the staff cared for their patients.

Sarah studied Joe's hand in hers. Familiar contours—tendon ridges, wrinkles on his knuckles, and faint scars—returned as the antihistamines continued to undo his allergic reaction to so much venom. "You're looking a hundred percent better already."

"I owe you my life," he said. "After all I've done to you, breaking your heart and the foot and driving you crazy..." Another spasm rocked him. "I wanted to keep you safe, protect you from any risk. If you had let me do that, I'd be dead."

"Those challenges were my seven rivers and seven mountains."

"And what did the Goddess of Love tell you?"

She snorted. "That I love tsuris. Funny, the goddess sounded just like my mom: 'You should have a lifetime of suffering, Feygela, nu? Joe you deserve.'"

"Now that's what she'd say to me, about you. You know Mom loves me more."

"'Oy, such a deal I have for you, Joseph, my golden son. Take my only daughter. Well, seven-eighths of her anyway. Mneh, don't get me started.'"

Joe's grin turned into a wince as he jolted. "I think it's supposed to be a yes or no answer."

"Yes, Joe. She said yes."

He glanced away. "But you'll never forget what I've done."

"No, I won't. And I haven't forgiven you, either. But I remember what Rita told me yesterday." That got him to look at her, and Sarah continued, "She said you were a lousy lay because you wouldn't stop blathering about me." Her eyes moistened. "You were in bed with her, but kept thinking of us. I guess that counts for something."

"How many times should I say I'm sorry?"

"That doesn't matter now." She leaned across him and took his other hand as well, careful not to dislodge the IV needle. His spasms subsided. She said, "Instead, I want your promise—swear on the life you will owe me forever—that you will go to therapy with me, trust me to do what's right for my life, and listen to me. If you truly care about me, then help me take care of us."

"I promise. I swear. I totally trust you to take the wheel."

She kissed him gently. "I feel so glad when you say that."

☙

After the doctor released Joe into Sarah's care, he fell asleep in the passenger seat, so she ferried him on her errands, heedless of her bare foot and exposed artificial leg. She filled his prescription for an EpiPen auto-injector—since he now could be extra-sensitive to any more insect venom—and stopped by the art boutique to collect her painting.

With Joe still sleeping when she drove into the garage, she hurried inside the house and killed the remaining yellow jackets while Dorothy danced around her. They would have to walk the bulldog in the front yard until an exterminator could wipe out the nest.

She helped Joe to his side of their bed, propped him up with lots of pillows, then sautéed vegetables for dinner and ate beside him, stretching out to rest her sore, tired body. For the first time, Joe let her do everything. He even complimented her cooking. The welts had vanished, as had his exotropia. Other than some blisters that marked the heaviest concentration of stings, he again looked like the gorgeous man she'd married.

Now that he was rested, she limped back to the car and returned with the picture wrapped in brown paper.

He asked, "You bought me a gift?"

"Hey, schmendrick, I'm the one who better get a helluva present—with fancy wrapping and a big ol' bow. No, this is the project you inspired me to paint."

She tore off the paper in long strips and dropped them to the floor, where Dorothy sniffed at the taupe-colored curls. Sarah's hips and back ached from hobbling on the crude prosthesis, so she sat on his side of the bed, her bottom pressed against his leg. After giving the framed work a final once-over, she showed Joe the eagle in flight above its lair and her sunlit face beaming like a golden goddess in the sky.

"The colors are amazing," he said. "Can I touch it?" She gave him permission, and he grazed his fingers along the surfaces. He lingered on her image, feeling every inch of her. "What's it mean?"

"What does it say to you?"

"You're cheering for the bird. Like it's doing something new, maybe leaving home and safety, and you're proud of it. Are you the eagle, too?"

She said, "The eagle's both of us. I didn't know that until now. We're taking risks and soaring."

"We'll do that together?"

Sarah laid the painting across her side of the bed. "We'll do everything together."

"Everything?" He raised an eyebrow.

"Maybe not everything." She let Joe squirm for a few seconds and then said, "For instance, no more cold showers."

Sarah tried to keep the conversation light, but he soon lapsed into morose regrets and withering self-criticism. To focus attention away from his mistakes, she told him about the chance to sell her work through the art boutique and a new idea she had for custom-painting prosthetic sleeves, to give amputees a unique form of self-expression. She also related her adventures with the therapist and the ballet class.

Despite repeated assurances that she wanted to look ahead and not dwell on the past, he brought all discussions around to his guilt. She recognized the choreography of leading every conversation back to a masochistic vortex. After her amputation, those same steps had sent her plummeting time and again into depression.

Unable to think of another option, she sighed and took the plunge. "Joe, you know you're not the first person to ever commit adultery."

"Of course other people have. That doesn't ma—"

"I mean, you're not even the first person in this room."

He jolted as if from a new shot of epinephrine. "So there was another guy!"

"Did I say that?"

"But…really? With a woman?"

"That would be the only other choice. Right where you're sitting."

He felt the sheets nearby, maybe expecting to find a lingering wet spot. Sarah rolled her eyes, and then he asked, "Who? When?"

"Isn't 'why' the most important question? Same reason you gave. I thought we were through. But unlike you, I wasn't trying to get my confidence back so I could rescue our marriage—in a twisted way, your cheating was nobler than mine." She took a breath and went ahead with the rest of the confession. "I just wanted to forget the world for a while and try something new. And, like you, I got propositioned by someone who was guaranteed to be awesome."

"Oh my God—Rita?"

"Yup, she bagged us both. And I didn't impress her either. In my case it was a lack of skill, not a lack of focus."

"Right here?"

"And all over the rest of the bed and on the floor and in the kitchen and on the dining room table and back here again for a nightcap." She shrugged as Joe gaped at her. "So now you can say you feel mad and sad when I cheat on you with the woman you later slept with. And I can break your foot and then get attacked by a thousand yellow jackets and you can save me. In the end, all we'll do is move this conversation about three feet to the left and switch positions."

"So you're saying we're even and everything is OK?"

"No, I'm saying we're both in the wrong, so we need to make it up to each other. Forever." She gave his leg a bump with her butt.

He grinned. "You know, you looked smoking hot in the Acura, pinning Rita to her seat. I sort of like the idea of you on top. In control."

Sarah pulled back the covers and crawled up his body. "You should see me when I have sex on my mind instead of homicide."

"Show me."

She did.

Chapter 32

THE MORNING OF THEIR SECOND ANNIVERSARY, Sarah balanced with more difficulty than ever on the bathroom scale. Joe had purchased a new model that announced the weight so she wouldn't struggle to try to see the display. The electronic voice said, "145.4 pounds." It didn't announce that this was her all-time high.

She gripped the counter edge and eased her foot back onto the tile floor. Nightmares about falling had begun to disrupt her sleep.

In the huge vanity mirror, she saw the woman in whom she recognized her past, present, and future. Her hair was its natural burnt sienna again and had grown halfway down her back, but comparisons to her old days in ballet ended there. She pivoted sideways to study how she had ballooned. The transformation continued to startle her, but this was no stranger's body. She smiled as the baby moved again.

The previous week, the twenty-seventh of her pregnancy, she'd begun to experience swelling in her face, hands, and foot. Her residual limb exhibited edema as well, making her left leg impossible to wear. Joe had encouraged Sarah to get fitted with a temporary prosthesis, despite the expense, to carry her through the final trimester. He refused to let anything slow her down.

She missed wearing the repaired version, since she enjoyed it more than ever. It stood beside the hall tree in the bedroom, stripped of all cosmetic camouflage, a masterpiece of industrial artistry that even Joe now admired. Over the standard dressings she always wore one of her decorative sleeves—a thin nylon hose that stretched from the socket up to mid-thigh—chosen from the variety she painted with Impressionistic and abstract designs. In the past few months, sales of them on her website had tripled. She was developing a following among avant-garde amputees.

After cleaning up, she pulled on the new maternity dress she'd hung from the back of the bathroom door, a habit of Joe's she adopted. He loved to shop for the latest in pregnancy fashions. Most often, she went with him, but sometimes he still came home with a surprise for her.

Having resorted to crutches, she swing-stepped barefoot to the kitchen. At the spotless table in the breakfast nook, she leaned on the right crutch and picked up a list written on graph paper. Joe had helped her compile it for their trip to Atlanta the next day:

√ 1. LUGGAGE: CLOTHES, TOILETRIES, BOTTLED WATER,
   FRUIT SNACKS
√ 2. ATLANTA FORECAST—UMBRELLA?
√ 3. APPOINTMENT WITH DR. RAMOS
√ 4. CONFIRM FOUR SEASONS ALLOWS DOGS
√ 5. FOOD & BOWLS FOR DOROTHY
√ 6. FINAL PREP AND SHOW AT PENUMBRA ART GALLERY

As she considered the items, her left hand trembled, rippling the page. Her first show in Atlanta, at the Penumbra Art Gallery, had taken six months to set up. The gallery owner had passed through Aiken, purchased the plaster bust of Rita, and offered Sarah a more prominent venue for her work. Sarah believed her celebration with Joe that night had produced their daughter.

For the trip to Atlanta, she planned to drive Joe's present. He had given her the gift the way she'd demanded, with fancy wrapping paper and a big bow. These covered a small jewelry box into which he'd put an empty key ring. The actual choice of vehicle he left to her. She had picked a hybrid SUV suitable for hauling bulky artwork in all kinds of weather. With her pregnancy, she'd also come to appreciate the roominess behind the wheel.

They'd taken it on a road trip to Savannah to attend the memorial for Michael. Her parents could hardly wait for their little Jewish-American Princess to be born. Everything she'd accomplished up to that point was easy compared to the challenge of the next two decades: to keep them from totally spoiling the girl.

Recalling Joe's presentation of the empty key ring touched her once more. As she had done many times, she wondered when he started caring *about* her—rather than *for* her—again.

Changes in his behavior had not come immediately or without effort. Nor would the process ever be complete. He attended Dr. Teraphim's couple therapy with her and saw a psychiatrist on his own to help him come to terms with past decisions. As a result, he suffocated less and listened more. While no one could live "happily ever after," they waltzed through most days, and when they didn't dance in harmony, they practiced the steps together and tried harder.

Through the windows, she watched Joe talk with Helen O'Malley over the low fence. They'd agreed to keep the back yard contained so Dorothy, and eventually their daughter, could have some freedom without endangerment. Birds cleared the short barrier with ease whenever the bulldog chased them.

Their neighbor stuck her liver-spotted hand between the slats to pet Dorothy, who wiggled and pawed like a cat at the proffered fingers. Helen finally had reached a settlement with Rita's insurance company a few months earlier. Rita had resigned from Matryoshka a week after the confrontation—four days after Joe quit.

Still absent from the corporate world, he assisted local charities and helped Sarah with the business aspects of her website, art sales, and the ballet school where she had become partners with Barbara. He said something in parting that made Helen laugh and followed Dorothy to the patio door.

The French bulldog preceded him inside and lay on the cool oak floor of the kitchen, beaming at them both. Yard work had left dewy perspiration on Joe's face. His musky scent teased her from across the room. He said, "I found you."

"And such a find, a real bargain—there's more of me than ever before." She presented her impressive profile. Their daughter turned inside her with a controlled spin. The baby already had learned to spot like a prima ballerina. She set the checklist back on the table. "Is there anything we're forgetting about?"

"Probably, but we'll deal with it. You're still nervous about the art show." Rather than re-center the paper, he stepped close and kissed her.

Sarah tasted his sweat along with basil and thyme he'd sampled from his garden. A longer kiss, slow and deep, revealed spicy oregano on his tongue. She set the crutches aside and let him support her. "A little, is all. I'll go back to pondering baby names."

"It'll come to us when the time's right. Relax."

Her fingers grazed the front of his jeans. "Is that a deluxe EpiPen in your pocket, or are you just happy to—" She yielded to the circular movement of his lips and the warmth that spread over her face and body.

Coming up for air, Sarah noticed Helen had turned her attention from a flowerbed to their kitchen bay. She murmured, "Sometimes I miss that privacy fence."

Joe eased her into the deep shadows near the front windows and shielded her with his body. He unbuttoned the top of her dress. "Happy anniversary," he said. "Have you ever been happier?"

"No, but ask me again in an hour." She turned their embrace into a stationary dance, humming Ravel's "Bolero" as she led. He caressed the arc of her abdomen and bent to kiss the tops of her breasts. She glimpsed their reflection framed in the glass, the way they curved around each other, neither one dominant, both vital to creating the balanced whole.

Was it better to capture the scene with paint or in sculpture?

Neither, Sarah decided. It was best just to appreciate these moments of living art. She and Joe could reproduce them countless times if they took care and mastered the art of loving.

Acknowledgments

MY GRATITUDE ALWAYS BEGINS WITH KATE, WHOSE stories from the world of ballet sparked the idea for this novel. She sometimes has to put up with my Joe-like tendencies, and always does so with good humor and patience. As the Dedication states, she continues to teach me how to love instead of merely to care.

Readers of any of my books know I enjoy languages and dialects. I grew up hearing a lot of Yiddish from my father and his mom. In fact, I think my first exposure, quite young, was an outraged "Oy gevalt!" uttered by my grandmother when she was trying to help me cut my food, and I snapped, "George do it." That's always been my motto, much to my family's dismay, but they did teach me a variety of colorful curses and to tell dreck from bupkes. A dank, y'all!

Thanks, too, to my critique groups from a decade ago, when I wrote the first draft, to present day for continuing to make me a better writer and editor. I am grateful as well to the prosthetists, amputees, physical and psychological therapists, dancers, and artists who shared their stories and insights.

Bob, Jan, and Mark Babcock of Deeds Publishing deserve praise for their unflagging belief in me and the many other authors they support. Their love of words only is exceeded by their deeds in continuing to bring books into the world.

I also thank you, the reader, for your attention and engagement with my work. I hope you found this and my earlier books to be journeys worth taking with characters who live on in your mind long after the final sentence.

—George Weinstein
Roswell, GA
September 2014

About the Author

George Weinstein is the author of the contemporary novel *The Caretaker*, the multi-cultural historical novel *The Five Destinies of Carlos Moreno*, and the Southern historical novel *Hardscrabble Road*.

His work has been published locally in the Atlanta press and in regional and national anthologies, including *A Cup of Comfort for Writers*. His first book, the children's motivational adventure *Jake and the Tiger Flight*, was written for the nonprofit Tiger Flight Foundation, which is dedicated to the mission of leading the young to become the "Pilot in Command" of their lives. He wishes that there had been such an organization in Laurel, Maryland, where he misspent his youth.

George is the former President of the Atlanta Writers Club (AWC) and former everything-else there too. Having run out of term-limited positions for him, in 2012 the AWC Board bestowed on George the lifetime title of Officer Emeritus, which means he can never leave. Not that he would, but it's nice to be wanted. The accompanying author photo was taken at the centennial celebration for the AWC in 2014. George insists he's as old as the Club, but has a self-portrait in his attic that does the aging for him.

More credibly, he also claims to be the lifetime Atlanta Writers Conference Director for the AWC, bringing top literary professionals each year to meet with Club members so they can avoid the mistakes he made early and often on his writing journey. An increasing number of writers have received publishing deals and agent contracts as a result of these conferences, ensuring George always will have a supply of author blurbs and book sales, courtesy of those who owe him big time. This is called enlightened self-interest and is his primary motivation in every aspect of his life.

George lives in Roswell, GA with his remarkable wife and their furry, four-legged children.

Read reviews and excerpts of his novels, download book club questions, and discover extras on his website:

www.georgeweinstein.com

CPSIA information can be obtained
at www.ICGtesting.com
Printed in the USA
BVOW01s0204301016
466415BV00002B/128/P